Augustus Antoine Cornelius Meves

The Authentic Historical Memoirs of Louis Charles

Prince-royal, dauphin of France, second son of Louis XVI. and Marie Antoinette,

who subsequently to October 1793

Augustus Antoine Cornelius Meves

The Authentic Historical Memoirs of Louis Charles
Prince-royal, dauphin of France, second son of Louis XVI. and Marie Antoinette, who subsequently to October 1793

ISBN/EAN: 9783337212667

Printed in Europe, USA, Canada, Australia, Japan

Cover: Foto ©Raphael Reischuk / pixelio.de

More available books at **www.hansebooks.com**

THE AUTHENTIC HISTORICAL MEMOIRS

OF

LOUIS CHARLES, DAUPHIN OF FRANCE,

AND

COMMENTARY.

The Authentic Historical Memoirs

OF

LOUIS CHARLES, PRINCE-ROYAL, DAUPHIN OF FRANCE,

SECOND SON OF

LOUIS XVI. AND MARIE ANTOINETTE,

Who, subsequently to October 1793, personated through supposititious means,

AUGUSTUS MEVES.

THE MEMOIRS, WRITTEN BY THE VERITABLE LOUIS XVII.,

ARE

Dedicated to the French Nation.

THE COMPILATION AND COMMENTARY

BY HIS TWO ELDEST SONS,

WILLIAM, AND AUGUSTUS MEVES.

LONDON:
WILLIAM RIDGWAY, 169 PICCADILLY, W.

1868.

PREFACE.

THE object in writing the Authentic Historical Memoirs of Louis Charles, Prince-Royal, Dauphin of France, firstly, is to place on record an authentic historical fact, which, on the part of the French Republic, has been purposely falsified, and tacitly acquiesced in by the European Powers, for political motives. Secondly, parental consanguinity involving us in this monarchical mystery, thereby holding us responsible to dispel the error which has hitherto surrounded the second son of Louis XVI., it would be impolitic, ungenerous, and pusillanimous on our part, to refrain advocating the cause here bequeathed to us as an heirloom. In promulgating the truth which surrounds the second son of Louis XVI. and Marie Antoinette, we shall have fulfilled a duty devolved upon us by filial ties, for were we to remain silent on this hitherto historical mystery, it would be a continual self-reproach and dishonour to our name and descent while living, whilst, for such silence, posterity would award us naught, but an inglorious and ignoble epitaph.

Our aim has been to divest this historical question of all mystification. It irrefutably proves the Dauphin's deliverance from the Tower of the Temple, and the only question remaining to be decided is, whether sufficient proof is brought forward to guarantee the recognition of Louis XVII. in the author of the present Memoirs.

Let our critics before passing judgment on the present work, attentively scrutinize its contents, and not assign, previous to reading it, either their condemnation or acquiescence, but resolutely adhere to equity in pronouncing their opinion on the claims advanced. The only desire sought is an impartial investigation of the question now brought under notice, and that its accuracy or inaccuracy may be attested to, by reason and justice.

The Dauphin's escape from the Tower of the Temple is no longer a mysterious problem. The truth that has hitherto been enveloped in a labyrinth of obscurities is now substantially removed. The demise of the son of Louis XVI. and Marie Antoinette in the Tower of the Temple was but a Republican assertion and not an historical fact, which has benefited the ruling sovereigns of France, since the sacrifice of Louis XVI., to acquiesce in, namely, Napoleon Bonaparte, Louis XVIII.,* Charles X., the Dukes of Angoulême and Berri (the sons of Charles X.), Marie Thérèse (the daughter of Louis XVI. married to the Duke of Angoulême, consequently in the interest of the house of Charles X.), le Comte de Chambord, the acknowledged legitimate sovereign of France (son of the Duke of Berri), Louis Philippe, the Orleans Family, and, lastly, Louis Napoleon—all have had, and still have, an interest in recognising the authenticity of the Republican announcement, that the son of Louis XVI. died in the Temple. Nevertheless, with all this apparent antagonistic array of political influence, with its attendant legions, to annihilate truth, such will be impotent and ineffectual, for sooner or later it will manifest itself; and though it may be lulled to sleep for a while, time will eventually dispel the illusions, that chicanery and artifice have invented.

The Memoirs are written by the Claimant to the Throne of France, as the legitimate heir, and were completed during his life. A sequel is now added, so that all particulars connected with this hitherto historical mystery should be thoroughly explained.

WILLIAM, AND AUGUSTUS MEVES.

LONDON, *September* 1868.

---

* See subject "Under what Auspices Louis XVIII. ascended the Throne of France," page 291.

ARRANGEMENT OF SUBJECTS

IN THE

Authentic Historical Memoirs of Louis Charles, Dauphin of France, and Commentary.

CONTENTS.

RECOLLECTIONS AND CAREER OF THE DAUPHIN TILL THE YEAR 1823.

CONTENTS.

INFORMATION RESPECTING THE CROWLEY FAMILY, AND MARIANNE CROWLEY'S CAREER, AND ACQUAINTANCE-SHIP WITH MR. WILLIAM SCHROËDER MEVES.

CONTENTS.

HISTORICAL RECORDS.

CONTENTS.

EVIDENCES OF THE MEMOIRS REVIEWED.

MRS. MEVES.

CONTENTS.

MRS. SPENCE, MRS. FISHER, AND MISS POWELL.

MR. GEORGE MEVES.

CONTENTS.

THE DAUPHIN'S RECOLLECTIONS OF THE TOWER OF THE TEMPLE.

HOW THE DAUPHIN WAS BROUGHT UP AFTER HIS ARRIVAL IN ENGLAND, TILL THE YEAR 1823.

THE DAUPHIN'S CONVERSATIONS WITH THE PRETENDER NAÜNDORFF.

AN OUTLINE OF THE PUBLISHED LIFE OF THE PRETENDER NAÜNDORFF.

COMMENTARY AND INFERENCES ON THE PUBLISHED LIFE OF THE PRETENDER NAÜNDORFF.

A WORD TO HISTORIANS : WHAT PROOFS AUTHENTICATE THE DAUPHIN'S DEMISE IN THE TOWER OF THE TEMPLE ?

UNDER WHAT AUSPICES LOUIS XVIII. ASCENDED THE THRONE OF FRANCE.

RECOGNITION OF THE SON OF LOUIS XVL AND MARIE ANTOINETTE BY PERSONAL IDENTITY.

REASONS WHY THE DAUPHIN DID NOT PROCLAIM HIMSELF.

CONCLUSION : WHAT IS THE DECISION ?

THE AUTHENTIC HISTORICAL MEMOIRS

OF

LOUIS CHARLES, DAUPHIN OF FRANCE.

IN placing my Narrative before the world, my only wish is to solve the truth, and circumstances of my chequered life, commencing with my recollections of the Tower of the Temple ; but it must be distinctly understood, that all recollections, as much as possible, have been destroyed in me regarding such a place.

I well remember in my boyhood being at a strange kind of place, surrounded with high walls. There were several houses, and a large garden divided into squares or quarters, in which were trees, and flowers in a wild neglected state. Near the garden was a building, " La Rotunda," rounded at each end, in which was established a school where several boys attended. I attended this school for a while. The teacher sat at one end of the schoolroom, and I sat alone at a desk. Opposite me were two firelocks, the muzzles of which pointed into the garden, and the butts were supported on a table or desk. When I left the schoolroom two boys used to accompany me across a piece of ground to a strange kind of high square tower, like a turreted building, when I ascended a flight of stone steps with an iron railing, and at once entered a good-sized dark parlour, in one corner of which was a cupboard, and on the opposite corner was a door, which led to a circular winding staircase connected with the upper part of the building. On entering the parlour I was received by a well-dressed portly woman.

This, I suppose, was Madame Simon, who used to give me slices of brioche, a kind of cake made with flour, eggs, and honey. I have no recollection of this person ever having ill-used me. Her husband was many years older than herself. He used to take me up the winding staircase, into which the door led from the parlour, to a large-sized room at the top of the building. The middle of this strangely built room was remarkably high in the centre, being of a conical shape, in which a swing was placed to a beam, and here it was where this dark-faced old man, "with furrows in his cheeks," used to swing me, and make me run round the room as fast as I possibly could. It was there, likewise, that I used to get on a chair, and mount a table fixed against the wall, and jump on the pavement of the room, which was not boarded, but had a kind of stucco or plaster-of-Paris flooring, of a dull red colour. I have no recollection that ever this person ill-treated me. Once when he was showing my dexterity and swiftness of running to some of his friends, whom he was entertaining in the parlour, he had a handkerchief, or possibly a damask napkin, in his hand, with which he was stimulating me, when the napkin swung round my face, and tore the skin from my left cheek, and occasioned a wound, which was some time in healing. A surgeon attended me, and Madame Simon used a kind of white powder to heal the wound.

Upon one occasion I recollect seeing an entertainment given in the Palace of the Temple, where a kind of play was performed with Marionnette figures. Some person read the drama, and I was seated on the stage, next to the person who had the care of me, from where I saw all the movements on the stage, and could observe the company.

I also recollect being taken out one afternoon by Simon and his wife to the house of some friend of theirs — I think a Marchand Chapelier,—whose wife took me into her petit cabinet, and gave me some delicious comfiture, spread on a slice of brioche, and upon her leaving the room she placed the jar containing the comfiture on the upper shelf of the cupboard, and left me in the room to do as I pleased. After she had been gone some time, I got upon a chair to get some more of the comfiture, but being unable to reach it, I mounted a high round muff-box, and in attempting to reach the shelf I over-turned the muff-box, and fell down on the floor. The noise brought the company into the room where I was ; the muff-box was then examined, which contained a quantity of large white feathers, which were found not in the slightest manner injured by the fall. Upon leaving the house, I was mounted on Antoine Simon's shoulders, and began singing. This attracted a crowd of persons, who followed us across the Pont Neuf, in La Rue du Temple, cheering us until we came to the entrance of the Temple.

As regards the Small Tower, the only part I recollect is the parlour, where a great deal of company, friends of the Simons, used to visit, most of them persons of repute as political men. Hébert and Danton were constant visitors. I am quite sure Danton was in the habit of frequenting the parlour occupied by Antoine Simon, for whenever I examine the portraits of the characters of the French Revolution, that of Danton always strikes me as having been familiar to me in my youth, as his features strike me as being those of the person who used to take me from the parlour to the step of the door on a starlight night, and explain the mysteries of the planetary system to me, and the course of the moon over the earth in its monthly orbit. I think I was taught astronomy according to the theory of Descartes, as his system agrees with my notions.

The only instance of extreme ill-usage that strikes forcibly my imagination, is that which regards the person who had the chief power over me at the Temple. This person was a very tall, powerful man. "Jacques Réné Hébert is the person I allude to." On one occasion he was desirous of my signing some papers which contained accusations of an infamous character, reflecting on the virtue of the most innocent and amiable of women, whose virtue is without a stain. I refused to obey the infamous commands of this man, when he, in his rage and disap-pointment, seized me by the hair of my head, and burst the door open leading to the upper chambers on the stone stairs, where I received a

wound over the eye on the left temple. "This scar is still visible."*
From this cruel treatment of Hébert I date the determination of
Madame Simon to save me, whenever a fair opportunity occurred to
do so.

On the 1st of August 1793, the unfortunate Marie Antoinette, Queen
of France, was removed from the Tower of the Temple to the prison of
the Conciergerie. This being a public prison, a greater chance existed
to save the Queen than when she was confined in the Tower of the
Temple. A lady of the name of Mrs. Charlotte Atkyns, of Kettringham
Hall, Norfolk, went to Paris, accompanied by the Marquis of Bonneval,
with the object of saving the life of the Queen of France, by extricating
her from the prison of the Conciergerie, previous to her trial, in October
1793. The Queen refused her proffered service, unless she could be
accompanied by her children. This being impossible to accomplish,
Mrs. Atkyns returned to England for safety, and the Marquis of Bonneval took refuge at the château of his mother, the Dowager Marchioness of Bonneval, in Normandy, September 1793.

About this time a letter was addressed to a lady of the name of
Carpenter by Tom Paine, the author of the *Rights of Man*. He
was a member of the French National Convention. His letter contained a desire for a youth to be found answering the description he
gave, and to be brought to France, "to Paris," for purposes required
by him. Mrs. Carpenter was a friend of Mrs. Marianne Crowley Meves.
These two ladies went in search of the youth, as required by Paine,
but it was found not to be so easy a task to accomplish.

Mr. William Meves, who resided in London, at 44 Great Russell
Street, Bloomsbury Square, with his son, who was born in France, the
16th of February 1785; and this youth answering in many instances
the description required, his father determined to take him to Paris.
This was accordingly done; and on Mr. Meves's arrival in Paris, he
obtained an interview with the Queen, in the prison of the Conciergerie,
and it was agreed that he should introduce his son into the Temple at

* See Appendix, Note A, for Medical Certificates.

Paris, and place him under the care of Antoine Simon, till a good opportunity occurred to extricate Louis XVII. from the Temple. A strong resemblance existed between Augustus Antoine Cornelius Meves and Louis Charles, "the Dauphin," in point of features, except in the eyes and hair—"*Louis Charles having brown eyes and hair*," and Augustus Meves having blue eyes and light hair.

In the month of January 1794, Mrs. Schroeder Crowley Meves went to Holland, to the Abbé Morlet, "who had emigrated to the house of his brother, Claude Morlet, a Chevalier of the Order of St. Louis," who had taken refuge at a village called Buren, near Utrecht,* having taken with her a deaf and dumb boy, the son of a poor woman, named Maria Dodd, who gained her livelihood as a charwoman, in the parish of St. Martin's. With this boy Mrs. Meves penetrated to Paris, for the purpose of extricating her son from the Tower of the Temple.

On the 19th January 1794, Simon obtained his discharge from the Municipality of Paris, from his position as Concierge du Temple, and quitted the Tower with his wife.

When Mrs. Meves arrived in Paris in January 1794, she stayed at the Hotel de Bussey, Rue de Bussey. She was attended by the Abbé Morlet. She then set about obtaining the release of her son. Her desire was to release him by introducing into the Temple the deaf and dumb boy she had brought with her to Paris. How this was accomplished I cannot tell, but that it was accomplished is positively true, as certainly a deaf and dumb boy was introduced into the Tower of the Temple. This boy was the son of Maria Dodd, and was the boy seen by Messrs. Harmand, Reverchon, and Mathieu, when they were sent by the orders of the French Directory to report the state of health of Louis Charles, the Dauphin. Monsieur Harmand published in 1815 a brochure, in which is a description of his commission to the Tower of the Temple, February 27th, 1795, which account is appended to a work written by Her Royal Highness the Duchess of Angoulême, published at the Royal Printing Office at Paris, in 1817, entitled

* See Appendix, Note B, for Letter from the Abbé Morlet to Mrs. Meves.

" Récit des Événements arrivés au Temple."—See Commentary, *Historical Records.**

The son of Maria Dodd died in the Temple, the 8th June 1795. The authentic proofs of his death, and the examination of his body by the surgeons Pelletan and Dumangin, will be found in a work published at Paris in 1834, called " Preuves authentiques de la mort du jeune Louis XVII."—See Commentary, *Historical Records.**

As regards my first introduction to my most excellent and worthy reputed father, Mr. William Meves, it seems to my reflective powers that I was lying on the sofa, in the parlour of the Small Tower of the Temple, and was awakened by the female who had the care of me, " Madame Simon," saying, " Votre père est arrivé, votre père est arrivé "—" Your father has arrived, your father has arrived." She then aroused me from the sofa, and took the pillow therefrom, and placed it into a kind of hamper-basket, such as milliners use to carry ladies' dresses in. After placing me on the pillow she covered me with a light muslin dress, and carried the wicker-basket, with me in it, across the ground, where a coach was waiting at the gate, in which she placed the basket, and then got in herself, when we were driven to the street where Mr. Meves was residing. On our entering the room where Mr. Meves was, "who was then at supper," Madame Simon retired, and I remember seeing a well-dressed gentleman; but as he was not the person I was led to expect to see, I burst into tears, when he consoled me by giving me some of the delicacies of which he was partaking. After which I recollect being alone in an open boat, which was lashed to the shore, with a wide expanse of water before me ; and the motion of the boat, from the tide coming in, alarmed and frightened me, and I cried out, when a stout woman on the shore seemed to give notice to some men who were near the shore to hasten to my help. When the men came, and got into the boat, and I was placed in the folds of a large travelling cloak, the boat was then loosened from the shore, and a sail hoisted, when we proceeded across an immense expanse of water, towards the hospitable coast of England.

* Refer to Table of Contents, under heading *Historical Records*, for page.

I next remember being in a post-chaise with Mr. Meves; and, on our arriving in London, the post-chaise stopped at the house of Roger Palmer, Esq., at the top of Oxford Street, opposite the wall of Hyde Park; and, on our alighting, we passed through the hall, and went up a flight of stairs into the drawing-room, where Roger Palmer was at breakfast. In this room there was a side-table on which was placed a beautiful set of ivory chessmen, "red and white," with which I amused myself. During the time I was thus occupied, Mr. Meves and Roger Palmer were in earnest conversation, carried on, I suppose, in the German language, as I could not understand one word they said. I had something very nice given me for breakfast; and after some time Mr. Palmer's household steward announced the post-chaise was ready waiting. On re-entering the post-chaise we proceeded to the house where Mr. Meves had apartments—44 Great Russell Street, Bloomsbury. The house was kept by an elderly man, "a Mr. Page;" and was managed by his eldest daughter, "a Mrs. Johnstone," and a young lass, a daughter of Mr. Page's.

It will be now necessary to give some account of my reputed mother, Mrs. Marianne Crowley Meves, who then resided at 15 Lower Marylebone Street, "exactly opposite Welbeck Street," where, the following evening after my arrival at Great Russell Street, I was taken in a hackney-coach, by a maid-servant, "a tall person of the name of Milley," to see Mrs. Meves. On the coach arriving at her residence I followed the maid-servant up-stairs to the second floor, and on my entering the room she ran to embrace me. This rather alarmed me, as Mrs. Meves was then an entire stranger to me; but her kind and gentle manners soon restored confidence in me. Towards the dusk of the evening she went out for some time, and upon returning she brought with her a fine bunch of grapes, which she gathered from the stalk, and threw into the air; and, as they fell upon the carpet, I scrambled to pick them up, and ate them. The next morning, when I was dressed I went down-stairs, and whilst the housemaid was busily engaged cleaning the step of the door, I passed into the street, and amused myself by looking into a stationer's shop-window; and when I left the shop-window to return home, I passed the house where my amiable reputed mother resided, and strayed to the next door, where the housemaid was engaged cleaning the doorway. I mounted the stairs to the second floor, but on finding myself amongst strangers I began crying, which brought a gentleman to my assistance, who kindly took me by the hand and led me to the next door. This little incident made it necessary for me to be returned to the care of Mr. Meves.

On my return to Great Russell Street, I was placed at a girls' day-school, 25 Museum Street, and was left at the school by Miss Page, who likewise fetched me home when required. Here I was regularly taught the pronunciation of the English alphabet. After a time I unfortunately caught the measles. I was nursed by an elderly woman, who treated me very kindly.

On my recovery, Mr. Meves placed me at a boys' boarding-school at Wandsworth, kept by a Mr. Tempest. I was taken there by Mrs. Johnstone, and placed as a parlour-boarder, as I required extra attention on account of my not understanding the English language. Accordingly, a bed was made for me in the same room where the daughters of Mr. Tempest slept. I had nothing to complain of as far as regards the school, but I certainly did not like the diet. What I longed for was that which I had been accustomed to, namely, brioche.

I remember, during the morning school-hours, the boys were served with bread and cheese, or bread and milk; and, upon the servants leaving the schoolroom, they used to go into the kitchen, opposite the parlour-door, and empty the fragments of bread, etc., into a high window-cell, which was at least four feet from the ground-floor of the kitchen. I knew this; and when the servants were engaged preparing the beds for the boys, I used to go into the kitchen, in order to find a little bread, which I did by putting my hands into the high cell of the window, and pull down whatever my hands came in contact with. Upon one occasion, instead of pulling down pieces of bread, I pulled down three shillings; and, not being able to replace the money, unless

I threw it into the window-cell, which would have attracted notice, as they would have heard me in the parlour, in this dilemma I put the shillings into my pocket, and when I went into the schoolroom I threw two of them under the usher's desk, amongst the cuttings of the quills; and the other I threw under Mr. Tempest's desk, in a similar manner.

When the boys were questioned who had taken the three shillings, I at once confessed, and said what I had done with them. The two shillings under the usher's desk were easily found, but the shilling I had thrown under Mr. Tempest's desk, which was raised about a foot higher than the flooring, had gone so far back amongst the rubbish that it could not be found at the time. For this involuntary fault I was severely punished by Mr. Tempest.

Towards the latter end of May 1794, I was taken from Mr. Tempest's boarding-school by my reputed mother. We walked from the Wandsworth school to Battersea, where we got into a boat and landed at Hungerford Stairs. We then went to the Strand, to the house of Mrs. Jane Higginson, where we drank tea and supped, after which we went in a hackney-coach to Mrs. Meves's residence, 16 Vere Street, Oxford Street, where I well remember seeing from the windows the illuminations and rejoicings in honour of Lord Howe's victory, the 1st of June 1794.

The house where Mrs. Meves lived was kept by a hosier. "The man and his wife were dressed like Quakers." On the opposite side was Parmentier's, a large confectioner's shop; there my reputed mother gave orders for the cake called "brioche" to be made for me. During my stay in Vere Street, I went with the servant "Milley" to fetch home Miss Cecilia Meves, who was placed at a preparatory school at Craven Hill, Bayswater. We went as far as the Edgeware Road, when we crossed some fields to Craven Hill, and I saw for the first time my reputed little sister "Cecilia," who was about five years of age. We returned home to Vere Street,—Mrs. Meves's entire affection being devoted to Cecilia: with her she was kind and indulgent, with me, strict and severe. She gave me instruction on the harpsichord, and how to read music in a proper manner.

After I had been about a fortnight under her care, I returned to Mr. Tempest's to finish my half-year's education, which upon completing, I left, with many of my school-fellows, at the Midsummer quarter. On my arrival at the White Horse Cellar, Piccadilly, Milley was there waiting to conduct me to my reputed mother's care, who then resided at the corner of Woodstock Street and Oxford Street. I was given to understand—"that is to say, about twenty or thirty years after the period I am now writing upon, for then I was entirely ignorant of any such person as Mrs. Davenport, or that any such lady was interested in my welfare, more particularly as regarded my respected reputed mother, or the name of Marianne Crowley, or that of Madame Schroeter or Schroeder, which was a family name used by Mr. Meves when he followed the profession of a miniature painter "—that when my reputed mother came from France, in May 1794, that Mrs. Davenport had remitted from Shropshire four twenty-pound notes to Mrs. Jane Higginson for the services of Mrs. Meves; and also that Mrs. Davenport had given directions for a suite of rooms to be properly and substantially furnished for Mrs. Meves, with a power of attorney, made in Mrs. Jane Higginson's name, for her to receive, at Messrs. Hoare and Barnett's, bankers, of Lombard Street, London, £100 per annum, in quarterly payments of £25, for the services of Marianne Crowley Meves. This, together with Mrs. Meves's musical talent as a teacher of the harp and singing, made her quite an independent lady, she having a number of pupils amongst the highest circles of the English nobility; and from her superior education and manners, she was always well received in society. She spoke English in the most refined manner, she was a classic Italian scholar, and could translate the most difficult Italian poets into French or English without the slightest hesitation; but she could not speak the Italian language or converse with the same fluency as Mr. Meves, the difference being, Mrs. Meves having a theoretical knowledge through study, and Mr. Meves a practical knowledge—he having resided a considerable time at Portici, near Naples, where his friend and patron, Roger Palmer, Esq., resided for some time. Peace being concluded between England and America in 1782, Roger Palmer returned to England with Mr. Meves as his travelling companion.

I well remember Mrs. Meves intrusting me to the care of old Mr. John Baptist Meyer, a teacher of the harp, to take me to 49 Wilson Street, Moorfields, where Mr. Meves resided, in July 1794. He received me with great kindness, and the next morning took me with him to the Rotunda of the Bank of England, and introduced me to a Mr. Abraham Osorio, a stockbroker, who recommended him to place me at a Mr. Vale's day-school, in Old Bethlehem, Bishopsgate, where his nephew, Master Aaron Brandon, went to school. The schoolroom was at the back of Broad Street Buildings. At this day-school I was placed by Mr. Meves, who usually came for me about three o'clock, after he had finished his transfers at the Bank of England. We then used to cross Moorfields, and return to his residence in Wilson Street.

Mr. Meves made me practise the pianoforte very attentively; and when he observed me lost in thought, he would question me as to what I was thinking about. He then got into the habit to engage my attention whilst I was practising the scales, by reading entertaining works, such as *The Arabian Nights' Entertainment*, *The History of England*, and parts of the Bible. Certainly he treated me in my youth with marked and extreme kindness.

Mr. Meves being extremely fond of music, he used to have violin quartetts played by some German gentlemen, whose acquaintance he formed at Mr. Bett's, of the Royal Exchange. Here it was that he met with a young German musician, "Herr Leichter," a native of Leipzig, who played the violin in a very superior manner. Herr Leichter was engaged to attend me in my musical studies, and to accompany me on the violin, in order to make me keep my time correctly. We used to go out together into the Shepherd and Shepherdess Fields at Hoxton. Thus I passed my time; and through being so much in company with

Herr Leichter, I acquired the art of speaking the German language by ear, and could converse when I was a young lad very well upon all common subjects; but when I went to hear the worthy pastor preach at the German Chapel, St. James's, I could not understand what he said. After Mr. Meves had heard the sermon we left the Chapel, and crossed St. James's Park to Ray's Orange Coffee-house, Chelsea, near Ranelagh Walk, where Mr. Meves usually dined. Thus passed my time until the latter end of 1797.

Before the end of the year 1797, Mr. Meves took lodgings at 39 Goodge Street. The master of the house was a sergeant in the St. Pancras Volunteers. He placed a gun into my hands, and taught me how to handle it in a soldier-like manner. At that time Mr. Meves gave up having quartett parties at his house, and amused himself in painting pictures, both in oil and water-colours. I remember him taking a full-length portrait of me, with a gun in my hand, in his camera-obscura. I never saw Mr. Meves paint the picture. He may have done so whilst 1 was in Edinburgh, in 1802, where I stayed for about three months.

About the year 1805, I went one afternoon to the house of a Mr. Facius, an engraver in mezzotinto, who lived in Macclesfield Street, Soho; and, from what passed between them, I have always since imagined that Facius engraved the above portrait which Mr. Meves took of me. Likewise, I am highly impressed that a coloured engraving I possessed, entitled " L'Espoir des Français," was taken from the portrait which Mr. Meves drew in the first instance for me, as the character of the above portrait and that of " L'Espoir des Français " were identical in idea; but in this I may be mistaken, both as to who engraved the print, and of Mr. Meves's picture of me having been the origination of the engraving entitled " L'Espoir des Français." The print was an oval, representing a youth in the garden of the Tuileries, near the Terrace, with a gun in his hand, and as possessing brown eyes and hair, the latter hanging in abundance over his shoulders.

In 1802 I made my appearance at the Edinburgh Concerts—

" Urbani's Concerts "—at the George Street Rooms, as Master Augustus. Mr. Paul Alday was the Musical Director. He, having heard me play at Mr. Tomkinson's, in Dean Street, London, had induced me to go with him to Edinburgh. I obtained Mr. Meves's consent, but he would not allow me to use his name, remarking, as your mother says, " I am keeping you in trammels, and as Mr. Alday seems to be satisfied with your musical talent I have not the slightest objection for you to go to Edinburgh ; but mind, sir, I will not permit you to appear in the name of Meves, but only that of Master Augustus."

On my arrival at Edinburgh, Mr. Alday introduced me at a party given at Lady Betty Cunningham's, who lived in a château near Leith Walk. I played a trio, accompanied by Mr. Alday and Signor Bigghi Lolli, " violoncello player." I also played a sonata of Steibelt's with Mr. Yaniewicz, who accompanied me on the violin. The following day a compliment was paid me, in a critique upon Urbani's Concert, namely : " Master Augustus, the Piano Concerto Player.—This young gentleman's fine touch, taste, and execution, is only to be equalled by the great Mozart."*

At Lady Cunningham's I met a lady of the name of the Countess Lally, or " Lilley," who complimented me highly on my performance.

One evening at the George Street Assembly Rooms, I played Steibelt's concerto of " The Storm," and in the andante movement on the air of " The Yellow-Haired Laddie " I met with an encore. After which, as I was passing down the concert-room, the lady whom I call the Countess Lally spoke to me. Next to her sat a stout French gentleman. The Countess paid me a flattering compliment on my performance, and the gentleman took me politely by the hand and likewise complimented me. Upon my seeing Mr. Alday, he said : " Mr. Augustus, as you were passing down the room, after you had finished your concerto, you spoke to the Countess Lally, whilst she was in conversation with the King of France." I said, " Was that gentleman really the King of France who spoke to me ?" He answered, " Yes ; although he does

* See Appendix, Note C, for Biographical Notice of Meves' " Augustus.'

not take the title of King of France, nevertheless he is so since the death of his brother. He paid you a very high compliment, saying : ' that you played like an angel, and that truly you were full of talent.' "

On my return to London Mr. Meves seemed to have lost all desire to make a superior musician of me. A Mr. Possin, who, up to the time I went to Edinburgh, had been giving me lessons on counterpoint and composition, no longer instructed me ; and Mr. Meves thought fit to place me in the counting-house of a friend of his, a Mr. Beland, to whom he said he had advanced a sum of money. The firm was that of Beland and Beckman, 9 Budge Row, Cannon Street. Here I was employed for some time, with the intention of my being brought up as a merchant. The dull monotony of the counting-house greatly fatigued me, and Mr. Beland found great fault with me for writing so badly. Certainly my handwriting was sadly neglected in my youth, my whole time having been devoted to the study of the pianoforte. My education was altogether indifferent ; and I almost think it was designedly done, in order that I might feel a diffidence in my own resource of knowledge as I grew up in life.

Being disgusted with Mr. Beland's rude manner, and the routine of the counting-house, I complained to Mrs. Meves, who at that time resided at 32 Great Pulteney Street, next door to Messrs. John Broadwood and Son, the celebrated pianoforte manufacturers. When she introduced me to Mr. John Broadwood, this worthy gentleman was very kind to me. I frequently dined at his hospitable table. He introduced me one day, whilst I was practising, to the Dowager Duchess of Leinster, who was pleased to compliment me on my pianoforte-playing. Subsequently, he introduced me to other families of distinction, to whom I gave instructions on the pianoforte.

My amiable reputed mother one evening took me with her to Lady George Stuart's, Dover Street, Piccadilly. Lady George Stuart introduced me to the Dowager Marchioness of Lansdowne, in Albemarle Street, who gave me a general invitation to her Sunday parties, where I usually played duets for the pianoforte and harp with Lady George

Stuart, who was Mrs. Meves's favourite pupil. The Miss Giffards, daughters of the Dowager Marchioness of Lansdowne by her first marriage, were also her singing pupils.

One evening when I was leaving the drawing-room, Lord Lauderdale requested I should stay to supper, saying, " It is the Marchioness's command, and you must obey." I conducted the Miss Giffards to the supper-table, and sat next to Captain Chadd. Opposite to me were Sir George Warrender and Captain Mellish, all young persons at that time. At the head of the table sat the Marchioness, on one side of her ladyship sat His Royal Highness Prince Ernest, Duke of Cumberland, and on the other sat my Lord Lauderdale, who acted as chaperon to the Marchioness.

On another occasion, as I was entering the drawing-room, an elderly pale-faced gentleman rose, and made me a polite bow. I observed on his breast the insignia, " Le Saint Esprit." I returned his salutation, and then retired to the grand piano to join the young ladies. The Count de Cogneau, the adjutant of a French royal regiment established in London, in which Captain Grammont had a commission, who was in company with Mrs. Meves at the time, said it was the Duke de Bourbon who had made me the polite bow. I observed that I thought I had seen him before at a party at Dowager Lady Dalling's, in Harley Street, and that I thought the gentleman was a teacher of the French language to Miss Dalling, as when I had previously seen him he was without his order of knighthood, and in familiar conversation with Mr. Louis von Esh, who taught Miss Dalling music.

Mr. Meves had a great dislike to my frequenting such society, remarking I should never gain any money by it, and thought it would be much better for me to teach at schools, and gain a settled income. Accordingly a walk in the musical profession was purchased for me, from a Mr. Lord, which occupied me incessantly for six days in the week, and thus it was that I was taken from forming a fine connexion in life. In a few years I amassed above £600 in Mr Meves's hands.

In 1802, after my return from Edinburgh, I entered the St.

James's Volunteers. On one occasion, in the court-yard of Burlington House, where the regiment usually paraded, I, with many others in the regiment, took the oath of allegiance before His Grace the Duke of Portland and Colonel Lord Amherst, on account of there being so many disloyal characters that frequented debating-societies, etc.

In 1809, when I resided with my reputed father at 44 Rathbone Place, I entered the Loyal British Artificers, upon the recommendation of Adjutant Orr, as an officer. I had, after about two years' service, a commission granted me as Captain. The commission was dated in 1811, and signed by His Grace Scott Duke of Portland, as Lord-Lieutenant of the county of Middlesex.

In 1809, I determined to go through a course of medicine. Accordingly I placed myself under the advice of a celebrated surgeon, and as I lay in bed, thoughts of former occurrences came to my mind. I remembered having seen a wonderful display on the water, and that I was sitting on some terrace in a garden, from where I saw a large gilded barge coming down the stream. When it came near to where I was, the boat stopped, and I saw several characters habited like Druids, who were near an altar engaged throwing perfumed incense before a marble bust. Clouds of smoke filled the air, and numbers of dancers with garlands in their hands approached the bust, and hung their garlands in festoons, and knelt before the bust. The Druid priests then sang hymns of praise, when a female dancer ran with a crown of laurels in her hands up to the bust, and crowned it with garlands. I saw the oars from the portcullis, " below the stage erected on the boat," move the boat, which passed through the arches of the bridge and disappeared from my sight.

I told my reputed father of this, and asked him where I had witnessed this representation. He replied this must have taken place on some occasion of the opening of the season at Vauxhall, when we were sitting on the terrace of the Apollo Tea-Gardens at Vauxhall, where they generally gave some grand display on the water, representing the genius of the Thames.

Upon reflection, I think what I have just related was the funeral obsequies of Voltaire, when his remains were removed to the Pantheon for the illustrious dead, as when I read the account in *Prudhomme's Journal*, it seemed to correspond in many instances with my own recollections of the above event.

THE REMAINS OF VOLTAIRE.

"Twelve white horses, three abreast, drew the triumphal car of four wheels, which should have been of equal size, the more so in order to approach the Greek or Roman style; likewise they should have contented themselves with a sarcophagus, and not to have crowned it with a figure of Voltaire lying on the bed of death. The ancients were more chaste in ornamentation, and from the most simple objects knew how to obtain great effect. Voltaire seated in the curule chair would have produced more effect, and should have been complied with, for the people, by instinct, prefer nature to art. Arrived at the point which leads to the Quai Voltaire, the procession was obliged to make a halt under the windows of the Palace of the Tuileries. The hosts of this château so positioned themselves behind their lattices, in order that they might contemplate at leisure this spectacle so strange to them,—this movement not being the most agreeable in their lives. Louis Capet took every precaution to observe this spectacle without being observed himself. The plaudits given to the remains of Voltaire by the people alarmed Louis, as he conjectured seeing the people already crowding into the Palace, in order to carry off his inviolable person, and oblige him to follow on foot the triumphal car, along with his chaste half. The daughter of the Cæsars that day was dressed in sky-blue, and had taken refuge in the entresol, in order to lose nothing of the cortège, every circumstance of which was a torture to her.'—*Prudhomme's Journal*, 4th July 1791.*

In 1813 I took a dislike to the musical profession, on account of the monotonous and wearisome sameness I had experienced, "as my pupils were not all finished players," when I took to speculating in the funds at the Rotunda of the Bank of England, buying with my money omnium, on which I made a considerable amount of money. In 1814 I lost considerably in speculating in the consols.

At the restoration of the Bourbons, in 1814, I went to Calais with Mr. Meves and a Mr. Henry Page, who held an appointment under the Lord High Chancellor, "Lord Eldon." At Calais I was introduced to

* See Appendix, Note D, for Lamartine's description of this procession.

a Mr. Palyart, "Chef de Duanne." This led to an introduction to a Madame Grancourt Mates and to a Mr. Pigault Moubilliarque. Places had been taken for us to proceed to Boulogne-sur-Mer, but after being about ten days or a fortnight in Calais, Mr. Page received orders from the Court of Chancery to return to England. Mr. Meves likewise returned to England with Mr. Page, but I remained at Calais for some time, as I had received an invitation from a Mr. Laloutre, whom I had met at Mr. Halgous's, who kept the Maison roulage at Calais, to go with him to Dunkirk, where his daughters were on a visit. In a few days I returned to Calais, where I remained for about six weeks, spending my time very agreeably amongst the inhabitants. The return of Napoleon Bonaparte from the Island of Elba in 1815 prevented my going to Paris.

After my return to London in 1815, Mrs. Meves and I went together to the Old Argyle Rooms, in Regent Street, where French plays were performed. We sat together in the front row of the boxes. During the performance Mrs. Meves left the box, but before leaving she desired me not to leave the seat in which I was seated until she returned. During the interval she was away, I saw a lady looking very attentively at me, and shortly after I went down-stairs, when I observed several ladies and gentlemen bow and curtsey to the same lady whom I had before noticed observing me. Upon making inquiry of some persons, whom I had noticed curtsey to the lady, who it was, I was informed it was Her Royal Highness the Duchess of Angoulême.

At the time I did not take any notice of this, but in after years I could not help thinking that I was taken intentionally to the Argyle Rooms by Mrs. Meves, in order that Her Royal Highness might see me, and be convinced that her brother, the once prisoner of the Temple, was saved, and in trustworthy custody.

In 1816 I took a trip to Calais. Mr. Pigault Moubilliarque, "of Calais," brother to Pigault le Brun, gave me a letter of introduction to Talma, the celebrated French actor. I proceeded to Paris about the latter end of August 1816, and resided à la Rue de Cléry, near La

Rue Montmartre. I used to frequent the house of a Mr. Freuden-thaler, a celebrated pianoforte manufacturer in La Rue Montmartre, who received me in a very hospitable manner. I called at Sebastian Erard's manufactory, where I became acquainted with Mr. Herold, "the operatic composer," who gave me an invitation to meet him on the following Sunday at Mr. Erard's country-seat, at Sêve, near St. Cloud. I dined with the family of the Erards, and slept at their house on the Sunday night. After breakfast on the Monday morning, when I was about to leave to return to Paris, Mr. Sebastian Erard desired me to avail myself of the opportunity, and pay a visit to the Palace of Versailles. This I did ; and on my arrival at the long avenue leading to the Palace, I met with a guide, who offered his services to attend me. I procured an order of admittance in the court-yard of the Palace, and viewed the various grand apartments, and observed the exquisitely painted ceilings by Le Brun ; and entered La Grande Salle des Ambassades, and observed the magnificent gardens. An old Swiss, attached to the service of the Palace, attended me ; and at the end of the room he led me to the Grand l'Escalier des Ambassades, the staircase of which is made of the most exquisite and rare marble, or porphyry—"a red mottled Italian marble." Whilst looking over the balustrade of the staircase, and attending to the conversation of the old Swiss, who was recounting to me the attack the populace made on Versailles, the 5th and 6th of October 1789, suddenly I looked around very attentively, and observed the ceiling, the stairs, and the hall below, when it appeared to my recollective powers that I had been there before ; it seeming to me that, at such a place I then beheld, was the one where, in my youth, I was in the lap of some lady, from where, looking over the balustrade, I saw a band of music, of some cavalry regiment, who were performing various pieces of music ; and thus recalling to my mind the place that had often struck my reflective powers, where I had seen in my youth a man with a kettle-drum fixed on his back, and a musician beating the kettle-drum. The play of the drumsticks rebounding from the drum attracted my attention, and made a powerful impression on my boyish mind.

I turned to the guide, and asked him how it was that one of the stairs was of a different kind of marble. He replied : "As the populace were forcing their way in from the doors entering the hall, the guards, with their muskets, in defending the staircase, destroyed one of the stairs, and the marble being of so rare and expensive a quality, another kind of the same colour had been substituted." The Swiss then took me into the theatre of the Palace, where the entertainment was given by the Queen of France to the regiment from Flanders, who were on duty at Versailles. He told me the theatre, and the tables, which were covered with a kind of deep red baize, were exactly in the same state as when the Queen of France gave the entertainment. He then narrated the circumstance of the Queen having brought her son, the Prince Dauphin of France, from Meudon, in order to present him to the regiment from Flanders ; and on their seeing the young Dauphin, they, being intoxicated with joy at the Queen's kindness and condescension, in the height of their loyalty tore the tri-coloured cockades from their caps, and trod them under their feet. This it was, he said, that had occasioned the populace to attack the Palace of Versailles, in order to resent the insult offered to the national colours. He then said : "From the time the Royal Family had quitted Versailles, the Palace had been uninhabited by any branch of the Royal Family." He then took me into the grounds of Versailles, to see the gardens and the magnificent fountains. I strolled across the park, listening to the remarks of the guide, when I beheld the Marble Palace, once the residence of the Marchioness of Pompadour. We entered the grand hall of the château, but I took little notice of what I saw, except a beautiful ivory model of a ship of war. We continued our walk across the park of Versailles to the entrance of the Petit Trianon, when I felt fatigued, and returned to Sêve. When left to myself, I walked leisurely along, ruminating on what I had seen ; and the more I reflected, the more I felt assured I had seen L'Escalier des Ambassades before, for it appeared to me the very balustrade over which I had, in my childhood, witnessed the incident of the band playing, and of the drummer's drumsticks rebounding from the drum, thereby making a lasting impression of such on my recollective powers.

It likewise appeared to me I had been in the Salle du Théâtre before, and of being caressed, and seeing fireworks displayed there by some soldiers. In this state of mind I returned to the château of the Messrs. Erard, and the next morning returned to Paris.

Talma used to send me orders to see him in many of his characters; as Hamlet, also in a tragedy of Corneille's, and in Racine's "Andromache," when I saw him perform with Mademoiselle Deschendis. He also sent me orders to see the celebrated French comedian Fleury, and Mademoiselle Mars, in Molière's comedy of "Tartuffe." I frequently went to the Opera Français, to hear Gluck's "Iphigenie;" and to the Opera Italien, to hear Mademoiselle Sessi and Madame Pasta in Mozart's opera of "Figaro;" and also witnessed the exquisite dancing of Mademoiselle Biggottini in the ballet of "Nina."

I passed my leisure time at the house of Herr Freudenthaler, and in the society of a Miss Willett, who resided in the Place Vendôme, under the care of a lady of the name of Prior. An elegant carriage was kept for their services.

I frequently dined at the table-d'hôte in the Place Vendôme, with Miss Willett and Mrs. Prior. Miss Willett was a ward in Chancery, and a pupil of Mrs. Meves. After dinner I frequently expressed my opinions regarding French manners in too forcible language, remarking, that Frenchmen, who had suffered so much for the cause of freedom, were in fact a set of slaves,—that at every table where mixed society frequented were to be found agents and persons connected with the French police, who reported what they heard, and the sentiments and feelings of parties who frequented the table-d'hôte,—that a lady from Bath, a friend of the Baron de Bode, had been before a commissioner of police, for having expressed herself rather too freely on some political subject.

The Baron de Bode, who resided in Rue de Parc Royal, invited me to pass my disengaged evenings at his house, as his daughter, Miss

Adelaide de Bode, was a very accomplished musician. Miss Willett had sent her an order, signed by the Baron Ségur, to view the Palace of the Tuileries, and the private apartments of Louis XVIII. As she had no desire to see the Palace, she gave me the order, and I visited the Tuileries; but I saw nothing which reminded me of any object I might have seen before. I asked if I might be permitted to touch the organ, but was informed that no person was allowed to do so, except the organist, "Signor Cherubini." From the chapel I went into the private apartments of Louis XVIII. His bed was on a mattress in the corner of his bedroom. Opposite the windows, by the side of his bed, was a large easy-chair, and a bearskin muff was lying on the seat. On my questioning a valet, who was in the bedroom, "Is this the bed of his Gracious Majesty?" he replied, "Yes, sir; his Majesty, who is unfortunately troubled with the gout, cannot get into a higher bed." I observed the simplicity and unpretending character of the furniture. Every article was useful, but no appearance of grandeur or royalty was displayed. On leaving the apartment I entered the room of the Garde de Corps. I there observed a large painting, and examined it carefully. This picture I thought I had seen before.

At Mr. Freudenthaler's I met with MM. Mugnie and Mezot, whom I had known formerly in London. One morning, however, Mugnie came into the room, where I was playing the pianoforte, accompanied by a stout French gentleman, in a kind of military costume of light blue with silver epaulets. Mugnie commenced a dispute with me about my pianoforte-playing, and finished by saying, "If you do not leave Paris within twenty-four hours, you will be thrown into prison; I tell you the truth, I tell you the truth." I defied his threat by saying, "Sir, I shall place myself under the protection of the British ambassador, and on my leaving this house I shall at once go to the Hotel de Sebastiani, and demand protection as a British subject." This I accordingly did. On my arrival at the residence of the English embassy, I was shown into the room of the chief secretary attached to the service of the embassy, and saw my friend the Honourable Captain

Dawson, whose sisters, the Lady Anna Maria and Lady Louisa I had the honour to give lessons to at their residence in Grosvenor Street, London. Captain Dawson advised me to leave Paris, as my object of establishing myself as a professor of the pianoforte at Paris would not be crowned with success. On my leaving I called at the Place Vendôme, and saw Miss Willett. I told her my intention to leave Paris and to proceed at once to Calais; she consented likewise to leave Paris the next day, and requested me to get a passport for her and her friend.

On my return to my apartments I reflected on the occurrences of the day, and could not account for the strange behaviour of Mugnie. I ascribed it to the manner I had expressed myself at the public dining-table at the hotel in the Place Vendôme. What I had seen at the Palace of Versailles, together with the incidental narration of the old Swiss, awakened imperfectly in me early reminiscences. I felt quite certain that the Escalier des Ambassades was familiar to me; my first introduction to Mr. Meves then came to my mind, and I resolved to quit Paris. The next morning I made application for my passport at the Duke of Richelieu's office, and at the same time obtained one for Miss Willett and her friend. Some French gentlemen who were residing in the same house with me desired me to visit the grave of Marshal Ney in the gardens of the Luxembourg before I left Paris. We all proceeded to the Luxembourg, where I saw in a detached part of the garden a mound of earth, which contained the remains of that brave French officer. I lamented much the end of the brave Marshal.

The same afternoon, I, in company with Miss Willett and her female friend, took our seats in the diligence, and proceeded *en route* for Amiens. On arriving there a considerable time was allowed the passengers to get their dinner. I availed myself of the opportunity to view the city and the magnificent cathedral, and saw the celebrated marble statue of Le Petit Plurcier. I arrived at Calais, but greatly fatigued with the journey, and felt seriously ill. I took quarters at the Hotel de Kingston. The next morning I conducted the ladies on board the packet-boat for Dover, but I really felt too unwell to accompany them, and I remained for about a week at Calais to recover from the fatigues occasioned by the dull heavy motion of the diligence. After taking a farewell leave of my friends at Calais, who had treated me with so much hospitality, I went on board the packet, and arrived at Dover. The next morning I proceeded on by coach to London, and paid my respects to Mr. Meves, who received me with expressions of great satisfaction at my cautious conduct and general behaviour during my stay in France.

I then entered with determination the musical profession, and published several pianoforte compositions which I had written whilst in Paris. They became very successful. I dedicated one of Berton's elegant melodies, from his opera "L'Alene," to my friend Mr. Latour.* This rondo became highly popular.

At times I frequented the Bank of England and the Rotunda. One afternoon I was sitting on a subscription form in Capel Court, near the Stock Exchange, whilst Mr. Meves was transacting business with some gentlemen, "members of the Exchange," and upon his leaving to return to the Rotunda to make his transfers, a Mr. John Henderson took the liberty, as he was passing him, to knock his hat off—"a usage then very common at the Stock Exchange." Mr. Meves, who was a very proud man, said, "How dare you presume to knock my hat off? take liberties, sir, with men of your own stamp." As Mr. Meves passed me I said to him, "Dear sir, I am sorry to see you so angry and so much offended, but I certainly will not allow such conduct to pass without a proper apology." With this I returned up Capel Court to Mr. Henderson, stating that Mr. Meves had complained to me of his conduct in frequently taking liberties with him. This he denied, and said, "What does your father mean by saying, 'Take liberties with men of your own stamp?' I am just as respectable a man as Mr. Meves, and pay my differences with as much promptitude as your father." I then said, "Sir, you frequently, when Mr. Meves comes from his painting-table, take the liberty to unbutton his coat, and expose him in his painting

* A music publisher of Bond Street.

dress." This he denied, and used a vulgar expression. This insult I immediately resented, and struck him a slight blow, upon which he dealt a most violent blow at me, which I luckily warded off; nevertheless it grazed the skin, and brought some blood from my cheek, whereupon I retreated, and then ran in and gave him a violent blow, which knocked him down. Some of his friends who were standing by carried him into the subscription room next to the Stock Exchange. A German Jew, a man of considerable property, who saw the whole affair, ran across the street to the Rotunda, and said to Mr. Meves, "Your son has thrashed Henderson." Mr. Meves then came and spoke to me. We then went into the room where Henderson was, when I said, "Sir, I do not regret having resented the rude conduct you were guilty of towards my father; but believe me when I say, that I am sincerely sorry to find that I struck you in so violent manner." I then went home with Mr. Meves, and he promised to pay several expenses I was at. He placed about £3000 in our joint names in the Bank of England, and other share property, he to receive the dividends as long as he was living.

From that time nothing particularly transpired until about the latter end of the month of July 1818, when I went into the City, and sold to Mr. Meves £1500 omnium, on which 20 per cent. had been paid. It had cost me, with the premium, about £350; I sold them at about the same price. I dined that day with him; Mr. George Meves was also there. Mr. Meves made his dinner on craw-fish, of which he ate very heartily. I told him I thought it was very dangerous food, and requested him to take some brandy after it, which he declined. We had a few glasses of Cape wine, and as I had to give some lessons in Bond Street the next day, it was agreed that Mr. George Meves should leave the £1500 omnium at the Exchequer Bill Office, as there was 10 per cent. further payment to make. Mr. Meves gave the proper instructions for what his brother had to do. It being a remarkably fine afternoon, Mr. Meves walked with me to the west end of the town. On our coming near Berners Street he complained of feeling rather unwell, when we rested for some length of time. I was very desirous of his accompanying me home to my residence, 54 Great Marlborough Street, where Mrs. Meves lived, and partake of a glass of brandy, in which a quantity of peach kernels were steeped, which made it a very powerful stomachic. All my persuasions were of no avail. He said he felt quite well, and was determined to return home ; but he promised me he would take a glass of brandy-punch at the Furnival Inn Coffee-house, and read the evening newspapers. I left Mr. Meves at the corner of Museum Street, Holborn, as I had promised to spend the evening in Bond Street, which I accordingly did. The following morning I was awakened at an early hour by the bell ringing rather violently, when the servant of the house ushered into my bedroom the patrol from Cushion Court, Broad Street, who informed me that Mr. Meves had taken dangerously ill, and that I was to come with all convenient haste to see him.

On my arrival in the City, I observed he looked greatly exhausted. He then told me that during the night his stomach became greatly disordered, and gave him dreadful pains. In the course of the day he became much worse, and I went for Dr. Meyers, who said Mr. Meves was attacked with cholera morbus. He gave him some medicine, which seemed to do him good. Late in the evening my amiable reputed mother came to inquire the cause of my lengthened absence. She gave the necessary orders to the housekeeper for Mr. Meves's comforts ; and the adjacent room was prepared for her. During the night Mr. Meves was seized with violent cramps. I gave him his medicine, which seemed to quiet and relieve him. Towards the morning, when the servant came to prepare the fire for breakfast, my kind protector, and more than father, had ceased to exist.

About ten o'clock I went to the Bank, and told the porter to call Proctor Davis. When his partner, Mr. Taylor, came, I informed him of the decease of Mr. Meves, and that I was to put his will as early as possible into Mr. Davis's hands. On my return to Cushion Court with Mr. Taylor, upon searching the bureau, " part of my late reputed father's bookcase," I found in the upper drawer a will, open, but not signed. I put it into Mr. Taylor's hands. Mr. George Meves said, "This will is not signed." I replied, "That does not signify; my late father told me that I should find his will in the bottom drawer of this bureau." I then opened the bottom drawer, and found a will, on the outside of which was written : "The Last Will, and Testament of William Meves. A copy of this will, properly executed, will be found in the hands of Mr. Henry Page and Sons, of 8 Southampton Buildings, Holborn." Mr. Taylor then observed, "The will in Mr. Page's hands is the last will executed by the late Mr. William Meves." We all proceeded to Southampton Buildings, when Mr. Taylor partially read the will, and said, "This is an exact copy of the will in Cushion Court." On my return, Mrs. Meves was desirous of my leaving, and giving the key of the room to Mr. George Meves, which I did, and said to him, "I wish my late father to be buried on Wednesday next, 'he having died on Saturday, the 1st August 1818,' which is four clear days from his decease." This he consented to, if the parish authorities allowed it. I then accompanied Mrs. Meves home to Marlborough Street, having placed my late reputed father's pocket-book, with about twenty pounds, into her hands. I locked up the bureau and bookcase, and then gave the key to Mr. George Meves; and left the entire direction of the funeral in his hands. I then conducted Mrs. Meves to a coach, and returned to our residence, 54 Great Marlborough Street.

I retired to rest early in the evening; and on the following morning, whilst I was at breakfast, Mr. George Meves came, and desired me to accompany him to Cushion Court, as it was necessary for me to see the searchers. Upon our arrival, two elderly women came and carefully examined the body. They said to me, "Sir, has not this gentleman died rather suddenly?" I replied, "Yes; he was in perfect good health last Thursday;" when one of the women said, "There are strange appearances about the body of this gentleman. Who attended him at the time of his decease?" I replied, "Dr. Meyers of Broad Street Buildings;" to which they said, "It is all right, sir," and they made me a curtsey. I then remarked, "Are you both satisfied?"

They replied, "O yes, sir; O yes, sir." I then observed, "If you are satisfied, it is more than I am, as I must see Dr. Meyers on the subject, or have the body properly examined by a surgeon, before I can allow it to be interred." On my leaving the house with Mr. George Meves, I met Dr. Meyers, and told him what the searchers had said respecting the strange appearances on the late Mr. Meves's body. He answered by saying, "Your father died of cholera morbus, which will take off the strongest man in twenty-four hours."

In the course of the afternoon I called on a Mr. Brooks, a surgeon, of Blenheim Street, and requested him to examine my late father's remains, which he agreed to do. I told Mrs. Meves what I had done, which she considered quite unnecessary, as it was quite certain Mr. Meves had died a natural death.

Early the next morning Mr. George Meves came, and stated, as Mr. Meves had died of a most dangerous malady, his funeral was to take place that very morning—"Monday morning." I said, "Sir, consider my good father dying on Saturday morning; such haste seems like hurrying him into his grave." All that I could say was of no avail; and at last I consented, and entered a coach, and we drove into the City. On our arrival, it being then rather late, we at once proceeded, as the burial was to take place at St. James's Church, Piccadilly.

Some days after the funeral, my amiable reputed mother desired me to write to Messrs. Davis and Taylor, "the Proctors," and request a copy of the will to be sent to 54 Great Marlborough Street; and, by her advice, I consented not to interfere or do anything regarding my late respected father's affairs, as Mr. Taylor had already taken me to Doctors' Commons, where I was sworn to execute the testator's will as the sole executor. It was then agreed I should go into the country, in order to divest myself entirely of all painful recollections respecting my late father; and that I should not go into the City to administer to the funded property or shares for at least a month. To this proposal I agreed, as my reputed mother had great power of persuasion over me.

A copy of the will was sent to me in due course of time, according to request.

" IN THE NAME OF GOD. AMEN.

"I, Augustus Anthony William Meves, 'but for the brevity of the many transactions at the Bank, always subscribe by my last Christian name, William Meves,' living, at this time of making my last Will, and Testament, at 49 Wilson Street, in the parish of Shoreditch, in perfect health, and understanding, first recommending my soul to the mercy of the Almighty, desire a plain, but decent, burial. My property—which will be found in the Three Per Cent. Consols, Three Per Cents. Reduced Long Annuities, New Five Per Cents., and the cashiers of the Bank with whom I keep my cash: my clothes, furniture, etc., shall be publicly sold, except those things which I shall separately mention—shall be disposed of in the following manner :—

"Firstly, I leave to my natural reputed son, Augustus Antoine Cornelius Meves, born in the year One thousand seven hundred and eighty-five, and baptized in Saint James's Church, the half of all my property; a quarter part to his sister Cecilia; an eighth part to my brother, George Meves, now living in the service of Mr. Drummond Smith, in Piccadilly. The eighth remaining part, in equal shares, to a brother, and sister at Brunswick, in Germany," etc. etc.

On my reputed mother reading the will to me, she exclaimed : *" What could have induced Mr. Meves to make such a will as this, disgracing me, by naming you as being his natural reputed son, and making you appear to be his illegitimate son. You, my dear Augustus, are the fruit of lawful wedlock ; you are not the son of the late Mr. Meves, nor are you my son, for you, Augustus, owe your existence to the unfortunate Marie Antoinette, Queen of France. She was your mother, who, in your infancy, intrusted you to my care; and I have done more than a mother's duty to you. For you I have become estranged from society, in my determination to protect you; and have lost every one that was dear to me. Never let this disclosure escape your lips whilst I am living. Remember, two attempts have been made on your life, which nearly took fatal effect; and the third might be decisive. The circumstance of your conveyance to England is known to the Archbishop of Paris; and, should it hereafter be required, your identity can be proved as positive as the sun at noonday. The late Mr. Meves, at the hazard of his life, went to Paris, and obtained an interview with the Queen of France, in the prison of the Conciergerie, where he made the Queen a promise regarding you, which he kept to the latest hour of his existence."*

This disclosure kept preying on my mind. I then well remembered my first interview with Mr. Meves, and the woman who left me in the room where he was sitting at supper, and my bursting into tears at seeing an entire stranger, instead of the person I was led to expect to have seen, which was my beloved father. I well remembered Mr. Meves's great kindness to me, and his giving me some delicious wine to drink, and his striving to comfort me in my sad affliction. All this came in rapid succession to my mind, which, from the intensity and depth of my thought on these subjects, brought on a fever of the brain.

I now became more determined in having a post-mortem examination of the body of the late Mr. Meves, and called on Mr. Brooks for that purpose. He advised me to see the magistrate at Bow Street, and to ask for an order for the disinterment of the body. I did as I was directed. The chief magistrate, "Mr. Connant," said that he had no power to give the order, but that I must apply for such to the Lord Mayor and the magistrates sitting at the Mansion House, as the decease took place in the City, and that I should take a surgeon with me at the time I made the application. This I accordingly did, and obtained the order for the disinterment, which was placed in Dr. Brooks's hands. I now felt quite relieved, having obtained my earnest desire.

The fatigue and anxiety I underwent from the opposition I had experienced to my proceedings, brought me into a bad state of health; so much so that I requested Dr. Brooks to attend me. He advised my being cupped, which was accordingly done by a Mr. Mapleson; and I found a great relief therefrom. Towards the evening Mr. Brooks sent one of his assistants with a bottle of medicine and a large blister, which was to be applied to my back. The medicine, I afterwards ascertained from a Dr. Gower, an esteemed friend and medical adviser of mine, contained a quantity of laudanum, which, unfortunately for me, flew to the brain. Under these circumstances a Dr. Tuthill of Soho Square was called in, who directed that I should be taken to a private lodging.

Apartments were taken for me in Park Street, Upper Baker Street, and in the course of the afternoon I was removed from Great Marlborough Street to there, by two men who were appointed by Dr. Tuthill as my attendants. During the afternoon Dr. Tuthill came to see me. I fully expected to see Dr. Brooks, and was astonished to see Dr. Tuthill, who then was a stranger to me. He conversed with me some time, and questioned me in English, and in German such questions he did not wish the men, who were in the room at the time, should understand. Towards the evening a Mr. Viner came, and cupped me by order of Dr. Tuthill. I remember his saying, when he saw my back, " Mapleson has so lacerated him that I do not know where to place the glasses." After he had cupped me I went to bed, and my attendants retired into the front room. I think I fell asleep for some time, but was awakened by the noise and laughing of the two men. I got up and went into the front room, and said to them, "It is the doctor's order that I should be kept quiet, and you are making such a noise that I cannot sleep." While I was speaking, one of the men came behind me, and thrust his hand between my legs, and upset me, and carried me into the bedroom. I protested against such conduct, but uselessly. They at once placed me in bed, and then one of the men, " Richardson," jumped across the bed, and confined my legs to the bed-post, by tying them with his handkerchief, which he took from his neck, and the other man—"his name was Press"—held a pillow over my mouth to prevent my cries being heard. I shall now cast a veil over my sufferings, which were caused more from neglect than ill-usage, as ·I became perfectly unconscious of what was done to me.

I understood from Dr. Gower, the fever, "so he was informed by Dr. Tuthill," lasted nine days, during which time I was at the point of death. However, on the ninth day the fever turned, when Dr. Gower attended me with the assistance of Dr. Tuthill. Subsequently a carriage was hired, which came every day, morning and evening, to take me for a drive in the Park, and by degrees I was allowed to eat animal food.

After about a month I was permitted to go to the Bank to administer to my late reputed father's effects, as all the money in my amiable reputed mother's hands was entirely exhausted. A day was appointed by Dr. Gower for Mrs. Meves to come and see me, when we went to the Bank of England together, accompanied by the attendant Press, where I drew a cheque for about £20. We dined in the City, and after paying the expenses, I put the change out of one of the notes into my pocket, and the remaining notes I gave into my reputed mother's hands, together with my French gold watch, which had nearly occasioned a quarrel between me and the attendant "Press" in the morning, for when he handed me my watch it fell from my hands, when he said to me, "You cannot be trusted with your watch yet." I answered him very cautiously, "Probably not, sir."

After we had dined, we drove to my mother's residence, and Press left us, stating he should return late in the evening. After he left us I entered into a conversation with my reputed mother, and told her of the danger of my remaining in Press's hands, as he wished me to reside with him at his house. My reputed mother then recommended me to a house, 3 Crawford Street, near Baker Street, where I could get furnished apartments.

The next day I took apartments at 3 Crawford Street, from where I wrote a letter to a medical friend of mine, "a Mr. Armstrong, residing in Baker Street, Portman Square," whom I requested to attend me professionally, as I was just recovering from a dangerous illness, and that I required his immediate attendance. Mr. Armstrong returned with the messenger, and after some conversation he left me. During the day he sent me a composing-draught, and a bottle of medicine to take at night. My reputed mother came during the afternoon, and greatly approved of what I had done. My attendants also came, when I requested Mrs. Meves to pay them their demand, which she accordingly did.

I now became regularly installed in my new residence, and continued to improve in my health, but my constitution was most dreadfully shattered, so much so, that little hope was entertained of my ever recovering, but, thanks to Providence, I did recover, though it took two years at least before I was myself again. I then partially resumed the musical profession.

In 1821 I frequented the Rotunda of the Bank of England, where I did business chiefly in the Five Per Cent. Navy Stock. I also attended the House of Commons to hear the debates respecting the Reduction of the Navy Five Per Cents. In 1822 I invested nearly the whole of my property in Spanish dollar bonds, called " Hope of Amsterdam's Loan." By the immense rise which took place in these bonds, I cleared above 30 per cent., nearly doubling my property, and on the sale of them, I invested the whole amount in the purchase of Holdimand's New Spanish Loan, and took on the account day £15,000 stock, or rather fifteen bonds of £1020 each, which I paid for in bank-notes. As I transacted the whole of my business in the Royal Exchange, I took no cheque for payment, only bank-notes for my stock. After paying for my bonds, and placing them into my bankers, Messrs. Remington, Stephenson, and Toulmin, of 69 Lombard Street, I was advised by Mr. Toulmin to go out of town for at least a week or ten days, as the rise was inevitable. This kind advice I took, and went down to Canterbury to see the cathedral and the ancient city, and spent my time very agreeably there. The *Courier* and *Globe* newspapers gave a full account of the stock transactions at the Royal Exchange, and I saw the Spanish bonds were the favourite stock for speculation, which were rising about 2 per cent. every day. When they reached near 75, or about £750 per £1020 bond, I thought it high time for me to return to town, which I accordingly did. On my arrival at the Royal Exchange I sold my fifteen Spanish dollar bonds. After paying the moneys I received to my account with the cashiers of the Bank of England, and to my bankers in Lombard Street, I found my profits to amount to a sum above £1600. This was the most fortunate period of my life as regards stock transactions. Before leaving the City I purchased three thousand

Spanish bonds, after which I sauntered down Cornhill as far as the Mansion House, where I took a chariot to Bond Street, Piccadilly.

On my arrival at 30 Conduit Street, where Mrs. Meves and I then resided, I told her my intention of investing a large sum of money in the purchase of bonded shipping rums, which at the time I could have purchased at an unprecedented low price, as I had intended to give up all speculation in the Spanish bonds, for at least some time. Mrs. Meves strongly advised me not to enter into any speculation in West India produce, particularly rums, as I knew nothing whatever about the nature and habits of the business. Her advice prevailed; but had I invested my money in this speculation, I should have tripled the original amount invested. I had spoken to a West India agent of the probability of my investing about £3000 in rums, "the purchasing price being then at eighteenpence per gallon." When I went into the City I informed the agent I had not fully made up my mind what I should invest, and that therefore he would defer acting for me till I communicated with him.

I found, by consulting the newspapers, the Spanish bonds were falling daily, and a large army was formed on the French side of the Pyrenees, called, "Le Cordon Sanitaire." This name was soon altered into that of "L'Armée d'Observation." The Spanish bonds had fallen to about fifty-eight per cent., when I went into the City, and purchased on 'Change ten bonds, of £1020 each, which cost me £5800.

Here I must take an antecedent date, and narrate an incident that occurred in the year 1821, when I was residing with Mrs. Meves, at 101 High Street, Marylebone. The incident was a transaction I had with Rowland Stephenson, Esq., banker, 69 Lombard Street, from whom I received the following :—

"LOMBARD STREET, *March* 6.

"DEAR SIR,—If you happen to be coming into the City in a day or two, will you favour me with a call? I have an instrument left with me, belonging to a most particular friend, for whom I am anxious to have your opinion.—Yours very truly,

" ROWLAND STEPHENSON.

"A. MEVES, Esq., 101 High Street, Marylebone."

I called as desired; and my visit ended in his requesting of me a loan of £1600, as he was about to be proposed as M.P. for Romford, in Essex. As I had not a balance of £1600 in their, Messrs. Remington, Stephenson, and Toulmin's hands, I directed him to sell £1500 of my India bonds to make up the amount required. This was accordingly done; and I requested him to fill up a cheque for the amount of £1600, and I would sign it. He began to fill up a cheque, and wrote as far as "Rowland," when he said, "Mr. Meves, it would be better for you to write the amount, as I should not like the firm to know, that I had been borrowing money." So I wrote :—

"Lombard Street.

"No.   No. 69.—London, *March* 13, 1821.—Messrs. Stephenson, Remington, and Co., pay Rowland Stephenson, or bearer, Sixteen hundred pounds.

"£1600."   "Augustus Meves."

As I passed through I paid into their cashier's hands £1560. Mr. Rowland Stephenson gave me a memorandum, stating he held £1600 at five per cent., returnable at any time required, on three days' notice. I informed him I should require the money upon the opening of the Five Per Cent. Navy Stock, after the payment of the dividends. He then said, "I shall not require the money longer than six weeks."

Upon my coming home, Mrs. Meves blamed me for what I had done, and advised me to get the money out of his hands as early as possible, observing: "Although the firm, as a bank, is enormously rich, nevertheless Mr. Rowland Stephenson himself is a very poor man." Upon the opening of the Navy Five Per Cents., after the dividends were paid, I wrote a short note, and requested the £1600, with interest due, to be paid to my account. I put the letter into the post-office early on the Monday morning, and on the following Friday I called upon Mr. Stephenson, to know whether he had paid the amount to my credit, as I had to pay for £6000 stock, entered against me in two transfers. Mr. Stephenson affected to be very much surprised at my conduct, and said, "Sir, when I borrowed your money, did you think I did so merely to look at it? I bought Exchequer bills, which have depreciated amazingly in value; and I shall be a severe loser by the transaction." I then said, "Please keep the interest due, and merely pay the £1600 to my account." He then observed, "Can't you put off the stock, and destroy the ticket?" I replied, "No, sir, the tickets were put into the box early, and the transfers are gone forwarded into the inner office, and the brokers have applied for the receipts for me to pay them, for the transfer of the stock into my name; and I must have the money paid forthwith." Mr. Stephenson, finding all his evasions useless, rang the bell for his confidential clerk, " Mr. Lloyd ;" and said, " Bring up £1600 short, and make out the amount at five per cent. for two months." This was accordingly done, and I received £1600 in bank-notes. I was paid the interest in cash by the clerk, and I paid the bank-notes into their bank as I passed through.

In January 1823 my reputed mother was gradually becoming very feeble, and her constitution was giving way to natural decay. I gave up, for her accommodation, the second-floor at 30 Conduit Street, New Bond Street, which consisted of three rooms. The upper floor was occupied by an old woman, " a nurse," and "a Miss Powell," an old trust-worthy companion of my reputed mother's. These persons were, as I supposed, in constant attendance on Mrs. Meves, they having received my orders never to leave her by herself, as she had become very feeble and tottering, and required assistance in crossing the room, and in being waited upon. Upon giving up my rooms I took apartments in Park Street, Regent's Park.

One day, after I had dined with my reputed mother, Miss Powell having retired to her own room, she again informed me, that the Queen of France was the mother of two male children—the Dauphin and the Duke of Normandy; adding, " *The Dauphin, you know, is dead, but the Duke of Normandy is alive and well, and in sound understanding to this very moment.*" *She then placed her hands upon me, in confirmation of what she said, and looked me full in the face, saying, "You, Augustus, are that very person.*"

She continued by saying, " Augustus, at the period of the decease of the late Mr. William Meves, after I had read his will to you, in which he leaves the sum of £100 to his sister, ' Mrs. Bouer,' if she should be living, otherwise it was to come to you; but you promised me, if Mrs. Bouer was not living, you would give me the £100, and I refused to accept it, as I did not require the money at the time. But now, Augustus, I require it, and will you give me the £100?" I said, " For what purpose do you want the £100 at the present time?" She replied, " Miss Powell has been very long and faithful in her kind attendance on me, and I wish to reward her for the services she has rendered me during my long and painful illness." I replied, " Dear mother, I should be happy to give you the £100 for your own services, but my giving so large a sum of money for the purpose of giving it to Miss Powell—upon my honour, I cannot comply with your request; but I will give you whatever gold I have in my bureau, so that you may not be in want of money; and I promise you to present Miss Powell with £5, for her kind attention to you." I then went to my bureau and took out about £20 in gold, which I gave to my reputed mother. I then told her I had invested my property in the Spanish bonds, at fifty-eight per cent., and, on their depression to fifty-two per cent., I purchased bonds nearly to the extent of my whole property. She then severely blamed me for my want of prudence, and said, "I thought you had faithfully promised me not to have any more dealings in the Spanish bonds." She then observed, should I ever have occasion to write to the Duchess of Angoulême, all I had to write was this : " *That I had, on the instep of my left foot, a cicatrice,* which was occasioned by a prong of a buckle wounding me, when a child with her in France;*" adding, " *Mind, Augustus, not to enter into any particulars, for, if I did, I should be lost. Neither to be induced to read any private memoirs of the Queen of France, as it would only set my mind woolgathering ; for how was it possible that circum- stances could be known to historians, which were necessary to be kept secret ?*" Some oue coming into the room prevented any further conversation.

* See Appendix A, for Medical Certificates.

The next morning, before I went into the City, I called in Conduit Street to see Mrs. Meves. When I came to the house, I rang the house-door bell gently, and went up-stairs. On my entering the room she got up from her chair, and endeavoured to run to meet me, when, unfortunately, she fell to the ground. I called the nurse to come down immediately to her assistance. My heart was ready to burst at seeing her in so dejected a state. Shortly after, I went down-stairs and spoke to the proprietor of the house, after which I left, and proceeded to the City, having determined to sell my Spanish bonds if possible, at any loss, however great, rather than keep them. This determination, unfortunately, I could not put into practice. On my arrival in the City, I found the price below fifty per cent., and there were no longer any dealers in the Spanish bonds on the Royal Exchange. I took, rather late in the evening, the stage-coach to Piccadilly, and went to Conduit Street; but observing lights passing to and fro, and persons moving about in the second floor, I felt I might disturb my reputed mother by calling at so late an hour, so I went leisurely on towards my own residence.

The next morning, whilst I was at breakfast, a gentleman called, who wished to see me immediately. On his entering the room I saw it was Mr. Vollottin, "the landlord of the house in Conduit Street, where Mrs. Meves resided." He informed me that my respected reputed mother was no more, and that Miss Powell was having all the late Mrs. Meves's trunks removed to the Hanover Square Rooms; that there was a man with a truck at the door when he left, and he thought it his duty to apprise me of it. I lost no time, but went immediately to Conduit Street. On my arrival I went up-stairs, where the body of my most excellent, devout, amiable, and reputed mother was. I knelt beside the bed, and took her hand, and kissed it. I then turned to Miss Powell, and said, "By what authority have you presumed to take possession of my late mother's trunks?" "By Mrs. Meves's authority, as every one in this room can attest." I said, "If the trunks are not restored to me, I shall apply to the magistrates of Marlborough Street."

I then said, " Miss Powell, what does that box contain ? " She replied, " It contains my linen, sir." I then observed on the table a small writing-desk, which had belonged to my late reputed sister Cecilia. I opened the desk by means of a small key I had in my pocket. On examining which, the first paper I read contained the following :—

"LONDON, *April* 12, 1820, HIGH ST., MARYLEBONE.

" Being in my perfect senses, I make my will and testament, giving and bequeathing all I die possessed of—clothes, etc. etc.,—to Caroline Read, proclaiming her my sole heir, as witness my signature,

"MARIANNE CROWLEY MEVES.

"*Witness*—Elizabeth Collins."

This singular paper quite overcame me, and I asked Miss Powell what were Mrs. Meves's desires previous to her decease ? She replied, " Mrs. Meves wished her remains to be kept above ground for at least five days, and not to be buried on a Saturday." I then said, " As my mother has placed every confidence in you, I wish you to take upon yourself the whole management of the funeral, and to give what orders you think fit to Mr. Loudon, of Great Marlborough Street."

In due course of time the trunks were returned to Conduit Street. I then examined the papers, which were in rather large quantities. I selected a letter written by the Abbé Morlet, who had emigrated to Buren, a village near Utrecht, dated November 9th, 1793, to Mrs. Meves, 16 Vere Street, opposite the Chapel, as I did not know what this letter* might lead to.

On the 25th January I had my pictures and furniture removed to a suite of apartments in Newman Street, Oxford Street.

* For letter referred to, see Appendix B.

II.

INFORMATION RESPECTING THE CROWLEY FAMILY, AND MARI-
ANNE CROWLEY'S CAREER, AND ACQUAINTANCESHIP WITH
MR. WILLIAM SCHROËDER MEVES, AND CONTINUATION OF
AUTHENTIC HISTORICAL MEMOIRS, WITH INFORMATION
AND COMMUNICATION.

CORNELIUS CROWLEY, Esq., resident of the city of Bath, was the father of Jane Elizabeth Crowley and Mary Anne Crowley, by his wife Mary Ellison, daughter of Francis Ellison, Esq., of Newcastle-upon-Tyne.

Jane Elizabeth Crowley was born in 1742, and married Francis Turner Blithe, Esq. of Broseley Hall, Shropshire.

In 1771, Francis Turner Blithe died; and by his will, proved at Doctors' Commons, he left the whole of his valuable estates, called the Broseley estates, to his wife Jane Elizabeth; and an estate at Colebrook Dale, called the Whiteley estate. This estate, the widow Jane Elizabeth Blithe ordered to be sold, to pay off a debt of £7000 created on the Broseley estates. The sale realized £10,000.*

In 1772, Jane Elizabeth Blithe contracted a marriage with William Davenport, Esq. of Davenport House, Shropshire. Previous to her marriage with William Davenport, Esq., Mrs. Jane Elizabeth Blithe placed £3000 on mortgage on Mr. William Davenport's estates in Shropshire. Over this £3000 she had the power of appointment, under her marriage settlements, together with £200 a year allowed her as pin-money—over this income Mr. Davenport had no right,—also to a large sum in East India bonds, which were found in Mrs. Davenport's writing-desk, with many years' accumulated interest, after her demise.

* See Appendix E, for Francis Turner Blithe's will.

Mrs. Jane Elizabeth Davenport died in 1811. Her will is proved at Doctors' Commons. The East India bonds produced a Chancery suit after her decease, between Francis Turner Blithe Harries, Esq. of Benthall, in the county of Shropshire, "who was the heir by appointment under Mrs. Davenport's will," and Mr. William Davenport, "her husband," Francis Turner Blithe Harries claiming the right over the India bonds, as being the residuary legatee under the will.*

Marianne Crowley, the second daughter of the said Cornelius Crowley, was born in the city of Bath, and baptized at the parish church of St. Peter's and St. Paul's, at Bath, the 11th of April 1754. She was educated at the convent of St. Omer, in the Holy Catholic Faith, and on her return to the house of her father at Bath, she studied music under Mr. Linley.

In January 1777, Miss Marianne Crowley came to London,† and became the favourite pupil of Signor Sacchini, "the celebrated Italian composer."‡ Whilst studying music under Signor Sacchini, the affecting news arrived of the death of her mother at Bath. Her father then came to London, and took his disconsolate daughter to Paris, for the purpose of placing her at a convent. They resided whilst at Paris at Madame Gregson's, in La Rue Dauphine, as appears from a letter addressed to Mademoiselle Crowley, at Madame Gregson's, La Rue Dauphine, à Paris, from Madame l'Abbesse de l'Abbaye aux Bois, which ran as follows :—

"The Abbess of the Abbaye ux Bois is very sorry at not being able to receive Miss Crowley into the interior of the convent. She suggests to her an apartment outside, at 400 fr., on condition that she shall have a housekeeper, or lady's-maid, of mature age, and that she

* See Appendix F, for letter from Mr. Davenport to Mr. A. Meves, explanatory of Mrs. Davenport's conduct.

† See Appendix G, for Mrs. Crowley's letter to her daughter Marianne, in London.

‡ LADIES INSTRUCTED IN SINGING,
AND ON THE PIANOFORTE, OR HARP,
BY
MRS. MEVES,
Pupil of the late MR. LINLEY *and* SIGNOR SACCHINI.

shall receive the visits of those only approved by her father, and of whom the Abbess shall have the list."

Mr. Crowley shortly after returned to England.

In June 1781, Mr. Crowley being ill, he wrote the following letter to his daughter " Marianne," in Paris, acquainting her with such :—

"BATH, *2d June* 1781.

"MY DARLING MARIANNE,—Come to Bath with all convenient expedition.   My state of health is too weak, and too much reduced to admit of hopes of a tolerable recovery.   Come then, my affectionate child, and take possession of all my effects.   Your worthy sister came here from London to see me, stayed two or three days at Miss Pember's, and then returned to town, promising to come again to Bath the 2d of this month, to comfort me.   This day I received a letter from her, that Mr. Davenport and herself must set out for the country, and cannot make Bath in their road, but will come for me the beginning of August, and take me down to Davenport House.   I do not intend answering your sister's letter, therefore desire you will prove yourself the most loving daughter of   CORNELIUS CROWLEY.

" *P.S.*—If it is the will of God that I should survive this illness, I will return along with you to France, and spend the remainder of my days in the bosom of the Holy Church.   I have fully decided the point in my own mind.   I keep Lord Southwell in my eye."

Miss Crowley at once journeyed to England ; but upon her arrival at Bath, she found her father had succumbed under his illness, and was buried.

In January 1782, Miss Marianne Crowley was in London, residing at 3 Little Maddox Street, Hanover Square, when she accepted an invitation from the Dowager Caroline, Countess of Harrington, to reside with her ladyship, in Curzon Street, Mayfair.

" DEAR MISS CROWLEY,—I was writing to know how you did to-day, and hope you did not increase your cold.   I have had but a bad night, and am not out of bed.   We were very comfortable yesterday, and, if you think so, I shall hope to be so soon again.—Your sincere friend,

"C. HARRINGTON.

" *Sunday*, 12 *o'clock.*
    MISS CROWLEY."

" Lady Sefton presents her best compliments, and many thanks to Miss Crowley for her very obliging inquiries. She is pretty well, and hopes Miss Crowley is the same.

" HILL STREET, *Monday morning.*"

" To MISS CROWLEY.

" Give me leave to thank you, dear madam, for the music you sent me—the songs you had the trouble of writing out for me. You have added much to my amusement by it. Could I hear you play them, I think I should like the music better afterwards. I rejoice extremely Lady Harrington has added so agreeable a person to her society, as all accounts agree in making you ; and I hope some day or another to be presented to you ; and, in the meantime, beg you will believe me, your very humble servant,

" A. M. LINCOLN."

In the year 1783, during the time Miss Crowley resided with Lady Harrington, she became acquainted with Mr. Meves von Schroëder, who arrived in England as travelling companion to Roger Palmer, Esq. of Rush House, near Dublin ; and soon after it was reported that Miss Marianne Crowley was privately married, according to the ritual of the Roman Catholic Church.

At the death of Lady Harrington, in June 1784, Mrs. Meves von Schroëder left England, and went to Paris, where she was delivered of a son, the 16th of February 1785, by a surgeon-accoucheur of the name of Vincent d'Etionville.

The following is a letter from Mr. Davenport :—

" DAVENPORT HOUSE, *6th August* 1836.

" DEAR SIR,—I have had the perusal of a letter from you to my niece, Mrs. Davenport of Worfield, in which there is some inquiries relative to your late mother, and which, had it been in my power to have given a satisfactory account, it would give me great pleasure ; but it is so many years since any conversation on that subject might have taken place between Mrs. Davenport and myself, that I cannot bring anything to my recollection in respect to time, or any particular circumstance, more than I know she went to France under the patronage of Lady Harrington, in the name of Schroëder ; and I know likewise, that she was very partial to her, and proved her great friend, but farther than this, I have no knowledge.—And remain, dear Sir, yours truly,

"W. DAVENPORT.

"To Mr. MEVES,
    8 Bath Place, New Road, London."

Mrs. Marianne Crowley Meves was about the middle stature of women, about five feet in height, rather stout, full dark eyes, fine teeth, a fair complexion, and a profusion of dark hair.

Mrs. Jane Higginson was cousin to Mrs. Jane Elizabeth Davenport, of Broseley Hall, Shropshire, and to Marianne Crowley; the relationship was by Mr. Simpson, of Newcastle-upon-Tyne, marrying Barbara Ellison, eldest daughter of Francis Ellison, Esq., of Newcastle-upon-Tyne. Upon the death of her brother, William Ellison Simpson, who was in partnership with Mr. John Higginson, as watch and cock-spur makers in the Strand, Jane Simpson married Mr. John Higginson.

In continuing my narrative of events : shortly after my removing to Newman Street, I had a transaction with a Mr. Frederick Spackman on 'Change, in the Spanish bond market, by which I was a loser of several hundred pounds.

Shortly afterwards I opened an account with Messrs. Hammersleys, Brookbank, and Clark, of about £3000 in cash, and left in their hands £6000 in Spanish bonds. After which I left my bank-book with the Messrs. Remington, Stephenson, and Toulmin, in order to have it made up, on account of my having many transactions with Messrs. Hoare and Barnett, of Lombard Street, who received the money I was entitled to under Mrs. Jane Elizabeth Davenport's will. Upon my book being returned, I found an item of an amount placed to my credit with the banking house, amounting to £4750, and as I had not paid in so large a sum, when I went into the City I called at the Messrs. Remington, Stephenson, and Toulmin, and inquired of the cashiers how so large a sum was placed to my credit. The cashier referred me to the inner office, to the bankers themselves, to give me the information. I spoke to Mr. Remington, who said, "That sum, sir, has been placed to your account, and we have entered it in our ledger, and you can write for

whatever portion of the sum you may require in your transactions."
Mr. Toulmin then remarked, " Do you not expect money to be placed
to your account from Mrs. Jane Higginson?—£1000 was paid in here
from Messrs. Hoare, Barnett, and Co. to your credit." I answered,
" That is all right; I inherit that sum under my sister's will, being part
of a mortgage of £3000 on Mrs. Davenport's estates in Shropshire, and
certainly I am entitled to the whole of Mrs. Jane Higginson's property;
but she is alive and well; but about this sum of money, 'the £4750,'
I am really quite ignorant of its source." " Well, sir, we can only say
the money has been placed here to your credit, and you can write whatever cheques you may require in your speculations in the funds, and we
shall be proud to honour them."

Some time after, when I left my bank-book to have the various sums
placed to my credit, and my cheques returned to me, whilst I was
making inquiries of the cashier for my book, Mr. Rowland Stephenson's
confidential clerk, " Mr. Lloyd," came down to the counter and said, "Sir,
we have made inquiries respecting the £4750 placed to your credit, and
we find it was an error. The £4750 ought to have been placed to the
credit of a Mr. William Meysing." I fully believed what was told me, and
Mrs. Meves being deceased, I had no one to consult on the subject.*

Whilst I was residing at 13 Air Street, Piccadilly, Miss Powell called
on me respecting the bill for the interment of my late deceased reputed
mother, which amounted to £52. I considered the charge too exorbi-
tant, as I had paid for a similar one for Miss Cecilia Meves £14. I said,
" What excuse does Mr. Loudon make for sending me so extravagant a
bill?" " On account, sir, of there being so many attendants. Moreover,
sir, I received your late mother's orders respecting her interment; and
you have no reason to complain, for Mrs. Higginson paid you the half-
yearly dividend due to your late mother, and I received Mrs. Meves's
orders that the whole sum due to her from Mrs. Higginson was to be
expended in her funeral, and I have only obeyed her request." I

* See Appendix H, for Lord W. Lennox's description and acquaintance with
Rowland Stephenson, the banker.

changed the conversation saying, "Tell me, Miss Powell, when did you first know my mother?"   "I first knew her, sir, in 1787, she having just come from Boulogne-sur-Mer with you, then a little boy.   Your mother, 'Mrs. Meves,' at that time was called Madame Schroeter; she resided in Suffolk Street, Haymarket."   I remarked, "Why, Miss Powell, my mother's name was Meves, not Schroeter."   She replied, "Your mother's name, sir, in 1787 was Schroeter, and you were called Auguste Schroeter.   I remained in Madame Schroeter's service till 1788, when Madame left England, and returned to Boulogne-sur-Mer.   I then procured a situation in the family of Sir John Cosbey, of Portland Place. When Lady Cosbey died, she left me an annuity of £40 for my length of service.   I then came to London to reside with my niece, 'Mrs. Field,' who was housekeeper at the King's Concert Rooms, in Hanover Square.   This was in 1814.   I then made inquiry about Madame Schroeter, a musical lady, and could hear no tidings of her. A friend of mine, a Mr. Seguin, said the only lady he knew who answered the description I gave, was a Mrs. Meves.   One day, when I was walking with Miss Seguin in Oxford Street, she pointed out your mother as the probable lady.   When I accosted her, and said, 'Have I the honour of speaking to Madame Schroeter?' she answered 'No, my name is no longer Schroeter, but Meves.'   She then invited me to take tea with her, and I went to 54 Great Marlborough Street, and was introduced to Miss Cecilia Meves, who at the time was very ill from a violent cold on her lungs.   I attended poor Miss Meves until the day of her decease, and always found a true and kind friend in Mrs. Meves.

"At the time of your return from Calais, I was astonished when you came into the room to see what an alteration had taken place in you, for when you were a child you had *blue eyes, and light-coloured hair, and was a stout little fellow;* but when I saw you in Great Marlborough Street, you had *brown eyes, and dark brown hair.*"

Some time after Miss Powell's visit, Mrs. Spence called on me to know whether I would favour her with £10, as she wished to send her daughter to Bath to see her aunt.   I complied with her request, and before she left, I asked her whether she knew my mother by the name of Schroeter, and at what time she first knew her? She replied, " Sir, when I first came to live with Mrs. Meves, her name was Schroeter; she lived in Dartmouth Street, Westminster. In the year 1789, Madame Schroeter engaged me as nurse-maid to her daughter Cecilia. You, sir, were at that time residing with Mr. Meves von Schroeter, who followed the profession of a miniature-painter, in Margaret Street, Cavendish Square. You were then called Auguste Schroeter, and were about five years old, and had ' *blue eyes and light-coloured hair up to the year* 1793.' If you inquire of Mr. George Meves, he will testify the truth of what I have stated.

"When I entered Madame Schroeter's service, she but had just arrived from France, from Boulogne-sur-Mer. She to my certain knowledge received remittances from France. Mrs. Davenport, 'her sister,' likewise reduced an annuity she allowed from £200 a year to £40 a year, when she found that her sister had married contrary to her desire, and was the mother of two children. Mrs. Vital, who was your mother's most intimate friend, informed Mrs. Davenport of the fact, after which your mother went down to Davenport House, in Shropshire, in order to induce her sister to increase the annuity to what she had been accustomed to receive. This Mrs. Davenport determinedly refused, and said, ' Marianne, as you have made your bed, so you must lie upon it, therefore, you must make use of your talents for your support, as I shall allow you only £40 a year.'

"On Madame Schroeter's return from Shropshire, she taught singing. As Madame had always been accustomed to live as a lady, Mrs. Vital frequently came to her aid, observing how ungenerous it was for Mrs. Davenport to act so unkindly towards her sister, as to her certain knowledge Madame Schroeter was a married lady, and could produce her marriage certificate in any court of justice." I then observed, "Was this Mrs. Vital the wife of Mr. Vital, of Rupert Street?" She answered, "Oh no, sir; Mrs. Vital was of a very high family; her brother, Mr. Dickenson, was M.P. for Cheshire; but respecting the name of Schroeter, if you inquire of Mr. George Meves you will find that Mr. Meves's name was Schroeter; it was the family name.

"In the year 1792, Madame 'your mother' came into difficulties, she being indebted to her landlord for rent, and was arrested at the suit of Mr. Squires. My father, Mr. Waterhouse, bailed Madame when I was living as nurse-maid to Miss Cecilia. My name was Elizabeth Waterhouse, and I was called Betty.

"In 1792 Madame took furnished apartments in Lower Marylebone Street, and she said, 'As the name of Schroeter was the occasion of so many misfortunes to her, she was determined for the future to live under the name of Meves, as her husband was following his business at the Bank of England only under his name of Meves.'

"I believe, sir, a marriage between Madame Schroeter and Mr. Meves took place in 1792, in the Protestant Church, to please Mrs. Davenport, who, after the marriage, paid all Mrs. Meves's debts, and settled £100 a year upon her, which was paid by Mrs. Jane Higginson, in quarterly payments of £25. In 1793 I married William Spence, a surgeon in His Majesty's navy. My husband was son to Dr. Spence of Lower Marylebone Street. I then left Mrs. Meves's service, when Madame engaged a maid-servant, called Milley."

Mrs. Spence then said: Whilst she was in Mrs. Meves's service a letter came from France, written by Thomas Paine, the author of the *Rights of Man*. The letter was addressed to a Mrs. Carpenter, who was an intimate friend of Mrs. Meves's, which letter expressed a desire that a deaf and dumb boy, of about eight years old, should be sent to him, for purposes he required. Mrs. Carpenter and Mrs. Meves made every search and inquiry to obtain the sort of boy required by Paine, but were unsuccessful—the only chance they had being the son of a poor woman, named Maria Dodd, "a charwoman," who formerly lived in Marylebone Court; but she having removed, they were unable to gain information where she then resided.

I now called upon Mr. George Meves, in order to ascertain the particulars respecting the name of Schroeter. Upon questioning him, he said, "You do not pronounce the name correctly: it is Schroëder, not Schroeter; but I will satisfy, with pleasure, your inquiry respecting the name of Schroëder. When my brother followed his profession as a miniature-painter,* he called himself William Meves von Schroëder. Meves is the father's name, which is plebeian. Schroëder is the mother's name, which is patrician, the family holding landed property in Germany. Upon my brother first establishing himself as a miniature-painter, in Half-Moon Street, Piccadilly, he called himself Meves von Schroëder, which means, in German, a man of noble family, or gentleman by birth.

"As respects my brother's marriage, he may have married Miss Crowley in the name of Meves von Schroëder, but he did not allow her to live under his name of Meves, as she was so extravagant. When your mother came from France to have you baptized, she stayed at Hart's, 'a perfumer in Piccadilly.' My brother being from London at the time, your mother sent for me to stand as sponsor. I called upon a friend of mine, a Mr. Kranke, to stand as sponsor with me; and you were baptized at St. James's Church, Piccadilly. After early morning prayers, I gave the name at the baptismal font, as Augustus Antoine Cornelius Mevis. My brother adopted the manner of spelling the name Meves. The reason of your being baptized in England was to give you the right of inheriting landed property, as your mother was the heiress-at-law to immense estates in Shropshire, belonging to her sister, Mrs. Davenport, of Davenport House. The baptismal register states: 'Born, 16th day of February 1785; and baptized, 25th day of March 1785.' After the ceremony your mother went directly to the Tower Stairs, and took the packet for France."

I then consulted him respecting his knowledge of me in my youth, and especially as respected dates, and my early life, when he stated that the first time he saw me after my baptism was in 1792, in Great Russell Street, at the house of a Mr. Page, where his brother was residing, I

---

* We have a memorandum of Mr. William Meves's, giving a list of upwards of 200 persons, whose portraits he has taken.

having just arrived from a boarding-school, where my mother had placed me, and on which occasion he gave me half-a-guinea to encourage me. I observed, I did not recollect his ever having called upon Mr. Meves at the time he was residing in Wilson Street, Finsbury Square. To which he replied, " No ; certainly not. How could he call upon his brother when he was living in the service of Sir Drummond Smith? When he wished to see him he went to the Bank of England, or to the Long-Annuity Office." In 1802, when his brother lived in Goodge Street, at the time of his brother Dederick coming from Germany, he gave me two guineas as a present. In 1805 he came frequently to see his brother, at the time his sister came with her husband, Mr. Frederick Bower, to London. I then asked him this question : " Pray, sir, what coloured eyes, and hair had I when you saw me in 1792?" He replied, " You had *blue eyes, and light-coloured hair;* but there is nothing extraordinary in that, as children's eyes and hair change their colour as they grow older." I then remarked, " That might be the case, but I really thought I had *brown eyes at my birth, and that they, as well as my hair, were always of a brown colour, up to that day*, only, as I had advanced in years, my hair had grown darker." I then said, " Have the goodness to inform me what you know respecting my early youth, and information respecting Mr. and Mrs. Meves, as it is right that I should know after what has transpired." He replied, rather angrily, " Your mother was living at Boulogne-sur-Mer until the breaking out of the French Revolution, when she came to England for safety ; and it was then agreed that you were to be under my brother's care, and that Cecilia was to be under her care. My brother, in the autumn of the year 1789, went to Lord Stamford's, in Cheshire, but, previous to going, he placed you under the care of an old woman at Battersea; but during the time he was absent, your mother got possession of you from the nurse, and took you over to France ; and on her return with you to England, she placed you at a school at Horsham, in Sussex; and it was from this school my brother brought you, when I first saw you in 1792, ' meaning, the first time after his baptism.' My brother's visit to Lord Stamford's was professional, being engaged taking like-nesses of the family, and copying several portraits. Upon leaving Lord Stamford's he called on his friend Captain Lee, of Coten Hall, Shrop-shire, and passed about a month with him." "What you state, Mr. George Meves, as regards myself, I acknowledge to be true, as I well remember my father, when we lived in Rathbone Place, in 1809, showing me a music-book. On the outside cover was written : ' Augustus Meves began to learn the pianoforte in August 1792.' This was written in my father's handwriting, at the time he was living at 44 Great Russell Street, therefore its genuineness I cannot for a moment question."

Subsequently a Mrs. Fisher called on me, in Air Street, Piccadilly, respecting her son, a young man who was studying music, and requested my opinion regarding his abilities as a musician. After complying with her request I said, " Mrs. Fisher, how did you first become acquainted with the late Mrs. Meves?" She replied, "When I lived with my mother, who did needlework for Mrs. Meves, at the time Mrs. Meves lived in Lower Marylebone Street. I was then an apprentice in Jermyn Street, Piccadilly. When I was out of my time, in 1805, I called on Mrs. Meves, in Broad Street, opposite Dufour's Place, and she engaged me as companion to Miss Cecilia Meves. Do you not remember, Sir, Maria Dodd, a charwoman?" I answered, "No ; I did not; but I remembered a woman called Kitty, who used to do all that kind of work." "Well, Sir, Maria Dodd was the mother to Caroline ; and when she was dying in the workhouse, she sent for Mrs. Meves, and begged of her to protect her poor child Caroline, which she con-sented to do. When Mrs. Meves was residing in Vere Street, Oxford Street, she went to Holland, accompanied by Mr. Joseph Frike, in the month of January 1794, and took with her, to fill up her passport, a deaf and dumb boy, a son of Maria Dodd's, and went on to Paris with this boy, and was detained there through some cause or other, that she did not return to England till about the middle of the month of May 1794, by which she lost the teaching of Mrs. Warner's ladies' boarding-school, at Wandsworth, which produced Mrs. Meves above £80 a year regularly. On Mrs. Meves's arrival in London, Mrs. Davenport sent four twenty-pound notes from Shropshire ; and Mrs. Higginson, who received the remittances, paid the money into Mrs. Meves's hands."

In 1824 I went to reside with Mrs. Jane Higginson, an old widow lady. She was cousin to the late Mrs. Davenport, of Broseley Hall. In 1828 Mrs. Higginson died, when I inherited the whole of her property, which consisted of a freehold estate in the parish of Shoreham, in Kent, and the lease of her house, 38 Southampton Street, Strand. The estate called Romney Street Farm, of 160 acres of freehold-land, I sold to Captain Ryder Burton, in 1834.

At the time I was residing in Southampton Street, I made acquaintance with a Captain d'Oliviera, who said his father had been an ambassador to England in the reign of Louis xv. On my making some inquiries of him, he stated he had been appointed Page of Honour to La Princesse de Lamballe, and he well remembered the Queen of France introducing Madame de Courville Schroëder to La Princesse de Lamballe at the time the Princess came to England on the private affairs of the Queen, in 1787. I said, " Did you accompany La Princesse de Lamballe to England ?" He replied, " No, he did not ; for, through his father's influence, he obtained an appointment in the Portuguese Embassy."

In the early part of the month of June 1830, I observed, in going along the Strand, a French tavern, near Wellington Street ; and on my return from the City I went up-stairs to the coffee-room, and gave orders for several dishes, and some bottles of French wine, to be sent to my house, 38 Southampton Street, Strand, as I expected some friends to dine with me on the Sunday. I afterwards made inquiry, and found that at five o'clock an excellent dinner was served up there. This being the case, I made up my mind to dine there occasionally on my returning from the City.

One day, after I had dined at the French tavern, a Monsieur Lassleur, who had been dining there, and who I had noticed on several occasions, threw a French half-crown piece on the table, and observed, " Que cet gentilhomme ressemble à Louis Seize "—" How much that gentleman resembles Louis XVI.!" This observation was taken up by other French gentlemen present, amongst whom was a Colonel de Bigault Desfouchères, who gave me his card, on which was engraved, " De Bigault Desfouchères, Chef de Battalion." These gentlemen I invited one evening to come, and take coffee with me at my house. When they came, I showed them my collection of pictures, left me by my late reputed father, after which we entered into conversation regarding myself. They were very desirous of knowing whether I had any portraits of Mr. or Mrs. Meves, but I told them I had no portrait of either, at which they seemed somewhat surprised, and shortly after took their leave.

Some days after, Monsieur Lassleur, Colonel de Bigault Desfouchères, and some other French gentlemen, called on me, and after having ocular proof as to the marks and scars on my body, and entering into conversation with me, they made me a proposal to accompany them to France. The spokesman was Monsieur Lassleur. I told them I had no objection, only at that time I was about selling an estate I had in Kent, also, that I was in treaty with the Bedford Office for the sale of the lease of my house in Southampton Street; and I having only a short time previously become a father, it was my duty to make arrangements for my child's welfare and happiness, in the event of anything happening to me, therefore it was impossible for me to go to France until such business was settled. I then remarked, " Gentlemen, supposing I were to go to Paris, what are your intentions?" " Sir," they replied, " our intentions are, on your arrival to provide you with a suite of apartments, where you will have everything you may require; in return, all we have to request of you is to remain as silent as you possibly can, and not to enter into any conversation or explanation with any persons, except ourselves: for the proof of your identity must rest with us. We know perfectly well who you are, as your proof exists on your own person, and we are fully convinced you are the true Louis XVII. Moreover, when you were in Paris in 1816, the great resemblance you bore to Louis XVI. caused much conversation." In continuation they said, "Our wishes are to take you on some particular evening to the theatre, when it will be well filled with our adherents. You will be seated in some conspicuous box, when some one will rise in the pit, and observe to his friend, 'Que cet gentilhomme ressemble à Louis Seize'—'How much that gentleman resembles Louis xvi.!'—when his friend will answer, 'Comme deux gouttes d'eau'—'Like two drops of water.' This will be repeated and re-repeated in the theatre, when an old French gentleman, of the highest rank in France, whose veracity is unquestionable, will be appealed to for his opinion. He has a knowledge of your person, and is sure to be at the theatre in his box the night we intend taking you, and if he answers, after well observing you, that he fully believes you to be the son of Louis xvi., the true heir to the throne of France, we shall all raise the cry of 'Vive Louis xvii.;' and we shall carry our point, as the whole of Paris at the present moment is ripe for a change of Government, since the days of the Carlist party are at an end, and the consequence of which, is : there will soon be in France a change of Government." In reply, I said, "Gentlemen, to tell you the positive truth, I assure you I have no ambition to die the death of Prince Murat. The greater chance would be, were I to go to France with you, that I should be either destroyed or incarcerated where no one would be able to trace what had become of me, and I assure you I am too fond of my personal liberty to risk it on the chances of such a scheme. No, no, gentlemen, this will never do for me ; what I require is to be invited to France by influential persons, when I will at once arrange my affairs in England, and come to France as speedily as possible. I am ready to do my duty to the best of my ability, but do not think, gentlemen, I am so ignorant of myself as you imagine, or that I shall act in a manner to make the French nation think lightly, or indifferently, of my character." Monsieur Lassleur then said, "Très bien, Monsieur, mais la plus belle trône de l'Europe ne veut-il pas vous tenter?" —"Very good, sir, but will not the most beautiful throne in Europe tempt you?" In reply I said, "Gentlemen, I assure you no temptation in the world would induce me to leave a certainty for an uncertainty.

Here I am happy, contented, and independent, and have the full enjoyment of social liberty. What more can I desire on earth, so long as I have the means of supporting myself independently?"

After the breaking up of the party I considered over the events of the day, and shortly after I received from Mr. Healy, of the Bedford Office, the sum of £350, for the remaining term of my lease of the house in Southampton Street, and before the 25th of June 1830, I removed the whole of my pictures and furniture to 8 Bath Place, New Road. By this time the whole party of French gentlemen had disappeared from the French hotel in the Strand.

The days of July ushering in such startling events, made me request a friend of mine, "a Monsieur Jules Hurel," to write a letter in the French language to the Marquis de Lafayette, and also one to Prince Perigord de Talleyrand, "Bishop of Autun," simply stating my existence. He did what I requested, and wrote a letter of his own dictation, which he read to me, the tenour of which I approved, excepting such parts that reflected on the character of the former Government of France, as I did not wish the letters to be political, but only to give them the information where I lived, and for him also to state his own private opinion respecting me.

Shortly after the arrival of the Royal Family in England, I made inquiry at the banking-house of the Messrs. Wright, in Henrietta Street, Covent Garden, for the town address of Cardinal Weld. I was referred for information to Portland Place, where I was informed that Cardinal Weld was at Rome, and that the ex-Royal Family of France had chosen Lulworth Castle as a temporary residence.

I now determined to address a letter to La Duchess d'Angoulême, and in September 1830 I wrote a letter, which I enclosed in a small parcel, containing two or three pieces of music of my own composition, likewise a lithographic portrait of myself, painted by Cause, and engraved by Gaucy, which I had done while I was residing at 38 Southampton Street. These I forwarded addressed to Her Royal Highness the Duchess of Angoulême, Lulworth Castle. The letter ran as follows :—

"To the DUCHESS OF ANGOULÊME,
        Lulworth Castle."

" September 2d, 1830.

"YOUR ROYAL HIGHNESS, — Circumstances having arisen which emboldens me to address your Royal Highness, an imperative duty seems to impel me, which I hope your goodness will pardon, when I call your attention to the following memorial.

"It was my misfortune to lose my good father in the year 1818, and in reading over his will to my mother, after some bequests to his relatives in Brunswick, he leaves the remainder of his property to me, as his reputed son, Augustus Meves.   That my father, to whom I had ever shown the most affectionate duty, should have thus named me in his will as his reputed son affected me greatly, when my mother overcame my affliction by stating what I now write, and humbly request your serious attention to,—namely: 'Augustus, Mr. Meves was not your father, nor am I your mother, but you owe me a greater duty than if I were your mother.   For you I have been estranged from society in my determination to protect you, and have lost every one that was dear to me.   *You, Augustus, were born in France, and owe your existence to the unfortunate Marie Antoinette, Queen of France.   She was your mother, and the circumstance of your being conveyed to England is known to the Archbishop of Paris.*   Remember, two attempts have been made on your life, which nearly proved successful, the third may be entirely so, therefore be cautious, and never let this disclosure escape your lips so long as I am living.   Should it hereafter be required, the circumstance of your being alive is known, and your identity shall be proved as plain as the sun at noon-day.'

"This disclosure greatly affected me, which, together with my severe loss, brought me into a high state of fever, so much so, that I could not administer to my father's effects for nearly two months after his decease. During this melancholy period, my mother possessed herself of my father's letters, as my medical attendants stated to her that some circumstances connected with my father's decease weighed heavily on my mind.

"In January 1823 I lost my amiable mother.   Word was brought me that a Miss Powell, a friendly attendant of hers, was giving directions for the removal of her trunks to the Hanover Square Rooms. Upon my arrival at her residence in Conduit Street, Miss Powell stated to me, that Mrs. Meves's wishes were, 'that no papers of hers should be opened until after her interment,' and that in obedience to her desire she had taken Mrs. Meves's trunks under her care, and in due time they should be returned to me,—through which means I have hitherto never been able to ascertain the particulars of my mother's residence in the Court of France, from written documents.

"I have since learned that my mother, whose maiden name was Marianne Crowley, shortly after my birth went to France, under the name of Schroëder, which name is my deceased father's maternal family name, Meves being the paternal family name, which circumstance I never ascertained till very lately. Likewise ; that to Madame Schroëder's care was intrusted the Duke of Normandy, and that the Queen of France had the greatest esteem, and confidence in her, and introduced her to the Princesse de Lamballe when she came to England in July 1787.

"What I know concerning myself is this : I remember in my early youth having been extremely unwell, and that during a severe illness, on my arrival in England, where persons about me appeared as strangers. That on my recovery I was placed at a Messrs. Thornton's boarding-school, at Horsham, in Sussex, about the year 1790; and I well remember my unhappiness in not being able to understand what was said to me, as I only understood the French language at that time. Here I remained for nearly two years, and was kept at school during the holidays. On my return to the care of my father, in 1792, I had lost all knowledge of the French language, which my father completed by teaching me the German language. I have lately found a paper containing the baptismal register of Augustus Meves, together with some light-coloured hair, and a description of the moles and marks about his person, '*not one of which moles or marks I have.*' The moles and marks about my person are a mole below the chest, ' on the middle of the stomach,' and a cicatrice on the instep of my left foot, which my mother said was occasioned by the prong of a buckle wounding me when a child in France. Should any of these circumstances here related bring any recollection to the mind of your Royal Highness, and should you be pleased, on due reflection, to allow me the honour of an interview, I shall, on the receipt of your commands, wait on you, and whatever the result may be, I hope your goodness will pardon my presumption in thus addressing you, as I cannot help believing that my mother was too honourable to have deceived me, as to my knowledge the strength and ability of her mind were ever pre-eminent.—I remain, with the most profound feeling of respect, your Royal Highness's devoted, and obedient servant, AUGUSTUS MEVES.

"*P.S.*—A variety of occurrences, and conversations with persons who were acquainted with my mother in early life, would be better related than communicated by letter, and should your Royal Highness condescend to permit me an interview, it would at once set the matter at rest."

Not having received any answer to my letter, I imagined possibly it may not have reached the hands I had directed it to; and it being current that the Royal Family would shortly quit England, I determined to address another letter to the Duchess of Angoulême, which ran as follows :—

"To Her Royal Highness
       The Duchess of Angoulême.

                                        "London, *June* 6, 1831.

"Having lately read in the newspapers a report that your Royal Highness is about to quit England, to reside on your estates in Hungary, and under the impression that, by some mischance, a letter I addressed to Lulworth Castle may not have reached its destination, and some circumstances relating to me may still remain unknown to your Royal Highness, I therefore at once recur to the object of my addressing you, and hope your kindness and urbanity will pardon me.

"At the death of my father, in August 1818, my mother disclosed to me, *that I was not the son of Mr. William Schroeder Meves, or her son, but that I was the son of the unfortunate Marie Antoinette, Queen of France, the Queen having, in my infancy, confided me to her care, and the circumstance of my being conveyed to England was known to the Archbishop of Paris; and that she, in her determination to protect me, had been estranged from her family. Within a few days of Mrs. Meves's death, in January 1823, she again more fully related to me the fact, that the Queen was the mother of two male children, the Dauphin, and the Duke of Normandy, the latter of whom was still living; and she then, in the most solemn manner, declared to me, that I was that person. She reminded me of two attempts that had been made on my life, and of a singular circumstance that happened to me in Paris, where I was for a short time, in the year* 1816.

"I have, since her death, been informed that, shortly after my birth, in 1785, she went to Paris, under the name of Schroeder, and was engaged by the Queen of France to nurse a child the Queen had at that time given birth to; and that she received a pension from the French Court till 1792; and that the name of Schroeder was the family name of my father, on the female side.

"In the month of June 1830, when I resided at 38 Southampton Street, Strand, I became acquainted with several French gentlemen, who were very urgent in their invitations for me to accompany them to Paris. They remarked upon my great resemblance to the Bourbon family, and that my likeness to Louis XVI., was such: that I should excite the greatest attention, from the resemblance I bore to that unfortunate monarch.

"A French officer, Colonel de Bigault Desfouchères, who was introduced at my house, was pressing in his polite attentions to me.

"A Captain d'Oliviera, whose father had been ambassador to England in the reign of Louis xv., on my making some inquiries of him, stated : that he had been Page of Honour to the Princesse de Lamballe, and that he well remembered Madame Schroëder, and that the Queen introduced her to the Princesse de Lamballe, to accompany her when she came to England, in July 1787.

"I lately had occasion to write to Shropshire, to Mr. Davenport, and he, in a letter to me, states that Mrs. Meves went to France in the name of Schroëder, under the patronage of the Countess of Harrington.*

"I cannot suppose my mother deceived me, as she was a lady of the highest capacity, and honour ; and this belief, joined with corroborative evidence, makes me imagine that some peculiar mystery surrounds me.

"On my own part, I can trace my being in England to the year 1790, when I was placed by my parents at Messrs. Thornton's school, at Horsham, where I remained for at least two years.

"The extraordinary events which have lately taken place lead me to consider it a solemn duty to inform your Royal Highness of these circumstances ; and could an interview be brought about, or some confidential person be appointed to investigate the affair, some clue would doubtless be found, and the happiest result be the consequence.—I remain, with the most profound respect towards your Royal Highness, your respectful, and humble servant,

"Augustus Meves.

"8 Bath Place, New Road."

About this time a Carlist newspaper was established in London, entitled *Le Précurseur.* One of the editors, Le Comte Fontaine de Moreau, called at my residence one morning, and sent up his card requesting to see me. On his entering my drawing-room, he asked me, " If I was the gentleman who had communicated to Her Royal Highness the Duchess of Angoulême, at Holyrood?" I replied, " Yes, sir, I am the gentleman. What may your business be with me?" He answered by saying, " Will you allow me, sir, to examine your hands?" I complied

---

* See page 43, for Mr. Davenport's letter.

with his request; and after he had carefully examined them, he said, "By what means did the *scar on the wrist of your left hand occur?*" I replied, "Upon my word and honour I do not know, but I imagine it must have been from some tumour that afflicted me in my childhood."* He then requested me to take off my neckcloth, and to permit him to see my bosom. To this I rather objected, and said, "I had some blood-spots on my chest, and a dark-coloured mole on my right breast, and that his seeing them could not possibly be of any particular conse-quence;" when he remarked, "You will pardon me, sir, when I tell you that I am like St. Thomas. I must see, before I believe. I then took off my neckcloth, and allowed him to examine *the dark-coloured mole on my right breast, and my bosom, on which are several singular small blood-spots, which in appearance: resemble a constellation in the heavens.** These he carefully examined, after which he said, "Sir, if you are disengaged this evening, will you accept an invitation to the house of Monsieur le Camus, a professor of music, who has some friends to dine with him to-day; and in the evening there will be a little musical party, and you will there meet Le Comte de Jouffroy, a gentleman of the highest talents as a political writer; also the Chevalier de Verniëul, who is also engaged with me in writing various articles for *Le Précurseur* newspaper; and possibly you will also meet Le Comte de Crouy, who is attached to the service of Charles x. I answered Le Comte by saying: I should have much pleasure in availing myself of his invitation, when he respectfully took his leave.

I called that evening on Monsieur le Camus, who received me very politely, and entertained me with great hospitality. When I entered the room I was introduced to Le Comte de Jouffroy, who seemed to be a very intelligent gentleman; and also to Le Chevalier de Verniëul. Upon another occasion I was introduced to Le Comte de Crouy, by Le Comte de Jouffroy. I frequently visited Le Comte de Crouy at his resi-dence, 15 Cambridge Street, Edgeware Road. He appeared to me to be a nobleman of high honour, and respectability. The day after the party at Monsieur le Camus's, Le Comte de Jouffroy favoured me with a

* See Medical Certificates, Appendix A.

morning call, and wrote down his address, 21 Allsop's Terrace, New Road, where he invited me to come and see him. Upon my calling, I was introduced by him to his friend the Abbé Prince Charles de Broglie, who, the Count said, was the paymaster to the gentlemen employed in writing articles for *Le Précurseur*, which paper was devoted to the interests of Charles X., and his party.

Upon one occasion when Le Comte de Jouffroy called on me, he began the following conversation, and said, " Sir, upon due reflection, my opinion is, the British Government is perfectly well aware that at 8 Bath Place lives the true Louis XVII.; but, sir, the danger lies in acknowledging you, as, from the energy of your character, you might put the whole of Europe into a state of fermentation, as you are not only King of France in right of your birth, but you are also heir to Maria Theresa, Empress of Germany ; therefore, if you were acknowledged to be the King of France, you would have a right to interfere in the affairs of Germany ; and you could also claim the title of Emperor of Austria, as being a descendant of Marie Antoinette, the daughter of Maria Theresa, therefore entitling you in right of birth to the throne of Austria, as the rightful, and hereditary heir. You thereby see the difficulties, and dangers that might occur were you to be acknowledged as the rightful heir to the throne of France." I answered Le Comte by saying, it might possibly be the case what he had stated, but nevertheless I thought the Powers of Europe would settle what degree of power and authority Louis XVII. would be entitled to, were such a circumstance to take place, of my being acknowledged the rightful heir of Louis XVI. The Count then observed, " Sir, I see no way so ready to make your claims known to the world as the press. You should therefore devise some means, and publish a work, when I will commence a disputation on it. This will doubtless raise the question as to the existence of Louis XVII. ; likewise, I advise you to leave London, and take a trip to Jersey, as soon as you conveniently can, and there see the French parties, as their coming to London, and seeing you would be of little use, on account of your being known in London for so many years as a professor of music, and your habits and manners being so much, in consequence of your professional career, at variance with your assumption of so great a character, as that of Louis XVII. It would therefore be greatly to your advantage to see persons in Jersey, where they are totally unacquainted with you, and thereby could judge by seeing you personally, there being thousands of French families in La Vendée, Normandy, Brittany, and Gascony, who fully believe in the existence of the son of Louis XVI. They know perfectly well that the Prince-Royal of France did not die in the Tower of the Temple, therefore : *the striking resemblance you bear to the Royal Family of France, and the marks and scars which are known to have existed on the person of the Prince-Royal being found so accurately corresponding on your person, these will form a convincing argument as to whom you really are.*[*]

" Respecting the incidents, and accidents that occurred to the Prince during the period he was in captivity under Antoine Simon, and his wife, these are all duly registered and known, therefore it is impossible for any pretender to gain credence, as there were many youths and boys residing within the precincts of the Temple at the time the Royal Family were confined there, who could easily assume the character, and pass themselves off as being Louis XVII. Hébert, who was appointed the chief commissioner by the municipality of Paris, had two sons who resided with him in the Palais du Temple; these youths, and many others, must have known the Tower of the Temple much better than the unfortunate captive Prince."

I now thought it advisable to call upon Mr. Latour, at Craven Hill, Bayswater, as my reputed mother told me he knew many circumstances regarding me. I accordingly paid him a visit, when he observed : "What induced you to call on me to-day?" I replied, "My late reputed mother informed me you knew many circumstances regarding me." When he replied, he certainly did, as he knew Vincent d'Etionville, a surgeon, and accoucheur, who was attached to the service of the hospital of St. Omer, and who delivered my reputed mother of

* See Appendix A, for Medical Certificates.

a son, born in France in February 1785. This boy was taken to England by her to be baptized, so as to entitle him to the privileges, and rights of an Englishman, and enable him to possess landed property as a British subject. Vincent d'Etionville and he were boys together, both being born at St. Omer. Vincent d'Etionville's real name was Vincent de Bette, but he married a lady of the name of d'Etionville, after which he called himself Vincent d'Etionville. Mr. Latour then said, "Tell me, Mr. Meves, the maiden name of your late reputed mother." I replied, "It was Marianne Crowley." He then said, "Marianne Crowley was called Marianne de Courville at the Court of France. She was appointed one of the ladies in attendance on the Queen of France at the Petit Trianon, where your reputed mother chiefly resided, nevertheless she was at times in attendance at the Palace of Versailles." He then kindly invited me to stay and dine with him, which invitation I accepted. After dinner we retired to his music-room, in order to converse on the subject for which I had called upon him, he remarking, "No one comes into my music-room unless I ring the bell, therefore, we shall not be disturbed here." We then seated ourselves at a table, where a small dessert was already prepared. He then related to me that the Queen of France was the mother of three male children, Louis Joseph, the Dauphin of France, who was born at Versailles in October 1781, and who died in 1789, previous to the French Revolution. Likewise, that the Queen gave birth to a son in 1783, who was named Louis Auguste, who was subsequently created by the King, Le Duc de Bourgoyne—this child being known at Meudon as Le Petit Bossu. A proposal was made to Marianne de Courville to adopt Louis Auguste, Duc de Bourgoyne, and a large quantity of jewels and diamonds of great value, the property of the crown of France, were given to Madame de Courville, in order to elevate and bring up Louis Auguste. He then remarked, "If you go to the British Museum, and make inquiry for L'Affaire du Collier,—'the transaction of the necklace' —you will be able to trace your reputed father, Mr. Meves, who sold the diamonds intrusted to his care, under the name of Valois, in the months of April and May 1785; but, my dear Mr. Meves, be very cautious you do not confuse yourself, in examining the papers and documents, by mixing up the diamonds that were given to your reputed mother with the affair of the diamond necklace, which necklace probably exists to this very day in a perfect state, it having been purloined for political purposes."

Mr. Latour then said, "What did Mrs. Meves state to you at the period of her last illness? did she make any disclosure to you?" I replied, "She did.   About two days previous to her decease, whilst we were sitting together, in the course of conversation she said, ' Augustus, the Queen of France was the mother of two male children, the. Dauphin and the Duke of Normandy,' adding: ' The Dauphin, you know, is dead, but the Duke of Normandy is alive and well, and in sound understanding at this very moment."   She then placed her hand on me, and said : ' *You, Augustus, are that very person.*' "

I then requested Mr. Latour to tell me when and where it was he first saw me.   He replied, he first saw me when Mr. Meves was living in Wilson Street, Moorfields, in the year 1794, and he knew when he saw me, that I was not his son Augustus, as he had previously given instruction on the pianoforte to Mr. Meves's son, at the time he lived in Great Russell Street, Bloomsbury.   Mr. Latour continued the conversation by saying, " Mr. Meves, in my youth I was attached to the service of the Chapel of Versailles, and attended the priests in their duties at the Palace, and was present at the baptism of Louis Auguste, in 1783, with the incense; and also at the consecration of the infant when he was made a Knight of the Order of the Holy Ghost, and created by the King, " Le Duc de Bourgoyne." When very young I took a dislike to the clerical life, and entered the office of Monsieur de Calonne, in 1786, and was appointed his private secretary in 1787. I came with him to England, when he lost his position as Minister of Finance, Necker having been appointed in his stead, through the influence of the Queen of France.   This interference on the part of the Queen, Monsieur de Calonne never forgave ; nevertheless, after the death of the King his heart relented, and he sent me to Maestricht, to the house of Monsieur Gretry, 'a woollen draper,' who was the brother to Gretry, the great musician, when I became acquainted with all the branches of the family of the Gretrys, and I obtained a passport from the Prince, Bishop of Liége, in the name of Gretry, and travelled with a knapsack on my back, with plenty of money in my pocket, as Jean Grétry. I have the passport, Mr. Meves, and will show it you, and you will find therein all the peculiarities of my countenance and person named. On my arrival at Paris, in 1793, Beurnonville advised me to enter the National Guard, which I accordingly did, and at the Tower of the Temple I have done duty as a sentinel, where it was impossible to relieve any one from confinement, as it was so strictly guarded ; but when the Queen was removed to the Prison of the Conciergerie it was a much easier task, the Conciergerie being a public prison. At this prison I came on duty in the passage, near the door of the chamber where the Queen was confined. Beaugerard was at the gate, and I passed word into the Queen's room for her to make her escape ; but she declined, unless accompanied by her children. This was a total impossibility. The Queen herself might have escaped at that time, had she availed herself of the opportunity, but her only request was, ' That when I next came on duty I should conceal about my person, pen, ink, and paper.' The Queen then gave me a pen ; the nib was of gold, and the quill part was made of crystal, with a gold top to secure the ink, the crystal part contained sufficient ink to supply the nib for a moderate-sized letter.

"When I next went on duty at the Prison of the Conciergerie, I concealed the pen and paper about my person, which I handed to the Queen, who then commenced writing, and when the ink was expended she punctured her arm, and drew sufficient blood to finish the letter, after which the Queen gave me the pen, and I will show you it in the same state as when I received it. At the present moment it is at my bankers, Messrs. Wright's, with other valuable property, but I will get it from them, and show it you the next time you do me the favour to call on me." I then asked Mr. Latour what became of the letter.

He replied, " I brought it with me when I came to England, and it is now in the possession of the Royal Family at Holyrood."   The servant then announcing the arrival of the physician who then attended Mrs. Latour, I wished Mr. Latour good evening, and left with a very heavy heart, at the sad misfortunes of the Queen of France.

I called a few days after on Mr. Latour, who showed me the pen, which was in a shagreen case, exactly as he had described it.   He then said, " The Duc de Polignac is coming to town from Holyrood, and on his arrival I will introduce you to him ; probably he may recognise some feature in your face by which he may possibly recollect you, as he was one of your playmates in your infancy."

In the year 1832 I was in the habit of visiting in Frith Street, Soho, a Monsieur de Chermant, who was about eighty years of age.   He was married to an English lady many years younger than himself. He told me that his uncle, " Monsieur de Chermant," was Clerk of the Kitchen to Louis xv., and that he had seen, and well remembered Louis, the Dauphin of France, " son to Louis xv.," to whom he thought I bore a very strong resemblance.   One evening whilst in conversation with him I said, " Dear sir, do you recollect any one belonging to the late Royal Family of France called Le Petit Bossu ?"   He replied, " Certainly I do.   Marie Antoinette gave birth to a male child, who, from weakness, became *bossu*.   This child was known as La Fausse Couchée de la Reine.   He was nicknamed Petit Bossu, and lived until he was about four years of age, when he died.   There is a work published, which gives a full account of Petit Bossu up to his death at Meudon.   I frequently went to the gardens at Meudon to see the Dauphin of France, and his brother, the Prince-Royal of France, where I have seen the two brothers playing together in the gardens of the château."   He then described the Dauphin of France as being a very fine youth, but of delicate constitution ; and remarked, that the Duke of Harcourt, who was appointed governor to the Royal children, had made the Dauphin study too much.   This produced a malady of the spine, from the effects of which he died, at Meudon, in the year 1789. He remembered the funeral of the Dauphin, which he saw pass through the Bois de Boulogne ; and that the Dauphin was most sincerely regretted by every true and loyal Frenchman.   I then told Monsieur de Chermant the conversation I had with Mr. Latour, respecting his service in the Chapel at Versailles, and his attendance with the priests, and his conversation relative to the Duke of Bourgoyne—here remarking, I had never known that such a child as the Duke of Bourgoyne, belonging to the family of Louis xvi., had existed ; when he said, " My dear Mr. Meves, take care Mr. Latour does not confuse you in what he relates, as he has the greatest friendship for the late Duc de Berri, and is no doubt highly interested in the cause of Henri, Duc de Bordeaux, the son of the Duc de Berri."   He then rose from his chair, and went to his book-case, from which he brought a small octavo volume, out of which he read a letter from a royalist to his friends in La Vendée, giving an account of the writer having been at the Tuileries, and having seen the Prince-Royal in the apartment of Madame Elizabeth ; and describes him as having *small laughing brown eyes, and a profusion of brown curly hair*, and as possessing remarkably strong limbs, and as being a strong, healthy boy.   Monsieur Chermant then observed, " Here, sir, is a perfect description of yourself; and if you are not the Prince-Royal of France, then I believe he must have died in the Tower of the Temple." He then placed the book in my hands, from which I read the description given of the Dauphin.

Whilst residing at Bath Place, Mr. George Meves usually dined with me on Sundays, and previously spent very frequently his disengaged evenings with Mrs. Meves and myself, when I have often entered into conversation with him respecting the disclosure of my late reputed mother ; but he attached no credence to Mrs. Meves's disclosure, therefore I did not press upon him too frequent conversation respecting this perplexing question ; for I must confess it was perplexing, on account of the contradiction I met with when I was surrounded by several gentleman, who seemed very much interested in me, but who felt much surprised when I stated I arrived in this country in 1789.

Therefore, I requested Mr. George Meves to write me a letter, and therein state what he knew respecting Mr. and Mrs. Meves and myself, as then I could form my own opinions. The following is the letter written by Mr. George Meves :—

" 128 Long Acre, *February* 22, 1832.

"Dear Sir,—At your request I have looked over some papers I have, and from my own recollection give you the best information I can relative to your late mother. Where my brother formed Miss Crowley's acquaintance was in Maddox Street, in 1783. He afterwards visited her at the time she was living with Lady Harrington. I delivered some tea and grocery to Miss Crowley in 1784, at Lady Harrington's. Some time after, my brother told me she had left Lady Harrington's, and had gone to reside in Piccadilly. From there she went to France. My brother was at Lord Stamford's in the autumn of 1788, taking likenesses of the family. On his road through Shropshire he called on Captain Lee. The following year he went to Captain Lee's, in the autumn of 1789, and spent some months with him at Coten Hall. Where I saw﹅ you, on your return from boarding-school, was at Mr. Page's in Great Russell Street, where my brother was residing, in 1792, and I gave you half-a-guinea to encourage you. I remember taking some wine to Dartmouth Street, Westminster, at the time of the birth of Cecilia. Your mother was then living under the name of Mrs. Schroëder. When your mother, 'Miss Crowley,' formed the acquaintance of my brother, I knew very little of their proceedings. My brother might have married her in the name of Schroëder, at the time she was living with Lady Harrington, as she had good expectations at that time. A separation between them took place shortly after the birth of Cecilia. In 1785 I gave up the grocery business, and entered the service of Sir John Shaw, and travelled with him abroad. I afterwards entered the service of Sir Drummond Smith, and remained in his service for a number of years. Further than this, I cannot at the present time charge my recollection.—I remain, dear sir, your true and affectionate friend,

"George Christopher Meves.

"Mr. Augustus Meves,
  8 Bath Place, New Road."

Shortly after, I was informed by the gentlemen connected with *Le Précurseur* newspaper, that two gentlemen were about to proceed to Edinburgh on the affairs of Her Royal Highness the Duchess of Berri; and they could therefore take any message I wished to send to the

Duchess of Angoulême. I called, and saw a gentleman of the name of Curten, "called Captain Curten, a French officer;" also, a gentleman of the name of Rogiers, an agent to the Duchess of Berri. Both these gentlemen resided at the French hotel in the Strand; and the same evening I was introduced to them they paid their passage-money for Leith Harbour, and early the next morning they went on board for their voyage to Edinburgh.

On their return to London they called at my house, 8 Bath Place, New Road. Upon their entering my drawing-room, Captain Curten addressed me in the French language with these words, " Monsieur, votre nom est en bon odeur à Holyrood "—" Sir, your name is in good odour at Holyrood." He then stated, that the communication he had to make to me did not come direct from the lips of the Duchess of Angoulême, but from the Cardinal de Latil, " confessor to Charles x.," who said, that the Duchess of Angoulême desired him to state that the gentleman who had written to her was mistaken, when he asserted that an exchange of persons had taken place in October 1789, as she, " the Duchess," was quite positive it was her own brother that got into the carriage with her when the Royal Family left Versailles; and that she had never lost sight of him from that time, until their unfortunate separation in the Tower of the Temple. The Duchess assures the gentleman who wrote to her, that nothing on earth could afford a greater consolation to her heart, than to know that her brother was still in existence; but she believes he died, and that his death was accelerated by poison in the Temple. She confesses she did not see her brother in death, but the proof was so positive as not to leave the slightest doubt on her mind; but, respecting the circumstance related of her brother having broken a small enamel box, which was beautifully painted, was true. Captain Curten then observed, " But, sir, the circumstance you have related of your having destroyed a beautiful enamel box in your youth, which you believe belonged to Her Royal Highness the Duchess of Angoulême, very probably, sir, you may have heard of the circumstance from Madame your mother." I replied, " Oh no, gentlemen, I assure you it comes entirely from my own recollection; besides which, when I was a young man, I spoke to my reputed mother respecting this circumstance, when she replied, 'Augustus, that must have occurred when you were at the Messrs. Thornton's boarding-school, and very likely the enamel box belonged to one of the Miss Thorntons, for which, no doubt, you were punished.' I said, 'No, I was not punished; for I remember putting the lid of the box into my pocket, and the box part I threw over a high wall.' On my honour, gentlemen, I tell you the truth, as I certainly broke a beautiful enamel box in my early youth, which occasioned great distress at the time, but to whom it belonged I have quite forgotten; and respecting the Tower of the Temple, during the time the Royal Family were confined there, I assure you I never as yet have read any work relating to that portion of the history of France."

They then resumed their conversation, and said, "The name of Marianne de Courville Schroëder is known, and there are now persons at Holyrood who remember such a lady as being in the service of Marie Antoinette, as a confidential friend, in whom the Queen placed great trust and confidence." They then observed, "Pray, sir, did you not, shortly after the decease of your reputed mother, receive a large sum of money?" I replied, "No, gentlemen; I did not." They then informed me, that a large sum of money was left for my services in such hands, that it must have come into my possession, as the Duchess, considering that I might by possibility have some claims on her, directed that a sum of money should be placed where it was certain to come into my hands. I then informed them that I had never received any sum of money; nevertheless, I did not doubt the kind intentions, or the goodness of heart, of the Duchess of Angoulême. Monsieur Rogiers then showed me some small packets containing the hair of the young Duc de Bordeaux, with his signature of "Henri" on the papers; and, in conclusion, said, "They should both leave London the next day for France, *en route* for La Vendée." I then wished them a safe and prosperous voyage, and we parted in a very friendly manner.

One morning I called on Le Comte Fontaine de Moreau, and the Chevalier de Verniëul, at 6 Grafton Street, when they informed me that

Le Précurseur newspaper was about to be given up, as the Royal Family of France were going to leave Holyrood for Germany, and that I had therefore better make up my mind and go at once to Edinburgh, and endeavour to see the Duchess of Angoulême herself, and should I think fit, either of them would accompany me and procure me a proper introduction to Her Royal Highness, through the medium of the parties with whom they were in the constant habit of corresponding. I then arranged for Le Comte Fontaine de Moreau to accompany me, and named Tuesday in the following week as the probable day.

This determination I disclosed to Mr. George Meves, when we were at coffee in the evening, telling him it was my intention to leave London for Edinburgh in about four or five days. He endeavoured to persuade me against such a resolution on account of the great expense I should incur, to which I replied, " Probably I shall go alone, when I get letters of introduction from the proper parties," as it was my full determination to seek an interview with the Duchess of Angoulême if possible. He, finding he could not dissuade me from proceeding to Edinburgh, said no more on the subject, but to my great astonishment, the next morning before I went out, a medical gentleman called on me, and said, " Sir, I have been sent here by Mr. George Meves to take blood from your arm." I said, " I shall not allow you to do anything of the kind, and I request, sir, you will do me the favour to tell Mr. George Meves not to trouble himself about me or my business."

On the following Sunday Mr. George Meves dined with me, but I said nothing further on the subject of my going to Edinburgh. During the evening I went out, and on my return home, when I was about undressing myself to go to bed, a Mr. Knight, of Hope House, Hammersmith, walked into my room with a paper in his hand, and said, " Mr. Meves, I have authority to take you under my charge for a short time ; here is my authority, which you can read if you please ; there is a carriage at the door, and you had better follow me without any opposition, or you may probably get into hands that might ill-treat you." I remonstrated at the illegality of the proceeding, but being fearful of

disturbing my family, and frightening them at so late an hour, as they
had all retired to rest, I thought under such circumstances it was best
to submit to this unwarrantable proceeding, and watch my opportunity
to escape and make a statement before a magistrate of the illegality of
being taken from my own home, and my detention without having
committed any act contrary to law, beyond that of my desire to go to
Edinburgh in order to procure an interview with the Duchess of
Angoulême. Upon my entering the carriage, Mr. Knight gave orders
to be driven to his son's house at Brook Green. I had a good bedchamber on the first floor, which looked out upon a garden. Not the
slightest compunction was used towards me. The next morning I
breakfasted with young Mr. Knight and his wife. In the course of the
day I walked about the garden to observe the locality, and saw that the
gate was securely barred and well locked, except when the tradespeople
came to deliver the necessary articles for the service of the establishment. Here I was placed, having been taken from my own house,
and from the bosom of my family, which I considered a most shameful
proceeding on the part of Mr. George Meves, especially so in his pre-
venting my seeking an opportunity of an interview with the Duchess
of Angoulême. After I had been there a few days I watched my
opportunity, and as some articles were being delivered at the door, I at
once made the best of my way through the gate, and ran towards the
Hammersmith road, and hid myself in a passage. My pursuers passed
down the road running after an omnibus, supposing that I had entered
one, after which I saw an omnibus approaching, when I left my hiding-
place and walked up the road to meet it, and seated myself very quietly
inside, when my pursuers mounted the step and claimed me, upon which
the ladies became very much alarmed, but luckily a French gentleman,
" a drawing-master," was in the omnibus, with whom I was acquainted,
who said, "I will become answerable for the good conduct of this
gentleman, who has been kidnapped from his house and family." After
the omnibus had proceeded some distance, I said, " I trust, ladies and
gentlemen, you will have the goodness to pardon the abrupt manner in

which I entered the omnibus. This gentleman knows the cause which occasioned my detention, and I shall now go as far as Southampton Street, Strand, and at once proceed to Bow Street, and lay my complaint before the magistrate for my illegal detention."

This I accordingly did, but first I called and requested two trades-people to come as witnesses before the magistrate, and the French drawing-master likewise accompanied me. The magistrate approved of my conduct, and said, "You have no right to detain this gentleman unless he has committed a breach of the peace, or misconducted himself; therefore you detain him at your own peril, and he can bring an action at law against you, unless you can show good cause for his detention." I then left the office and called in the Strand. The man, "my pursuer," said he would not leave me. I then called a coach, and told him he could ride outside with the coachman, and I then returned to Mr. Knight's.

When I entered, Mrs. Knight was much vexed at my having ran away. She informed me Mr. Knight had gone to town to my house. I then said, "I am not in the slightest degree angry with Mr. Knight; he only obeyed the orders he received; the man who attended me will explain my conduct, likewise the magistrate's opinion respecting my illegal detention." Shortly after, Mr. Knight returned, and was much provoked at my laying the complaint before a magistrate. He then said, "Sir, you are entirely your own master. Mr. George Meves will be here to-morrow, and you must leave; and as to the complaint you laid before the magistrate, that you were kidnapped from your house and your family, that is not correct, for you came here of your own free-will, and never made the slightest resistance when I showed you my authority to take charge of you." I answered, "Of course, I knew you would not act unless you had proper authority, and under such circumstances I submitted, on account of not desiring to create any disturbance at my residence." After some further altercation I retired to rest, and the next morning I left Mr. Knight's.

A few days after, the Royal Family of France arrived in London, from Holyrood.   The ex-King, Charles X. and suite, put up at Grillion's Hotel in Albemarle Street, Piccadilly, and her Royal Highness the Duchess of Angoulême, "daughter of Louis XVI.," with her Royal Highness Mademoiselle d'Artois, and his Royal Highness Le Duc de Bordeaux, stayed at Grillion's Hotel in Charles Street, Grosvenor Square.

At about eleven o'clock I contrived to procure the use of a first floor in Charles Street, from where I wrote the following note :—

"*14th September* 1832,
8 BATH PLACE, NEW ROAD.

"Mr. Augustus Meves respectfully presents his congratulations on the safe arrival of Her Royal Highness the Duchess of Angoulême in London, and earnestly requests that Her Royal Highness will condescend to allow him the honour of an interview, previous to her departure from London."

I then delivered the letter to one of the attendants at the hotel, and said, "should my request be granted, I should be waiting at apartments opposite."   I then returned and seated myself near the window, and observed the various carriages that came.   Amongst the visitors to the Duchess of Angoulême were Le Comte de Jouffroy and Prince Charles de Broglie.   The window I was at was directly opposite the antechamber, from where I observed the company, but the room where the Duchess of Angoulême was in was too distant for me to see minutely their features.   His Royal Highness the Duke of Cumberland came with his Duchess to pay their respects.   After a short levée I could just see Her Royal Highness the Duchess of Angoulême take leave of her numerous friends, and pass from her room to her chamber. I then descended to the street, and saw the Duc de Guiche enter his carriage, and recognised him, as I had often seen him when he was Captain Grammont, at the parties of the Dowager Marchioness of Lansdowne.   I made inquiry at Grillion's Hotel, and was informed that the Duchess would leave England *en route* for the Continent early the next morning.

Nothing particular occurred to me until the year 1835, when, one afternoon while I was walking in Regent's Park, I accidentally met the

Abbé Prince Charles de Broglie. We entered into conversation ; and he then informed me Le Comte de Jouffroy had been appointed banker to the Pope of Rome, and that a friend of his, the Marquis of Bonneval, was very desirous of being introduced to me. Shortly after I received a letter from Prince Charles de Broglie. The following is the translation :—

"SIR,—Monsieur le Marquis de Bonneval having appointed Wednesday, ' to-morrow,' to take tea with me at my house, wishing to meet you together, if you have no other engagement, I shall be delighted if you will be there with him. Should it be agreeable to you, I shall expect you between eight and nine o'clock.—I beg you to accept the renewed assurance of my distinguished consideration,

" PRINCE CHARLES DE BROGLIE.

" This 13*th*, P.M.
    Monsieur MEVES, Bath Place, New Road."

I went according to invitation, and was introduced to the Marquis of Bonneval ; and, before leaving, I invited both gentlemen to honour me with a visit at my residence. The Prince de Broglie said, he would write and let me know the evening the Marquis would appoint. A short time after I received the following note :—

" PRINCE CHARLES DE BROGLIE has the honour of presenting his compliments to Mr. Meves. He has been waiting for an opportunity of meeting the Marquis before replying to his invitation. The latter unites with the Prince in thanks, and if Tuesday evening be convenient to Mr. Meves, they will be at his house about eight o'clock.

" This 4*th October*."

They came, and we passed a very agreeable evening. I did my best to entertain them, and played several elegant compositions. The Marquis before leaving gave me an invitation to breakfast with him at his house, 90 Norton Street, Portland Place. Accordingly I paid the Marquis a morning visit ; and after breakfast he narrated the following : —" Sir, during the process against Louis XVI., L'Héritier passed from the Tower of the Temple into La Rue du Temple, and the guards at the gate presented their muskets, in order to prevent him passing into the street, when he cried out, 'Laissez moi passer, pour que je demande grace pour mon père'—'Let me pass, that I may ask pardon for my father;' and in his agitation, while throwing his arms about and wringing his hands, he accidentally struck his left wrist on one of the points of the bayonets of the guards at the gate, and consequently wounded his left wrist.* *Now, sir, it is extraordinary, but you have on your left wrist a scar corresponding with such that must exist on L'Héritier. This scar, and particularly your features and general appearance, which so exactly correspond with those of L'Héritier,—these to me are the most convincing proofs, and not your conversation, as apparently you are quite ignorant of the circumstances which regard yourself."*

The Marquis then said, "What do you recollect of your arrival in England, and when have you been led to suppose that you first came under your reputed father's care?" I replied, "I was led to believe I first came under his care in 1792, from a boarding-school at Horsham, in Sussex, called the Messrs. Thornton's boarding-school, which school I had been given to understand had formerly been a county prison, and on a new county prison being built, the Messrs. Thornton had taken the old county prison, and converted it into a large boarding-school for boys; and, in consequence of Mrs. Meves getting into pecuniary difficulties, Mr. Meves came to Horsham and paid for my schooling, and took me with him to Great Russell Street, where he was then residing: but, respecting my own recollection, I am quite positive of being placed at a boarding-school at Wandsworth, kept by a Mr. Tempest, and that I was a parlour boarder at this school. I used to sleep in the same bedroom as the daughters of Mr. Tempest; likewise, when my schoolfellows during the holidays went home to their parents, I remained at this school. It was during this vacation that Mrs. Meves came to Wandsworth and took me from school to her residence, 16 Vere Street, Oxford Street; and it was from the windows of her apartments that I saw some illuminations, *which illuminations I have since been fully assured were those given in honour of Lord Howe's victory in June*

* See Medical Certificate in Appendix, Note A.

1794." These incidents I declared to the Marquis I knew were positive, for they emanated from my own recollective powers ; therefore I had not to depend, nor had I gained the knowledge of these incidents from any other person, who might have misled me on the subject. The Marquis then requested me to write a short narrative of what I thought the truth, and give it to the Abbé Prince de Broglie. He then gave me an invitation to call on him any morning before twelve o'clock, when he should be always most happy to see me.

I wrote a short memoir comprising the subject of the letters, as written to the Duchess of Angoulême, and what I had stated to Charles x.'s party, and adopting the dates I had received from Mr. George Meves, from the information he had given me respecting my reputed father and mother, to my recollections, which I left with the Abbé Prince de Broglie. *The occurrences I had stated were in themselves correct, but the dates were incorrect, on account of having been misled as regards time and place, of which I was under a misconception at the time.** Some time after, I received the following note from the Prince de Broglie :—

"Sir,—I beg you to be kind enough to accept my excuses. I cannot possibly fall in with the proposal you have made me at this moment, to come to tea at your house, on account of the coldness of the evening. I am compelled to take great care of myself in consequence of my fall. I shall endeavour to compensate myself for it as soon as I can, and it will be with great pleasure. I avail myself of this opportunity to send you back the interesting papers that you confided to me, and trust you will accept my thanks.—I have the honour to be, sir, your very humble and obedient,

"Prince Charles de Broglie."

One morning I called on the Marquis, when we entered into conversation, during which the following transpired :· That he had emigrated to England in the year 1791, he having left his mother, the Dowager Marchioness of Bonneval, with his brother, the Count de Bonneval, at the family château in Normandy, near Elboeuf; and in 1793, during the time the Queen of France was confined in the Prison of the Con-

* See Appendix, Note I, for Narrative.

ciergerie, he accompanied an English lady, a Mrs. Atkyns, to France, who proceeded on to Paris, and he for safety took refuge at the château of his mother in Normandy, as he was fearful of being recognised in Paris, on account of his being known to be a royalist. The cause of her going to Paris was to aid and assist the Queen of France to escape from the Prison of the Conciergerie, and make her way if possible to England. The proffered service of this noble and intrepid lady the Queen declined to accept, unless she could be accompanied by her children, who were confined in the Tower of the Temple. This being impossible to accomplish, the lady returned to England, as it was dangerous for her to remain in Paris.* The party to which the Marquis of Bonneval belonged, finding all their endeavours ineffectual in delivering the Queen, now determined to use all their efforts to save the heir. They had access to Simon, " in whose custody the Dauphin was," and Hébert, whom they bribed, as any sum of money required was at their command. The escape of the heir from the Temple was effected, and he, the Marquis, had guarded the carriage which contained the heir, with a guard of undoubted courage, through a certain pass in Normandy leading to the coast; and upon arriving on the coast in safety, he spurred his horse and returned to the château of his mother, and soon after came to England, on account of the danger he laid himself open to by remaining in France. I then said, " My dear Marquis, at what time did this occur, and to where did the carriage proceed?" He replied, " During the process against the Queen ; and the carriage proceeded on to La Vendée, for Charette to certify the identity." I then asked the Marquis whether he saw into the carriage, to which he answered, No, he did not ; but he knew perfectly well the carriage contained the heir, with a guard of undoubted courage. The Marquis then made me a very kind offer, saying, " There is a very fine house to let in Norton Street, with a good-sized garden attached to it," and desired to know whether I should like to live there, as he thought it would be more comfortable for my children, on account of the garden attached to

* See Appendix, Note K, for account of the Atkyns family of Kettringham Hall.

it, as where I resided in Bath Place there was no garden.   I returned many thanks to the Marquis for his kind offer, but I thought the rent of the house would be more than I could conveniently afford ; when he observed, If it is too expensive, he should feel proud, if I would permit him, to pay for it.   I thanked him for his kindness, and said, " I could not think of accepting such ; " when he observed, It was not for me, but for the advantage of my children.

Upon another occasion when I called to see the Marquis, he asked me if I had read the trial of Mathurin Bruneau ? I replied, " No, Monsieur le Marquis, I have not."   He then said, "Have you ever read the trial of the Baron de Richemont ? "   I answered, " No ; really I have not, nor any works of that kind."   He then gave me two French newspapers, *Le Constitutionnel*, dated the 1st and 2d of November 1834, containing two days' trial of the Baron de Richemont; and he read some portion of the trial to me, and observed : There was a paper published at Paris, established by a person of the name of Thomas, for the purpose of receiving any evidence concerning the Prince-Royal, Dauphin of France, and that an aged person had given the following information at the office : That he had been in the service of Her Royal Highness Madame Adelaide at Versailles, and had frequently been in the apartments of the nurses, and held the Prince-Royal in his arms, and saw the child quite naked when the nurse was washing him, and had observed that the Prince-Royal had an appearance on his right breast resembling *two teats*. The Marquis then said, " Sir, have you any such mark, as it will be a singular proof ? "   I replied, " I have certainly many singular marks on my chest, but I have not two teats on my right breast, *nevertheless— over the nipple on my breast is a kind of mole, which in my youth may have greatly resembled two teats*."*   The foregoing is the substance of my interviews and conversations with the old Marquis of Bonneval, at his house in Norton Street, Portland Place.

Some few days after, I paid a morning visit to the Abbé Prince Charles de Broglie, when he informed me that the Marquis of Bonneval,

* See Medical Certificate in Appendix, Note A.

while walking in the Regent's Park, was seized with a fit of paralysis, and was taken to his own house in a most dangerous state.

On my leaving the Abbé Prince I went direct to the Marquis's, and made inquiry of the housekeeper as to the state of my friend the Marquis, and was informed that the old Marquis was in a dying state, the fit having rendered him quite speechless, yet he had still the use of his senses. I was shown into his bedchamber, and I then beheld him in a most deplorable state. I said, "Dear Marquis, I am sorry to see you suffering, and have come to offer you my sincere gratitude for your interest and kindness towards me." He seemed to understand perfectly what I said. I took from the side of his pillow his handkerchief, and wiped his mouth; his breast was heaving violently. I then made inquiry of the housekeeper, whether the Marquis had sufficient medical advisers, when she replied, "Most certainly, sir. The Marquis is attended by his own doctor, and the Marquis's solicitor has written to the Count of Bonneval, and he is expected here this evening from France." I then took my last adieu of the kind old Marquis. The next time I made inquiry, the Marquis was deceased.

I now made researches at Bosange's French library in Great Marlborough Street, and consulted the *Moniteur*, and purchased an abridged chronological History of France, likewise *Prudhomme's Journal*, from the year 1789 to 1794.

In the year 1835 I frequented the house of a Dr. Riofrey Bureaud, where I was introduced to a Monsieur Cabet and several other French gentlemen. One morning when I called on Dr. Bureaud, he gave me a French work published at the Royal French Printing-Office, entitled *Les Evènements du Temple* —"The Events of the Temple." The authorship of this work is attributed to her Royal Highness the Duchess of Angoulême, "daughter of Louis xvi." At the end of this work is appended Monsieur Harmand's report respecting his official visit to the unfortunate prisoner of the Temple, from whom he was unable to elicit a single word.* I made several extracts from the

* For Harmand's report, refer for page to Index, under heading, *Historical Records.*

Moniteur, and wrote them as marginal remarks to this work. On one occasion, when I was at Dr. Bureaud's, he informed me he expected Prince Louis Napoleon there that evening. During the evening I played Steibelt's "Storm." After which, as I was walking about the room in conversation with various persons, a young gentleman spoke to me in French, saying, "Est-ce que j'ai l'honneur de parler à Monseigneur le Dauphin?"—"Have I the honour of speaking to my Lord the Dauphin?" I replied rather abruptly, "On le dit"—"They say so"—and then passed to the room where Monsieur Cabet was surrounded by a number of French refugees, expatriated from their country by Louis Philippe. On my going home I reflected that my short reply was incorrect, as I should have entered into conversation with my questioner and ascertained whom in reality he was; but my supposing him to be Louis Napoleon, I did what I thought the best in order to avoid any explanation.

Time passed on, until one afternoon, on my return home, my good lady informed me that a French gentleman had left his card, and requested an interview with me the next morning, as he wished to introduce me to a party of French noblemen who surrounded a gentleman, who, in his mind, was the Dauphin of France, as the circumstances he related regarding the Temple at Paris proved that he must have been there. On seeing the card, I found it was an acquaintance of mine, a Monsieur Auguste Desjardin. Accordingly at about ten o'clock the next morning he visited me, when we proceeded together to Pagliano's Sablioniere Hotel, Leicester Square.

On my arrival at the hotel I was introduced to a gentleman called Naündorff, whose features in many points bore a resemblance to my own, with this exception, that he had blue eyes and light hair, and had full whiskers, which gave him a military appearance; and I had brown eyes and brown hair, and was deficient of the whiskers. After exchanging the usual courtesies, the topic of the Temple was soon alluded to, when Naündorff and myself entered into conversation respecting the Temple. I then observed, "Sir, in respect to my recollection of the

Tower of the Temple, I must in the first instance inform you that all recollection of such a place has been as much as possible destroyed in me by my reputed parents, by them substituting in its place a boarding-school at Horsham, which school had formerly been a county prison, where Augustus Meves had been placed in his youth; therefore, they have always accounted for circumstances that have occurred to me in reality at the Tower of the Temple, as if happening to me at this county prison at Horsham, for it is evident, had they allowed any suspicion to have entered my mind respecting the Tower of the Temple, or incidents prior, as if they in reality had happened to me at Paris or at the Tower of the Temple, they would have lost all power over me, therefore, the school at Horsham, and the Tower of the Temple, through their 'in many instances similitude to each other,' rendered it easy for them to account for all my recollections in a natural, and, as it were, conclusive manner, thereby all my questions were readily and plausibly answered, and consequently my recollections of the Temple were to a great degree destroyed, or, correctly speaking, abused, and its place substituted as the recollections of the old county prison at Horsham, the boarding-school of the Messrs. Thornton; but since Mrs. Meves's disclosure, and what has come to my knowledge, of course I am aware that the positive source, as refers to my personal recollections, have been designedly misrepresented by my reputed parents, and erroneously endorsed by my reputed uncle, 'Mr. George Meves.' I will now recount to you, what in reality my recollections are—namely: I remember in my youth attending a kind of schoolroom, which, in order to reach, I had to cross a piece of ground, and I then entered a singularly built large room, rounded at each end; a little below the centre of this room I used to sit alone at a desk; opposite me were placed two firelocks, the muzzles of which pointed into the garden, and the butts were supported inside. This place had an appearance as if it had been some factory, as the windows were about a yard from the basement, or ground of the chamber." While I was speaking in this manner, very much to the satisfaction of Herr Naündorff, a French gentleman, called the Count,

interrupted me, saying, "C'est absurde, c'est absurde—It is absurd,
it is absurd,—there is not the slightest record that ever the Dauphin
went to school within the precincts of the Temple." When I replied,
"I beg your pardon, Count." Naündorff here remarked, "What you call
the schoolroom was a kind of oval rotunda near the garden, next the
iron gate of the entrance into the garden, and called 'La Rotunda.' It
was dismantled, and all the ornamental part destroyed and stolen after the
Comte d'Artois quitted the Temple in 1789." He then said, "Tell me,
Sir, when you left the Rotunda how did you enter the Small Tower of
the Temple where Antoine Simon and his wife lived?" I replied,
"When I left the schoolroom two boys used to accompany me across
a piece of ground, when I ascended a flight of stone steps with an iron
railing, and at once entered a good-sized dark parlour, where a woman
received me. In this room there was a large cupboard in one of the
corners, from which was given me slices of brioche; in the opposite
corner was a similar door, which opened to a circular staircase." Naündorff then said, "And what, Sir, was opposite to the door of entrance?"
To which I replied, "Upon my word I cannot say; what I have stated
is all I recollect of the room." He then observed, "There was a
door which opened to a corridor connected with the entrances of the
Great Tower." Here ended my first conversation with Naündorff.

On the following day I again visited Naündorff and his friends.
After I had been there a short time, Naündorff questioned me as
follows,—"When you entered the doorway which led to the spiral
staircase, where did that staircase lead to?" I replied, "The staircase,
of which I have a tolerable recollection, led to the upper chamber of
the Great Tower; but, Sir, I must acquaint you that I have lately purchased *Prudhomme's Journal;* also I have read a very interesting book,
entitled *Les Evènements du Temple*—'The Events of the Temple,'—
therefore my recollective powers are greatly assisted by the reading of
these works. The winding staircase of which you speak terminated in
a covered passage which led to the upper chamber of the Great Tower.
This room was very large, and in the centre of the ceiling there rose a

very high square-sided, conical kind of tower.   In this large cone a
swing was fixed to one of the beams which supported the cone, and it
was in this room that the person who had the care of me used to make
me run.   In this room, near the wall, was a German stove of an obelisk
shape, and likewise two large-sized glass Dutch bottles."   I then said,
" Herr Naündorff, have you by chance any recollection of the circumstance I am about to relate, which is, that I was placed in the swing
attached to the beam which supported the cone, by the person who
had the care of me ?   In order to gain greater velocity, I used when
swinging to strike the side of the cone with my feet, but upon
this specified occasion there was another boy in the room with the
person who had the care of me, who was watching, whilst I was thus
occupied, and after I had finished swinging, this youth was placed in the
swing, and upon his attempting to strike the side of the cone with his feet,
as I had done, he by accident struck the hooks which held the tube that
conveyed the smoke from the iron stove, and down came a portion of
the worm-eaten tube, and with it the soot, the accumulation of years."
Naündorff shrugged his shoulders and said, " The old iron stove, of
which you speak, was removed, and a French one was built in its stead.
The room itself also was divided into two chambers ; in one was placed
the French stove, which heated the chambers, and in the other was
a bed, two chairs, and a small-sized table."   He then added, " In
these two chambers it was, that he was confined, and the National
Guard used to challenge him, and he was obliged to answer them as
well as he could."   He then informed me that he and his friends
were busily engaged writing the events of his life, which would be shortly
published.   I then proposed that the gentlemen I had the pleasure of
meeting should accompany me to my house and take tea with me, to
which they consented.

Naündorff admired my beautiful paintings, and likewise two valuable
prints of Louis XVI., and a painting representing an itinerant musician,
with dancing dogs, and a chained monkey. Having met with an
accident with the thumb of my right hand, I could not perform any

pieces of music, and to my astonishment Naündorff sat down at my pianoforte, and played several pieces of music, and modulated very correctly. I called his attention to an oval print of a youth in the dress of the National Guard of Paris in 1792. The print represented a boy standing in the Garden of the Tuileries near the terrace, with a gun in his hand. This picture was entitled " L'Espoir des Français, Louis Charles de Bourbon, Prince-Royal, née à Versailles, Mars 1785," which picture represented the Prince-Royal as having " *brown eyes and brown hair, the hair hanging in abundance about his shoulders.*" Naündorff then remarked, " Sir, this print is no proof for you, as it certainly is not a genuine French print of the year 1792, and very probably this is engraved, and painted in England, and if so, such would constitute it a surreptitious print; moreover, it represents a youth of at least twelve years of age, and therefore it cannot be a genuine French print." He called his friends' attention to it, and they all agreed that it represented a boy of at least twelve years of age, and consequently it could not be a genuine portrait of the Prince-Royal, as when the Prince was in the habit of amusing himself in the garden of the Tuileries he was not seven years of age. Having promised to lend Naündorff some volumes of *Prudhomme's Journal,* I took from my bookcase the three last volumes of·the *Journal,* of the years 1792, 1793, and 1794, also *Les Preuves Authentiques de la Mort de Louis* XVII., published at Paris in 1831. I then requested him to return me the volumes of *Prudhomme's Journal* after he had read them, as their loss would make the work incomplete. We then sat down and had some refreshment, and an agreeable chit-chat, during which Naündorff related in the German language, "which I understood tolerably well at that time," the following :—" The upper room of the Great Tower was divided into two chambers, and a large space was left behind for the purpose of containing old broken furniture. In these two rooms I was confined, in one of these was a bed, —'which had formerly belonged to Cléry'—a chair, and a table, and in the other, which was the larger one of the two, was a French stove which heated both the rooms." Having stated such, he proceeded as follows :—

"One evening a man who had succeeded Antoine Simon came into the room, and brought with him a mannikin, which he placed in the bed, after which he took down a portion of the partition, and desired me to follow him into the lumber-room. He cautioned me to be very silent, and not to make the slightest noise, as my life and deliverance depended upon my remaining quiet. The man then returned into the bedroom, and screwed up the boards of the partition. The next evening about dusk he came again with a bundle, containing a blouse and trousers, such as working men wear. These I put on, when he told me to follow him fearlessly. I was then taken down the spiral staircase into the parlour of the Small Tower, after which he led me across the piece of ground which divides the Palace of the Temple from La Rue du Temple. The guard at the gate allowed us to pass, as my conductor was well known as an honest republican, who was taking one of the workmen's boys to his home. I walked a considerable distance from the Tower of the Temple, when we entered a house, of which my conductor took me to the fourth storey, where a young woman received us, who treated me very kindly. I remained for some time under the care of this young person. One night I was taken from the house and placed into a carriage with a stranger, who said very little to me. We travelled night and day, until we came to the confines of Germany. Here I was placed with a family who were not unkind, but who seemed to care very little about me. In due time I was apprenticed to a watchmaker. My education in the meantime was not neglected. When I was eighteen years of age I was obliged to enter the Prussian army as a private soldier; from this life I was determined to escape, so also a young friend of mine, of the name of 'Naündorff,' into the King of Saxony's dominions. Having carried our design into effect, and as we were travelling through a dense forest, we were pursued by the Prussian military, who suspected us of being conscript deserters, when my companion and I parted, he entering the wood whilst I ran along the pathway until I came to the highroad, where an officer in the King of Saxony's service was travelling in his carriage, who took compassion on me, and allowed me a seat in his carriage.   I informed him that I was of a respectable family, and by trade a watchmaker.   The officer, whose name was Major Schiller, advised me to make my way into the interior of Saxony, to one of the large cities, where I should be sure to find employment if I was a good workman.   On my arrival at the town, which was fortified, I entered it in company with the Major, to whom I returned my respectful thanks.   I stayed there all night, and the next morning proceeded towards one of the principal cities in Saxony, where I soon found employment in my trade as a watchmaker, which I followed under the assumed name of my lost comrade 'Naündorff.'"   With this he finished his narration, when I observed, "Pray tell me, Herr Naündorff, were you not taken to Brunswick, and placed with a family by the name of Bouer, and had not Madame Anna Dorothea Bouer the care of you?" After some pause, he replied, "Most truly, Mr. Meves, you put such questions to me that I cannot consistently answer, but as respects yourself, you can say and do what you please, whilst I, you must be fully aware, must be cautious how I give answers to questions that are placed to me.   Now, Mr. Meves, will you answer me this question, Did you not receive from Germany a letter in 1818?   One was sent you, addressed to Mr. Augustus Meves, Poste Restante à Londres?"   I said in reply, "Dear sir, at that time I was under a severe illness, after the decease of my most excellent reputed father, whom I greatly loved ; his death, which was rather sudden, affected me, and I was in a very precarious state for some time after.   As I recovered I was in the habit of frequenting the Anti-Gallician Coffee-house, in Threadneedle Street, where a gentleman informed me that a letter was at the Dead-Letter Office at the General Post-Office, in Lombard Street, which had been there for some time, addressed to Mr. Augustus Meves, and it had the German Post-Office mark upon it, which I might procure if I made inquiry respecting it.   However, I do not know how it was, but I never made the slightest inquiry about it, and consequently it was entirely lost to me ; my being in so weak a state at the time, accounts for my indifference to anything that might have given me trouble or vexation."   Naündorff seemed surprised at this admission, and when he had expressed himself to that effect, and was fully convinced that I had not seen or read any letter from Germany, he went with me up-stairs to rejoin his friends. Before the party left, I wished Naündorff every success in the work he was about to publish.

When left to myself I reflected on the occurrences of the day, and could not help feeling, almost to a conviction, that Herr Naündorff, the watchmaker, was in reality the son of Mr. William Meves, as he so exactly corresponded with the description given me by Ann Powell, and Mrs. Spence, of my having, when a boy, blue eyes and light-coloured hair. His playing the pianoforte and modulating correctly, impressed me that, very possibly, he it was who was the pupil of Joseph Frike, the celebrated author on Thorough Bass, Counterpoint, and Modulation, who had instructed Augustus Meves in his youth. I now thought it advisable not to pursue any further acquaintanceship with Naündorff, but to leave all, as regarded myself, to the chance of circumstances.

In the year 1836 a gentleman of the name of Desanges called on me, respecting a quantity of letters and papers which had belonged to Mrs. Charlotte Atkyns of Kettringham Hall, Norfolk, these having been left in the care of the late Marquis of Bonneval by her, and that these letters and papers were now in the possession of her solicitor, and should I require them they would be delivered up to me, as it was the desire of the late Marquis of Bonneval. Shortly after, I received the following note from Monsieur Desanges :—

"8 UPPER RANELEIGH TERRACE, BELGRAVE ROAD.

"MY DEAR SIR,—I have to inform you that this morning I have seen Mr. Jenkins, and have fixed an appointment with him for Friday next, between two and three o'clock, and I shall on that day wait for you at the place appointed by you.—I remain, my dear Sir, your obedient servant,

"C. J. DESANGES.

" *Wednesday, 24th August* 1836.

"AUGUSTUS MEVES, Esq., 8 Bath Place, New Road."

I met Mr. Desanges as appointed, and we went to Barnard's Inn,

Holborn, to the office of Mr. Jenkins. I presented my card, and he then stated that he was the solicitor to the late Mrs. Charlotte Atkyns of Kettringham Hall, Norfolk ; that she had inherited the Kettringham Hall estates under the will of her husband, in trust for his son, a minor, and that Mrs. Atkyns had mortgaged her farms in Norfolk, which at one time produced her a rental of about £1500 a year ; that she had advanced considerable sums to various French emigrants, and had claims on the French Government for sums of money lent to Louis XVIII. during his residence at Hartwell ; that he had placed in the hands of an agent memorials to the French Government to see if anything could be obtained in liquidation of the demands ; that a sum of about £600 had been paid to Mrs. Atkyns during her lifetime, but that for the want of proper means to prosecute her claims she was obliged to give them up, and had died in very reduced circumstances at the house of her friend the late Marquis of Bonneval. He then took from his desk a large bundle of foreign letters, and said, " Sir, if you like to accept these, you are perfectly welcome to them." I accepted them with thanks, and then left the office. I invited Monsieur Desanges to dine with me, after which he arranged the letters for me, which dated from the year 1792, when the Royal Family were confined in the Tower of the Temple. Part of the correspondence was from Monsieur Peltier, the editor of the French newspaper *L'Ambegue*, and several from Monsieur de Cormier, whom I afterwards traced in the *Moniteur* to have held the appointment of Colonial Minister to Louis XVI. One of the letters written by Peltier, in the month of April 1793, stated, that Colonel Tarlington had left in despair, after having eyed the Tower of the Temple, and that he, " Peltier," had a model of the Tower made, sufficient to rescue the Queen of France from her confinement. Most of the letters from Monsieur Peltier, up to the month of July 1793, were addressed to Mrs. Charlotte Atkyns, Kettringham Hall, Norfolk, and those from abroad to the care of Mrs. Walpole, Hamilton Street, Piccadilly.

I had been given to understand by some friends of mine, that a gentleman, by the name of Franks, who had formerly been a magistrate in Ireland, and who was then confined in the Fleet Prison for contempt of Court, in a Chancery suit, that he in his youth had been a page attached to the service of Louis XVI., at the Palace of Versailles. Having a letter of introduction to Mr. Franks, from a French gentleman, I made inquiry for him at the Fleet Prison, and was shown into the coffee-room on the first floor. After exchanging the usual courtesies I explained to him the object of my visit, and we then entered into conversation, and he then told me that he had been in the service of Louis XVI. for above ten years, from the year 1779 till the month of October 1789; that he knew Mr. Cornelius Crowley of Spring House, County Tipperary, as being a branch of the family of the Macartys of Spring House, Tipperary; and that he saw Mr. Cornelius Crowley in Paris, where he was about placing his daughter, Miss Marianne, at a convent.* Subsequently, through the influence of Signor Sacchini, the celebrated Italian composer, Miss Marianne Crowley became a Lady-in-Waiting on the Queen of France,† and remained in the service of the Queen at ·Versailles till the period of her father's death, when she went to England to administer to his effects. Marianne Crowley returned to Paris in 1784, and re-entered the service of the Queen, and she was then called Madame de Courville Chroeder, and the Queen of France placed the highest confidence in her. He then said, he was a page appointed to attend the King's writing-table, at the Palace of Versailles; he then showed me an ivory carved penknife, which he took from a shagreen case, and said, "Do you remember ever having seen a similar penknife?" (I examined the handle, the top of which was an acorn that unscrewed, and there was in it three blades concealed. These blades had a screw, which fixed in a worm, at the lower end of the handle, which was of silver, and on screwing on one of the blades a perfect penknife was formed.) "Sir, a duplicate of this penknife was in the possession of the unfortunate Louis XVI. at the time His Majesty was taken to the Tower of the Temple, which was his favourite penknife, and was

---

* See letter from the Abbess of the Abbaye aux Bois, *ante*, p. 41-2.
† See Mrs. Meves's Professional Card, *ante*, p. 41.

taken from his person by the order of the National Convention." I answered, I had not the slightest recollection of ever having seen such a penknife.

Mr. Franks then said, "Sir, I recollect perfectly well, when in the service of the King, the inoculation of the Prince-Royal of France at the Palace of Versailles." I observed, "Who was it that inoculated the Prince; was it Dr. Brunier?" He replied, "Oh no, Sir. Dr. Brunier was appointed physician to the Prince-Royal by order of the Queen, but the person who inoculated the Prince-Royal was a Dr. —— (the name has slipped my memory), a celebrated inoculator of children; his custom was to inoculate boys on the right arm, and girls on the left; and, Sir, if you are the Prince-Royal, you must have a large scar on your right arm, from the effect of a deep wound that was given to the Prince-Royal by the lancet of the surgeon, for which incautious operation he received a reprimand." We then spoke upon this subject, when I, to satisfy his curiosity, took off my coat, and bared my arm for his inspection, on which existed "*a large scar, about the size of the bowl of a small teaspoon.*"* Mr. Franks was somewhat surprised when he beheld it, and said, "Certainly, Sir, this is a strong proof of identity, and your features, and whole person, bear a strong resemblance to Louis xvi." He then informed me he had been engaged with Sir George Rumbold, attempting to obtain a loan in Holland for the service of Louis xvi., but the attempt to raise money on the King's credit was totally impossible, as the credit of the French Government was at so low an ebb at that time, that Sir George Rumbold and himself had returned to England in despair of success. Most of the letters I had received from Mr. Jenkins I submitted to the care of Doctor and Madame Bureaud, as they were about leaving England for France, and it was their intention to reside at Paris for some time. Amongst the various letters was one from the faithful valet of Louis xvi., during his incarceration at the Temple, which I did not wish to part with, but Dr. Bureaud said, "It was *bien important,*" as Cléry in the letter said,

* See Appendix, Note A, for Medical Certificates.

"You who have suffered so much in the cause of Royalty, and devoted to the interests of the Queen of France." This coming from his hands, made it important.

At this distance of time, the greatest proof I can substantiate, is that of identity. About twenty years ago, "that is to say, about the year 1837," I caught the scarlet fever from one of my children, which raged so intensely with me that my skin entirely perished. The new skin does not show the cicatrices and scars upon my body so strongly as on the original, they having become considerably weaker. My likeness to the Bourbons of France was apparent to every one familiar with the portraits of that family.

In 1838 I came into pecuniary difficulties, in consequence of the South American Mining Shares—of which I held thirty Real del Monte, twenty United Mexican and St. John del Rey shares—having depreciated so considerably in value to what they had originally cost me, in consequence of which, together with pressing demands from inflexible creditors, I lost my remaining property; and since the year 1840 have followed the musical profession, in arranging for the pianoforte various works for different publishers. With this I close my Memoirs, having been actuated with no other motive throughout than recording the truth.

LOUIS CHARLES, DAUPHIN OF FRANCE,

Who, subsequently to October 1793, personated through supposititious means,

AUGUSTUS MEVES.

LONDON, 1858.

Such, then, is the history of events in the chequered life of the descendant of that long line of French kings, and such is the career of the veritable son of the martyrs, Louis XVI. and Marie Antoinette, as written by the Dauphin himself.

We here add a few words to the Authentic Historical Memoirs, and state, what we have undertaken in our late father's cause, has emanated solely from a pure and thorough conviction in its intrinsic reality, not being biassed on account of paternity, but by historical facts.

The following portrait recalls a few of the personal qualities of the veritable Louis XVII. :—

" He was a man humanity could have gazed on and been satisfied with ; open of countenance, cheerful in conversation ; of high faculties and irresistible manners ; upright, honest, charitable, and of surpassing accomplishments. On all subjects his conversation was entertaining, instructive, and edifying. Of most temperate habits, and of courage unquestionable. His smile illumined a most expressive and intelligent countenance. He was the *beau-idéal* of philanthropy and majesty."

In his professional career few excelled him. He was of the school of pianoforte executants of which the renowned Charles Hallé is now an example. It was masterly, and of exquisite finish. Whatever he played became enhanced, for his style and touch were most superior.*

Two days previous to his decease, on Saturday 7th May 1859, he seemed in good health, and went to Hammersmith, on a visit to his respected goddaughter, Miss Louisa St. Clare Dalton, a lady who has evinced great personal interest in this cause.

On Monday the 9th May, he went out in his usual cheerful spirits about eleven o'clock, and, at about two o'clock, being within two miles of home, and feeling unwell, he entered a cab, " a very unusual thing for him," and during its transit his soul passed into eternity.

Up to his demise he followed his usual avocation, and was active in

* See Appendix, Note C, for Biographical Notice of Meves' " Augustus."

such till within an hour of his decease.   Sudden, indeed, was his summons from mortality to immortality.   May his soul experience everlasting joy and felicity !

He was interred at Brompton Cemetery on Monday 16th May 1859, deeply regretted by a devoted wife, and the following family :—

WILLIAM, ...	*born in* 1829.
ADELAIDE CECILIA, . . .	„ 1830.
AUGUSTUS, ...	„ 1832.
CHARLES LOUIS, . . .	„ 1834.
ALEXANDER GEORGE, . . .	„ 1836.
FANNY ELIZABETH, . . .	„ 1838.
HENRY STEPHEN, . . .	„ 1841.

END OF AUTHENTIC HISTORICAL MEMOIRS.

COMMENTARY

TO THE

AUTHENTIC HISTORICAL MEMOIRS

OF

Louis Charles, Prince-Royal, Dauphin of France,

SECOND SON OF

LOUIS XVI. AND MARIE ANTOINETTE,

BY

WILLIAM AND AUGUSTUS MEVES.

"Many subjects that appear improbable at first, in the course of time are found to be undeniable truths."—A. MEVES.

COMMENTARY

TO THE

AUTHENTIC HISTORICAL MEMOIRS

OF

LOUIS CHARLES, DAUPHIN OF FRANCE.

III.

HISTORICAL RECORDS.

HAVING now placed the Memoirs of our late father before the world, it is necessary to discuss the different subjects therein contained, in order to arrive at a definite decision as to their reality. We do not guarantee to remove every single obstacle which surrounds the present question; nevertheless, the liberation of the Dauphin from the Tower of the Temple will irrefutably be proved to have taken place. Doubtless, many remarks in the Historical Records at first reading may appear futile, but as the work progresses they will be found otherwise, for howsoever irrelevant they may appear to the question at issue, they are in reality of transcendent importance, for they constitute the fundamental basis which will prove the Dauphin's escape from the Tower of the Temple—for it is the records of the Temple which will establish this fact.

Before now the world has been enlightened, as it were, from obscure persons, when the talent of an age has been ineffectual in solving definitely some important subject; so likewise in this historical problem the task has devolved on those whose obscurity is apparent, but yet whose imperative duty is to dispel the mythical, and substitute the positive history that appertains to the second son of Louis XVI., by

G

placing confirmatory and forcible evidence before the world, in proving that Louis XVII. was released from the Temple, and that he did not end his days there, as was reported by the Revolutionary Government,—the inducement being, the cause of justice and devotedness to the cause of the martyr King Louis XVI. and his lineal successor, the Dauphin, Louis Charles, Prince-Royal.

We know in a great measure we shall have to differ from received opinion ; still, we feel assured we shall be able to open a channel, whereby the whole truth of the complicity surrounding the Dauphin can be brought to light, if prejudice is thrown aside, and sincerity takes its place, by vindicating the cause of right.

It is not our intention to narrate the various sad catastrophes in connexion with this calamitous period of the history of France, which threw the kingdom into such unlimited excesses of cruelty.   These we pass as it were in silence, until the departure of the Royal Family from the Palace of the Tuileries, in August 1792, trusting our endeavours may be successful in placing the question in its true light, and in eliciting the truth respecting the mystery that surrounds the son of Louis XVI. ; for, did we not think confidently ourselves we were writing the truth, we should shrink from the responsibility of its advocacy, but feeling assured we have a firm basis to work on, stimulates us to advocate the cause imposed on us fearlessly.   Since conscience dictates the policy, and animates us with an undaunted resolution not to allow ourselves to be baffled, for alone we desire to promulgate the truth, and our perseverance will redouble, and with it courage in advocating this our father's cause, whatsoever obstacles politically assail us.

From the year 1789 France became openly in a most agitated state. The causes which led to this existed previous to the accession of Louis XVI. to the throne.   They had their origin from the libertine period when the Duke of Orleans was Regent, " during the minority of Louis XV."   This was the period from whence arose that spirit of profligacy and infidelity which pervaded France during the reign of Louis XV. and was bequeathed a legacy to Louis XVI.

Thus, then, on the accession of Louis xvi., was the Court and society, and from the rooted bad effects of which burst out into open rebellion in the reign of this innocent, generous, and magnanimous monarch.

During the Revolution all classes indiscriminately suffered. The kingdom was rent; vice and horror predominated; tyranny usurped all its administrative branches; the monarchy and aristocracy became a thing of the past; all honourable profession and liberal expression were treasonable in the eyes of the desperadoes. Alone, fanaticism was the ruling element. Onwards strode the Revolution. Chimeric philosophy was substituted for reason, which diverged into folly and audacity, and finally, by its atrocities and reckless tyranny, outraged society and humanity by its excess of cruelty. Nevertheless, the primary idea of the Revolution in a great measure has triumphed. Henceforth France, and alike all other countries within the pale of civilisation, must advance. Their vitality is in their progress.

On the night of the 9th August 1792, the Palace of the Tuileries was attacked, when the Royal Family of France quitted its threshold, and took refuge in the bosom of the National Assembly, where, in the gallery, they remained from half-past seven in the morning of the 10th August, till half-past two on the following morning, during which the Tuileries had been stormed, the Swiss guards massacred, and the King had seen some of his faithful troops brought prisoners into the hall of the Assembly. The provisional suspension of the Royal power had been voted, a governor had been named for the Dauphin, and the King "himself," and his family, had been committed to the Luxembourg, under the protection of the citizens and the law. Danton had been chosen Minister by a majority of 222 out of 284, the Royal Family thus witnessing in these nineteen hours its formal destruction.

From the hall of the Assembly the Royal party were conducted at three in the morning to the convent of the Feuillants. Here they remained till the 13th, when the Commune, to whom their custody had been intrusted, refused, through Manuel, longer to accept the responsibility of that duty, unless a surer place than the Luxembourg was assigned for their detention, when the Temple was suggested as being a secure habitation for the custody of Royalty, which proposition was carried ; and for the Temple, at four o'clock in the afternoon of the 13th August, in two carriages, escorted by National Guards, the Royal Family of France left the convent of the Feuillants.

In order to place lucidly the position of the Royal Family before the world, it will be necessary to give a brief sketch of their entrance in the precincts of the Tower of the Temple, and to narrate, partially, the conduct pursued towards the Royal prisoners during their confinement there, as then their position will be clearly understood, and our endeavours comprehended.

The Temple where the Royal Family were consigned had originally been the abode of an ancient order of Knight Templars, founded at Jerusalem in the year 1118—"during the reign of Louis XVI. the Palace of which had been occupied at times by Le Comte d'Artois." When the Royal Family arrived at the Temple they were conducted to the Palace of the Temple, and after remaining there some hours, while apartments were being prepared, an order came from the Commune for them to be removed from the Palace of the Temple, and to be transferred to the Small Tower of the Temple. After waiting till midnight the Royal prisoners were escorted to the Prison of the Temple, and were lodged on separate floors. Persecution was now the law predominant, renegades triumphed, and terrible was the result for France.

The Royal Family occupied the Small Tower till the month of October, and at appointed hours took exercise in the garden of the Temple, under the escort of the Guards. The privations and insults they experienced were one succession of taunts, reproaches, and vile indignities, which were left unchecked by the officers in command; therefore, their recurrence took place daily, and thus the captives' few hours of exercise were converted into hours of studied abuse, by which the national honour of France became doubly stained by its contemptible treatment of the defenceless monarch and his family.

"The nation should have been magnanimous in its conduct towards its imprisoned King, whose only fault was the too great love he bore his subjects; for had he been what the malcontents of his country had pronounced him, his throne and his country would have been saved. But alas! irresolution was his great defect. The epoch demanded a stern and unforgiving judge, but in Louis XVI. it found one incapable of determination when such called forth extreme severity. He had the power at command, but not the willingness to use such against his subjects. He trusted in them; their amelioration was his cherished idea—his deeds prove such; he took the partisans of the new idea for honourable; he thought reform was the object sought, and not desolation, which caused him to vacillate when he should have been firm; he was courageous, but indecisive; he forgave when he should have punished; virtue and sensitiveness were his ruin; he possessed the noblest and purest attributes susceptible to man, which unqualified him to contend against the incessant machinations of his enemies. His nature was conspicuously philanthropic—had it been otherwise, he could have stopped the Revolution at its outset. The French nation should have hesitated before causing a single pang towards so benevolent a monarch. Many will be the tears which will fall over the sufferings of this forgiving King, whose memory must be sacred to every true-hearted Frenchman. He was by nature a patriot king, not from compulsion, but choice." The Royal Family, although experiencing this ruthless behaviour from their oppressors, nevertheless welcomed their hours of exercise, as it relieved them from the monotony of the prison—especially so, as at times they thought they recognised from without, " at the windows overlooking the garden of the Temple," the faces of former friends, which gave them temporary alleviation and hope in their captivity.

The most bigoted revolutionists were selected as commissaries at the Temple—their predominant principle, the degradation of the King. Such was the conduct pursued to the Royal Family till the month of September 1792, when, after the Royal Family had supped as usual, and the King was about to leave the Queen's apartments to ascend to his own, he was detained by a municipal guard, who desired him to wait, as the Council had something to communicate to him. Shortly after, six municipal officers entered with a retinue into the Tower, and read to the King an arrest from the Commune, which ordered his removal into the Large Tower of the Temple, and for his complete separation from his family. On the morning of the same day the Royal Family were deprived of all means of correspondence. Their paper, pens, ink, and pencils were taken from them. The King was conducted to an apartment which they had destined for him in the Great Tower. The workmen were still employed there. This room contained a bed and a chair, in the midst of dirt, rubbish, planks, and bricks ; such formed the whole of the furniture they had assigned for the apartment of Louis xvi.

The King was precluded from seeing his family, and his keepers were immovable to his requests respecting this sudden separation. The authorities should have disdained such ignoble acts; for how severely they punished the children of their Sovereign. Their tender ages should have protected them from such barbarity.

This separation caused the Queen and Royal Family the greatest affliction.. The Queen vowed she would allow herself to perish with hunger if they persisted in keeping her separated from the King, and refused to touch the food provided for her. This startled and intimidated the municipals, as the responsibility of the lives of their prisoners weighed upon them. The entreaty of the Queen and Royal Family were by dint of perseverance complied with by the municipals, and their request was afterwards referred to the Commune, who did not oppose the reunion of the prisoners. From this time the captives met three times a day in the Great Tower, where they took their meals. The municipal guard present at these meetings prevented all confidential conversation with the Royal Family, who were interdicted from speaking low, or in foreign languages. The order was to talk aloud, and only in French. The Royal Family continued to take their meals and walks together, while apartments were being prepared for the Queen and the rest of the Royal captives above that of the King. During these preparations the King remained with Cléry, " his valet de chambre," in the Great Tower, and the rest of the Royal captives in the Small Tower. During this interval the King attended to the education of his son at appointed hours. On the 26th October, while the Royal Family were dining, they were interrupted by a municipal entering, accompanied by a registrar, and an usher, followed by six gendarmes, sword in hand, and arrested Cléry for conspiracy. He was taken before the revolutionary tribunal, but was acquitted of the charges preferred against him. He proved himself a devoted servant to the Royal Family. The same day the arrest of Cléry was effected, the Queen, and the rest of the Royal captives, were removed from the Small to the Great Tower, and on the very evening the Queen took possession of her new apartment her son was taken from her, and placed under the entire care of the King.

It is necessary to give a description of the Great Tower, to which the Royal Family were consigned.

The ground floor was occupied by the municipal officers not on duty at the King's or Queen's apartments.

The first floor served as a guard-room. It was a repetition of the ground floor, with the exception of the beds placed there, for the use of the guards.

The second floor was occupied by the King, the Dauphin, and Cléry.

The third floor was occupied by the Queen, Madame Royale, and Madame Elizabeth. " Tison and his wife were in attendance."

The fourth floor was not occupied. This floor was somewhat larger than the other storeys, its ceiling being loftier, and being deficient of a central pillar which ran through each of the other stories. A quantity of planking and old furniture tenanted this floor. Between the battlements and the roof of the Great Tower ran a gallery, sometimes used as a promenade. The openings between the battlements were afterwards boarded up, so that a person walking there could not be seen outside the Temple. Such then, was the habitation of the Royal captives.

The assembling of the Royal Family in the Great Tower made little change in the usual routine—for the meals, the walks, the lessons, and education of the children were all regulated as before. In this Tower the captive family met with unmanly insults, which must make the most bigoted republican blush at the excesses of these devotees of harsh treatment. At this epoch, the French nation seemed void of reason, cruelty and devastation alone being the predominant passion. Had they reasoned with themselves, and thrown aside party faction, they would never have imperilled their compliant King, but the thirst of all factions was power and popularity, and the Girondists, who in reality desired advanced innovations, "but within the Constitutional Charter," and likewise to check that recklessness pursued by the extreme faction. However, they did not contend manfully and resolutely against the pernicious doctrines of the terrorists at the proper time, and as the furorists did not meet with stern and decided opposition, their audacity redoubled with their success, and ultimately they usurped all power and popularity. They did not wish to appease, but excite revolt. They had everything to gain, and nothing to lose, by causing insurrection. Riches, the accumulation of honest industry, virtue, integrity, justness, mercy, honourable position in life, and all objects that honour was attached to, or ancient usage, were emblems of tyranny in their eyes; and the faction of the Girondists, in which were enrolled men of un-doubted and rare talents, instead of uniting and resolutely opposing false measures, wavered when they should have been firm. Their anta-gonists, perceiving their vacillation, grew daily more vehement, verging on dictating. Had the Moderates made use of the talent they undoubtedly possessed, in opposition to anarchy, they would have intimidated their foes, and have averted the baneful consequences that befel France.

In November, the King became ill, through a severe face-ache and cold, and was refused the attendance of his dentist. On the 22nd of November, fever set in. The Commune, informed of this, became alarmed, and permitted Monsieur le Monnier, first physician to the King, to enter the Tower, accompanied by Monsieur Robert, "a surgeon." Monsieur le Monnier bestowed the greatest attention on the captive King. During the King's illness the Queen requested to have the charge of her son, but the Commune refused her this request. The Dauphin now fell ill, and the Queen's supplications were still unheeded. Thus they persecuted a helpless child and a faithful mother. Can such conduct be excused ? No ; it was execrable. The Queen then became ill through anxiety, and so likewise the Princess-Royal, and the devoted, and pious Elizabeth.

Cléry, the faithful servant of the Royal Family, in his turn fell ill. This devoted and noble servant met with all the kindness from the Royal Family that lay in their power. Louis XVI. would have been a blessing to France had the originators of the Revolution appreciated his virtues, and what national misery would have been averted had they not persecuted this upright monarch.

"However, in proportion as the hate and persecution of their captors increased, so did the anguish for their fall, and grief for their situation, inspire some of their friends with interest and daring. The daily spectacle of the sufferings, the dignity, and perhaps the touching beauty of the Queen, had caused even members of the Commune to turn traitors. If great crimes sometimes tempt ardent souls, great devotions equally tempt generous minds, and compassion has its fanaticism. To snatch the family of the King from their prison, their persecutors, and the scaffold, by an heroic stratagem, and restore them to liberty, happiness, and perhaps to the throne, was a temptation destined to seduce men, by the very magnitude of the perils, and dangers, and to rouse imaginations capable of meditating and daring such attempts.

"At this period, there was amongst the Commissaries a young man named Toulan, born at Toulouse, in an inferior position. Passionately attached to those literary pursuits that elevate the mind, he had established at Paris. The trade of bookseller, which he followed, satisfied at once his tastes and his wants. His volumes, which he was constantly turning over in his business, had fired his imagination with the love of liberty, and those romantic emanations that intoxicate the mind. He had cast himself into the Revolution as a waking dream ; his ardour and eloquence had rendered him popular in his section. One of the foremost in the attack on the Tuileries on the 10th of August, he had also been one of the first in the Council of the Commune. Marked by his inveterate hatred of tyranny, he had been chosen as one of the Commissaries of the Temple, which he entered with the most profound horror of the tyrant, and his family, and quitted the first day with passionate adoration for the victims. His was one of those minds whose emotions carry them from one extreme to another; and before he had taken time to reflect, he had already devoted himself in his heart—for everything that was noble seemed in his eyes possible. He had sought on every occasion to attract the attention of Marie Antoinette by signs, which, without exciting the suspicions of his colleagues, would yet acquaint the Queen that she had a friend amongst her persecutors; and he had succeeded.

"Toulan was very young, of small stature, and possessed one of those delicate and expressive faces of the south, in which the eyes reveal the thoughts, and sensibility speaks in the mobility of the features. His look was a language which the Queen had long since comprehended. The presence of a second Commissary had prevented Toulan from fully declaring his sentiments; but he at last succeeded in gaining over one of his colleagues, named Lepitre, by the greatness of the project and the splendour of the recompense, to join in a plan of escape.

"The Queen beheld the two Commissaries fall at her feet in the gloom of her prison, and offer her a devoted attachment, which the place, the peril, and impending death elevated above all that had been shown her in her prosperity. She accepted and encouraged it, and gave Toulan a lock of her hair, with this device in Italian: 'He who fears to die, knows not how to love.' This was the letter of credit she gave Toulan to her friends. Soon after she added a billet in her own hand to the Chevalier de Jarjais, her secret correspondent, and the chief of this plot. 'You may fully confide,' she wrote, 'in the person who remits you this; his sentiments are well known to me; they have not varied during five months.' A certain number of trusty royalists, concealed at Paris, and distributed in the ranks of the National Guard, were vaguely initiated into this plan of escape. It consisted in bribing some of the Commissaries charged with the surveillance of the prison, drawing up a list of the most devoted royalists in the National Guard, in order that these men might, on a fixed day, compose the majority of the troops on guard at the Temple, disarm the rest of the detachment during the night, set the Royal Family at liberty, and escort them by relays, prepared beforehand, to Dieppe, where a fishing bark would convey them to England, with their principal liberators.

"Toulan, intrepid and indefatigable in his zeal, and furnished with considerable sums, which a word from the King had procured him from his adherents in Paris, matured his plans in obscurity, transmitted intelligence of his partisans, sounded the principal leaders of the Convention, and in the Commune strove to obtain the aid even of Marat, Robespierre, and Danton, tempting the generosity of some, and the cupidity of others ; and, each day more fortunate in his enterprises, and more certain of success, already reckoned several of the guardians of the Tower, and five members of the Commune amongst the accomplices of his perilous designs.   Thus a ray beamed into the hitherto dark dungeon, and kindled, if not the hope, at least the dream, of liberty."—Alphonse de Lamartine's *History of the Girondists*, vol. ii. p. 278.

While this activity was prevailing within and without the Temple, the discussions at the Commune were not of so turbulent a character against the King, and his treatment in the Temple was more endurable, especially as fortune seemed to be favouring his escape, with the rest of the Royal Family.   While the plot of escape was maturing, and all seemed to be progressing satisfactorily, the re-elections for the municipality took place, and then came emulation for severity towards the Royal Family, and with it redoubled surveillance, which shut out every hope of escape, as the most bigoted were placed on duty at the Temple, thereby frustrating the project that was entertained of effecting the escape of the Royal captives.   The Royal Family soon again became accustomed to the harsh treatment of their inveterate foes, and now the Commune thundered forth its abhorrence of Royalty, and demanded that the King should be brought to trial.   Deep-rooted animosity pervaded this unjust tribunal.   Record shows how many voted against the King for party's sake, sacrificing their honour, conscience, and principle ; whereas, had they acted as their consciences dictated, they would have immortalized their names in the cause of nationality, and have stopped the fatal impetuosity and indiscriminating guillotine from the atrocities which followed.

The King was demanded to be brought before the Convention on the charge of conspiracy, etc. etc.   Accordingly the authorities proceeded to the Temple to conduct the King to the Assembly, — the whole of Paris being rife with the republican army, in order to insure the King's uninterrupted progress to the treacherous and tyrannous

Assembly. Early on the morning of the 11th December 1792, distant drums, and the roll of artillery-waggons, became audible to the ears of the Royal Family. The commotion became greater and greater; at last it arrived at the Temple. The King anticipated this movement, as he had been informed of the intentions of the Commune, and while the Royal Family were awaiting the indignities of their inexorable oppressors, suddenly the door opened, and the King was commanded to take leave of his family, as he would not be allowed further intercourse with them until after his trial.

The King was then conducted to a room where he was left to ruminate on the treatment he was about to receive, but the most poignant troubles he experienced were the imprudence of his subjects, and that of being separated from his family until the arrival of the civic authorities. Upon their arrival, Chambon, the Mayor of Paris, read the Act of Accusation the Commune had drawn up against the King. After which the King was conducted to a carriage, and his cortége of oppressors conducted him to the presence of an unjust and impious assembly of malcontents. The route was one line of armed military, ready to sacrifice life to any amount had there been an effort made in the King's favour. Each face wore a gloomy and sadly determined cast, but many were there who deeply lamented and repented the indignities thus heaped on their King and his family, but rash indeed would the voice have been, that had openly proclaimed such sentiments during the King's progress to the presence of his accusers. On the King's entry in the Commune, the frivolous and malignant Act of Accusation was read, which accused him of conspiracy against the nation, and of like fabulous charges. The King pleaded his innocence, but nothing could move his inexorable foes. After the King had withdrawn from the bar, the turbulent gave full vent to the animosity they bore to Royalty in any shape.

The King was re-conducted to the Temple. Meanwhile the Commune was one scene of uproar; the members menacing each other; no voice was tolerated that expressed justness; each section was fearful of the issue of this day. It was a day of triumph, and each party made desperate efforts to maintain its popularity. After much discussion, and by the persevering advocacy of Pétion and Trulhard, the King was allowed the privilege of choosing the counsel to undertake his defence. The King selected the two most celebrated advocates of Paris, MM. Tronchet and Target. Tronchet unhesitatingly accepted the mission of defending the King, but Target, an imposing orator, wrote a pusillanimous and cowardly letter to the Convention, in which he declined the honour of defending the King, saying his principles did not permit him to undertake such a cause. This refusal caused the populace to vent its disgust against this weak, ungenerous, and frail law-apostle. He ultimately fell dishonoured, a victim to the Revolution, and mounted the scaffold unmourned and undefended. Several competitors offered themselves in Target's place. The King chose Desèze, an advocate of Bordeaux. The faithful and honourable men who conducted the King's defence, discharged their duties with perseverance and bravery, which will for ever redound honour to their memories.

"Amongst many who tendered the King their services, was one Malesherbes. He was seventy-four years of age, and had twice been Minister to Louis XVI., and his ministry had been repaid by ingratitude and exile, not by the King, but from the hatred of the clergy, the aristocracy, and the court. A liberal and a philosopher, Malesherbes was one of those precursors who outstrip, in an age of arbitrary power, and abuse the application of the rules of justice and reason, which ideas demand, but which things resist.

"A disciple of Jean Jacques Rousseau, the friend of Turgot, Malesherbes had rendered himself popular amongst philosophers by favouring, when Director-General of the Library, the introduction of the Encyclopædia, that arsenal of new ideas, into France. Under a legislation of legal darkness and censure, Malesherbes had boldly exposed present abuses, by declaring himself the accomplice of light, and this the Church and the aristocracy had never forgiven him. In his heart he was a republican, but his manners and sentiments were yet monarchical, and he was a living example of that internal contradiction which exists in men, born as it were on the frontiers of a revolution, whose ideas are of one age, and whose customs are of another. The republicanism of Malesherbes was to the French republic what the philosophical idea of a sage is to the tumultuous ardour of the people. The misfortunes of the King had awakened his liveliest sympathy—for this Prince had been the hope and the illusion of Malesherbes. A witness and confidant of the desire of the King for the happiness of his people and the reform of the monarchy, Malesherbes imagined he beheld in the youthful King one of those imperial reformers who voluntarily relinquished despotism, who lend their aid to revolutions to accomplish and moderate them, and by their actions legitimate Royalty. A secret and occasional correspondence had conveyed to Louis XVI. the recollections, the hopes, and the commiseration of his old servant. At the intelligence of the trial of the King, Malesherbes had quitted his country residence, and wrote a letter to the Convention, which the President, Barrère, read to the Assembly.

"'Citizen President,' said Monsieur de Malesherbes, 'I am ignorant whether the Convention will give Louis XVI. an advocate for his defence, or permit him to choose one. In this case, I wish that Louis XVI. may know, if he chooses me for this post, I am ready to undertake it. I do not ask you to acquaint the Convention with my wish, for I am far from believing myself a sufficiently important person to occupy their attention. But I have twice been summoned to the council of him who was my master, at a time when everybody was ambitious of that post, and I owe him this service, now that this office is in the eyes of most persons one of danger; and were I aware of any means of acquainting him with my wishes I should not take the liberty of addressing you, but I thought that from the position you hold you would possess the surest means of informing him of this fact.'

"At the name of Malesherbes the whole Convention felt that electric shock which the name of a man of lofty soul creates, and the emotion caused by an act of courage and virtue. Hatred itself recognised the holy rights of friendship in the demand of M. de Malesherbes, and it was granted.

"Malesherbes, introduced the same day into the prison of his master, was compelled to wait some time at the last gate-house, in which the Commissaries, whose duty it was to see that no arms or poison were conveyed to the King, by which he might cheat the scaffold of its prey, detained him. The name and aspect of the aged Minister inspired them with respect. He himself showed them the contents of his pockets, which merely consisted of some diplomatic papers, and the journal of the sittings of the Convention. Dorat Cubières, a member of the Commune, a man rather vain than cruel, and totally out of his element amidst the tragedies of the Revolution, was on guard in the ante-chamber. He knew M. de Malesherbes, and reverenced him as a philosopher, whom his master Voltaire had often held up to the gratitude of all ages. 'Malesherbes,' said he, 'you are the friend of Louis xvi., how can you bring him papers in which he will read the expressions of the wrath of the people against him?' 'The King is not like other men,' returned M. de Malesherbes; 'he possesses a great mind, and a faith that raises him above everything.' 'You are an honest man,' said Cubières, 'but if you were not, what is there to prevent you from bringing him poison, or a weapon, or advising him to commit suicide?' The features of M. de Malesherbes betrayed at those words a reserve, which seemed to indicate the thoughts of one of those voluntary deaths of olden time, which rendered a man in desperate situations, in some sort, his own judge and liberator; then, as if checking the idea, 'If the King,' said he, 'were of the religion of the philosophers—were he a Cato or a Brutus, he might kill himself, but he is pious, he is a Christian,—he knows that religion forbids him to take away his own life, and he will not commit suicide.'

"The door of the King's chamber opened, and Malesherbes advanced with faltering steps towards his master. Louis xvi. was seated reading Tacitus, that Roman evangelist of the mighty dead. At the sight of his former Minister he sprang from his seat, and clasped him in his arms. 'Ah,' said he, 'in what a situation do you find me; see to what my passion for the amelioration of the state of the people, whom we have both loved so much, has reduced me. Why do you come hither? Your devotion only endangers your life, and cannot save mine.' Malesherbes assured the King, with tears, of his joy at devoting to his service the last short remains of his life, and of displaying an attachment to him in prison, which in a palace was always suspected. He endeavoured to give the prisoner some hope in the justice of his judges, and the pity of the people, weary in persecuting him. 'No,' replied the King, 'they will condemn me; for they possess both the power and the will. No matter; let us occupy ourselves with my cause, as though I were to gain it,—I shall gain it, in fact, since I shall have no stain on my memory.'"—Alphonse de Lamartine's *History of the Girondists*, vol. ii. p. 315.

This worthy and venerable man, by his honour, justness, and perseverance in the King's cause, has for ever made memorable his name, which will echo to the remotest posterity, and surround his memory with an everlasting halo of admiration for his nobility of soul. Tronchet,

Desèze, and Malesherbes repaired to the Temple daily to prepare the King's defence.

On the 26th of December 1792, Louis XVI. was conducted to the Convention, and on entering this corrupt and atrocious assembly, he seated himself between his counsel, and surveyed, with a benignant eye, the crowded benches of his adversaries. In the speech which followed, Desèze ably argued the inviolability of the Sovereign, and proved that if it was destroyed, the weaker party in the Convention had no security against the stronger,—a prophetic truth which the Girondists soon experienced at the hands of their implacable enemies. He examined the whole life of the King, and showed, in every instance, that he had been actuated by the sincerest love of his people.

"The Convention listened in silence to the pleading of Desèze. It being evident, from the attitude of the Montagne, there was no longer any agitation, because there no longer existed any doubt. The judges had the patience of certainty, and they thus gave an hour to a King whose life was already forfeited in their minds. Desèze spoke with dignity, but without passion, and preserved the calmness of reason before the ardour of public passion, and his language, always on a level with his duty as a defender, was but rarely on a level of the occasion.

" He disputed a point when he should have struck a decisive blow, and he forgot that the people possess no other conviction than that of their emotion ; that temerity is in some cases prudence, and that on desperate occasions there is no hope save in a despairing eloquence, which risks everything in the hope of saving it.

"It was one of the fatalities of the life of Louis XVI. that he did not find, to dispute his death with the people, one of those voices which elevate the occasion to the level of the misfortune, and which make the fall of thrones, catastrophes of empires, and the stroke of the axe that spills the blood of kings, to resound from age to age, by language as grand, as solemn, and as majestic as the events themselves. Had the place of Desèze been filled by Bossuet, Mirabeau, or Vergniaud, Louis XVI. would not have been defended with more zeal, more prudence, or more logic ; but their language, political, and not judicial, would have sounded like the accent of vengeance in the ears of the judges, like remorse in the hearts of the people ; and if the cause had not been gained before this tribunal, it would have been for ever rendered illustrious before that of posterity."—Lamartine's *History of the Girondists*, vol. ii. p. 322.

Desèze concluded the King's defence, saying, "On the 10th August was the monarch under the necessity of submitting to an armed multitude. Was not the power which he held in the Constitution a deposit for the preservation of which he was answerable to the nation? If you yourselves were surrounded by a furious and misguided rabble, which threatened, without respect for your sacred character, to tear you from this sanctuary, what could you do other than he has done? The magistrates themselves authorized all that he did, by having signed the order to repel force by force. Notwithstanding their sanction, the King was unwilling to make use of this authority, and retired into the bosom of the Assembly to avoid the shedding of blood. The combat which followed was undertaken neither for him nor by his orders. He interfered only to put a stop to it, as is proved by the fact that it was in consequence of an order signed by him that the Swiss abandoned the defence of the château, and surrendered their lives. There is a crying injustice, therefore, in reproaching him with the blood shed on the 10th August. In truth, his conduct, in that particular, is above reproach." His conclusion was in these words :—" Louis mounted the throne at the age of twenty, and even then he set the example of an irreproachable life. He was governed by no weak or corrupted passion ; he was economical, just, and severe. He proved himself from the first the friend of his country. The people desired the removal of a destructive tax ; he removed it. They wished the abolition of servitude ; he abolished it in his domains. They prayed for a reform in the criminal law ; he reformed it. They demanded that thousands of Frenchmen, whom the rigour of our usages had excluded from political rights, should enjoy them ; he conceded them. They longed for liberty ; he gave it. He even anticipated their wishes ; and yet it is the same people who now demand his punishment. I add no more. I pause before the tribunal of history ; remember it will judge your decision, and that its decision will be the voice of ages." The King then rose and addressed the Assembly as follows :—" You have heard my defence ; I will not recapitulate it. When addressing you, probably for the last time, I declare that my conscience has nothing to reproach itself with, and that my defender has said nothing but the truth. I have no fears for the public examination of my conduct, but my heart bleeds at the accusation brought against me, of having been the cause of the misfortunes of my people, and most of all, of having shed their blood on the 10th August. The multiplied proofs I have given in every period of my reign of my love for my people, and the manner in which I have conducted myself towards them, might, I had hoped, have saved me from so cruel an imputation." The King then withdrew with his defenders. Whereupon the Convention was all disorder, for it was not justice the infamous Montagne required, but the condemnation, and that speedily, of the King. So matters proceeded till the 15th January, which determined the Appel Nominal under the following headings :—

First.—Is Louis guilty ?

Second.—Shall the decision of the Convention be submitted to the ratification of the people ?

Third.—What shall be the sentence ?

Bertrand de Moleville, " Minister of State," in his Private Memoirs relative to the Last Year of the Reign of Louis xvi., says—

"When the King's process was first deliberated upon in the Convention, Danton—the infamous Danton,—whose services had been so highly paid by the Civil List, was one of those who showed the most violence and inveteracy. This alarmed me greatly, because the popularity which that villain then enjoyed gave him great influence in the Assembly. My ardent desire of saving the King made me consider every measure as justifiable which tended to that end, and I made no scruple of employing falsehood in order to tame the fury of that monster. On the 11th December I sent him the following letter :—

"'You ought no longer to remain ignorant, sir, that amongst the papers intrusted to my care about the end of last June, by the late M. de Montmorin, and which I have brought to this country with me, I find a note of different sums which you received from the funds for secret expenses of the Foreign Department. The occasions on which you received these sums, and the different dates, are specified, as also the person who negotiated that affair. Your connexion with this person is clearly proved by a letter in your own handwriting, pinned to the note in question, which is entirely in the handwriting of M. de Montmorin. I have not hitherto made any use of those papers, but I warn you that they are joined to a letter I have written to the President of the National Convention, and which I send by this same courier, enclosed to a confidential friend, with orders to send the letter to the President, and to cause your billet and the note to be printed and placarded in the corner of every street, if you do not conduct yourself in the King's affair as a man who has been so well paid ought to do. But if, on the contrary, you exert yourself to render him the services which you have in your power, be assured they will not pass unrewarded. You need have no uneasiness with regard to this letter, as nobody shall know I have written to you. (Signed) BERTRAND.'

"The truth of this matter was, that M. de Montmorin had communicated the affair to me, and showed me the papers, but never gave them into my hands, as I had asserted to Danton, who, knowing the intimacy in which I had been with M. de Montmorin, could not doubt, after what I had written, of my having them in my possession. I received no answer to my letter, but I saw by the public papers that two days after that in which he must have received it, he caused himself to be deputed to the Northern Army, and did not return to Paris till the day before sentence was pronounced on the King. He voted for death at the Appel Nominal, but without supporting his opinion, as was his custom, by reasoning, or any discourse whatever.

"How much was it to have been wished that at this dreadful crisis, some means had also been devised for terrifying or alluring from the capital, Robespierre, Marat, Barrère, Pétion, and all those consummate villains, who, that they might assassinate Louis XVI. with more certainty, got themselves constituted his judges, and associated in their design all the obscure vagabonds of the provinces, by giving them to understand that this crime was the only means left for them to emerge from want and obscurity to wealth and power."—Bertrand de Moleville's Private Memoirs relative to the Last Year of the Reign of Louis XVI., vol. iii. p. 231.

On the 16th January, Danton, the infamous revolutionary peculator, demanded that the Convention should not break up till the sentence of the King had been pronounced, which proposal terminated in the Assembly declaring the sitting permanent until such was passed, and at eight P.M. began the Appel Nominal.

Each approach, corridor, and lobby leading to the judgment-hall, was filled with armed and paid bravos, to intimidate and threaten the members who were favourably disposed to the King. Under such dastardly means was the King judged, which terminated in his condemnation. Evil was the decision that proclaimed his death, as the infuriated gained ascendency, and France was governed by the lawless, whose whole usurpdom was naught but tyranny.

The venerable Malesherbes, on the 19th of January, repaired to the Temple, when the King learnt the result of the trial; after which the authorities from the monstrous Commune wended their way to the Temple, and informed the King the decision of the Commune, that his execution would take place in twenty-four hours.

"The King then demanded of the Convention a respite of three days, in order to prepare himself to appear before God; and further, that he should see freely a priest, whom he would name to the commissaries of the Commune, who should 'be protected in the act of charity which he shall exercise towards me. I demand to be freed from the perpetual surveillance which has been exercised towards me for many days. I demand, during these last moments, leave to see my family, when I desire it, without witnesses. I desire most earnestly that the Convention will at once take into consideration the fate of my family, and that they be allowed immediately to retire unmolested whithersoever they shall think fit to choose an asylum. I recommend to the kindness of the nation all the persons attached to me. There are amongst them many old men, women, and children, who are entirely dependent on me, and must be in want.—Given at the Temple, the 20th January 1792.'

"At the same time the King handed to Garat a second paper, containing the address of the ecclesiastic whose offices and whose consolation he desired for his last hours. This address, written in a handwriting which was not the King's, was, 'M. Edgeworth de Firmont, Rue de Bac.' Garat having taken the two papers, the King retreated some few paces, and bowed as when he dismissed an audience at Court, intimating his desire to be left alone. The Ministers retired.

"After their departure, the King walked up and down his chamber with a firm step, and then demanded his repast; and, as he had no knife, he ate with a spoon, and broke his bread with his fingers. He was more indignant at these precautions than at hearing his death-warrant. 'Do they think me such a coward,' said he, 'as to snatch my life from my enemies? Crimes are imputed to me, but I am innocent, and shall die fearlessly. I would that my death could render France happy, and avert the evils I foresee for the nation!'"—Lamartine's *History of the Girondists*, vol. ii. p. 342.

Many members desired that the King's requests should be complied with, and contended fearlessly with the malign Jacobins to delay the execution. However, their efforts were in vain. At six o'clock the authorities informed the King that he was at liberty to send for any priest he pleased, and to see his family without any one else being present, but that the demand of three days' respite was refused, and that therefore the execution would take place within four-and-twenty hours. Thus did these unmerciful monsters refuse their King's last request.

In the afternoon of the 20th January, the Abbé de Firmont was summoned to attend the Executive Council; after which he was conducted to the Tower of the Temple by the Minister of Justice. In this reverend and worthy man the King found great comfort and consolation in his last moments.

In the evening the King had his last and sad interview with the Queen, his sister, and children. Sad were the pangs and remembrances of the Royal group during these last moments, and affecting was the parting struggle, which, when consummated, the King returned to his room exhausted, and conversed with his confessor; after which the King retired to rest, and slept his last sleep in this corruptible world. The Abbé occupied Cléry's room. At five o'clock the next morning the King rose, when the Abbé attended him in his cabinet, and whilst there an altar was erected in the King's apartment. Upon leaving the cabinet the King heard mass, and then received the sacrament; after which the King passed into his cabinet, and the Abbé into Cléry's room, when Cléry followed the King, and on his knees requested his blessing. Louis XVI. gave it him, and desired him to convey it in his name to all who were attached to him, and especially to those of his guardians, who, like Turgy, had shown pity on his captivity, and softened its rigours. Then, leading him into the recess of the window, he gave him, unseen, a seal which he detached from his watch, a small parcel which he took from his bosom, and his wedding-ring, which he removed from his finger. "After my death," he said, "you will give this seal to my son, this ring to the Queen. Tell her I resign it with pain, in order that it be not profaned with my body. This small parcel contains locks of hair of my family that you will give her. Say to the Queen, my dear children, and my sister, that I had promised to see them this morning, but that I desired to spare them the agony of such a bitter separation twice over; likewise, how much it has cost me to depart without receiving their last embraces." Sobs impeded his utterance. "I charge you," he added, in a tone of tenderness which nearly choked his words, "to convey to them my last farewell." Cléry then withdrew, overcome with tears.

A moment after, the King left his cabinet, and asked for a pair of scissors, in order that his servant might cut off his hair—the only legacy he could leave his family. Cléry then entreated to be allowed to accompany his master, in order to undress him on the scaffold, that the hands of a faithful servant might replace that of the brutal executioner, which was refused.

The King then sent for the Abbé, and on his entering the room, he found the King seated near his stove, where he could scarcely warm himself, appearing to reflect with sad joy on the termination which had at length arrived to his sufferings. "Mon Dieu," he exclaimed, "how happy I am that I maintained my faith on the throne! Where should I be to-day but for this hope? Yes; there is on high a Judge incorruptible, who will award to me that measure of justice which men refuse to me here below."

After the heartrending separation on the night of the 20th January, the Queen had scarcely sufficient strength to undress the Dauphin and put him to bed. She had thrown herself in her clothes on her own couch, where, throughout the night, her daughter and the sister of Louis XVI., stretched on a mattress in her room, heard her trembling with mental agony and cold.

On the King taking leave of the Queen the evening before, he had promised to see her again next day, and he wished earnestly to keep his word, but the Abbé de Firmont entreated him not to put the Queen to a trial under which she must sink. He hesitated a moment, and then said: "You are right, sir. It would kill her; therefore, I must deprive myself of this melancholy consolation, and let her indulge in hope a few minutes longer."

"The Royal Family rose before daybreak, thinking they were about to be led to a last interview. They were soon undeceived. Each minute seemed to mark ages on the prison clock. Language is powerless to describe the agonizing scene which then presented itself. Poor heart-rent woman, essaying a last effort to arouse sterile pity. *The Dauphin escaping from his mother's arms, and rushing, supplicant, wild, and frantic, to the municipal officers, to the guards, from one to another, embracing this man's knees, clasping that man's hand, and exclaiming, ' Let me pass, gentlemen; let me pass !' ' Where do you want to go ?' ' To speak to the people, that they may not kill my father. In the name of God, let me pass !'* To such entreaties the jailers were deaf."—Beauchesne's *Louis XVII.*, p. 8, vol. ii.

"*The Dauphin, his voice lost in sobs, rapidly traversed the outer apartment, descended the stairs without any one being able to stop him, and reached the courtyard of the Temple. He addressed the guards in the most pitiful terms of supplication, his hands clasped, and throwing himself on his knees; ' Let me pass, gentlemen; let me pass ! I want to speak to the people, to entreat them not to kill my papa, the King. Ah, let me pass, gentlemen ! In the name of God, do not hinder me !'* His entreaties were vain, and he was compelled to return."—Necker on the Revolution, vol. i. p. 106; likewise Echard, p. 127, *Mémoires Historiques sur Louis XVII.*

Early in the morning the military were in motion for the Temple, armed to the teeth, and determined to carry into effect the decree of the Convention, who were fearful the King would be rescued, or that he would receive the sympathy of the people; consequently they took every precaution that would insure the carrying into effect their tyrannous decree.

"At nine o'clock there was a tumultuous noise of armed men on the staircase leading to the King's apartment, when suddenly the doors were opened, and Santerre appeared, attended by twelve municipals, and with ten gendarmes, whom he arranged in two lines in the apartment. The King opened the door of his cabinet, and said in a firm voice, and with an imperious gesture to Santerre, 'You are come for me; I will be with you in an instant; await me there.' He pointed with his finger to the threshold of the chamber, closed the door, and knelt once more at the priest's knees. 'All is consummated, my father,' he said; 'give me your blessing, and pray to God to sustain me to the end.' He then rose, opened the door, advanced with a serene air, the majesty of death on his brow and in his looks, and placed himself between the double row of gendarmes. He held a folded paper in his hand. It was his last will and testament. He addressed himself to the municipal guard in front of him, saying, 'I beg of you, transmit this paper to the Queen,'—a look of astonishment at this word on the republican countenance made him recollect that he had mistaken the word—'to my wife,' he said, recovering himself. The municipal retreated, saying savagely, 'That is no affair of mine. I am here to conduct you to the scaffold.'

"This man was Jacques Roux, a priest, who had left his order, and cast off all feeling with his frock. 'True,' said the King, with a saddened air; then looking at all the guards, he turned to the one whose countenance expressed some tenderness of heart. His name was Gobeau. 'Transmit, I pray you, this paper to my wife. Read it, if you will; these are wishes that the Commune should know.' The municipal, with the assent of his fellows, took the testament.*

"Cléry, who feared, like the valet of Charles I., that his master, shaking with cold, might seem to tremble at the sight of the scaffold, gave him his cloak. 'I do not require it,' said the King; 'give me only my hat.' When he took it, he grasped the hand of his faithful servant, and squeezed it, as a token of intelligence and farewell; then turning to Santerre, and looking at him full in the face, he said, with a gesture of resolution, and in a tone of command, 'Let us go.'

" Santerre and his troop seemed rather to follow than to escort him. The King descended the staircase of the Tower with a firm tread, and meeting in the passage the turnkey Mathey, who had been disrespectful to him over-night, and whom he had reproached for his impertinence, he went towards him, and said, with a kindly look, 'Mathey, I was somewhat warm with you yesterday; excuse me for the sake of this hour.' Mathey, instead of replying, pretended to turn his head away, and retreated, as though contact with the dying prince had been contagious.

"As he crossed the first court on foot, the King turned round

---

* See Appendix, Note L, for Louis XVI.'s will.

twice towards the Tower, casting each time on the windows of the Queen's apartments a look in which his whole soul seemed to breathe forth its mute farewell to all so dear to him, that he left in the prison.

"A carriage awaited him at the entrance of the second court ; two gendarmes were standing by the steps. One mounted first, and seated himself in the front; the King then got in, and his confessor seated himself by his side. The second gendarme then entered, fastened the door, and the vehicle moved forward."—Lamartine's *History of the Girondists*, vol. ii. p. 354.

Surrounded by the hirelings of his tyrannous persecutors, his carriage was encircled with one mass of military, armed, and ready for action, as on a day of battle. Cannon loaded with grape-shot guarded the main streets on the line of route. An order of the day prohibited any citizen, who did not form a portion of the armed militia, to cross the streets leading to the Boulevards. Every order was given to insure the King's uninterrupted progress to the scaffold. Each man's thoughts were locked in his bosom who entertained sympathy towards the oppressed monarch, as it would have been dangerous to have given utterance to such ; each feared his neighbour, for few were to be trusted ; fanaticism alone was only tolerated, and that fanaticism cruelty to the King. On proceeded the carriage which bore the persecuted monarch, who sat calm and inspired on his road to martyrdom, forgiving his enemies for their cruelties, and trusting for forgiveness from God for the follies that mankind are heir to. The multitude, meaning the well-disposed, were entranced at the demeanour of the King, whose brow was composed and confident, and, in the words of Lamartine, " Had it been asked of each of these two hundred thousand citizens, actors, or spectators of this funeral of a living man, 'Must this man, one against all, die?' not one would have replied, 'Yes.' On rolled this vast assemblage, until the carriage which contained the King reached the numerous streets which meet on the Boulevard between the Portes St. Denis and St. Martin. At this point, several young persons, rushing from the Rue Beauregard, made way through the crowd, breaking the line, and dashing sword in hand towards the carriage containing the

King, exclaiming, ' Help, those who would save the King !' Amongst these was the Baron de Batz, and his secretary Devaux ; likewise, three thousand young men were enrolled for this *coup-de-main* who were to respond to the signal of these brave men, and afterwards to attempt an insurrection in Paris, supported by the popular General Dumouriez ; but seeing that no one followed them, these loyal heroes made their way, amidst the surprise and confusion, through the line of the National Guard, and were speedily lost in the neighbouring streets. Some were captured, and paid dearly for their effort, whilst others escaped unharmed." Blessed be the memory of these loyal patriots !

After a moment's delay, on again marched this cruel and mercenary cortége, until it reached the Place de la Revolution, where it was everywhere surrounded by the most pitiless souls of Paris, " the Commune having influenced this vile proceeding." On the arrival of the carriage at the foot of the scaffold, the King raised his eyes from the book he had hitherto been reading. He was then in the hands of his executioners. These inhuman monsters offered fresh indignities to the King, which, by his noble confessor's advice, he submitted to. He then ascended the scaffold, and as he passed along he looked at the instrument which was to terminate his life. He then turned his face towards the Palace, making a gesture of silence to the drummers, " whose office was to drown by dint of noise any sentiments that might be aroused of affection." They obeyed, when the King addressed the multitude with firmness, and in an impressive voice, in language which came from his heart, saying, " People, I die innocent of all the crimes imputed to me. I pardon the authors of my death, and pray to God that the blood you are about to shed may not fall again on France." He would have proceeded, had not the heartless Santerre interrupted him by saying, " I brought you here to die, and not to talk." Upon which the drums were ordered to be beaten, which drowned the voice of the King, and at the same time checked the multitude from expressing any feeling in favour of the King. In another moment he was in the hands of the executioners, and shortly after Louis the Martyr was no more. He gave up his life to his Creator, in whose clemency he trusted, and his soul divested itself of mortality for immortality, at the words of his honourable confessor, "Soul of St. Louis, ascend to heaven." Thus died Louis XVI., the Martyr King, at twenty minutes past ten, on the morning of the 21st January 1793.

His death was accomplished, but was this attended with any beneficial result to France? "No." It was but the ushering in of the vilest tyranny and cruelty with which the pages of history are blemished. All well-intentioned men were struck with remorse at this sacrilege. The satellites of anarchy wore sinister looks, such as marks those incapable of feeling, and which recoils twofold on the possessor when it meets not applause or recognition from its beholders. Desperation now reigned in France, its constitution ever since being restive and insecure, and the cup filled to the brim with State stratagem.

The Queen and Royal captives heard the return of the artillery that had announced the consummation of Louis, and now despair and desolation were the friends of this unhappy circle, who were left without mourning till the 23d of the month, and desponding in the gloom of their captivity.

After the execution of the King, the Queen, Madame Elizabeth, the Princess-Royal, and the Dauphin, remained in the Prison of the Temple, the Queen having the charge and education of her son.

We will pass over the sufferings of the Royal captives, while without despotism with avenging death was reigning wide and near. Time passed on, and the Queen's health was fast giving way. Shame to France for so persecuting a woman !

"Still bold and loyal hearts entered the Temple. The old sentiment of French loyalty was still to be found, as we have seen, even in the commissaries placed in charge of the Temple. Amongst these, history will preserve the name of Toulan, who, a thorough republican, was gained over to the Royal cause by witnessing the patience and courage of the captive Queen of France. It was he who conceived the project of effecting the escape of this Princess and her children from the

Temple.   He submitted his plan to the Queen, who, pleased with its daring, would not, however, adopt it without the previous sanction of a grave and able man, who had worthily fulfilled several secret and important missions which Louis XVI. had confided to him—the Chevalier de Jarjayes, a lieutenant-general, husband of one of the Queen's ladies, and who, in the hope of being useful to his benefactors, had not quitted the perilous abode of Paris.   Marie Antoinette sent Toulan to this general officer, who received the trusty messenger with full confidence, and examined his plan with intelligent attention.

"After two protracted conferences, the possibility of success having been established, it became indispensable to admit into the secret of the enterprise another commissary of the Temple.   But who among the municipals would be found sufficiently devoted to sacrifice his life for the Royal Family?   Our readers have already named him—the perilous honour appertained of right to Lepitre.   In a third conference, at which Lepitre was present, the basis of the plan was adopted.   M. de Jarjayes undertook to have male attire prepared for the Queen and Madame Elizabeth, and the two municipals were to convey this attire secretly into the Tower.   The two Princesses were in this disguise—heightened by the addition of the tri-coloured scarf—to quit the Tower, furnished with the pass-cards carried by the commissaries and all other persons who had access to the Temple.   So far, everything seemed clear enough and of ready execution, but the escape of the two children presented difficulties that seemed insurmountable.   Louis XVII., in particular, was so closely watched that it was almost impracticable to effect his deliverance.   An idea, however, occurred; the genius of devotion is a great worker of miracles.   There was a worthy man, named Jacques, who came every morning, we know not whence, to clean the lamps, and again every evening to light them.   He was usually accompanied and assisted in his work by two children, of about the same age and size with the Royal children.   Prudence precluded the admission into the secret of this stranger, who, in the execution of his subordinate functions, silently obeying his orders, never exchanged a word with the persons employed in the Temple, to whom, consequently, he had remained almost wholly unknown.   But this plan presented itself:—Jacques was in attendance at between five and six o'clock in the evening, and his last lamp was lighted, and he himself departed from the Temple, when, at seven o'clock, the sentinels were changed.   After his departure, then, and the change of sentinels, a man, dressed like him, was to pass, by favour of an admission-card, the first gatekeeper, and, on reaching the Queen's apartment, his tin-box under his arm, was to be soundly rated by Toulan for not having come himself to trim his lamps, and for having sent his children to do his work for him. The two Royal children were then to be handed over to him scoldingly, and the pretended lamp-man and his young apprentices were then to quit the Tower and proceed to the corner of the Boulevard, where they would find M. de Jarjayes waiting to receive them.

" This plan adopted, it became necessary to associate with it another confidant, worthy of admission into this holy conspiracy, and of playing the exceedingly important part of lamp-lighter. Toulan proposed a friend of his own, a discreet and courageous man, who, on being accepted himself, accepted with enthusiasm his share of danger and of devotion. This new confederate, equally resolute with the chiefs of the design, was an inspector of the national domains, named Ricard.

" Toulan was to have special charge of all the arrangements for the escape from the Tower; Jarjayes, of all those for flight from the French territory. The latter had, for this purpose, secured three cabriolets, which, at a fixed place and hour, were to be ready, with vigorous horses. The Queen and her son were to get into the first of these carriages, driven by M. de Jarjayes; Madame Royale into the second, driven by Lepitre; and Madame Elizabeth into the third, driven by Toulan. Ricard, his part acted, and his disguise laid aside, was to return home, no one being in a position to suspect the successful share he had taken in an event which would occupy the attention of Paris, of France, of Europe, while his colleagues would reach the frontier with the precious charge they had achieved by their liberating zeal.

"Everything seemed to assure the success of the enterprise. The requisite money was provided, the passports ready, signed by Lepitre himself, as President of the Passport Department in the section of Police ; every arrangement made, every incident duly calculated, so that the pursuit of the fugitives might not commence until many hours after their departure.

" It was at first proposed to direct their steps to La Vendée, where insurrection was already on foot. But it was considered, on mature reflection, that this would only be an asylum in a camp, and that, while on the one hand the presence of the Royal Family would communicate a powerful impulse to the enthusiasm of the Royalist army, it would, at the same time, create for that army fresh difficulties. M. Jarjayes pointed out these objections to the Queen by the medium of Toulan ; and Marie Antoinette, influenced by maternal love, more than ambition, and who was anxious to save the head rather than the crown of her son, at once adopted them. It was then determined to proceed to the coast of Normandy—a route shorter, and less impeded with obstacles. Arrived there, Jarjayes had provided the means of transit to England, in a vessel which lay at his disposal off a point of the coast near Havre. In short, all the means best calculated for frustrating the mischances of fate were taken ; but that sad fatality, which was precipitating into the abyss the old house of France, was more ingenious than all the precautions of man, more potent than all his efforts. Had Toulan and Jarjayes been intrusted with the conveyance of the Royal Family in the journey to Varennes, I have no doubt they would have placed it beyond danger ; but others, equally devoted perhaps, though less intelligent, or less able, had the management of that fatal affair. And so, for some time past, had all things befallen this family, marked with the seal of calamity, the enterprise that was to destroy it was carried into effect. That which would have saved it never took place.

"The circumstance which prevented it was this :—The 8th March was the day fixed upon for the escape. On the 7th, there was in Paris an almost universal rising, excited, on the one hand, by the scarcity of provisions, and, on the other, by the intelligence just received of the rapid progress of the foreign armies. After a battle on the Rhoer, where they had been compelled to abandon their entrenchments, the French had evacuated Aix-la-Chapelle, and raised the siege of Maëstricht, leaving more than four thousand of their number dead on the field. After another battle, not less sanguinary, the Austrians had retaken Liége. The blood of France, when she is wounded at her extremities, flows back to the heart. Paris was roused, excited, and infuriated, under the twofold apprehension of invasion, and of famine by the Mountain, who had resolved to massacre, in the Convention itself, the Gironde, and all who opposed their projects, more especially that of the creation of a revolutionary tribunal to try all conspirators, without appeal. The extremity of the circumstances called for extreme men ; the Mountain, who appreciated the situation, determined to profit by it. Forewarned in time, the menaced deputies did not attend the sitting of the evening of the 9th March, at which the decree in question was noted. In the same sitting the Convention ordered the appearance at its bar, of Generals Stingel and Lanoue, charged with treachery in the rout of Aix-la-Chapelle. Envoys of the National Convention passed through the departments, loudly proclaiming the fresh perils of the country. Each section set loose its agitators, who daily, hourly, beset the Council of the Commune with vehement demands for the closing of the barriers, in order to prevent the departure of the suspected, that is to say, of all who desired to withdraw themselves from the action of sanguinary laws, and domiciliary visits, or to avoid the contingent imposed on the city of Paris, in the levy of three hundred thousand men ordered on the 24th February. Despite

all clamours, and all menaces, however, the Council contented themselves with suspending the issue of foreign passports, declaring that
until the Convention should otherwise decide, the barriers should remain
open, the law prohibiting, under pain of death, their being closed, except
by order of the Convention ; and Pache, Mayor of Paris, and General Santerre, having made that same day a satisfactory report at the bar of the
Convention, on the situation of the capital, the barriers remained open.

"The excitement of the populace, however, had awakened all the
solicitude of power, all its watchfulness. Whenever anything stirred
about it, its uneasy attention became at once directed to the Temple.
The enterprise of Toulan's could not, therefore, be essayed on the day
which had been assigned for it ; too many hostile eyes, too many jealous
ears, were on the watch, in and around that State prison.

"The succeeding days were characterized by the same movement
out of doors, and presented, consequently, the same danger. On the
12th March, General Dumouriez, whose conduct was also regarded by
the populace as treasonable, was denounced by the section Poisson-
nière to the avenging justice of the Convention. On the 13th, for the
first time, La Vendée, which had been long in a state of fermentation,
openly raised its head, and uttered that cry which, with its echoes, was
destined frequently to disturb the slumber of the dictators. Moreover,
Toulan and Lepitre's turn of service at the Tower not recurring for
several days, any attempt at escape was inevitably suspended.

"When he entered the Tower on the 8th, Toulan had found the
Royal Family deeply agitated. Since the preceding evening the thousand clamours of the great city had been confusedly sounding around
the Temple ; the prisoners knew not the cause of the tumult, and they
were fearful that some calamity had occurred compromising the noble
friends who had devoted themselves to their deliverance. The presence
of Toulan re-assured them, and the joy of learning that no one had
become involved in peril for their sake, more than compensated for
their grief at finding their captivity prolonged. 'I should have deeply
regretted to leave this place,' said the Queen to him, 'without removing also several articles that are extremely precious to me, as the
bequest of one who was very dear to me while he lived, and whose
memory, now that he is gone, is sacred. I speak of the wedding-ring,
and the seal, which the King always wore, and which he charged Cléry
to deliver to me, with his sister's hair, and that of my children.'* Toulan

* The ring was of gold, and on opening it presented this inscription :—"M. A.
A. A., 19 Aprilis 1770, jour des fiançailles à Vienne, de Marie Antoinette, Archi-
duchesse d'Autriche, et de Louis-Auguste, Dauphin of France." The unhappy
Prince had, ever since his marriage, worn it, and when he relinquished it for the first

made no definite reply; but he knew that the municipal officers had required from Cléry, when he was restored to liberty in February, restitution of the effects which the Council of the Commune had left in his care on the 21st of January; and that these effects, among which were those of which Marie Antoinette had spoken, had been placed under seal in the late King's apartment. Next day, before quitting the Temple, Toulan brought to the Royal widow the articles she so earnestly desired. He had skilfully managed to procure other articles somewhat resembling them, and these he had as skilfully substituted for the originals, which he had removed from under seal. Assuredly the Queen of France, in all the splendour of her glory at Versailles, could not have been served with equal zeal and ability. The devotion of the heart performs greater miracles than selfish interest, or the unmeaning adulation of the courtier, which says to queens, when, in the hour of their prosperity, they make a request : 'If it be possible, it is done ; if impossible, it shall be done.'

"The system of intimidation developed itself in every direction. On Thursday, 14th March, the Convention ordered the revolutionary tribunal to try, *par contumace*, as they did not appear to defend themselves, the brothers of Louis XVI. On the 18th it decreed the demolition of the châteaux of the emigrants, and the partition of the national property. Still, Jarjayes and Toulan would not abandon their noble project. They watched in silence, with incessant and anxious attention, for the moment wherein to carry it into execution. Unhappily, each day brought with it some event, which infused fresh vigilance into the guard of the Tower, and especially into the surveillance of the Royal infant. It would have been imprudence—madness, in fact—to have attempted an escape, which had become almost impracticable. The virtuous conspirators did not allow themselves to be blinded by their vast desire to accomplish a good action. They calmly resolved to confine their enterprise within the limits of the possible, and to concentrate their ideas of deliverance upon the Queen and Madame Elizabeth, whose exit from the Temple presented difficulties of a less insurmountable character. But how induce these two mothers to separate themselves

time, on the morning of the 21st January, he charged Cléry to deliver it to his wife, and to tell her from him, that he had parted from it with pain. He parted from it, in fact, only at the moment of parting from life.

The seal was a silver ring, with three openings, one of which exhibited an engraving of the Shield of France, another the letters L L, and the third the head, helmeted, of the Dauphin.

The hair, separately enclosed in three small papers, was enveloped in one larger paper, on which was written, with the King's own hand, " Hair of my wife, of my sister, and of my children."

both from their beloved children? The very attempt indeed could not be made. The devotion of Madame Elizabeth was well known. Her soul was too beautiful, too lofty, not to forget itself when any other interest presented. Hers was the purest expression of that single-hearted candour, of that holy affection, which Raphael has given to the mother of Jesus,—an angelic grace, a Christian serenity, that never occurred to the imagination of antiquity. She employed the entire eloquence of her love to persuade her sister that it was her duty to profit by the resources which still remained at her disposal for escaping from her enemies. She impressed upon her that her very life might be endangered by her stay, whereas the lives of her children and that of her sister were under no peril. She even ventured, as a conclusive inducement, to whisper in her ear all the rumours current in the city, which, though stamped with popular exaggeration in their details, but too truly represented the public animosity that had been excited against the Queen. M. de Jarjayes himself conveyed to Marie Antoinette his earnest supplications that she would concur in the execution of the new project, every feature of which was carefully explained to her by Toulan. In that new plan it was still the faithful Toulan, and this time Toulan alone, who undertook to effect the exit of the Royal prisoner from the Tower, and to conduct her to a secure retreat where she would meet Jarjayes. The latter, on his part, had taken measures which seemed to place that august head beyond the reach of assault. The tender entreaties of Madame Elizabeth, the fervent zeal of Toulan, at length produced their effect upon the Queen, who approved of the plan, and consented to conform to it. The day fixed upon at length approached. On the evening preceding it, the mother and the aunt were seated beside the bed of the sleeping King. Madame Royale was also in bed, but the door of her chamber was open, and the young Princess, intent upon the mournful and meditative air which her mother had worn throughout the day, had not yet closed her eyes. Thus it was that she heard the words which at a later period she repeated. Resolved upon the sacrifice demanded at her hands, the Queen, as we have said, was seated beside her son's bed. 'God grant that this child may be happy!' she exclaimed. 'He will be so, my sister,' replied Madame Elizabeth, pointing to the open, candid, gentle, yet proud features of the King, who seemed to smile as he slept. 'Youth is brief as joy,' murmured Marie Antoinette, in heart-breaking tones; 'happiness comes to an end as everything else.' Then, rising, she walked to and fro in the chamber—'And you, my dearest sister, when and how shall I see you again? No; it's impossible, it's impossible.' The youthful Marie Thérèse did not, at the time, comprehend these words, the meaning of which was explained to her afterwards. The Queen had made up her mind not to avail herself of the door which Toulan had undertaken to open for her on the morrow. Her resolve was irrevocable. Love for her children was more potent than all other considerations,—than the prayers of her sister, than the instinct of her self-preservation, than the promise she had given to the devotion of her courageous friends. But reproaching herself as for a breach of faith, for that promise given and which she would not observe, she felt that she owed reparation to the generous hearts who had resolved to imperil themselves for her. Next morning the municipal Toulan presented himself, full of emotion at the idea of the great action he deemed himself about to accomplish. So soon as it was possible to speak with him, Marie Antoinette said to him, ' You will be angry with me, but I have reflected. There is nothing but danger in this. Better death than remorse.' Later, she said to him these words, which Toulan recalled to mind as he ascended the scaffold on the 30th June 1794: 'I shall die unhappy if I have not first an opportunity to prove to you my gratitude.' 'And I, Madame, unhappy indeed, if I have not first been able to prove to you my devotion.'

"Alas! towards these noble hearts justice was impartial. Devotion and gratitude obtained the same recompense. There was, at that period, a place at which all the virtues assembled together—the scaffold.

"The Queen desired also to thank M. de Jarjayes, and to explain to him the motives of her refusal. She wrote to him with her own hand this note, which she charged Toulan to transmit to him—a memorable note, which M. de Chauveau Lagarde was the first to publish, in his *Note Historique sur les Procès de Marie Antoinette, et de Madame Elizabeth:*—

"'We have had a pleasant dream; that is all. But there has been this great gain to me from it, that it has furnished to me a fresh proof of your entire devotion towards me. My confidence in you is boundless. You will ever find in me firmness and courage; but the interest of my son is my sole guide. However great my happiness in quitting this place, I cannot consent to separate from him. I could feel no enjoyment apart from my children, and this idea leaves me without even a regret at my resolution.'

"The Queen, as if filled with a sinister foreknowledge, said further to Toulan, "As matters are now proceeding, I may at any moment be deprived of all communication with others. There are the wedding-ring, the seal, and the packet of family hair, for the recovery of which I am indebted to you alone. I request you to place them in the hands of the Chevalier de Jarjayes, entreating him to convey them to Monsieur and to the Count d'Artois, with the letters which my sister and I have just written to our brothers.' "—Beauchesne's *Louis XVII.*, vol. ii. p. 18.

"M. Hue, valet-de-chambre to the King, who had remained free and forgotten in Paris, was in communication with these Commissioners, and thus transmitted to the Princesses the facts, the reports, the hopes, and the plots outside, which affected their situation. These communications, verbal or written, could not reach the captives without precautions and devices, which blinded the eyes of the other Commissioners. The Commissioners mutually watched each other. A look, or a gesture of intelligence, surprised by one, would have conducted the other to the scaffold. Toulan and Lepitre borrowed the hand of Turgy, and the mediation of inanimate objects. A stove, pierced with heat-holes, was destined to warm a hall on the first storey, which served as a common antechamber to the Queen and Madame Elizabeth. It was in the pipes of this stove that Turgy deposited the notes, the advices, or the fragments of the public papers, which could inform the Princesses of what was wished to be made known to them. The Princesses, in their turn, concealed their notes, written with sympathetic ink, the colour of which was only revealed by exposure to the fire. The events within and without, the disposition of men's minds, the progress of La Vendée, the success of foreign armies, the glare of false hopes, which enlightened chimerical conspiracies for their deliverance ; and, lastly, some letters, bathed in tears of real friendship, entered thus into the prison of Marie Antoinette. But hope entered not into her soul. The horror of her situation was precisely that of having nothing more to fear, and nothing more to hope. She possessed not even the agitation of that suffering which struggles. She combined the peace of despair and the stillness of the sepulchre with the sensibility of life."—Lamartine's *History of the Girondists*, vol. iii. p. 139.

Tison and his wife, the Arguses of the Temple, discovered that a plot existed for the liberation of the Royal Family, and denounced Toulan, Lepitre, Beugneau, Vincent, Bruno, Merle, who were suspended from their duties, and which brought these intrepid souls to the scaffold. The wife of Tison, who had denounced the Municipals, troubled by remorse, ultimately lost her reason.

Shortly after, another plan of escape was formed by Michonis, who had fortunately escaped being denounced to the tribunal.

"The Baron de Batz was again at the head of this dangerous enterprise. The incessant search after him ever since the attempt of the 21st January, had not driven from Paris this intrepid servant of a cause that misfortune had rendered so noble, and which, besides, presented the allurement of danger, irresistible to all generous spirits. The obstinate struggle maintained by this man against the fearful power that oppressed the nation is one of the marvels of those times. Everywhere present, though nowhere to be seen, as skilful in laying his own snares as in avoiding those of the enemy, he had the most prudent agents at his devotion, and the most active spies in his pay. His words were even more insinuating than the arguments of his purse were persuasive, and, with admirable address, he had gained over several members of the Convention, who, if circumstances did not allow of their rendering him any useful assistance, at least remained faithful to him by preserving inviolable silence upon his affairs. Unwearied in conspiracy, no sooner had his enterprises failed, than he began again with renewed ardour, and fearlessly remained in a town where a price had been set upon his head. His name was the signal for serious measures being taken, and the strictest possible search being made. The trackless conspirator had many impenetrable places of refuge in Paris and its environs, but his most usual, and perhaps securest, retreat, was in the house of Cortey, a grocer in the Rue de la Loi, whose reputation for civism had recommended him to the suffrages of his fellow-citizens, by whom he had been chosen Captain in command of the National Guard of the Lepelletier section. Cortey also enjoyed the friendship of Chrétien, a member of the Revolutionary Tribunal, whose influence was all-powerful in the committees of that section. It was in consequence of his recommendation that Cortey was appointed one of the officers of the post to whom the guard of the Temple was intrusted, whenever a detachment from their battalion formed part of the armed force there. Sheltered by the revolutionary renown of his host, and concealed in his house, Baron de Batz confided his plans to him, and Michonis, and, in concert with them, took all the measures relating to their execution. The first time that Cortey was on guard at the Temple, after this disclosure, Batz desired him to include him, under a fictitious name, in the list of the men whom his company furnished to the post, in order that by being thus introduced into the Tower, he might, as a preliminary step, be enabled to form an exact idea of the locality. The officer yielded to his desire, and having put him down on the roll of the men on duty, under the name of Forget, he thus gave him admission into the Temple, where he mounted guard. It was also necessary, for the execution of the plan agreed upon, to wait until Cortey's turn on guard should coincide with Michonis's turn on duty. The mutual understanding of the two authorities was indispensably requisite, and several days passed before the Captain and the Civil Commissary were on duty together. Batz took advantage of this delay to secure, conjointly with his host, the assistance of thirty men of the section, whose sentiments either one or the other had discovered, whose character they had had cause to appreciate, or whose discretion they had tried. The good-nature of Cortey seduced some, while the flattering words of Batz persuaded others. Michonis, with his customary prudence, did not appear in person in this dangerous recruiting. However, he reserved as bold a part for himself when he took upon him to direct everything within the Tower.

"The expected day arrived. The officer and the municipal were on duty at last together. Cortey entered the Temple with his detachment, among whom figured De Batz, under his assumed name. The officer of the post arranged the turns of duty in the manner the most favourable for the success of the enterprise. Twenty-eight men on whom he could depend were to be on patrol, or sentry, from midnight until two o'clock A.M., while the Civil Commissary, on his part, was to take his measures for being on guard himself in the apartment of the Royal Family at the same hour. The men on sentry on the staircase of the Tower were to wear above their uniforms ample military cloaks. Michonis was to take this extra clothing from them, and dress the Princesses in it, who, under this disguise, and with arms in their hands, were to be incorporated with a patrol, in the midst of whom the child-King would be concealed. The sentries on guard in the courtyard, who were acquainted with the secret, would be silent, if the night turned out bright, or the lamps not discreet. Cortey was to command the numerous patrol in person, and have the great gate of the Temple opened for them—a prerogative which during the night, belonged only to the officer commanding the post. Once without the walls, the safety of the Royal Family was certain. Carriages were placed ready in the Rue Charlot, to insure a rapid flight. By this street the patrol would pass, and was then to leave the prisoners, together with De Batz, Michonis, Cortey, and several others, who, like them, had entered on this forlorn hope.

"The day, which had passed over without any sign of bad weather, seemed to give hope of a favourable night. It was half-past eleven o'clock. Michonis had been on duty some time in the apartment of the prisoners, and his colleagues were resting or playing in the council-room, with the exception of Simon, who had left the Tower about an hour before. All the men who were to enter upon their turn of duty at midnight were at their post, when suddenly Simon arrived, and noisily entering the guard-room, he roughly ordered the roll of all the men present to be called. 'I am most happy to see you here,' said he to Cortey. 'I should not be easy without your presence.' M. de Batz saw that all was discovered, and the thought came into his head to blow Simon's brains out, and to attempt the escape by force.   But speedily mastering his first impulse, he reflected that the explosion of fire-arms, by causing a general stir, would ruin his enterprise, and probably aggravate the sad condition of the Royal Family.   He reflected that the posts on the staircase and on the Tower were not yet in his possession, and that the very men around him, on whom he might rely for passive co-operation, would perhaps fail him if the question became one of a struggle, and, after all, of almost certain death.   Batz remained immoveable after the roll-call.   Simon went up to the Tower, and displayed an order from the Council-General, commanding Michonis to give over his charge to him, and instantly repair to the Commune.   Michonis heard it without surprise, and unhesitatingly obeyed.   He met Cortey in the outer court.   'What is the meaning of all this?' said he to him.   'Be easy,' replied the Captain, in a low voice, 'Forget is gone.'

"The head of the post had not indeed lost a minute.   As soon as Simon had left him to go up to the Tower, he had, on pretence of a noise in the next street, sent out a patrol of eight men, who were but seven in number when they returned.   The coolness of Batz, and presence of mind of Cortey, had saved the lives of all.   Simon had not been idle; he had instituted a strict search in the apartment of the Princesses in the Towers, and in all the outbuildings within the enclosure; he had examined all the men on duty—but all his inquiries were fruitless.   Nothing at all suspicious was visible within the Temple bounds, where all was as quiet as usual.   Ashamed of the useless alarm he had occasioned, Simon then doubled the number of men on duty, endeavouring to give weight to an idea of danger in which he no longer himself believed, by the precautions he deemed it prudent to take.

"We will now relate all that had occurred, according to the account given by Simon.   A gendarme on duty at the Temple had, at about nine o'clock that evening, found a paper, without any address, lying on the pavement before the great gate, within the second fold of which were written these words :—'Michonis will betray you this evening—Watch.' The gendarme having opened the paper, gave it to Simon, the only one of the six commissaries with whom he was personally acquainted. Simon repaired with this note in all haste to the Council-General, who ordered him to relieve his colleague, and desire him to repair without delay to the bar of the Commune.

"Obedient to the summons, Michonis had to undergo a most rigid examination.   He answered all questions skilfully; refuted, with authoritative honesty of manner, the testimony of an anonymous paper, forged by some political adversary, and also—'which was indeed the case'—represented Simon to be his personal enemy.   The open countenance and apparent candour of the accused had already won him an acquittal from his supposed crime, when next evening, his adversary of the previous night having given an account of the meagre results of his mission, the Council-General remained impressed with the conviction, that although Simon, with his restless temper, might be capable of imagining a conspiracy, Michonis, with his frank disposition, was quite incapable of forming one."—Beauchesne's *Louis XVII.*, vol. ii. p. 53.

Thus misfortune followed the efforts of these brave royalists, at the moment when their heroism seemed crowned with success.

"On the 30th June some municipal officers of the Pont-Neuf presented themselves to the Committee of Public Safety, and deposed that a plan had been formed for the re-establishment of monarchy; that it was evident that this plot had numerous ramifications in the south and west; and that, in every section of Paris, some trusty associates were labouring to gain over the majority, on pretence of restoring order, and re-assuring well-intentioned persons that General Dillon, in concert with several other general officers who were ready to second him, was to take the command of the insurgent army, which, after spiking the alarm-gun and overpowering all the guard-houses, was to re-assemble on the Place de la Révolution with the guns carried off from the different posts, and march thence in two columns, one by the Boulevards on the Temple, whence they would take the young King, and the other on the Convention, where they would cause him to be proclaimed King of France under the regency of Marie Antoinette during his minority. Lastly, to give their revelation a more positive character, they added, that all the agents armed in this revolution were to be formed into the privileged guard of the monarch, and to receive medals suspended by a white-watered ribbon.

"In consequence of these street rumours converted into formal denunciations, without attempting to inquire into their truth, the Committee of Public Safety signed, on the 1st July, an order for the arrest of General Dillon and his supposed accomplices, and then another decree, the tenour of which was as follows :—

"'The Committee of Public Safety decrees that the son of Capet be separated from his mother, and committed to the charge of a tutor, to be chosen by the Council-General of the Commune.'

"These two measures sanctioned by the Convention were carried out on the 3d July."—Beauchesne's *Louis XVII.*, vol. ii. p. 59.

After the separation of the Dauphin from his mother, on the 3d

July, he was escorted by six commissaries and a porter to that part of the Tower formerly occupied by Louis XVI., where he was placed under the custody of Antoine Simon, " a shoemaker," who had been appointed by the Council-General to be the tutor to the Prince.   Simon was shortly afterwards joined by his wife.

The shoemaker now had the charge of the Dauphin.   The municipals no longer did duty in the room of the Royal captives.   The turnkeys alone ascended to take the Queen and Princesses their provisions.

" On Sunday, 7th July 1793, the report was circulated in Paris that the conspiracy formed by General Dillon had, notwithstanding the arrest of that General and of his principal accomplices, been entirely successful; *that the son of Louis* XVI. *had been carried off from the Tower, that he had been seen on the Boulevards, and had been carried in triumph to Saint Cloud.   Crowds hastened towards the Temple, eager to assure themselves of the truth.   The Temple guard, who had not seen Louis* XVII. *since he had been given up to Simon, replied that he was no longer in the Tower;* and from that time the popular falsehood gained ground and strength continually.

" In order to put a stop to this rumour, which excited every one, a numerous deputation from the Committee of Public Safety repaired in all haste to the Temple, in order to make an official report of the presence of the Royal child in that place."—Beauchesne's *Louis XVII.,* vol. ii. p. 74.

On their arrival at the Temple they ordered the Dauphin to be taken instantly into the garden, in order that he might be seen by the guard coming on duty.   After which, the authorities assembled in the council-room to investigate how Simon acquitted himself of his duties, which ended in Simon demanding to know what they desired him to do with his charge,—" Do you want him transported ?"   " No."   " Killed?"   " No."   " Poisoned?"   " No."   " Then, what am I to do with him?"   " *We want to get rid of him.*"   After which they visited the Queen and Princesses, and on returning to the Convention, Drouet expressed himself as follows :—

" Some evil-disposed or senseless persons have been pleased to spread a report that Capet's son had escaped, and had been carried in triumph to Saint Cloud.   Although they were convinced of the impossibility of such an escape, your Committee of Public Safety directed us, Maure, Chabot, Dumont, and myself, to make an official report of the presence of the prisoner.   We repaired to the Temple accordingly, and in the first apartment found Capet's son, quietly playing at draughts with his Mentor.   We then went up to the women's apårtment, and found there Marie Antoinette, her daughter, and sister, all three enjoying perfect health.   There are persons who still make it their delight to spread reports among foreign nations, to the effect that they are ill-treated ; while from their own confessions, made in presence of the commissaries of the Convention, it appears that nothing is wanting to their comfort."—Sitting of the National Convention of Sunday, 7th July 1793 ; *Moniteur* of Tuesday, 9th July 1793.

"Shortly after the Dauphin was separated from the Queen, *his long ringlets, which fell profusely over his shoulders, were cut off by the wife of Simon.*"—Beauchesne's *Louis XVII.*, vol. ii. p. 86.

After a time the Queen and the Princesses used to walk on the platform of the Tower, in the hope of catching a glimpse of the Dauphin, and once only did the Queen catch a glimpse of her son through the crevices of the planks, on the 30th July, when she became aware of the treatment he had to endure, and which caused additional pangs to her desolate position.   So proceeded events till the 2nd of August, when, at two o'clock in the morning, the Queen was awakened to be conducted to the prison of the Conciergerie.   These barbarians violated decency by remaining in her room while she was half-dressed.   When dressed, she blessed her daughter, and then gave her in the care of Madame Elizabeth, saying, " Behold the person who will be henceforth your father and your mother ; obey her, and love her, as she were myself."   And then she said to Madame Elizabeth, throwing herself into her arms, "I leave in you another mother to my poor children ; love them as you have loved us, even in the dungeon, and even unto death."

She then left the room, and on issuing from the wicket of the Temple, she struck her forehead against the beam of the low door.   She was asked if she had hurt herself.   She answered, " Oh no ; nothing now can further harm me."   She then ascended the carriage with two municipals, and was escorted by gendarmes to the Conciergerie.   Upon her arrival she was conducted to an apartment, which must have struck chillness to her very soul. We shall now insert a description of the new home to which these inveterate and dishonourable foes consigned their suffering and magnanimous Queen :—

"Having descended the steps of a large staircase, and having passed by two large doorways, you enter into a cloister, the arcades of which open upon a court, the promenade of the prisoners. A series of roughly planed oaken doors, fastened with bands, locks, and massive bolts, ranged on the left under these corridors. The second of these doors, on issuing from the wickets, looked into a small subterraneous chamber, the floor of which was lower by three steps than the threshold of the corridor. A barred window borrowed light from a court, narrow and deep as an empty cistern. On the left of this first cell, a door still lower than the first, but without fastenings and bolts, led to a kind of sepulchral vault, paved, and walled in freestone, blackened by the smoke of torches, and incrusted by dampness. A window, taking its light from the same meadow as that of the antechamber, and garnished with trellis-work of interwoven iron bars, allowed a light always similar to twilight to filter through. At the bottom of this little cellar, on the side opposite the window, a miserable pallet, without canopy or curtains, with covering of coarse cloth, such as that which passes from one bed to the other in hospitals and barracks, a small deal table, a wooden box, and two straw chairs, formed all the furniture. It was there, that in the middle of the night, and by the light of a tallow-candle, the Queen of France was thrown, fallen from grade to grade, from misfortune to misfortune, from Versailles and from Trianon, even into this dungeon. Two gens d'armes, with naked swords in hand, were placed on duty in the first chamber, with the door open, and their eyes fixed on the interior of the Queen's cell, being charged not to lose sight of her, even in her sleep.

"Men cannot, however, always find implacable instruments for their ferocity. Even dungeons have their mitigations. A respectful gesture, a look of intelligence, the sound of a sympathizing voice, a stolen word, made the victim comprehend that she was not as yet totally shut out from humanity. This communication with that which breathes and feels on earth, gives to the unfortunate, even in the last hour, a link with existence. The Queen found in the countenance, in the eyes, and in the soul of Madame Richard, the wife of the Concierge, this feeling concealed under the rigour of her duties. The hand ordained to bruise her became softened, in order to comfort her. Everything which the arbitrary law of a prison permitted to be adopted, all alleviation of the rules in captivity, nourishment, and solitude, was essayed by Madame Richard, to prove to her prisoner that, even in the depth of her misfortunes, she still reigned, through pity and devotion, over one heart.

"Madame Richard, a royalist in remembrance, felt less pride in having the guardianship of the daughter, the wife, and the mother of kings consigned to her mercy, than in the happiness of being able to dry her tears. She introduced some necessary or convenient furniture into the dungeon of the Queen. She sent to the Temple to seek the tapestry work, the balls of wool, and the needles which Marie Antoinette had left there. Madame Richard herself prepared the prisoner's food. She brought her news of her sister, her daughter, and her son, which she procured by correspondence with the Temple. She transmitted, through the medium of Commissioners, who were accomplices, news from the Queen to her sister and the children. The concierge Richard, although apparently more austere, shared in all the feelings of his wife, and joined her in all these consolations.

"People without were ignorant of the period at which Marie Antoinette was to be tried. This adjournment of the Committee of Public Safety caused a hope that they would deceive the ferocious impatience of the populace, or wear it out by delay. Many municipals joined secretly in plots of escape. Madame Richard favoured the introduction of these devoted men into the cell. She cleverly engaged the attention of the gens d'armes on guard in the antechamber, during these rapid interviews. Michonis, a member of the municipality, and administrator of police, who had already proved his devotion to the Royal Family in the Temple, at the peril of his life, continued the same devotion in the Conciergerie. By his favour, a royalist gentleman, named Rougeville, was introduced into the prison, saw the Queen, and offered her a flower, which contained a note. This note spoke of deliverance, and was detected in the hands of the Queen by one of the gens d'armes. Michonis was arrested. Madame Richard and her husband, deprived of their functions, were cast into the dungeons, where they had permitted indulgence to enter. The Queen trembled."—Lamartine's *History of the Girondists*, vol. iii. p. 145.

Monsieur Hue, valet-de-chambre to Louis XVI., in his work, *The Last Years of the Reign and Life of Louis XVI.*, describes how the loyal Rougeville gained his entry to the cell in the Conciergerie, which contained the magnanimous Queen. He says :—

"Rougeville confided in a woman, with whom a municipal, 'Michonis,'* was in love, and engaged her to assist his views. She redoubled her attentions to the municipal, and invited him to dinner, at which M. de Rougeville, who passed for a foreigner, was one of the guests. During dinner, the conversation increasing in freedom, it was gradually turned on the events of the day. 'A Queen,' said M. de Rougeville, ' and especially a Queen of France, shut up in one of the dungeons of the Conciergerie, must be a strange sight.' 'Do you know her?' said the municipal. 'No,' replied the Chevalier, with seeming indifference. 'Should you like to see her? I can let you go into her cell.' M. de Rougeville showed no eagerness to accept the offer, but, urged to it by the guests who were in the secret, he consented. The hour was fixed for the very same day. In the intervening time, on pretence of its being the lady's birthday, M. de Rougeville purchased a nosegay, which he presented to her. She took out a pink, and gave it to the Chevalier, who withdrew for a few minutes, and dexterously placed in the cup of the flower a paper rolled up, on which were written these words, ' I have at your command men and money.' At night the municipal conducted M. de Rougeville to the Conciergerie. On entering the Queen's cell, the Chevalier perceived that Her Majesty recollected him. After some words of no consequence, he pretended to believe that his pink must be agreeable to the Queen, and presented it to her. She accepted it, and being apprised by a look to secrete it, withdrew to a corner, found, and read the paper. Her Majesty had begun to trace with a pin a negative, when one of the gendarmes, on duty at the door of the cell, suddenly entered, and seized the paper. The prison was immediately in a great uproar, and a denunciation was made to the Commune, and to the Committee of Public Safety. The warden's wife and son were at first arrested as accomplices, sent to the Convent of the Magdelonettes, and confined in separate dungeons, but were liberated in a few days.† M. de Rougeville escaped. A reward was offered for his head." —Hue's *Last Years of the Reign and Life of Louis XVI.*, p. 482.

Monsieur and Madame Bault, the former concierges of La Force, took the positions of Monsieur and Madame Richard at the Conciergerie, they having solicited this position in order to assuage the last moments of the Queen. The Commune had enjoined them to act in

---

* This municipal was one of the magistrates for the prisons of Paris. As such, he entered them at all hours, day and night. He perished on the scaffold.

† ' These particulars were communicated to me by M. Pommier, one of the lady's guests. I was a prisoner with him in the Hôtel de la Force. He perished on the scaffold.'

the most unfeeling manner, nevertheless these brave hearts did everything in their power to ameliorate the sad condition to which their
suffering Queen had fallen, assisted by their loyal daughter, who attended
the Queen.

"One day, ' the 19th August,' Simon, as was his custom, was being
served at table by the young Prince. Simon was drunk, and being displeased with the manner in which the Royal child obeyed his orders or
interpreted his intentions, *he very nearly put out one of his eyes with a
blow with a napkin.*"—Beauchesne's *Louis XVII.*, vol. ii. p. 111.

Monsieur Alphonse de Lamartine, in speaking of the above treatment
the Dauphin received from Simon, says :—

"He made the child wait upon him at table, himself seated, the
former standing. One day in cruel sport *he nearly tore an eye from
the Dauphin's head, by striking him on the face with a knotted towel.*"—
History of the Girondists, vol. iii. p. 142.

The following is from Madame the Princess-Royal's Private
Memoirs :—

"On the 21st September, at one in the morning, Hébert arrived
with several officers to execute an order of the Commune, that we should
be confined more strictly than heretofore ; that we should have but one
room ; that Tison, who did the coarse house-work, should be put in
prison in the turret ; that we should have nothing but what was strictly
necessary ; that there should be a kind of slide made in the door of our
room, by which our victuals were to be conveyed to us ; and finally,
that, except to bring us water and firewood, no person should be
allowed to enter the room. The slide in the door was not made, and
the officers still continued to come three times a day, and examine very
carefully all the bars and bolts, and every kind of furniture. We were
obliged to make our own beds and sweep the room. This was a long
work at first, from our awkwardness at it, but we were obliged to do it, for
we had at last absolutely no one to assist us. Hébert told my aunt that
equality was the first law of the French republic, and other prisoners not
being allowed attendants, we could have no longer Tison. In order to
treat us with all possible severity, they deprived us of even the most
trifling accommodations—an armed chair, for instance, in which my aunt
used to sit, and several other little matters of the same kind. Nay,
things of strict necessity were denied us.

"When our meals came the doors were suddenly clapped to, that we might not even see the persons who brought them. We no longer heard any news except by the hawkers, whose cries now and then reached us, but, in spite of all our attention, indistinctly. We were forbidden to go on the leads, and were deprived of our large sheets, lest, notwithstanding the gratings, we should escape from the windows. This was the pretext alleged, but the real cause of the change was— a desire to substitute coarse and dirty sheets.

"I believe it was about this time that the Queen's trial began. I have learnt since her death, that there was a plan for effecting her escape from the Conciergerie, which unhappily failed. I have been assured that the gendarmes who guarded her, and the wife of the gaoler, had been gained over ; that she had seen several well-affected persons in the prison, and amongst others a clergyman, who had administered the sacrament to her, which she received with the utmost devotion.

"The opportunity of escape failed, once because, instead of speaking to the second sentinel, as she had been desired to do, she addressed the first. Another time she had already got out of her dungeon, and had passed one of the corridors, when a gendarme obliged her to turn back, and the whole scheme failed. These attempts will not surprise us if we recollect that all honest men took an interest in the Queen's fate, and that (with the exception of the vile and ferocious wretches, who were, alas! too numerous) every one who was permitted to speak to her, see her, or approach her, were touched with pity and respect, so well did her affability temper the dignity of her manners. We knew none of those details while they were passing. We had only heard that a Chevalier de Saint Louis had given her a pink with a note concealed in it, but, as we were confined closer than ever, we could not learn the result."—*Private Memoirs of what passed in the Temple*, by Madame Royale, Duchess of Angoulême.

"On the 21st September, after Hébert and his party had visited the Princesses, they went down into Simon's room. It will be seen that the object of his visit was more the little prisoner than the captive ladies. He had a long conversation with Simon, looked at the child without speaking to him, took leave of the Master with the words, ' *Very soon,*' and withdrew.

"No official order or direction was given on that floor. ' *Very soon,*' is the sole portion of the visit that we have heard of ; a farewell word, simple and common enough, but which, under these circumstances, seems frightfully significant."—Beauchesne's *Louis XVII.*, vol. ii. p. 122.

On the 3d of October the following decree was passed :—" The

National Convention, on the proposition of a member, decrees that the Revolutionary tribunal proceed without delay or interruption to the trial of the widow Capet." But the materials for the trial were wanted; it was necessary to invent a foundation. The following is from Madame the Princess-Royal's Private Memoirs :—

"At noon, on the 8th October, while we were employed in dressing ourselves, and arranging our bedroom, Pâche, Chaumette, and David, members of the Convention, with several officers of the municipality, arrived. My aunt, who was not quite dressed, refused to open the door till she was. Pâche, addressing me, begged me to walk down stairs. My aunt would have followed, but they stopped her. She asked whether I should be permitted to come up again. Chaumette assured her that I should. 'You may trust,' said he, 'the word of an honest republican; she shall return.' I embraced my aunt, who was greatly affected, and went down, greatly embarrassed at finding myself for the first time in my life alone with men. I did not know what they wanted with me, but I recommended myself to the protection of God. On the stairs Chaumette affected to offer me certain civilities. I made him no answer. *I found myself in my brother's room, whom I embraced tenderly, but we were soon torn asunder, and I was obliged to go into another room.* Chaumette desired me to sit down, which I did. He sat down opposite to me, while a municipal officer took out his pen. Chaumette asked me my name, but Hébert continued the interrogatory.

"'Tell me the truth,' he said, 'it is not intended to affect you or your friends.'

"'Not to affect my mother?'

"'No, but some other persons who have not done their duty. Do you know the citizens Toulan, Lepitre, Breno, Brugnot, Merle, Michonis?'

"'No, sir.'

"'That is false—particularly Toulan, that little young man who used to come so often on duty at the Temple?'

"'I know nothing of him, nor of the rest.'

"'Do you remember that you were one day alone with your brother in the turret?'

"'Yes.'

"'Your parents had sent you thither that they might be more at their ease to speak to these people?'

"'No, sir, but to accustom us to cold.'

"'What did you do in the turret?'

" 'We talked, and played with one another.'

" ' When you came out, did you not observe what these men had brought to your parents ?'

" ' I did not see anything.'

" Chaumette then questioned me about a thousand shocking things of which they accused my mother and my aunt. I was so shocked at hearing such horrors, and so indignant, that, terrified as I was, I could not help exclaiming that they were infamous falsehoods, but, in spite of my tears, they still pressed their questions.

" There were some things which I did not comprehend, but of which I understood enough to make me weep with indignation and horror.

" He then asked me several questions about Varennes and other things, to all which I answered as well as I could, without implicating anybody. I had always heard my parents say, that it was better to die than implicate anybody.

" At last, about three o'clock, the examination was finished. It had lasted from noon. I entreated Chaumette to let me rejoin my mother, saying, with truth, that I had often made the same request of my aunt. ' It is out of my power,' said he. 'What, sir ! could you not obtain this favour from the General Council ?' ' No ; I have no authority there.' He then sent me back to my apartment with the municipal officers, desiring me not to speak of what had passed to my aunt, whom they were going to examine also. When I reached my room I threw myself into her arms, but we were soon separated, and she was desired to go down stairs.

" They put the same questions to her as they had done to me, relative to the men before mentioned. She answered that she knew the persons and names of the officers and others, but that she had no kind of intercourse with them. She denied having any correspondence without the Temple, and she replied with still more contempt to the shocking things about which they examined her also.

" She returned at four o'clock. Her examination lasted but an hour, though mine had lasted three, because the deputies saw that they had no chance of intimidating her, as they had hoped to be able to do a young person, by the length and grossness of their inquiries. They were, however, deceived. They forgot that the life which I had lived for four years past, and, above all, the example shewn me by my parents, had given me more energy and strength of mind.

" Chaumette had assured us that this interrogatory had no concern with my mother, nor even ourselves, and that they were not thinking of trying her. Alas! he deceived us. She was immediately after put upon

her trial and condemned to death, but we were aware of neither."—
Madame Royal Duchess of Angoulême's Private Memoirs.

They had, previously to examining the Princess-Royal and Madame
Elizabeth, interrogated the young Dauphin, endeavouring by threats to
make him comply with their demands; but in this they failed, as the
child resolutely refused to comply with their infamous requests; whereupon the brutal Hébert turned his spleen on the defenceless and harmless youth, and ill-treated him.   After which, Simon gave him intoxicat-
ing drink, by which foul means they obtained what they had failed to
do by threats and blows.

"On the 13th of October, Fouquier-Tinville came to notify to the
Queen his Act of Accusation.   She listened to it as a form of death,
which was not worth the honour of discussion.   Her crime was, being
a queen, the consort and mother of a king, and the having abhorred a
revolution which deprived her of a crown, of her husband, her children,
and her life.   To love the Revolution, she must have hated nature, and
destroyed all human feeling.   Between her and the republic there was
no legal form; it was hatred even to death.   The stronger of the two
inflicted it on the other.   It was not justice; it was vengeance.   The
Queen knew it, the woman received it.   She could not repent, and she
would not supplicate.   She chose, as a matter of form, two defenders—
Chauveau-Lagarde and Tronson-Ducoudray.

"These advocates, young, generous, and of high repute, had secretly
solicited this honour.   They sought, in the solemn trial of the Revolutionary Tribunal, not a despicable salary for their eloquence, but the
applause of posterity.   Nevertheless, a remnant of that instinct of life,
which causes the dying to seek a chance of safety even when impossible, occupied the Queen the remainder of the day and the following
night.   She noted some answers to the interrogatories to which she had
to submit.

"The following day, 14th of October, at noon, she dressed herself,
and arranged her hair with all the decorum which the simplicity and
poverty of her garments permitted.   She did not affect a display of the
rags which should have made the republic blush.   She did not dream of
moving the regards of the people to pity.   Her dignity as a woman and
a queen forbade her to make any display of her misery.

"She ascended the stairs of the judgment-hall, surrounded by a
strong escort of gendarmerie, crossed through the multitude, which so

solemn a vengeance had drawn into the passages, and seated herself upon the bench of the accused. Her forehead, scathed by the Revolution and faded by grief, was neither humbled nor cast down. Her eyes, surrounded by that black circle which want of rest and tears had graved, like a bed of sorrow, beneath the eyelids, still darted some rays of their former brilliancy upon the faces of her enemies. The beauty which had intoxicated the Court and dazzled Europe was no longer discernible; but its traces could be still distinguished. Her mouth sorrowfully preserved the folds of Royal pride, but ill effaced by the lines of long suffering. The natural freshness of her northern complexion still struggled with the livid pallor of the prison. Her hair, whitened by anguish, contrasted with this youth of countenance and figure, and flowed down upon her neck as in bitter derision of the fate of youth and beauty. Her countenance was natural,—not that of an irritated queen, insulting, in the depth of her contempt, the people who triumphed over her,—nor that of a suppliant who intercedes by her humility, and who seeks forbearance in compassion; but that of a victim whom long misfortune had habituated to her lot, who had forgotten that she was a queen, who remembered only that she was a woman, who claimed nothing of her vanished rank, who resigned nothing of the dignity of her sex and her deep distress.

"The crowd, silent through curiosity rather than emotion, contemplated her with eager looks. The populace seemed to rejoice at having this haughty woman at their feet, and measured their greatness and their strength by the fall of their most formidable enemy. The crowd was composed principally of women, who had undertaken to accompany the condemned to the scaffold with every possible insult. The judges were Hermann, Foucault, Sellier, Coffinhal, Deliége, Ragmey, Maire, Denizot, and Masson. Hermann presided. 'What is your name?' demanded Hermann of the accused. 'I am called Marie Antoinette of Lorraine, in Austria,' answered the Queen. Her low and agitated voice seemed to ask pardon of the audience for the greatness of these names. 'Your condition?' 'Widow of Louis, formerly King of the French.' 'Your age?' 'Thirty-seven.'

"Fouquier-Tinville read the Act of Accusation to the Tribunal. It was the summing-up of all the supposed crimes of birth, rank, and situation of a young Queen—a stranger, adored in her Court, omnipotent over the heart of a weak King, prejudiced against ideas which she did not comprehend, and against institutions which dethroned her. This part of the accusation was but the act of accusation of fate. These crimes were true, but they were the faults of her rank. The Queen could no more absolve herself from them than the people from accusing her of them. The remainder of the Act of Accusation was only an odious echo of all the reports and murmurs which had crept, during ten years, into public belief—of prodigality, supposed licentiousness, and pretended treason of the Queen. It was her unpopularity converted into crimination. She heard all without betraying any sign of emotion or astonishment, as a woman accustomed to hatred, and with whom calumny had lost its bitterness, and insult its poignancy. Her fingers wandered heedlessly over the bar of the chair, like those of a woman who recalls remembrances upon the keys of the harpsichord. She endured the voice of Fouquier-Tinville, but she heard him not. The witnesses were called and interrogated. After each evidence, Hermann addressed the accused. She answered with presence of mind, and briefly discussed the evidence as she refuted it. The only error in this defence was the defence itself.

" Many of these witnesses, taken from prisons in which they were already confined, recalled other days to her, and were themselves affected at seeing the Queen of France in such ignominy. Of this number was Manuel, accused of humanity in the Temple, and who gloried in the accusation ; Bailly, who bent with more respect before the downfall of the Queen than he had done before her power. The answers of Marie Antoinette compromised no one. She offered herself alone to the hatred of her enemies, and generously shielded all her friends. Each time that the debates of the trial brought up the names of the Princesse de Lamballe, or the Duchess of Polignac, to whom she had been most tenderly attached, her voice assumed a tone of feeling, sorrow, and regard. She evinced her determination not to abandon her sentiments before death, and that if she delivered her head up to the people, she would not yield them her heart to profane. The ignominy of certain accusations sought to dishonour her, even in her maternal feelings. The cynic Hébert, who was heard as a witness upon what had passed at the Temple, imputed acts of depravity and debauchery to the Queen, extending even to the corruption of her own son—'with intention,' said he, 'of enervating the soul and body o that child, and reigning in his name over the ruin of his understanding.' The pious Madame Elizabeth was named as witness and accomplice in these crimes. The indignation of the audience broke out at these words, not against the accused, but against the accuser. Outraged nature aroused itself. The Queen made a sign of horror, not knowing how to answer without soiling her lips. A juryman took up the testimony of Hébert, and asked the accused why she had not replied to this accusation. 'I have not answered it,' said she, rising with the majesty of innocence and the indignation of modesty, 'because there are accusations to which nature refuses to reply.' Afterwards, turning towards the women of the audience, the most enraged against her, and summoning them by the testimony of their hearts and their community of sex, 'I appeal against it to all mothers here present,' cried she. A shudder of horror against Hébert ran through the crowd. The Queen answered with no less dignity to the imputations which were alleged against her of having abused her ascendency over the weakness of her husband. 'I never knew that character of him,' said she ; 'I was but his wife, and my duty, as well as my pleasure, was to conform to his will.' She did not sacrifice by a single word the memory and honour of the King for the purpose of her own justification, or to the pride of having reigned in his name. She desired to carry back to him to heaven his memory honoured or avenged.

"After the closing of these long debates Hermann summed up the accusation, and declared that the entire French people deposed against Marie Antoinette. He invoked punishment in the name of equality in crime, and equality in punishment, and put the question of guilty to the jury. Chauveau-Lagarde and Tronson-Ducoudray, in their defence, excited posterity without being able to affect the audience or the judges. The jury deliberated for form's sake, and returned to the hall after an hour's interval. The Queen was called to hear her sentence. She had already heard it in the stamping and joy of the crowd which filled the palace. She listened to it without uttering a single word, or making any motion. Hermann asked her if she had anything to say upon the pain of death being pronounced upon her. She shook her head, and arose as if to walk to her execution. She disdained to reproach the people with the rigour of her destiny, and with their cruelty. To supplicate would have been to acknowledge it; to complain would have been to humble herself; to weep would have been to abase herself. She wrapped herself in that silence which was her last protection. Ferocious applause followed her even to the staircase, which descends from the tribunal to the prison."—Lamartine's *History of the Girondists*, vol. iii. p. 148.

The Queen was re-conducted to her loathsome cell, but her magnanimity and self-possession never forsook her, and in the depths of the dungeon, with the condemnation of death sealed on her, the forgiving and noble Marie Antoinette, at half-past four in the morning of the 16th October, wrote for the last time to her sister. She therein recalled the King's injunction to his son, and forgives her enemies the injustices they had heaped upon her. Thus wrote the noble Marie Antoinette :—

"Let my son never forget the last words of his father, which I repeat to him here on purpose that he may remember them : 'Never let him think of avenging our death, for I forgive all my enemies the injuries they have done me.'"

The guillotine terminated the sorrows and the indignities the troubles of the time, in its rancour and malignity, had unjustly and ungenerously heaped on the heroic and noble Marie Antoinette. She expiated such by the sacrifice of her life on the scaffold, the 16th October 1793, and thereby left a monument of eternal opprobrium to the craven-hearted and detestable monsters who then constituted the authority of France. On her road to immolation, royalists, dressed so as to avoid suspicion, followed the Queen from the Conciergerie to the foot of the scaffold, in the hope that some signal might be given to liberate her from the hands of her assassins.

The spirit of chivalry guiding the pencil of genius has left the following portrait of Marie Antoinette at the period of her accession to the throne :—

"It is now," says Mr. Burke (in a passage which will live as long as the English language), "sixteen or seventeen years since I saw the Queen of France, then the Dauphiness, at Versailles, and surely never lighted on this orb, which she hardly seemed to touch, a more delightful vision. I saw her, just above the horizon, decorating and cheering the elevated sphere she just began to move in, glittering like the morning-star, full of life, and splendour, and joy. Oh what a revolution ! and what a heart must I have to contemplate without emotion that elevation and that fall ! Little did I dream when she added titles of veneration to those of enthusiastic, distant, respectful love, that she should ever be obliged to carry the sharp antidote against disgrace concealed in that bosom ; little did I dream that I should have lived to see such disasters fallen upon her in a nation of gallant men, in a nation of men of honour and of cavaliers. I thought ten thousand swords must have leaped from their scabbards to avenge even a look that threatened her with insult. But the age of chivalry is gone. That of sophisters, economists, and calculators has succeeded, and the glory of Europe is extinguished for ever. Never, never more shall we behold that generous loyalty to rank and sex, that proud submission, that dignified obedience, that subordination of the heart, which kept alive, even in servitude itself, the spirit of an exalted freedom. The unbought grace of life, the cheap defence of nations, the nurse of manly sentiments and heroic enterprise, is gone. It is gone, that sensibility of principle, that chastity of honour, which felt a stain like a wound, which inspired courage whilst it mitigated ferocity, which ennobled whatever it touched, and under which vice itself lost half its evil by losing all its grossness."—Edmund Burke's *Reflections on the Revolution of France*, p. 149.

We must here draw attention to the fact that the Dauphin's escape was effected from the Prison of the Temple during the Queen's trial, which we shall fully substantiate in a subsequent chapter.

On marched the reign of tyranny, with all its attributes of dishonour, sacrilege, heartlessness, and corruption, whilst, as reported by the Revolutionary Government, the Dauphin was under the sole care of Simon.

On the 2nd of January 1794 the municipal body passed a decree, which prohibited the duties of a member of the Council-General being performed by any person holding a paid office under Government. Simon became affected by this decree, as he was a member of the Council, and in accordance with such, he tendered his resignation as tutor to the Dauphin, which was accepted. A decree was then passed that the Dauphin should thenceforth have no preceptor.

Chaumette and Hébert, who had the direction of everything concerning the Temple, agreed to this resolution, by which no intermediate power was appointed between the Temple and the municipal authority.

On the 20th January 1794 the captive was placed in solitary confinement. The door of his room was fastened up with nails and screws, and grated from top to bottom with bars of iron, in which, half-way up, was placed a shelf on which the bars opened, forming a sort of wicket, closed by other moveable bars, and fastened with an enormous padlock, through which his coarse food was passed.

"On the 20th January, the evening before the anniversary of the King's death, the Dauphin was entirely sequestered, like a wild animal, in a high chamber of the Tower, wherein no one entered. Simon, alone, threw to him his provisions, half opening the door. A flask of water, seldom replenished, was his beverage. He never got out of his bed, which was never made. His clothes, his shirt, and his shoes had never been changed for more than a year. His window, closed by a moveable fastening, opened no more to the air without. He continually inhaled his own infection. He had neither book, nor plaything, nor tools to occupy his hands. His active faculties, repelled in him by idleness and solitude, had become depraved. His limbs stiffened. His intelligence became suspended under the continuance of his terror. Simon appeared to have received orders to try to what degree of brutality and misery it was possible to make the son of the King descend.

"The aunt and sister, also prisoners, incessantly deplored and wept over this child. Their interrogatories respecting him were always answered with insult. During Lent, they brought them only coarse, fat viands, to force them to violate the precepts of the prescribed religion. They ate nothing during forty days but the bread and milk reserved by them from the superfluity of their breakfast. They deprived them of candles in the very first days of spring, from national economy. They were compelled to retire to repose at the close of day, or to watch in darkness. This savage captivity, nevertheless, did not alter the dawning beauty of the young Princess, nor the serenity of her aunt's temper. Nature and youth triumphed in the other over misfortune. Their mutual affection, their conversation, and their sufferings, felt and comprehended mutually, inspired them with a patience which almost resembled peace.

"The order to try Madame Elizabeth was a challenge of cruelty between the ruling men, as to who would be the most pitiless towards the blood of the Bourbons.

"On the 9th of May, at the moment when the Princesses, half-undressed, were praying at the foot of their beds, before retiring to slumber, they heard such repeated and violent blows at the door of their chambers as made it tremble upon its hinges. Madame Elizabeth hastened to dress herself, and to open it. 'You must descend instantly,' said the turnkeys to her. 'And my niece?' replied the Princess. 'We shall attend to her by and by.' The aunt foresaw her fate, rushed towards her niece, and encircled her in her arms, as if to dispute this separation. Madame Royale wept, and trembled. 'Be tranquil, my child,' said her aunt to her; 'I shall come up again, without doubt, in an instant.' 'No, citoyenne,' rudely replied the gaolers; 'you will not re-ascend. Take your bonnet and come down.' As she delayed, by her protestations and embraces, the execution of this order, these men loaded her with invectives and injurious apostrophes. She uttered her last adieu and pious exhortations to her niece in a few words. She invoked the memory of the King and Queen, to give more authority to her words. She bathed the face of the young girl with her tears, and went out, returning to bless her for the last time. Having descended to the wickets, she there found the Commissaries. They searched her anew. They made her ascend a carriage, which conducted her to the Conciergerie.

"It was midnight. It has been said, that the day did not contain hours sufficient for the impatience of the Tribunal. The Vice-President awaited Madame Elizabeth, and interrogated her without a witness. They left her afterwards, to take some repose upon the same couch where Marie Antoinette had slept out her agony. On the following morning they conducted her to the Tribunal, accompanied by twenty-four accused, of every age, and of both sexes, selected to inspire the people with the remembrance and resentment of the Court. Of this number were, Mesdames de Sénozan, de Montmorency, de Canisy, de Montmorin; the son of Madame de Montmorin, aged eighteen; M. de Loménie, the former Minister of War; and an old courtier of Versailles, the Count de Sourdeval.

"'Of what should she complain?' said the public accuser, on seeing this cortége of women of the most illustrious names grouped around the sister of Louis XVI. 'In seeing herself at the foot of the guillotine, surrounded by this faithful nobility, she may imagine herself again at Versailles.'

"The accusations were derisive, the answers disdainful. 'You call my brother a tyrant,' said the sister of Louis XVI. to the accuser and to the judges. 'If he had been what you say, you would not be where you are, nor I before you.' She heard her sentence without astonishment, and without grief. The only favour she asked, was a priest faithful to her faith, to seal her death with the Divine pardon. This consolation was refused her. She supplied it by prayer, and the sacrifice of her life. A long time before the hour of punishment, she entered the common dungeon, to encourage her companions.

"They then cut her long fair hair, which fell to her feet, like the crown of her youth.

"The females of her funeral suite, and the executioners themselves, divided it among them.

"They bound her hands. They made her then mount upon the last bench of the car which closed the cortége. They desired that her punishment should be multiplied by the twenty-two blows which fell upon these aristocratical heads. The people, assembled to insult, remained dumb upon her passage. The beauty of the Princess, angelic by interior peace ; her innocence of all the disorders which had rendered the Court unpopular ; her youth, sacrificed to the affection she bore to her brother ; and her voluntary devotion to the dungeon and the scaffold of her family made her the purest victim of Royalty. It was glorious to the Royal Family to offer up this spotless victim ; impious in the people to exact it. A secret remorse gnawed every heart. The executioner presented in her, relics to the throne, and a saint to Royalty. Her companions already venerated her before heaven. Proud of dying with innocence, they all humbly approached the Princess before ascending one by one to the scaffold, and asked the consolation of embracing her.

"The executioners dared not to refuse to females what they had refused to Hérault de Séchelles and to Danton. The Princess embraced all the condemned as they ascended the ladder. After this funereal homage, she yielded her head to the axe. Chaste in the midst of the seductions of beauty and of youth, pious and pure in a frivolous Court, patient in the dungeon, humble in greatness, proud upon the scaffold, Madame Elizabeth bequeathed by her death a model of innocence upon the steps of the throne, an example to affection, and admiration to the world, and an eternal reproach to the republic."— Lamartine's *Girondists*, vol. iii. p. 420.

During the time that marked the captive of the Temple's incarceration in solitary confinement—"*when commenting on this period, we shall prove it was a substitute confined in the Temple, and that it was on this especial account that the captive was placed in solitary confinement, so that no one should detect this substitution,*"—many and bitter were the crimes of the Convention, and many Revolutionary favourites forfeited their corrupt lives. The slightest suspicion or attachment to Royalty sufficed to open the prison and lead the proscribed to the scaffold. Terrible were the events that transpired ; all classes were indiscriminately condemned to death.

Irrepressible must be the indignation of humanity against the atrocities of the French Revolution ; for what acts have the perpetrators of that sad epoch placed on record but insatiable thirst for blood and self-aggrandizement, which has, and will re-echo and re-echo, with bitterness and dishonour to their memories, to the remotest posterity ?

Wisdom and prudence forsook their unfeeling hearts, and barbarity and desolation reigned supreme. What has been the track of their footsteps but ambition, fostered to crush and annihilate each other, their hearts being shut to justice or pity. Their liberty and constitutional ideas were to crush and despoil every idea that honour was attached to. The friend of the day was but the enemy of the morrow, for the proscribed found no advocate. His hours were numbered, the guillotine his fate. Horror after horror followed the reign of fanaticism. Nothing could expiate the conduct of the accused. Its sole interpretation was death, and the cry was—instant vengeance.

Thus, the detestable Hébert and the Hébertists were suddenly arrested, and were condemned to death on the 24th of March 1794. The ruling party in the Convention accused them of a plot between Madame la Comtesse de Rochechouart and Hébert, for the escape of the.Royal Family; that Hébert, as a reward for joining this plot, had already received one million, paid by the Allied Princes, and that another million would be bestowed on him after the successful issue of the enterprise. Couthon accused Hébert, at the Tribunal of the Convention, for attempting to send a letter and a packet of fifty gold louis to the children of Capet, for the object of facilitating the escape of the Dauphin.

On the 5th April 1794, Danton was sent to the scaffold, with fourteen of his companions, for endeavouring to re-establish Royalty in France. Danton had established the Revolutionary Tribunal on the 5th July 1793; and this Tribunal, in conformity with a peculiar rule introduced by himself, had the right of commanding the accused to be silent when such silence suited the judges. When Danton was endeavouring to justify himself, the judges, and jurors, and members of the Committee, who were present watching the proceedings, being fearful that if Danton was allowed to continue his defence, the voice of the people might decide in his favour, they enforced the very law which Danton himself had so much contributed, in his popularity, to render effective—namely: that whenever prisoners had rebelled against the Tribunal, the trial might be closed at once by the summary condemnation of the mutinous parties. Thus Danton and his followers' doom were sealed as it were from the mouth of Danton himself.

On the 13th April 1794, Chaumette and Arthur Dillon, with nineteen others, were sent to the scaffold ;—the accusation brought against them, that of "the conspiracy of the prisons."

On April 22nd and June 17th, 1794, sixty-six persons perished on the scaffold ;—the crime of which they were accused, "that of attempting the re-establishment of Royalty." Alarm, embarrassment, and depression reigned triumphant. France was frantic. Terror was on all sides. Nobles, generals, clergy, citizens, and peasants, perished together. Anarchy was supreme ; commerce and progress at a stand-still ; France deserted by its ablest men ; no opinion tolerated which did not coincide with the Revolutionists. It was dangerous to utter an opinion. All was exaggeration.

On marched the reign of folly, and where would it have ended had not that heartless, unmerciful, and execrable horror " Robespierre," in company with several of his demoniac supporters, amongst whom was Simon, the once guardian of the Dauphin, ascended the scaffold, and forfeited their corrupt lives. Whilst popular they used their influence in creating insurrection and crime, instead of ennobling the cause and prestige of the Revolution and France. Their courage, audacious in authority, forsook them with their fortune. Imprecations and reproach followed them on their road to expiate their polemical follies, by that same multitude who had once apparently adored them. They had taught the people to systematically revile men, majesty, misfortune, and worth, and to cancel from their hearts pity, clemency, and justice. The day came when many of those excessive monsters of the Revolution experienced the wage of their fanatical delirium, and were themselves hailed with that brutal derision they had engendered whilst popular with the misguided populace. They saw their error and repulsive policy too late, and lived to see their once enthusiastic partisans become their most strenuous and implacable enemies.

On the 29th July 1794, Laurent, a member of the Revolutionary Committee of the Temple section, was appointed keeper of the imprisoned captives. On his repairing to the Temple on the evening of his appointment, the municipals received him in the Council-room, and it was not till two o'clock in the morning that they conducted him to the door of the captive's apartment. On reaching the door, and peering through the wicket into the dungeon, one of the municipals summoned the child; but no amount of threatening could make the captive rise from his miserable pallet to come to the wicket, and it was thus, at the wicket, by the light of a candle turned upon the incarcerated innocent, that the municipals presented the unfortunate captive to the charge of his new keeper.

Laurent, seeing the condition the child was in, and knowing the responsibility of his office, the next day addressed a request to the Committee of General Safety, that an examination should be made to ascertain the child's condition. His official request was attended to.

On the 31st July 1794, several members of the Committee of General Safety, accompanied by municipals, repaired to the Temple to examine into the state of the captive. On arriving at the door of his room, they called him, but he answered not; they then ordered the door to be opened, when one of the workmen attacked the bars of the wicket, which soon enabled him to put his head into the room. And seeing the unfortunate child, he asked him why he had not replied. The child still remained silent. The fastenings of the door were removed, and the visitors entered this deplorable kennel, which had contained the captive from January till July, when he was found all but dead, and in the most deplorable condition; and, as recorded by Beauchesne in his work of *Louis XVII.*, vol. ii. p. 224,

"his discoloured lips and hollow cheeks had a sort of greenish tinge, in their ghastly paleness, and his *blue eyes*, enlarged by the thinness of his face, but from which all brightness was gone, now that they no longer reflected the azure light of heaven, seemed to have taken a greyish, greenish, tint in their immobility; and his beautiful *fair hair*, once destined to wear the crown of France, was now, to the shame of France, given up to the attack of vermin."

Respecting the colour of the eyes and hair of the captive, we shall have occasion to comment thereon in a subsequent chapter.

Laurent appears to have behaved very kindly to his charge ; notwithstanding, the captive remained almost entirely silent.* The duties being too onerous, and he not desiring to have the entire responsibility of the captive, he complained several times to the Commissaries, and requested that the Committee of Public Safety would appoint in conjunction with him a colleague. In October, Laurent addressed himself directly to the Committee of Public Safety, when his request was granted. On the 8th November 1794, the Committee of Public Safety, on the presentation of the Administrative Committee of Police, selected citizen Gomin to be attached to the Temple.

"He entered on his duties the 9th November, when Laurent asked him 'if he had ever seen the Prince-Royal,' to which he replied, ' *I have never seen him.*' ' *In that case,' replied Laurent, ' it will be some time before he will say a word to you. The municipal on duty and his keepers had imperative injunctions not to permit the brother and sister meeting, or take their walks at the same time.*' "—Beauchesne's *Louis XVII.*, vol. ii. p. 239.

The following is the routine observed towards the prisoner of the Temple :—

"About nine o'clock every morning the two keepers and the Commissary usually went up together into the Dauphin's room, accompanied by Gourlet. The latter dressed the Prince, and while the child was at breakfast, made his bed, and swept the room, in presence of his superiors.

"The breakfast, consisting of a cup of milk, or of fruit, was brought in by Caron, the kitchen assistant.

"When the room was arranged, and he had taken his breakfast, *the Prince was left alone until dinner-time, that is, about two o'clock.* The keepers then went up again, accompanied by the new civic Commissary. The dinner consisted of soup, a small piece of boiled meat, and a plate of dry vegetables, usually lentils. *The child was then left alone till eight o'clock in the evening.*

"When the evening came, one of the keepers, generally Gomin,

* The condition of the prisoner of the Temple was ameliorated under Laurent's charge. Nevertheless, up to June 1795, the captive of the Temple was subjected to almost solitary confinement. For routine enforced at the Temple towards the captive see pp. 157 and 168, *Historical Records.*

went up with Caron or Gourlet to light the lamp, which was placed in the front room, and which lighted the bedroom through a glass window.

"Supper was brought at eight o'clock, and was the same with the dinner, except that there was no boiled meat. *After this the child was put to bed and left alone until nine o'clock next morning.*"—Beauchesne's *Louis XVII.*, vol. ii. p. 241.

"On the 14th November 1794, six days after Gomin's entrance into the Temple, there came a Commissary on duty named 'Delboy.' His manner was blunt, and his speech brief. He had everything opened for his examination, with almost brutal despatch, but under this disagreeable and arrogant outside, there was soon visible a certain elevation of sentiment, for he expressed his indignation at the conduct pursued towards the imprisoned captives; and when he saw the diet the captive boy was subjected to, he reproved his keepers by saying, 'Why this bad food? if they were at the Tuileries we might contend against them having any food, but here, in our own hands, we should show clemency towards them; the nation is generous.' 'Why exclude the light under the reign of equality, the sun shines for all, and they ought to be allowed their share of it?' '*Why prevent the children from seeing each other under the reign of fraternity?*' *Then addressing the child, he said, '* *Would you not, my boy, be very glad to go and play with your sister? I do not see why the nation should recollect your origin, if you forget it yourself.*' Then turning towards Laurent and Gomin, he said, 'It is not his fault that he is the son of his father; he is nothing but an unfortunate child, therefore do not be hard upon him; the unfortunate belong to humanity, and the country is the mother of all her children.' *But it had been expressly forbidden to allow of any meeting taking place between the children of Louis XVI. Mathieu had signified this prohibition in the most formal manner, and for this reason no notice was taken of the philosophizing Delboy. Since their separation on the 3rd July, and their meeting on the 7th October 1793, Madame Royale had not once seen her brother.*'—Beauchesne's *Louis XVII.*, vol. ii. pp. 243 and 245.

All were not as Delboy, for generally the municipals' hearts were incapable of the smallest degree of moderation or pity, for the sufferings of the captives.

Proposals were made to the Convention by foreign Powers, and the chiefs of the Royalist army of La Vendée, for the release of the children of Louis XVI.

"Several members of the Convention, who had not voted for the death of Louis XVI., were employed in carrying on negotiations with the chiefs of the Catholic and Royal Army. Le Chevalier de Charette and his brave companions in arms, lacking the most necessary war stores, skilfully profited by the overtures made by the Committees of the Convention, and concluded with them a treaty of peace—at least an armistice. Hostilities ceased, and at a stated period the young King and the Princess-Royal were to be given up to the Vendeans. Some people assert that shortly before the death of Louis XVII. the Committee of Public Safety had treated with the chiefs of La Vendée, and had engaged themselves to place the heir and his sister in their hands before the 15th June 1795 at the latest. These persons positively assert that M. Dessolteux, Baron de Cormatin, Major-General in the Catholic Royal army of Brittany, had the honourable mission to go to Paris for the children of Louis XVI."—Eckard's *Mémoires Historiques sur Louis XVII.*, p. 278.

"The published Articles of the Armistice stipulated that the Vendeans should be allowed the free exercise of the Catholic religion, that the sequestrations imposed on the estates of the insurgents should be taken off, and that the republican Government should reimburse notes to the amount of two million francs, mostly bearing the head of Louis XVII., which had been signed and circulated by the chiefs of the Royal army.

"At the conclusion of this suspension of arms, several chiefs of the Vendeans, having at their head the celebrated Chevalier de Charette, repaired to Nantes, where they assisted at the Assembly with their white cockades and their Royal uniforms. All was to remain thus until the secret articles, settled between the Vendeans and the deputies of the Committees, had been ratified by the Convention.

"These Articles stipulated, between other things, that Louis XVII., and Madame his noble sister, should be given up to the Catholic and Royal army of Vendée and Brittany, and that the re-establishment of the Catholic religion should be proclaimed in France before the 15th June."
—Eckard's *Mémoires Historiques sur Louis XVII.*, p. 435 ; likewise, Beauchesne's *Louis XVII.*, vol. ii. pp. 303 and 367 ; and Hue's *Last Years of the Reign and Life of Louis XVI.*, p. 501.

Spain had demanded the liberation of the prisoners of the Temple as the preliminary condition of peace. Simonin, a Government commissary, who had been sent to Madrid to treat for an exchange of prisoners, had listened to the following proposals, which he transmitted to the Government :—

"The King of Spain is disposed to treat of peace on the following terms :—1st, Spain will recognise the French republic. 2nd, France will give up the children of Louis XVI. to his Catholic Majesty. 3rd, The French provinces bordering on Spain will form an independent State for the son of Louis XVI., which he will govern as King of Navarre."

The Committee of Public Safety immediately recalled that agent in the following terms : — "Simonin to be recalled instantly ; he compromises the dignity of the French people."

When the Government, on the 22nd January 1795, resolved to retain the rallying-point and the hope of the Royalists in their custody, fearing there would be much to be apprehended were they to set the imprisoned children at liberty.

The captive boy's health becoming in an extremely dangerous state, " a municipal, who was a surgeon, and had been employed to attend the young invalid, made a report to the Council of the Commune respecting his condition, and they judged it expedient to acquaint the authorities. On the 26th of February, several civic Commissaries repaired to the Council of General Safety to inform them of the danger of the prisoner's life. Upon being interrogated as to the nature of the danger, the municipals replied, ' that little Capet had swellings at all joints, particularly at his knees, *and that it was impossible to extract a word from him;* and that always, either sitting or in a recumbent position, he steadily refused to take any sort of exercise.' Upon being interrogated as to the period from which this obstinate silence and systematic inactivity might be dated, they answered, ' *Ever since the 6th October* 1793, *that day of disgraceful memory, when Simon had induced the son of Marie Antoinette to sign the horrible interrogatory invented by Hébert.*'"—Beauchesne's *Louis XVII.*, vol. ii. p. 264.

The Committee of General Safety directed Harmand "of the Meuse," one of its members, who was attached to the police section of Paris, to proceed to the Temple, with two of his colleagues, and satisfy himself as to the real state of the case, and make out a detailed report of everything relating to the imprisoned child.

The next day, " 27th February," the Commissaries, Messrs. Harmand, Mathieu, and Reverchon, repaired to the Temple to see the suffering captive. The following is M. Harmand's published report of this visit :—

"We arrived at the doors, the bolts of which confined the innocent boy, the only son of our King—our King himself. The key turned with a grating noise in the lock, and on the door being opened, we discovered a small anteroom, perfectly clean, with no other furniture in it but an earthenware stove, communicating by an opening in the wall with the adjoining room, and which stove could be lighted only in the anteroom. The Commissaries observed to us that this precaution had been taken in order not to leave a fire in power of a child.

"The room so adjoining was the Prince's chamber, containing his bed; the door was fastened on the outside, and we had again to wait for its being opened. These sounds of locks and bolts inspired a gloom, the more painful from being increased rather than dispelled by reflection.

"The Prince was sitting near a small square table, on which were scattered a number of playing cards, some turned up into the shapes of trunks and boxes, and others raised into houses. He was occupied with these cards when we entered, and did not leave off his play. He had on a sailor's dress, new, and made of slate-coloured cloth; his head was uncovered, and the room was clean and well lighted. The bed was a small wooden one, without curtains, and the bedding and linen seemed to us to be good, and of a fine quality. The bed was behind the door, on the left hand on going in, and farther on the same side was another bedstead without bedding, placed at the foot of the first. Between them there was a door which was shut, leading into another apartment, which we did not see. The Commissaries told us that the second bed had been that of the shoemaker Simon.

"After having become acquainted with these preliminary details I approached the Prince, but our motions did not appear to make any impression upon him. I told him that the Government, informed too late of the bad state of his health, and of his refusal to take exercise, or to answer the questions put to him upon that subject, as well as his rejecting the proposals made to him to take some remedies, and to receive the visit of a physician, had sent us to him to ascertain these facts, and, in its name, to renew all those proposals; that we hoped they would be agreeable to him, but that we should take upon ourselves to offer him advice, and even to add reproaches, if he should persist in remaining silent, and in not taking exercise; that we were authorized to

L

offer him such objects of diversion or recreation as he might desire; and that I requested he would tell me whether that pleased him.

"*While I was thus addressing him he looked at me steadfastly without any change of position, and he listened to me apparently with the greatest attention, but not one word in reply.*

"I then began afresh my proposals, as conceiving that he had not understood me, and I detailed them pretty nearly in these words :—

"'I have perhaps explained myself badly, or perhaps you have not understood me, Sir.   I have the honour to ask whether you wish for a horse, a dog, birds, toys of any kind whatever ; or one or more companions of your own age, whom we will present to you previously to their being permanently attached to you ? Will you, at the present moment, go down into the garden, or ascend the turrets ? Do you wish for sweetmeats, cakes, etc. ?'

"I exhausted in vain the list of all the things that are usually wished for by children of his age. *I did not receive a word of answer, not even a word or a motion, although his face was turned towards me, and he looked at me with an amazing fixedness, denoting the most utter indifference.*

"I then took upon me to assume a more decided tone, and I ventured to say to him, 'Sir, so much obstinacy at your age is a fault that nothing can excuse. It is the more surprising, since our visit, as you must perceive, has for its object the affording some relief to your situation, some attentions and succours to your health. How can we attain this object if you persist in refusing to answer, and to say what is agreeable to you? Is there any other way of making the proposal? Have the goodness to state it, and we shall adopt it.'

"*Still the same fixed look and the same attention, but not a word.* I resumed :—

"'If your refusal to speak, Sir, involved none but yourself, we would wait, not without pain, but with more patience, until you might be pleased to speak, as we must conclude that your situation is less displeasing to you than we imagined, since you will not change it ; but you do not belong to yourself, all those about you are responsible for your person and your condition. Do you wish that we ourselves should be blamed ? For what answer can we give to the Government, of which we are only the delegates ? Have the goodness to answer me, I entreat you, or we must finish by commanding you.'

"*Not a word, and always the same fixedness.* I was in despair, as well as my colleagues ; that look had especially so strong a feature of resignation and indifference that it seemed to say, '*What does it matter to me? Despatch your victim.*'

" I could bear no more ; my heart was full, and I was near giving way to tears of the bitterest grief, but some steps which I took about the room recovered me, and I resolved to try the effect of a tone of command. I tried it accordingly, placing myself close, on the Prince's right hand, and saying to him, ' Give me your hand.' He gave it me ; and extending mine up to his arm-pit I felt a swelling at the wrist, and one at the elbow. It seems that these swellings were not painful, for the Prince gave no sign of their being so.

" ' The other hand.' He gave it me likewise, but there was nothing.

" ' Allow me to touch your legs and knees.' He rose, and I found the same swellings under both knees.

" In this position the young Prince had the appearance of rickets and a bad formation. His legs and thighs were long and thin, his arms the same ; his neck short, his chest raised, his shoulders high and narrow ; his head was in every respect finely formed, and beautiful ; his complexion clear, but without colour ; *his hair long and handsome, well kept, and of a light chesnut colour.*

" ' Now, have the goodness to walk.' He did so immediately, going towards the door, and returning at once to his seat.

" ' Do you think, Sir, that that is exercise ? And do you not perceive, on the contrary, that this apathy is alone the cause of your ill-health, and of the disorders with which you are threatened ? Pray believe in our experience and regard for you. You cannot hope to recover your health but by attending to our proposals and advice. We will send you a physician, and we trust that you will consent to answer him ; at least make us a sign that it will not be disagreeable to you.'

" *Not a sign, not a word.*

" ' Be so good, Sir, as to walk again, and for a little longer time.'

" *Silence and refusal. He remained on his seat, his elbows resting on the table; his features did not change for an instant, not the least motion apparent, not the least mark of surprise in the eyes ; just as if we had not been present, and as if I had not spoken.* I must observe that my colleagues said nothing.

" We looked at each other in amazement, and we were advancing towards each other to exchange our reflections, when the Prince's dinner was brought.

" A new scene of grief,—it should have been seen and felt to be believed.

" A porringer of red earthenware contained a black soup, on the top of which floated a few lentils, and on a plate of the same material lay a small bit of boiled meat, also black and shrivelled, the bad quality of which was sufficiently apparent. There was a second plate of lentils, and a third, in which were six chesnuts, rather burnt than roasted, a pewter fork, but no knife. The Commissaries told us that this was by order of the Council of the Commune. And there was no wine.

"Such was the dinner of Louis XVII., of the successor to so many kings ; and such was the treatment suffered by innocence.

"Whilst the illustrious prisoner was eating this shameful meal, my colleagues and myself expressed by our looks to the Commissioners of the Municipality our astonishment and indignation ; and in order to spare them, in the Prince's presence, the reproaches they deserved, I made them a sign to come into the anteroom. There we explained our sentiments, but they repeated that it was the order of the municipality, and that it was worse before their time. We ordered that this execrable system should be changed for the future, and that they should begin that moment to improve his dinner, and particularly to give him some fruit. I desired that grapes, which were then scarce, should be procured for him.

"Having given these orders we went back into the room, and found that he had eaten everything. I asked him whether he was satisfied with his dinner ?

"*No answer.* Whether he wished for some fruit ? *No answer.* Whether he liked grapes ? *No answer.*

"Shortly after the grapes were brought they were placed on the table, and he ate them without speaking.

"'Do you wish for more ? ' *No answer.*

"We could then no longer doubt that every effort on our part to induce him to speak would be useless. I told him the conclusion we had come to, and I said to him that it was the more painful to us, as we could attribute his silence towards us only to our having had the misfortune to displease him. I added, that we should in consequence propose to the Government to send other Commissioners who might be more agreeable to him.

"*The same look, but no reply.* 'Do you wish, Sir, that we should withdraw ?' *No answer.*

"After these words we retired. I have stated that the motive to which the Commissaries attributed the obstinate silence of the Prince, was his having been forced by Simon to give evidence against his mother and his aunt. *I inquired of them in the anteroom, whether that silence really began on the day upon which that atrocious violence had compelled him to sign the odious and absurd deposition against the Queen. They repeated their assertions on that point, and protested that the Prince had not spoken since the evening of that day.*

"My colleagues and I agreed that for the honour of the nation, which was ignorant of these unhappy circumstances—for that of the Convention, which indeed knew them not, but which ought to have known them, and for that even of the criminal Municipality of Paris, which knew all, and which caused all these evils—we should confine ourselves to the ordering some steps of temporary alleviation 'which were immediately carried into effect;' and *that we should not make a report in public, but in a secret committee,* and it was so done."— Harmand's Report. †

After the authorities heard the report of the Commissioners, no physician was employed to endeavour to restore or alleviate the condition of the suffering captive. Harmand, a few days after his visit to the Temple, was sent from Paris on a mission to the Armies, which hindered him from seeing adopted the measures he had recommended to improve the state of the neglected captive of the Temple.

Doubtless the authorities sent him away from Paris on account of his report, and the measures he had recommended, for they did not desire to ameliorate the condition of their prisoner, as they had resolved on his death.

---

* This accounts for the extraordinary circumstances stated in this report being only to be found in M. Harmand's publication.

† John Baptiste Harmand, one of the Commissioners of the Convention appointed to inquire into the state of the son of Louis XVI.

Few men in the Revolution have suffered greater vicissitudes of fortune than J. B. Harmand. He was of a respectable family, and an advocate at bar before the Revolution. In 1792 he was elected to the Convention, where he voted for the exile of the King, which was equivalent, under the circumstances, to a vote of acquittal. Though he sat on the Mountain, he was really a Modéré, not to say a Royalist. After the fall of Robespierre he became a member of the Committee of Public Safety, in which capacity he made an official visit to the prisoner of the Temple.

Harmand became a member of the Council of Ancients, and secretary of that body; he was afterwards elected to the Council of Five Hundred, and when the accession of Bonaparte began to produce a regular Government, M. Harmand was appointed Prefect of a Department, and created successively a Member of the Legion of Honour and a Baron of the Empire. He, however, does not seem to have been a more cordial partisan of the Usurpation than he was of the Revolution, for he seems to have been deprived of his Prefecture and reduced to an obscure and severe, but not dishonourable poverty. In 1814 he published a pamphlet on the treatment of the Royal Family in the Temple, from which his visit to the captive is an extract. Towards the end of 1815, this man, who had sat in all the Legislatures of regenerated France, was found, in December 1815, starving of cold and hunger in the streets of Paris, and lived only to be conveyed to the public hospital.

Laurent resigned his position as keeper of the captive, and on Sunday, 30th March 1795, he quitted the Temple.

On Monday the 31st March 1795, Etienne Lasne was informed of his nomination as keeper of the Temple captive by a message from the Police, and as he did not immediately obey the order by repairing to the Temple, two gendarmes proceeded to his residence, and conducted him to his new occupation.

"After Lasne enters on his duties, he reports he had not been able to extract *a single word from the Dauphin during three weeks he had been at the Temple.*"—Beauchesne's *Louis XVII.*, vol. ii. p. 294.

The captive became worse and worse in health, and the keepers wrote on the register, "Little Capet is unwell." No notice was taken of this. The next day they wrote, "Little Capet is dangerously ill," which was still unheeded. They then added, "It is feared he will not live."

On Wednesday 7th May 1795, three days after their first report, they were informed of the decision of the authorities, who appointed M. Desault to attend the captive. On Desault arriving at the Temple, after having written down his name, he was admitted to see the captive. He made a long and attentive examination of the unfortunate invalid, whom he considered attacked with the germ of a scrofulous affection. *He asked the captive many questions, without being able to obtain an answer from him,* and without giving an opinion as to the captive's state before the Commissaries, he left the Temple.

He did all in his power to recruit the health of his unfortunate patient, and proposed to the authorities that he should be removed from the Temple to the country, where he thought the healthy air, together with assiduous treatment, and constant care, might possibly succeed in prolonging his life.

This advice on the part of the physician met with no attention. "*It is stated that he did not recognise in his patient of the Temple the Dauphin, but a substitute who was enacting the Dauphin's part, which discovery he disclosed to the apothecary Choppart.*"

On the 30th May, Desault visited his patient, when the doctor was
well in health.   The next morning, at the hour he should have arrived
to attend the captive, he did not come to the Temple.   The Commissary for the 31st May was Bellanger, an artist, who remained with the
captive alone, awaiting the arrival of Desault.   On the 1st June, Desault again failed to attend at the Temple, and on the 2nd June, when the
Commissary for the day arrived at the Temple, and hearing the keepers
of the captive express their astonishment, that Desault did not come to
attend his patient, he informed them that Desault was no more, he
having died on the 1st June.   Consequently, there were six days that the
invalid was without medical treatment, as a surgeon did not attend the
young sufferer till the 5th June, his guardians in the interim being his
two keepers, and the Commissary for the day.

It is asserted that the authorities caused the assassinations of the
physician Desault and the apothecary Choppart, who both died suddenly, and within four days of each other, whilst the captive was under
their medical treatment.   The reason assigned for the authorities in-
stigating such, was on account of Desault having expressed himself,
that the captive he was attending in the Temple *was not the Dauphin*,
and that they, in fear of being denounced, caused the medical men's
death, as they could not rely on their silence.*

There seems something very mysterious connected with this strange
coincidence, which we shall point out in the proper place.

No notes were found, "we should say, not made public," amongst
Desault's papers, respecting his attendance on the captive.

The Princess-Royal again and again supplicated the authorities to
permit her to see and attend her brother during his illness, but with no

---

* The following may be read in a pamphlet published in 1831, by M. Labreli de
Fontaine, formerly librarian to the late Duchess Dowager of Orleans :—

" M. Abeillé, medical pupil under Dr. Desault at the time of his violent death,
declared to whoever would hear it, in France, and in the United States, where he
has since sought refuge, that the death of that doctor immediately followed the report
which he made, to the effect, that the child to whom they had introduced him in
the Temple, was not the Dauphin, whom he knew perfectly well. *The American
Bee*, edited by M. Chaudron, mentions this fact in an article inserted in 1817."

avail ; the order was imperative, that no meeting, under any pretence, should be allowed to take place ; the reason is conclusive why the order was so.

" The Dauphin's state grew more and more alarming. The affection of Madame Royale for him increased. One might have said that she guessed his danger. She was continually questioning the keepers and commissaries without being able to obtain anything from them but vague words, which, though intended to reassure her, only alarmed her the more. Her entreaties to see her brother, and to be allowed to nurse him, were always refused."—Beauchesne's *Louis XVII.*, vol. ii. p. 307.

Monsieur Hue, formerly valet-de-chambre to Louis xvi., thus writes respecting his petition to be allowed to attend the captive of the Temple :—

" Being informed of the declining state of Louis xvii., I petitioned the Committee of General Safety as a favour to be allowed to shut myself up again with the Prince to take care of him. My prayer was rejected, on pretence that the Commissioners of the Temple took care of him."—Hue's *Last Years of the Reign and Life of Louis XVI.*, p. 501.

On the 5th June, M. Pelletan, head surgeon of the Grand Hospice de l'Humanité, was appointed by the Committee of General Safety to continue the medical treatment of the son of Louis.

He went to visit his patient at five in the afternoon. He was entirely (so it is stated) unacquainted with the Dauphin. He found the captive in a most distressing condition, that he demanded instantly the co-operation of another member of the profession, as he did not wish to bear such responsibility alone, and desired that the captive might be removed into *another room where light and air was.* His request was attended to.

On the 7th June, M. Dumangin, chief physician of the Hôpital de l'Unité, was appointed to attend the captive in conjunction with M. Pelletan. They both repaired to the Temple to see their patient, and saw that his death was inevitable. *They expressed their astonishment at the solitary state in which the captive was left during the night and part of* *the day*, and strongly insisted in their bulletin that the captive should be allowed a nurse to attend him.*

The Committee next day complied with this request, but, alas ! poor child, this day was his last, as he passed from the power of his tormentors ; and, according to the testimony of Etienne Lasne, "his last keeper," the captive Prince died in his arms at half-past two in the forenoon of the 8th June 1795 ; and upon visiting his lifeless prisoner, at his supper hour, he says :—

"*His eyes, which, while suffering, had half closed, were then open, and shone as pure as the blue heaven, and his beautiful fair hair fell like a frame around his face.*"—Beauchesne's *Louis XVII.*, vol. ii. p. 324.

According to the testimony of the guardians of the captive, " Gomin and Lasne," as recorded in M. Beauchesne's *Louis XVII.*, an entire change takes place in the manner of the captive after the death of the physician M. Desault, for up to the entrance of M. Bellanger, the acting Commissary at the Temple, the 31st May, "the first day M. Desault missed attending the captive," it had been impossible to elicit any word or conversation from the imprisoned invalid (M. Harmand's report likewise testifies this systematic silence), but, subsequent to the entrance of M. Bellanger at the Temple, "the 31st May," the captive, who had hitherto been dumb, and who had an aversion to strangers, all of a sudden finds his tongue, and instead of waiting to be spoken to, he at once begins to converse with the strange physicians.

This will be commented on hereafter, which may throw some light on the mysterious movements surrounding the imprisoned captive.

The captive's death is attested to in the following extraordinary manner :—

"We, the undersigned, Jean-Baptiste-Eégenie Dumangin, head physician of the Grand Hospice de l'Unité, and Philippe-Jean Pelletan, head surgeon of the Hospice de l'Humanité, assisted by citizens

---

* For description of the lonely condition to which the captive of the Temple was subjected, see page 157, *Historical Records*.

Nicolas Jeanroy, professor in the medical schools of Paris, and Pierre Lassus, professor of legal medicine in the École de Santé of Paris, whom we associated with ourselves, in obedience to a decree of the Committee of General Safety of the National Convention, dated yesterday, and signed Bergoing, president, Courtois, Gauthier, Pierre Guyomard, for the purpose of proceeding together to examine the body of the son of the late Louis Capet, and verifying its state, have acted as follows :—

"Having, all four, arrived at eleven o'clock A.M. at the outer gate of the Temple, we were received there by the Commissaries, who admitted us into the Tower. On attaining the second floor, we found, on a bed —in the second a suite of rooms there,—the dead body of a child, apparently about ten years old, *which the Commissaries declared to be that of the son of the late Louis Capet, and which two of our number recognised as that of the child they had been attending for several days. The said Commissaries declared to us that this child had expired at about three o'clock P.M. the day before*, on which we proceeded to seek for the signs of death, which we found in the general paleness and coldness of the entire body, etc. etc.

"This report was made and closed at Paris, in the above-mentioned place, by the undersigned, at half-past four P.M., above-named day and year.

"J. B. E. DUMANGIN, P. J. PELLETAN, P. LASSUS, N. JEANROY."

The remains of the captive were interred, or were reported such, in the cemetery of Saint Marguerite, on the night of the 10th June. No persons were allowed in the grounds but the authorities. "Mystery was the watchword, and strict watch was kept over the resting-place of this unfortunate child, till no trace was visible where he had been interred."

The Princess-Royal had not seen her brother since October 1793, therefore it was no more difficult for her to believe in his death than in that of her mother, Marie Antoinette, and her aunt, Madame Elizabeth, as she was informed from the same channel of all that had befallen her relatives ; thus the same tongue pronouncing her "motherless, brotherless, and that of her martyred aunt, the devoted Elizabeth, long after those sad events had taken place." Therefore it was no more difficult for her to believe one than the other. Sad indeed, was such deplorable news to fall on the ears of a young, persecuted, and imprisoned daughter of France, and pitiless were the times that had occasioned such.

The Princess now alone remained in the Temple. Negotiations were ratified between Austria and France for an exchange of prisoners, the result being that the Princess regained her liberation from the Temple at midnight on the 19th December 1795, and repaired by coach *en route* for Vienna, thus escaping from the power of the heartless oppressors of the family.

Having reached that period of French History which is connected with our late father's Memoirs, we will now comment on his work, and on the preceding Historical Records, and then leave it to public opinion to decide whether the Dauphin died in the Temple, or escaped therefrom.

END OF THE HISTORICAL RECORDS.

IV.

EVIDENCES OF THE MEMOIRS REVIEWED.

MRS. MEVES.

IT is seen, antecedent to the demise of Mr. William Schroëder Meves, that both Mr. and Mrs. Meves had never alluded in any way that our father was the Dauphin, for they had done all in their power, if his thoughts reverted to circumstances of his youth, to quell suspicion, or to give him the slightest clue which may have brought any light on his real origin ; and it was not till after the decease of Mr. William Schroëder Meves, and on his will being read, wherein he designates him as his natural reputed son, that makes Mrs. Meves make the declaration that our father was not her son, but the son of Marie Antoinette, Queen of France.   Unquestionably, no person could have known better than herself, whether she was addressing her own son, or the son of another person.

It is seen, page 41, in the Memoirs, that Marianne Crowley was educated at the convent of Saint Omer, and on her return to her father's at Bath, she studied music under a Mr. Linley.   In 1777, she went to London, and studied music under Signor Sacchini, " the cele-brated Italian composer ;" * and whilst there, pursuing her studies, her

* See Appendix, Note G—Mrs. Crowley's letter to her daughter in London in January 1777, thereby showing that Miss Crowley was residing in London during Signor Sacchini's *séjour* in England.

mother died. Mr. Crowley then took his daughter to Paris for the purpose of placing her in a convent. Whilst in Paris, it appears that a certain Mr. Franks (a page appointed to attend at the King's, " Louis XVI.," writing-table), who was acquainted with Mr. Cornelius Crowley, states that he saw Mr. Crowley in Paris, with his daughter, Mr. Crowley having come there for the purpose of placing her in a convent.

There can be no doubt but Miss Crowley was in Paris for this purpose, for the note of the Abbess, directed to " Miss Crowley, at Madame Gregson's, La Rue Dauphine, Paris " (see *Memoirs*, page 41), decides positively that it was so.

Admitting Mr. Franks filled the functions at the Court of France, as stated in his evidence, and of his acquaintance with Miss Crowley, who he states was afterwards in the service of the Queen, she having obtained her admission into the service of Marie Antoinette, through the influence of Signor Sacchini, whose pupil Miss Crowley had formerly been in London, and he, knowing her qualifications, had procured her an appointment.

This seems highly feasible, for Signor Sacchini held a high position as a maestro of music, his operas being played at Versailles, under the patronage of the Queen, therefore, his recommendation could have obtained all that Mr. Franks has stated.*

* Signor Sacchini, a celebrated Italian composer, born in 1735 at Naples, studied under Durante at the Conservatory of Saint Onofrio, in that capital. On quitting this seminary he soon raised himself into notice, and in 1762 obtained an engagement as composer to the principal theatre in Rome. This situation he filled about seven years, when he proceeded to Venice, and in 1769, succeeded Galuppi in the superintendence of the Conservatory of l'Ospedaletto. In 1772 he came to England, where he remained nine years. His dramatic works, amounting to seventy-eight in number in 1778, and his superior talents, were acknowledged, but a cabal was formed against him through jealousy of his superior abilities, and in the summer of 1781, Sacchini went for the first time to Paris, where he was almost adored. In 1782 he returned to London, and in 1784 he took a final leave of England and settled in Paris, where he not only obtained a pension from the Queen of France, but the theatrical pension, in consequence of three successful pieces. In 1786 this talented musician died in Paris, and was honoured with a public funeral, and with every mark of respect and distinction which sensibility and gratitude could bestow on a person who had contributed so largely to the public pleasures."

Thus, then, Miss Crowley's, "Mrs. Meves'," appointment in the service of Marie Antoinette was apparently attributable to the influence of Signor Sacchini. Mr. Crowley's letter to his daughter in Paris, in 1781, shows that his daughter was at Paris at this period. In the postscript he writes :—"If it is the will of God that I should survive this illness, I will return along with you to France," etc.—*Memoirs,* p. 42.

Respecting the statement of Mrs. Meves, that Mr. Meves, at the hazard of his life, had made the Queen a promise, whilst she was incarcerated in the Conciergerie, regarding the Dauphin, which he kept to the latest hour of his existence—this promise assuredly was, never to let the son of Marie Antoinette know his real origin.

The likelihood of Mr. Meves parting with his son, and placing him in the Temple as a substitute of the Dauphin, and of bringing the Dauphin to England and adopting him as Augustus Meves, seems, at first, a very improbable resolution. This we shall endeavour to explain.

The decease of Mr. Crowley in England brings his daughter from Paris to England to administer to his effects.

Subsequent to Miss Crowley's arrival in England she became acquainted, whilst residing at Lady Harrington's, with Mr. Meves, in the year 1783. It was supposed Miss Crowley had been privately married to Mr. Meves. After which, she quitted England and returned to Paris, in 1784, as a married lady, and re-entered the Queen's service, and was known there by the name of Madame de Courville Chroeder.

Mrs. Meves gives birth to a son on the 16th February 1785, which son is brought to England to be baptized, in order to guarantee to him the right of inheriting landed property, as Mrs. Meves's sister, Mrs. Davenport, possessed much landed property, and she having no issue, the probability was, that he would be heir to her property.

In March 1785 the Queen of France gave birth to a son, the Duke of Normandy. Mrs. Meves in 1818, and again before her decease, assured the subject of the present Memoirs that he was in reality this same Duke of Normandy, and that he had been intrusted to her care in infancy, and that she had been more than a mother to him, and telling him by what means to make himself known to the Duchess of Angoulême, namely, " a cicatrice on his left instep," * as this would be a convincing proof to the Duchess in recognising him. This, then, points out her connexion with the Court, and accounts for the interest of both her and Mr. Meves in the affairs of the Royal Family of France.

Respecting Mr. Meves taking his son Augustus to Paris, with the idea of placing him in the Temple and of extricating the Dauphin, this seems assuredly an unnatural course for a father to adopt : this we admit, and the only reason we can account for his having done so is, " that Augustus Meves appears to have been, from the evidences of the Memoirs, an illegitimate child." We must state our reasons for inferring such. Did we consult our own feelings we should omit doing so, but our duty is to unveil this mystery, howsoever unpleasant the task may be.

After the supposed marriage of Miss Crowley and Mr. Meves, it is seen Miss Crowley adopts the name of Madame Schroëder, being the family name on the mother's side of Mr. Meves. After the birth of a daughter, " Cecilia Meves," according to the evidence of George Meves, a separation, or something similar, took place. Mrs. Meves has the care of her daughter, and Mr. Meves that of his son. Subsequently they always seem to be living apart, for right through the evidences of the Memoirs there is no one place where they appear to be living together as husband and wife, for each, although residing in England at the same time, appear to have lived at different residences ; now, whatever was the occasion for such we know not.† A sister of Mrs. Meves had married a Mr. Blithe of Broseley Hall, Shropshire, and upon the decease of Mr. Blithe she inherited his property, and

---

* See Medical Certificates, Appendix, Note A.
† See Appendix, Note M, for letter from Mrs. Meves to Mr. Meves.

afterwards married a Mr. Davenport of Davenport House, Shropshire.

Upon Mrs. Davenport learning her sister Marianne had formed a connexion with Mr. Meves, and was the mother of two children, she was much displeased, and curtailed an annuity she had hitherto allowed her from £200 a year to £40. Apparently this reduction was on account of her not being thoroughly convinced of her sister's marriage, for when requested, Marianne would not show her marriage certificate.

In Mrs. Spence's evidence it is seen a marriage was contemplated between Miss Crowley—" Mrs. Meves "—and Mr. Meves, according to the ritual of the Protestant Church, in order to please Mrs. Davenport, and the letter subjoined to the Commentary * seems, by its tenor, to allude to something of such a nature, the handwriting being that of Mr. Meves. Whether such was carried into effect, or ended with contemplating, we know not. However, it appears Mrs. Davenport subsequently augmented the allowance to her sister to £100 a year (see *Memoirs*, page 47).

On the widow Mrs. Blithe's marriage with Mr. Davenport, it is seen she sold the Whiteley estates to pay off a mortgage of £7000 on the Broseley estates. The sale realized £10,000. The surplus, £3000, Mrs. Davenport placed on mortgage on Mr. Davenport's estates, over which Mr. Davenport had no power, likewise over £200 a year pin-money. Subsequently she called in £1000 from the £3000, and invested such in East India Bonds.

Subsequently a disagreement took place between Mr. and Mrs. Davenport respecting the coal and iron mines, which being out of lease, she desired Mr. Davenport to let them for their lives to a Mr. Harries, her adopted heir to the property. Mr. Davenport objected to this proposal, as it would have been against the interest of Harries, her adopted heir, to work the mines like a person whose sole interest was in embracing every possible advantage in well working the mines, during the time of his tenure. Therefore, as a great deal of money would

* See Appendix, Note X, for letter referred to.

accrue to Mr. Davenport by the mines being well worked, he thought it highly detrimental to acquiesce in Mrs. Davenport's proposal. The issue of this was, that a misunderstanding arose between them, which ended in Mrs. Davenport altering her will, and she left all she possibly could to Harries, her heir by appointment.

Mrs. Davenport died without issue, and her property came to her adopted heir "Harries." She left £1000 to each of her sister's children, Augustus, and Cecilia Meves.

Whether Mrs. Davenport's wishes were unattended to by her sister and Mr. Meves, that remains undecided, but it seems Mrs. Davenport had no satisfactory proof in concluding that the marriage of her sister was *bonâ fide.* The question then is: was Augustus Meves an offspring of legitimate wedlock, or no? and if not, would this account for Mr. Meves parting with his son in order to extricate the Dauphin from the Temple?

The question may be asked, can you account for your father not asking, even insisting, upon receiving more information from Mrs. Meves, than the statement at the reading of the will in 1818, and the similar one in 1823? The following is the answer:—

After the disclosure of Mrs. Meves in 1818, her reputed son, much against her own wish and that of the family, and likewise those who had been professionally employed to attend the late Mr. William Meves, had the body disinterred, in order to have a minute examination made, as he was not satisfied as to the real cause of his death. The fatigue and anxiety he underwent consequent on this resolution, together with the revelation of Mrs. Meves, brought him into a nervous state, when he called in medical advice, as he thought a composing-draught and quietness would soon restore him ; but, unfortunately for him, he was prescribed for incautiously, and the medicine instead of giving him relief flew to the brain, the consequence of which was, that it laid him on a bed of sickness for some time. He was placed in hands, as he has explained, from whom he received abominable treatment. All supplication on his part was unheeded by those under whose immediate care he was placed. He remained in this state for some time, and upon his convalescence, Mrs. Meves closed her lips on this subject until 1823, when she again reiterated his true origin.

Had not such a revelation come from Mrs. Meves, and had not his reputed father so strangely alluded to him in his will, he would never had thought to have had such an examination; but different ideas entered his head, and even lent import to the remark of the searchers; but certainly the only real import that can be attached to their remark is, their endeavour to ingratiate themselves into his favour, in the hope of receiving pecuniary consideration. Thus, then, this illness after the reading of Mr. William Meves's will was caused unquestionably directly through the revelation of Mrs. Meves, for that unsettled him, together with the excitement he consequently underwent in ascertaining precisely and conclusively the cause of his reputed father's demise. Therefore, his determinate resolution was compatible, when the circumstances are considered which gave rise to the course he adopted.

Certainly what Mrs. Meves revealed intrinsically was a substantial basis to work from, but it was insufficient testimony to guarantee it solely on such a revelation. Had she felt inclined, doubtless she could have made it more than clear, but apparently she was disinclined to reveal further information on this point, possibly on account of the suffering her revelation had already caused her reputed son.

Many may remark, had they been placed in similar circumstances, the result would have been different; that is, from 1818 to 1823 they would have gained more information, howsoever disinclined Mrs. Meves would have been to give it. Those who read have the advantage to accumulate without much trouble the experience of those who have worked. Had they been the actual working party, and similarly positioned, they would have found their theories impracticable. Willingness alone on Mrs. Meves's part would have been the only inducement for her fully revealing the mystery surrounding her reputed son, and this willingness, it is seen, did not exist in Mrs. Meves.

Mrs. Meves's reputed son was of a sensitive disposition. He could not bring his feelings to be antagonistic to woman; he could not torment or persecute; he preferred to suffer rather than give pain; he was the essence of delicateness with woman; kindness found no tyrant in him; and upon Mrs. Meves he looked as one he ought never to give pain to. Gratitude is a virtue of inestimable value. If we possess it not, let us not condemn such.

It is apparent in his writing to the Duchess of Angoulême, how he had been misled by his reputed parents' misrepresentation as to time and place occurrences had happened to him. His errors have arisen solely from this source. As regards the cicatrice on his left instep,* this must have been characteristic of some incident happening to the Dauphin, and well known to the Royal Family; and the existence of such on our father must have been a more convincing fact in establishing to the Duchess's mind who in reality her correspondent was, much more so than the recapitulating recollections; for did the Dauphin receive such an incision on his left instep in his infancy, as Mrs. Meves stated, this must have been indisputable evidence to the Duchess. In his letters to the Duchess, which every reader we think will admit to be candid and upright on his part, the scar on his left instep is the only one he mentions, in conformity to the directions of his reputed mother.

We have every reason to conclude that the Duchess, long prior to Mrs. Meves's demise, knew perfectly well that our father was her brother, through the medium of Mrs. Meves.

Respecting what Mrs. Meves stated, that the Archbishop of Paris was aware of the liberation of the Dauphin from the Temple, and of the circumstance of his being conveyed to England, the plausibility of this is apparent, for after the restoration of Royalty in France, the head of the Gallican Church did not commemorate the annual obsequies in memory of Louis Charles the Dauphin that his birth demanded, which were celebrated in memory of the martyred King Louis XVI. Probably, the obstacle in the head of the French Church not openly recognising the existence of the Dauphin was, "that he was a Protestant;" therefore

* See Medical Certificates, Appendix, Note A.

there was a probability, had the Archbishop revealed the secret of the existence of the Dauphin, that possibly he may have raised a dangerous antagonist to the established faith; likewise, it was uncertain what might come to light in showing the Church were cognisant of the existence of Louis XVII., consequently the expiatory service was omitted.

Without a shadow of a doubt, the Historical Records prove the Dauphin's liberation from the Temple.

From some people it is impossible to gain any clue to a secret. which you know they possess; neither threats, violence, or death itself can induce them to alter their determination. Sometimes the secret is held in revenge, or from obstinacy, etc., and at other times from the oath of secrecy. And apparently Mr. William Meves's secret was held in observance of the latter, for, as Mrs. Meves said, "He made the Queen a promise in the Conciergerie, which he kept to the latest hour of his existence."

MRS. SPENCE, MRS. FISHER, AND MISS POWELL.

At the time our father received the communication from Mrs. Spence, Mrs. Fisher, and Miss Powell, respecting Mrs. Meves, he did not attach much importance to their information, on account of his not then seeing how intricately he was interwoven with such mysterious movements on the part of his supposed mother, and it was not till he had read the work that Dr. Riofrey Bureaud had presented him with, in the year 1835, entitled, *Les Evènements du Temple*, which contained M. Harmand's report respecting the captive the Convention delegated him, in company with two other commissioners, to visit at the Temple, and report upon,* that he was aware of the importance, and likewise the application of the evidence of Mrs. Spence, Mrs. Fisher, and Miss Powell.

In referring to Mrs. Spence's statement (page 48, Memoirs), it is seen

* See Harmand's Report, page 161 *Historical Records*.

whilst she was in the service of Mrs. Meves, in 1793, that a letter was sent from France to London by Tom Paine to a Mrs. Carpenter—"this lady was a friend of Mrs. Meves's,"—requesting that a deaf and dumb boy, of about eight years of age, should be brought to Paris for purposes he required. His wish could not be complied with, as a boy answering the description could not be found.

It seems a singular resolution on the part of Paine to have desired to adopt, if this deaf and dumb boy was really required by him in order to extricate the captive Prince from his imprisonment by such a substitution; nevertheless sufficient indication exists to warrant the conclusion that such in reality was the case, on account of what transpired subsequently in the Temple, of a deaf and dumb boy enacting there the part of the Dauphin.* As regards Paine writing such a letter as Mrs. Spence states, there is every probability of his having done so, with the intention as above attributed. Though Paine was an inveterate and inflexible foe to Royalty, or any form of government that was aristocratical or hereditary, his opinions, nevertheless, were that Louis XVI. was a good man, and meant well to his country, and had he been otherwise the Revolution would never have gained the acme it did—therefore in reality it was not against the integrity of the man, but the title of King, where his animosity was directed.

"It was not," says Paine, "against Louis XVI., but against the despotic principles of the Government, that the nation revolted. These principles had not their origin in him, but in the original establishment many centuries back, and these were become too deeply rooted to be removed, and the Augean stable of parasites and plunderers too abominably filthy to be cleansed by anything short of a complete and general Revolution. When it becomes necessary to do a thing, the whole heart and soul should go into the measure, or not attempt it. That crisis was then arrived, and there remained no choice but to act with determined vigour, or not to act at all. The King was known to be the friend of the nation, and this circumstance was favourable to the enterprise. Perhaps no man bred up in the style of an absolute King ever possessed a heart so little disposed for the exercise

* See Harmand's Report, page 161 *Historical Records.*

of that species of power as the present King of France, but the principles of the Government itself still remained the same. The monarch and the monarchy were distinct and separate things, and it was against the established despotism of the latter, and not against the person or principles of the former, that the revolt commenced, and the Revolution has been carried."—Paine's *Rights of Man*, p. 20.

When it is considered the aid Louis XVI. rendered to the Americans in gaining their independence, every patriot of America should honour his memory.   As Paine then was a stanch republican, could he not have been susceptible to some degree of mitigation for the sufferings of the imprisoned captive Dauphin, whose martyred father had given such signal proof of his sincerity for freedom, as it was in a great measure through the countenance Louis XVI. had given to the American struggle that its independence was realized, and by being susceptible to reforms in France, had caused his own overthrow?   Thus Lamartine writes of Tom Paine :—

"Thomas Paine, born in England, the apostle of American independence, the friend of Franklin, author of *Good Sense, The Rights of Man*, and the *Age of Reason*—three pages of the new evangelist, in which he had brought back political institutions and religious creeds to their primitive justness and lucidity.   His name possessed great weight among the innovators of the two worlds.   His reputation had naturalized him in France—for that nation, who thought, who combated not for herself alone, but for the whole universe, recognised as countrymen all those zealous in the cause of reason and liberty.   The patriotism of France, like that of religion, was not in the same language, or the approximation of frontiers, but in the fellowship of ideas.   Paine, the friend of Madame Roland, Condorcet, and Brissot, had been elected by the town of Calais.   The Girondists consulted him, and had placed him in the Comité de Surveillance.   Robespierre himself affected for the cosmopolite radicalism of Paine the respect of a neophyte for ideas that are but dim and indistinctly understood.   Paine had been loaded with favours by the King at the time when he had been sent to Paris to entreat succour from France for America, and Louis XVI. had given the nascent republic 6,000,000 francs (£250,000).   It was into the hands of Franklin and Paine that the King had confided this gift, and gratitude for past kindnesses should have sealed the lips of the philosopher, but he had neither the memory nor the dignity befitting his station.

Unable to express himself in French at the Tribune, he wrote and read to the Convention a letter, ignoble in its language as cruel in its intentions, a long series of insults, heaped, even in the depths of a dungeon, upon a man whose generous assistance he had formerly solicited, and to whom he owed the preservation of his own country. 'Considered as an individual, this man is unworthy the notice of the republic, but as an accomplice of the conspiracy against the people, you are bound to judge him,' said Paine. 'As regards inviolability, that must not be mentioned. Only look upon Louis XVI. as a man of limited abilities, badly brought up, like all kings, subject, it is said, to frequent fits of intemperance, and whom the Constituent Assembly would imprudently re-establish on a throne for which he was never fitted.'

"It was in these terms that the voice of America, freed by Louis XVI., resounded in the dungeons of that monarch. An American, a citizen, a philosopher, demanded, if not the life, at least the ignominy of the King who had sheltered with French bayonets the cradle of liberty of his country. Ingratitude expressed itself in outrages, and the philosopher degraded himself below despotism in the language of Paine. Madame Roland and her friends loudly applauded the republican rudeness of this act and these expressions, and the Convention unanimously voted the impression of this letter ; but public feeling was indignant—it was rather the world that should hate Louis XVI., than the apostle of America and the friend of Franklin."—Lamartine's *History of the Girondists*, vol. ii. page 284.

In referring to the Historical Records, page 107, it will be seen that Marat, Robespierre, and Danton were, to a certain degree, implicated, or cognisant of a plan to effect the Royal Family's escape from the Temple. Mirabeau, the firebrand orator and leader of the Revolutionary party, the foremost in striking at the power of the monarchy, whose eloquence had inflamed the masses against the monarchy, and hurried on the Revolution, who would suppose that such a man as this at last repaired secretly to nocturnal conferences with the King and Queen, and that he was profusely paid by the King, and allowed a monthly income from the Court, to undo what he himself had so greatly contributed to enforce ? The following account of Mirabeau will partially explain the above :—

"Since the month of February 1791, the King, who had the most entire confidence in the Marquis de Bouillé, had written to this general that he wished him to make overtures to Mirabeau, and through the intervention of the Count de Lamarck, a foreign nobleman, the intimate and confidential friend of Mirabeau. 'Although these persons are not over estimable,' said the King in his letter ; 'and although I have paid Mirabeau very dearly, I yet think he has it in his power to serve me. Hear all he has to say without putting yourself too much in his hands.'. The Count de Lamarck arrived soon after at Metz. He mentioned to the Marquis de Bouillé the object of his mission, confessed to him that the King had recently given Mirabeau 600,000 francs (£24,000), and that he also allowed him 50,000 francs a month. He then revealed to him the plan of his counter-revolutionary conspiracy, the first act of which was to be an address to Paris and the Departments demanding the liberty of the King. Everything in this scheme depended upon the rhetoric of Mirabeau. Carried away by his own eloquence, the salaried orator was ignorant that words, though all-powerful to excite, are yet impotent to appease. They urge nations forward, but nothing but the bayonet can arrest them. M. de Bouillé, a veteran soldier, smiled at these chimerical projects of the citizen orator ; but he did not, however, discourage him in his plans, and promised him his assistance. He wrote to the King to repay largely the desertion of Mirabeau. 'A clever scoundrel,' said he, 'who perhaps has it in his power to repair through cupidity the mischief he has done through revenge.'"—Lamartine's *History of the Girondists*, vol. i. p. 50.

"Mirabeau plainly perceived that his popularity was on the wane— not because his eloquence was less powerful, his arguments less cogent, his energy less commanding than when he reigned the lord of the ascendant, but because he no longer headed the popular movement, and now strove to master the passions he had excited among the people. The failure of the Duke of Orleans to take advantage of the revolt of the 6th October had entirely alienated him from that pusillanimous leader, and he sighed for the offices and favour of the Court. Already the cry had been heard in the streets : 'Grande trahison du Comte Mirabeau !' and the populace followed the career of less able but more reckless leaders. Disgusted with the fickleness of the multitude, and foreseeing the sanguinary excesses to which they were fast approaching, he had, since the beginning of February, made secret advances to the Constitutional party, and entered into correspondence with the King, for the purpose of restraining the further progress of the Revolution.*

* In the beginning of February he opened these communications by the following note to M. Malouet, one of the King's ministers :—" I follow more your advice than you think, and whatever opinion you may entertain of me, mine has been unalterable to you. It is time that sensible people should approach and understand each other.

He received for a short time a pension of 20,000 francs, or £800 a month, first from the Comte d'Artois, and afterwards from the King; but it was not continued till the time of his death, from its being found that he was not so pliant as the Court party expected. He was even honoured with a private interview with the Queen in the gardens of St. Cloud, who was with reason most anxious to secure his great abilities in defence of the throne.* Her fascinating manner secured his unsteady affections, while the Royal bounty provided the supplies for his extravagance. His style of life suddenly changed. Magnificent entertainments succeeded each other in endless profusion, and his house resembled rather the hotel of a powerful minister than that of the leader of a fierce democracy. Yet mere venality was not the motive for this great change. He allied himself to the Court, partly because he saw it was the only way to stop the progress of the Revolution. He took their pensions because he regarded himself as their minister to govern the Assembly; and he would have rejected with disdain any proposition to undertake what was unworthy of his character. His design was to support the throne and consolidate the constitution by putting a stop to the encroachments of the people. With this view, he proposed to establish in reality, and not in name, the Royal authority, to dissolve the Assembly, and re-assemble a new one, restore the nobility, and form a constitution as nearly as possible on the English model—a wise and generous object, entertained at different times by all the best friends of freedom in France, but which none were able to accomplish, from the flight of the great and powerful body by whom it should have been supported.

"The plan of Mirabeau was to facilitate the escape of the King from Paris to Compiègne or Fontainebleau; that he should there place himself under the guidance of the able and intrepid M. de Bouillé, assemble a Royal army, call to his support the remaining friends of order, and openly employ force to stem the torrent. He pledged himself for the immediate support of thirty departments, and the ultimate adhesion of thirty-six more. Between the contending parties he

Would you have any reluctance at being present with me at the house of a friend of yours, M. de Montmorin? Acquaint me with the day, and let such be after an evening's sitting."—Bertrand de Moleville, vol. iv. p. 174.

* So charmed was Mirabeau with the Queen's manner, that he took leave of her with these words :—"Madame, when your august mother admitted any of her subjects to the honour of an interview, never did she dismiss them without first presenting her hand for them to kiss." Mirabeau knelt, and then raising his head, he said, with an accent full of soul and pride, "Madame, the Monarchy is saved."—Campan, p. 127, and Weber, vol. ii. p. 37.

flattered himself he should be able to act as mediator, and restore the Monarchy to the consideration it had lost, by founding it on the basis of constitutional freedom. 'I would not wish,' said he, in a letter to the King, 'to be always employed in the vast work of destruction.' And, in truth, his ambition was now to repair the havoc which he himself had made in the social system. He was strongly impressed with the idea, which was in all probability well founded, that if the King could be brought to put himself at the head of the Constitutional party, and resist the further progress of democracy, the country might yet be saved. 'You know not,' said he, 'to what a degree France is still attached to the King, and that its ideas are essentially monarchical. The moment the King recovers his freedom the Assembly will be reduced to nothing. It is a colossus with the aid of his name. Without it, it would be a mountain of sand. There will be some movements at the Palais-Royal, and that will be all. Should Lafayette attempt to play the part of Washington at the head of the National Guard, he will speedily and deservedly perish?' He relied upon the influence of the clergy, who were now openly committed against the Revolution, with the rural population, and on the energy and intrepidity of the Queen, as sufficient to counterbalance all the consequences of the vacillation of the King. But, in the midst of these magnificent designs, he was cut off by death. A constitution naturally strong sank under the accumulated pressure of ambition, excitement, and excessive indulgence."— Alison's *History of Europe*, vol. ii. p. 63.

The inveterate and corruptible Danton, who embraced the extremest principles of the Revolution as the means of raising himself from obscurity, was always available to the highest bidder. The following will speak for itself of the venality of this demagogue trickster :—

"Danton was the first leader of the Jacobins who rose to great eminence in the Revolution. Born poor, he had received, as he himself said, no other inheritance from nature than 'an athletic form, and the rude physiognomy of freedom.' He owed his ascendency not so much to his talents, though they were great, nor to his eloquence, though it was commanding, as to his indomitable energy and dauntless courage, which made him rise superior to every difficulty, and boldly assume the lead when others, with perhaps equal abilities, were beginning to sink under apprehension. As was said of Lord Thurlow, self-confidence, or, in plainer language, impudence, was the great secret of his success.* At first ambition was the mainspring of his actions, individual gratification the god of his idolatry. Situated as he was, he saw that these objects were to be gained only by a zealous and uncompromising support of the popular party, and hence he was a Revolutionist. But he was ambitious, not philanthropic ; a voluptuary, not a fanatic : he looked to the Revolution as the means of making his fortune, not elevating or improving the human race. Accordingly, he was quite willing to sell himself to the Court, if it promised him greater advantages than the popular side ; and at one time received no less than 100,000 crowns (£25,000) from the Royal Treasury, to advocate measures favourable to the interest of the Royal authority—an engagement which, as long as it lasted, he faithfully kept.† But when the cause of Royalty was evidently declining, and a scaffold, not a fortune, promised to be the reward of fidelity to the throne, he threw himself without reserve into the arms of the democracy, and advocated the most vehement and sanguinary measures."‡—Alison's *History of Europe*, vol. ii. page 135.‖

Thus said the noble Marie Antoinette to the devoted attendant Hue, during her captivity in the Tower of the Temple, on the return of the Royal Family from their walk in the garden, in which the notorious Santerre had accompanied them :—

"'That man,' said she to Hue, 'whom you now see our jailer, has several times solicited and obtained of the King considerable sums

---

* "A moderate merit with a large share of impudence is more probable to be advanced than the greatest qualifications without it. The first necessary qualification of an orator is impudence, and as Demosthenes said of action, the second is impudence, and the third is impudence. No modest man ever did, or ever will, make his fortune in public assemblies."—Lady M. Wortley Montague, in Southey's Edition of Cowper, p. 254.

† Through the hands of Durand, Danton had received more than 100,000 crowns, to propose or support different motions at the Jacobins' Club. He fulfilled faithfully enough the engagements he undertook in this respect, as he stipulated in reserving to himself the liberty always of employing the means that he judged best to attain the passing of his measures. His ordinary mode of accomplishing his ends in this respect was to advance his motions with the most abusive invectives against the Court and the Ministry, in order to avoid arousing suspicion of his being sold to them.—Bertrand de Moleville, *Mémoires*, vol. i. p. 354 ; Lamartine's *Histoire des Girondins*, vol. i. p. 139. See Lamartine's *History of the Girondists*, Bohn's English Edition, vol. i. p. 83, and vol. ii. p. 10.

‡ See Bertrand de Moleville's letter to Danton, threatening to expose his venality, by forwarding the proofs of such to the President of the National Assembly.—*Historical Records*, p. 114.

‖ For Lamartine's description of Danton, see Appendix, Note O.

from the funds of the Civil List.   How many others in the National Guard, and even in the Assembly, have under various pretences obtained pecuniary assistance, and yet are at this moment our mortal enemies! Before the 10th of August, the conduct of Dumouriez, the pusillanimity of M. de Lafayette, and the errors of the Duke de Liancourt, having disappointed our hopes, of what use to us were the large sums * distributed by our friends to Pétion, Lacroix, and other conspirators? They took the money and betrayed us.'"—Hue's *Last Years of the Life and Reign of Louis XVI.*, p. 394.

The above gives some insight into the principles of a few prominent Revolutionists, and thus it was that many who in public denounced the Royal Family, in private, through the stimulant of gold, planned to serve them ; whilst others, animated by nobler and more chivalric sentiments, who had been inveterate against the Royal Family at a distance, when brought in immediate proximity with them saw the fallacy of their opinion as regarded the conduct of the Royal Family, and thenceforth became secretly their confidential and devoted friends, thereby showing their secret principles were opposed to their open or public avowed protestations; therefore there can be no great strain of imagination in supposing Paine to have entertained the desire to liberate from the Tower of the Temple the son of the King who had sheltered with French bayonets the cradle of American liberty. Duplicity in the leading men of this direful Revolution is apparent throughout. Why then should we hesitate in drawing our conclusions as to the duplicity of Paine, as the Revolutionary area was but a struggle for precedency? and we see no reason to discredit that Paine wrote to Mrs. Carpenter for her to send him a deaf and dumb boy to Paris, especially as subsequently such a boy was introduced into the Tower of the Temple, as we will now proceed to prove.

Monsieur Harmand's report then opens our father's eyes as to the importance of what Mrs. Fisher had communicated to him, namely, "that Mrs. Meves, in the month of January 1794, went to Holland

---

* These large sums were advanced principally by the Procureur-General of the Order of Malta (Baillé d'Estourmel), by the Duke du Châtelet, M. Bertrand de Moleville, and some other faithful subjects.

accompanied by a Mr. Frike, and took with her, to fill up her passport, a deaf and dumb boy, the son of a Maria Dodd, and went on to Paris with this boy, and was detained there from some cause or other, that she did not return to England until about the middle of the month of May 1794.

There is every reasonable probability to infer that Mrs. Meves did make this journey to Holland and Paris, as stated by Mrs. Fisher, with a deaf and dumb boy. On referring to the Appendix, Note B, it will be seen that Mrs. Meves received a letter from the Abbot Morlet in the month of November 1793, whilst residing in Vere Street, and it is to the Abbot Morlet, who, in January 1794, was residing at the house of his brother Claude, at Buren, near Utrecht, that Mrs. Meves proceeded with the deaf and dumb boy, "the son of Maria Dodd," the same lad that Mrs. Carpenter and Mrs. Meves went in search of, after the letter that was received from Paine. This boy was now taken to Paris by Mrs. Meves, to make use of him, in order to extricate her son Augustus from the Temple, for it is seen that he, "Augustus," was taken to France by Mr. Meves, unknowingly to Mrs. Meves; and upon her learning this she went in quest of the deaf and dumb boy, as had been previously required by Paine, whom she finds, and he is placed in such hands at Paris, who, at the most convenient time, places him in the stead of Augustus Meves at the Temple. Through whose hands the deaf and dumb boy passes, that is impossible for us definitely to say, but it is most apparent that a deaf and dumb boy was confined in the Temple when Harmand and his colleagues made their official visit.

It is stated in the pretender Naündorff's work that the Empress Josephine and Barras carried this into effect,* but on this we offer no

---

* "J— P— was employed to attempt my deliverance from the Tower of the Temple, for which purpose some individuals, high in the Revolutionary Government, had received large sums from a powerful personage. J—. P— presented himself, and received not me, but the dumb child in my stead. In accordance with the orders which had been given him, he took the child to Madame Josephine Beauharnais, who became afterwards Empress of the French. On seeing the child, she exclaimed, 'Unhappy man, what have you done? By this mistake you have given up the son of Louis XVI. to his father's murderers.' Josephine had been well

opinion. The only remark we have to make is,—there is every reason to suppose that it was a deaf and dumb boy confined in the Temple at the period when Harmand and colleagues made their official visit; and we naturally conclude that this deaf and dumb boy was the son of Maria Dodd, for the evidence of Mrs. Fisher respecting Maria Dodd's son, and the journey of Mrs. Meves with a deaf and dumb boy to France, previous to the apparent substitution of such a boy in the Temple, gives ample reason for such a conclusion.

The full particulars of Harmand's report is given in page 161, where it is seen that, when the deputation entered the room where the captive was confined, they found him amusing himself with a pack of cards. He did not give up playing as they entered. Harmand approached him, but the captive took no notice of him. He then spoke to him, *but he answered him not.* He promised him toys, etc., *but he still stared with steady and vacant indifference, and to all the questions Harmand put to him, he answered him neither by gesture, expression, nor word.*

Harmand then tried peremptory commands, after which he proposed that a physician should be sent to him, and trusted that he would consent to answer him. He then requested the captive to make a sign, whether it would be disagreeable or otherwise, to which *he neither answered by sign nor word.* Harmand then desired him to walk again, to which request *the captive remained silent on his seat, his elbows resting on the table. His features did not change for an instant, not the least mark of surprise in the eyes, not the least motion apparent; his demeanour was just as if the deputation had not been present, and as if Harmand had not spoken.*

Harmand, in his report, here observes, that his colleagues Reverchon and Mathieu said nothing. They looked at each other in amazement, and they were advancing towards each other to exchange their reflections, when the captive's dinner was brought, at which Harmand

acquainted before with the real Dauphin, and also with the dumb child, for it was she who had procured him for Barras, when he was substituted in the place of the wooden figure. The truth of these facts will be undeniably proved in a court of justice."— Naündorff's *Misfortunes of the Dauphin*, p. 67. Translated from the French by the Hon. and Rev. C. J. Perceval.

and his colleagues expressed by their looks to Laurent and Gomin their astonishment and indignation. They made a sign for the keepers to retire with them to the anteroom, where they expostulated with them on the inhuman system exercised towards a helpless child, and ordered that such a vile system should be changed for the future, and that the captive should have fruit given to him. They having given all the necessary orders, etc., again returned to the captive, and found that he had eaten all that was brought him, when Harmand asked him, "Whether he was satisfied with his dinner?" *He gave him no answer.* "Whether he wished for fruit?" *No answer.* "Whether he liked grapes?" *Still no answer.* Grapes were then placed on the table, and the captive ate them *without speaking.* Harmand then requested to know whether he wished for more. The young captive still gave *no answer.* Finding all his efforts in vain to induce the captive to speak, he added, that he and his colleagues should in consequence propose to the Government to send other Commissioners, who might be more agreeable to him. To these threats, says Harmand, "*the captive neither changed his look nor gave an answer, or any indication of an answer.*" Harmand then resumed: "Do you wish that we should withdraw?" *He still answered not.* The Commissioners then withdrew. Harmand then inquired of his keepers in the anteroom, whether such silence had commenced, as they had reported to the Committee of Public Safety, from the 6th October 1793? They repeated their assertions on that point, and protested, "*That the child had not spoken since the evening of that day.*"

Evidently this was the deaf and dumb boy Mrs. Meves had taken with her to Paris in the month of January 1794, and explains at once why Harmand and those who approached the captive could not gain any response from him. No child could have carried such a resolution into actual force, as described and reported to the Committee of Public Safety—of a child not having spoken for so many months, on account of such a ridiculous deposition being extracted from him. This is too much to believe, and could not have been carried into effect by any child who had the use of his tongue and ears, for kindness such as Harmand exhibited would have sufficiently interested any child who had the power of speech, to have given some kind of answer in token of thankfulness ; but as this was the deaf and dumb boy, the son of Maria Dodd, it was physically impossible for this child to answer the Commissioners, or understand them.   Therefore the authorities, who were in the secret of the Dauphin's liberation, were assured that no secrets would be divulged by the then captive of the Temple.

Laurent must have been personally aware of the substitution of the deaf and dumb boy in the place of Augustus Meves, as this must have been effected after his appointment at the Temple, and previous to Gomin's appointment.   Mark the singular interrogatory Laurent placed to Gomin upon his installation at the Temple, namely,—" Have you ever seen the Prince-Royal ?" " *I have never seen him.*" " *In that case,*" replied Laurent, " *it will be some time before he will say a word to you,*" which seems to be quite correct by the admission of Gomin to the Committee and the Commissioners.   As he, " Gomin," did not know the Dauphin by sight, as a matter of course any one who was introduced to him as the Dauphin, him alone would Gomin recognise as such, but as for either one or the other saying the Dauphin had not spoken since October 1793, that was impossible for either of them to know positively, because they could be only certain from the time he had been in their custody ; nevertheless, it seems to amount to certainty, not probability, that it was a deaf and dumb boy who was confined in the Temple upon the visit of Messrs. Harmand, Reverchon, and Mathieu, for it is undeniable that the keepers of the captive and the Commissaries, in their report to the Committee of Public Safety, acknowledged that the young captive *never even spoke to them*, and it is seen that Harmand and his colleagues were unable to obtain from him *a word in reply to questions*, and that Laurent and Gomin acknowledged to the Commissioners when on their visit, that the captive *never spoke ;* therefore there can be little difficulty in arriving at a definite conclusion as to who the captive really was.

As regards the name of Madame de Courville Schroëter, it appears Mrs. Spence, Mrs. Fisher, and Miss Powell first knew Mrs. Meves under the name of Madame Schroëter, and Mr. George Meves explains from whence the name of Schroëter was derived. Captain d'Oliviera also states that Madame de Courville Schroëter accompanied the Princess de Lamballe to England in 1787, which year is seen to be that in which Miss Powell in her information states that Mrs. Meves came from France to England, and that Mrs. Meves at that time was known by the name of Madame Schroëter. Latour also states, that Mrs. Meves went by the name of Madame de Courville at the Court of France, and Mr. Franks the same, with the addition of Schroëder or Chroëder, on her return to the Court of France as a married lady. Captain Curten, on his return from his visit to the ex-Royal Family at Holyrood in 1832, stated that the name of Madame de Courville Chroëder was well known at Holyrood, as a confidential friend in whom the Queen of France, " Marie Antoinette," had placed much confidence. Mr. Davenport, in his letter, also states, that Mrs. Meves went to France, under the patronage of Lady Harrington, in the name of Schroëder ;* therefore, in speaking of the lady who was known as being in the private and confidential service of Marie Antoinette, as Madame de Courville, or Madame de Courville Schroëder, the above shows every probability of Mrs. Meves having been that lady.

Respecting the information relative to the colour of the eyes and hair Augustus Meves possessed as a child, as stated by Miss Powell and Mrs. Spence, namely, *blue eyes and light-coloured hair*, and on their seeing him in manhood possessing *brown eyes and brown hair*, to such there is attached much importance.

In the important particulars regarding the colour of the eyes and hair, will be found to exist essential testimony in proving the subject of the present Memoirs to have been the Dauphin, for it will be found, on investigating authentic sources, that the Duke of Normandy possessed in reality brown or hazel-coloured eyes and chestnut-coloured hair, up

* See Mr. Davenport's letter, page 43, Authentic Memoirs.

to the period of his separation from his mother, in the Tower of the Temple 1793, and the error that many have fallen into, in representing the second son of Louis XVI. as having possessed blue eyes and light-coloured hair, has arisen on account of the many substitutions that were effected in the captive of the Temple subsequently to October 1793.

Having devoted a special chapter to this subject, under heading, " Colour of the Dauphin's Eyes and Hair," to which we refer our readers for full particulars, wherein it is shown that the colour of the prisoner of the Temple's eyes and hair, subsequent to October 1793, will prove positively that the Dauphin was liberated from the Temple, and that substitutes thenceforth enacted his part.

MR. GEORGE MEVES.

In respect to Mr. George Meves's particulars we shall have much to say, for after the demise of our father's reputed parents, he being as it were in great perplexity how to proceed in this business, the most likely person he concluded to have recourse to for information was his reputed uncle Mr. George Meves, as most probably he could acquaint him with the movements of his late reputed parents, and the places of their residence, with the dates.   Mr. George Meves then is the person upon whom, on his setting out in this perplexing path of establishing his claims as the lineal descendant of Louis XVI. of France, to whom he applies for information ; and, moreover, on whom he relied for the dates he has assigned he arrived in England from the kingdom of France.

We will now summarize the dates and circumstances of Mr. George Meves's letter, namely,—" That his brother formed Miss Crowley's acquaintance in 1783, in Maddox Street, and visited her when she was living with Lady Harrington.   After a time his brother 'William' told him she had left Lady Harrington's and had gone to reside in France.

At the time his brother made Miss Crowley's acquaintance he knew very little of their proceedings, and as regards his marriage with Miss Crowley in the name of Schroëder, that he did not know. In 1785 Mr. George Meves entered the service of Sir John Shaw, and went abroad. On quitting Sir John Shaw's service, he entered that of Sir Drummond Smith, in whose service he remained for many years. At the time of the birth of Cecilia Meves, Mrs. Meves was living in London under the name of Schroëder, and shortly after the birth a separation took place between Mr. and Mrs. Meves. In the autumn of 1788, his brother was professionally at Lord Stamford's taking likenesses, and in 1789 at Captain Lee's of Coten Hall, Shropshire."

He then says he saw our father, in the year 1792, in Great Russell Street, on his return from boarding-school, on which occasion he gave him half-a-sovereign, having written the above in his letter. We will give the particulars of his evidence, which are as follows :—" Mr. William Meves von Schroëder followed the profession of a miniature painter, and on the occasion of his son being baptized, Mrs. Meves having brought him from France for this express purpose, she sent for him to stand as sponsor for her child, in consequence of the father being in Derbyshire at the time. The baptism took place at Saint James's Church, Piccadilly, and after the ceremony Mrs. Meves at once proceeded to France with her son."

The next time Mr. George Meves saw his brother's son was in 1792, in Great Russell Street, Mr. William Meves having just brought him from a boarding-school, where Mrs. Meves had placed him. Upon the subject of the present Memoirs asking him what coloured eyes and hair he had when he saw him in 1792, he replied, " You had *blue eyes and light-coloured hair;*" adding, "but there is nothing extraordinary in *your eyes and hair having changed their colour to brown*, as eyes and hair change their colour as people grow older." He then asked Mr. George Meves to favour him by writing a letter, and therein state what he knew respecting the name of Schroëder, which is entered above, as several gentlemen, who then surrounded him, doubted the time that he supposed he arrived in England from France.   To which Mr. George Meves replied,—" That Mrs. Meves was living at Boulogne-sur-Mer until the breaking out of the French Revolution, when she, for safety, came to England.   Mrs. Meves then took her daughter, Cecilia, under her charge, and Mr. Meves that of his son.   In 1789, previous to Mr. Meves going to Lord Stamford's, he placed his son under the care of an old nurse at Battersea.   During his stay from London Mrs. Meves got possession of the boy, and took him with her to France, and on her return to England she placed him at a school at Horsham, in Sussex, and it was from this school his brother brought his son in 1792."   It is upon the above statement that our father, in the first instance, based the period of his arrival in England from France.

In commenting on Mr. George Meves's statement, it will be well to observe, in the first instance, that it was through our father having depended implicitly on all his dates for authority, that he was in his outset in this, to him, perplexing question led astray.

The statements as respects dates when he wrote to the Duchess of Angoulême, and during the period he was surrounded · by the adherents of Charles x. till after his acquaintance with the Marquis of Bonneval, were not narrated as having originated from his own recollections, but were the adapted dates as received from Mr. George Meves, thinking by adhering to such he should not go astray ; therefore, it was upon Mr. George Meves that he relied as a warranty for affixing dates and place to his recollection.

We will now account why the Duchess of Angoulême and Charles x.'s party was attached to his person, " as undoubtedly they thought very highly of his claims," but repudiated his statements, that is, in respect as to when he stated he arrived in England from France.

In his writing to the Duchess of Angoulême, in 1830, it is seen he merely acquainted her with the disclosure of his reputed mother " Mrs. Meves," and it is apparent throughout his letters that there was not the slightest intention on his part to deceive, but only to endeavour to elicit the truth.   As a matter of course he could not depend upon himself for the specified dates, but his reliance has been in those who he naturally concluded could acquaint him with such. Here then has originated the mistake, for he has confounded himself with Augustus Meves, and accounted to the Duchess of Augoulême in his letters, and likewise to the Royalists, who, previously and subsequently to his writing the letters, had surrounded him, as having arrived in England after the attack on the Palace of Versailles in 1789, and he has informed them of incidents that in reality have occurred to him, but he has substituted the place of action as having happened in England instead of France, in accordance with the dates of Mr. George Meves, who stated that Mrs. Meves arrived in England in 1789. After the breaking out of the French Revolution, and that subsequently, she got possession of her son from the person to whom Mr. Meves had intrusted his care, and took him with her to France, and on her return to England she placed him at a boarding-school at Horsham, which school had formerly been a county prison.

As the Dauphin was only four years of age in 1789, and Augustus Meves the same, whether he was the Dauphin or Augustus Meves, he was too young to have any lucid or reliable recollection of the events of his life at such an early age.

We will now insert the portions of the two letters to the Duchess of Angoulême, where the mis-statements have occurred :—

FIRST LETTER.

"*September 2nd*, 1830.

"I remember in my early youth having been extremely unwell, and that during a severe illness on my arrival in England, where persons about me appeared as strangers. On my recovery I was placed at a Messrs. Thornton's boarding-school at Horsham, in Sussex, about the year 1790, and I well remember my unhappiness in not being able to understand what was said to me, as I only understood the French language at that time. Here I remained for nearly two years, and was kept at school during the holidays. On my return to the care of my father in 1792, I had lost all knowledge of the French language, which my father completed by teaching me the German language."

SECOND LETTER.

"*June 6th*, 1831.

"On my own part I can trace my being in England to the year 1790, when I was placed by my parents at Messrs. Thornton's school at Horsham, where I remained for at least two years."

We will compare subjects in order to arrive at a definite conclusion respecting the letters. In the first place, he says, on his arrival in England those about him seemed as strangers. Although he states in his letters that he arrived in England in 1790, nevertheless in this he was in error, for the actual time of his arrival was in October 1793, after his liberation had been effected from the Tower of the Temple, through the instrumentality of Madame Simon, during the trial of Marie Antoinette; consequently, the hands he then came into were all strange to him, both Mr. Meves's, in whose care he was placed by Madame Simon in Paris, and Mrs. Meves's in England, likewise all those that then surrounded him.

Respecting the illness he writes of having during his early youth, and upon his arrival in England :—

In referring to the Historical Records, page 105, it is seen that the Dauphin, whilst under the care of the King in the Temple, fell ill, and again whilst under the care of the Queen. The Princess-Royal, "the Duchess of Angoulême," writes as follows concerning the Dauphin's illness :—

"My brother had for some days complained of a stitch in his side, but on the 9th of May, at seven in the evening, he was seized with a violent fever, accompanied with headache and still the pain in his side. During the first days he would not lie in bed, for he complained that he was suffocating. My mother was alarmed, and asked the officers to send for a physician. They assured her the illness was nothing, and that her maternal anxiety had alarmed her unnecessarily. They, however, mentioned it to the Council, and asked in my mother's name for our physician Brunier. The Council laughed at my brother's illness, because Hébert reported that he had seen him at five o'clock, and that he had then no fever. They therefore positively refused the attendance of Brunier, whom, it will be recollected, Tison had lately denounced. The fever, however, grew worse and worse. My aunt had the goodness to take my place in my mother's room, in order that I might not be exposed to the infectious air of the disease, and that she might assist her sister in attending upon the poor sick boy. She therefore took my bed, and I slept in her room. The fever lasted several days, and was always most violent towards evening. My mother continued every day to request the attendance of a physician, but could not obtain it. At last, on Sunday morning, Thierry came. He was the physician of the prisons, and appointed by the Commune to attend my brother. As he came in the morning, he did not perceive much fever, but my mother having requested him to call in the afternoon, he found it violent, and he undeceived the municipal officers as to their opinion that my mother was alarmed at a trifle. He said, on the contrary, that it was more serious than she believed, etc."—*Private Memoirs of what passed in the Temple.*

"Whilst the Dauphin was under Simon's charge, he changed the mode of living of his Royal scholar. He obliged him to eat more than usual, and to drink a great deal of wine ; he allowed him to take but little exercise, shortened the time of his recreation in the garden, and put a total stop to his walks upon the Tower. These new regulations ended by making him quite ill. At last he was attacked by a violent fever," etc.—Beauchesne's *Louis XVII.*, vol. ii. p. 109.

Shortly after the Dauphin's arrival in England, he was placed at a day-school in Bloomsbury, in 1794, where he was taught the English alphabet, and whilst attending there he caught the measles ; therefore the illness he writes of in his letter to the Duchess of Angoulême must have been on one of the above occasions. Although the Dauphin had three attacks whilst confined in the Temple, doubtless the slight illness he had after his arrival in England made the most impression upon him, on account of being surrounded by total strangers, and not knowing the English language.

He then states in his letter, " On my recovery I was placed at Messrs. Thornton's boarding-school, at Horsham, in Sussex, about the year 1790, and I well remember my unhappiness in not being able to understand what was said to me, as I only understood the French language at that time. Here I remained for nearly two years, and was kept at school during the holidays. On my return to the care of my father, in 1792, I had lost all knowledge of the French language, which my father completed by teaching me German."

It is through this school at Horsham that the errors in the letters respecting dates and place arise, for this is the school which has enabled his reputed parents to deceive him, on account of its semblance in many respects to the Tower of the Temple. As it had formerly been an old county prison, therefore all his interrogatories to his supposed parents in respect to incidents of his youth, which had happened to him in reality at the Tower of the Temple, have been specified as having happened to him at this school, and incidents prior, as having happened at public entertainments. Thus it was that he was confounded, as everything certainly appeared natural and feasible, and for further proof on their part they have shown him copy-books, etc., on which has been written the dates, "such as are alluded to in Mr. George Meves's evidence," and thus it was that all reminiscences in connexion with his early career, as refers to date, were incorrect, for he appropriated the dates and place as pertaining in reality to Augustus Meves, and has specified the incidents that have happened to himself as the Dauphin, whilst he was in the Palace of Versailles, the Tuileries, and the Tower of the Temple, which in fact had happened to him up to the month of October 1793 in the kingdom of France. These he has accounted for as happening to him in England, therefore his error has been in saying England, instead of France, and this has only been done on his part in conformity with the assertions of his supposed parents, and furthermore corroborated by Mr. George Meves, who in truth stated that which was correct, if the person he had addressed had been Augustus Meves, but as it was the Dauphin all was incorrect.

On what are his, "Mr. George Meves's," opinions based, that our father was not the Dauphin, but Augustus Meves? Certainly he knew, "that Augustus Meves was born in France in 1785, and brought to London to be baptized, and that after the ceremony the mother at once returned to France with her son. Likewise, of the separation that occurred between Mr. and Mrs. Meves, and of Mrs. Meves gaining possession of her son from the old nurse, in whose care Mr. Meves had placed him, and with whom she proceeded to France, and after the breaking out of the French Revolution, in 1789, she for safety returned to England, and placed her son at a boarding-school at Horsham." This we do not discredit, but it refers to Augustus Meves. When Mrs. Meves disclosed to our father that he was not her son, but the son of Marie Antoinette, Queen of France, she neither specified nor explained to him more than that he was the Duke of Normandy. She gave him no intimation at what period he was brought to England, only simply informing him, "that Mr. Meves had gained an interview with the Queen in the Conciergerie," not mentioning in any respect that he it was who had brought the Dauphin from Paris to England, but only that he had made the Queen an oath, which he kept till the latest hour of his existence. The Dauphin could have no knowledge from his own individual recollection that he was brought to England from France in 1789, for he was then but four years old. Why he stated in the first instance that an exchange of children must have taken place at the time of the assault on the Palace of Versailles, in October 1789, was on account of the statement of Mr. George Meves, as he stated Mrs. Meves returned to England on the breaking out of the French Revolution, in 1789. This statement therefore did not originate from his own individual recollections, as he was too young to have any, but this being the period he was given to understand that Mrs. Meves returned from France, caused him, when surrounded by parties, to state that this must have been the period of his arrival in England, which was a most unplausible statement, and will readily testify to the truth of his assertion to Captain Curten and Monsieur Rogiers on their return from Holyrood Palace, in 1832, "where the Duchess of Angoulême and Charles x.'s party were residing," respecting the enamel box, he commissioned them to state on their visit to Holyrood, he broke in his youth, which he imagined belonged to the Duchess of Angoulême. On their return they remarked, "that possibly he may have learnt this from Mrs. Meves, or read of it in some work." His answer was, "he begged to assure the gentlemen he had never read any works on the French Revolution." Had he done so, unquestionably he would have seen his error in stating, "that the Dauphin's escape was effected in 1789," for he would have learnt that it was the Dauphin who was confined in the Temple until his separation from his mother in 1793. This, then, explains why his claims were not admitted by the Duchess of Angoulême, and Charles X.'s party, on account of the mis-statement, which did not emanate from himself, but only from his having adhered to the dates of Mr. George Meves. Certainly Charles X.'s party were attached to his person, and undoubtedly were aware that he was the Dauphin ; nevertheless, politically, it was not to their interests to maintain and promulgate such.

On reflection, this statement respecting his arrival in England, in 1789, will testify his individual integrity, for this must be a convincing proof to the world that his object was not to deceive, but only to state that which he had been led to believe; for had his object been such, a superficial glance at the Revolutionary history would at once have convinced him of his egregious error in this particular—therefore this error should not be attributed as emanating from himself, but from the source, as he states in his letter to the Duchess of Angoulême, *from what he has been able to trace,* and the authority of such tracing has been his reputed parents and Mr. George Meves. He thereby, in accordance with information received, attributed incidents, etc., as happening in England from 1789, whereas they occurred actually in France up to October 1793, and in England subsequently.

In respect to the boarding-school at Horsham, although he states in his letter to the Duchess of Angoulême, that he was placed at Thornton's boarding-school at Horsham, in 1790, the school he in reality meant was Tempest's school at Wandsworth, where he was placed shortly after his arrival in England, after his having had the measles in 1794. He had no recollection himself of Thornton's, but only of Tempest's, of which he had a decided recollection, as is seen in pages 8 and 76 of his Memoirs ; therefore it is in truth the circumstances which happened to him on and after his arrival in England, in 1793—such as being ill, then being placed at a boarding-school, and all appearing strangers to him, and his not being able to understand what was said to him; these he has erroneously stated happened to him at Thornton's school at Horsham, but which actually had happened to him at the Tower of the Temple at Paris, up to the period of his quitting Tempest's school at Wandsworth, in 1794. Therefore all his recollections, what he recounts in his letter to the Duchess, were in point of action correct, but incorrect as respects dates and stated place of action, which errors alone are attributable to the sources from whence he received his information.

In respect to his recollection of being kept at school during the holidays, that in reality refers to the time he was at Tempest's school at Wandsworth, from where Mrs. Meves took him to her residence in Vere Street, in 1794, where, from his own positive recollection, he saw from Mrs. Meves's windows some illuminations. In reverting to this reminiscence he has been led astray, for when he has in the course of conversation with Mrs. Meves alluded to having witnessed these illuminations on the occasion of her having brought him from school, she has impressed it upon him that these occurred in the year 1792, and this was what made him state in the Duchess's letter that he remembered he was in England in 1792, for he knew perfectly well that he had seen these illuminations in England from Mrs. Meves's residence, after having been brought from school, and he was not aware of the misrepresentation of their date until after he knew the Marquis of Bonneval, and then all for a time was a greater mystery than ever.

He then well investigated in his own mind his recollections, not subjecting himself to be led by what others had told him in framing his statement in order to make it coincide with dates which pertained not to him, for this it was that had hitherto misled him, and made complicity where in reality none existed. He therefore resolved, now that he was aware of his former errors, to repudiate such, and thenceforth to depend solely on his own individual recollections, " which are," as he has written in his Memoirs, "which have not been written to deceive, but to elicit truth, and nothing but truth," and upon which, after mature consideration, we do not hesitate in pronouncing him to be the veritable son of Louis XVI. and Marie Antoinette.

The illuminations, as referred to above, were those given in honour of Lord Howe's victory, the 1st of June 1794, which took place for three successive days, the 13th, 14th, and 15th June 1794, which he traced from the information of Mrs. Fisher; therefore in this recollection he was two years in error as regards date, for they took place in 1794, and not, as represented by Mrs. Meves, in 1792.   For full particulars on this subject refer to page 230.

The next subject to allude to is: As Mr. George Meves did not see his brother's son from 1785—his baptism—till 1792, in Great Russell Street, and then not again till 1802 in Goodge Street, and upon his seeing him in 1792, *he had blue eyes and light-coloured hair*, and Mr. George Meves remarking, "there was nothing extraordinary in his eyes and hair having changed their colour as he grew up." Upon this we have a few remarks to make.   Certainly the infant Mr. George Meves stood sponsor for in 1785, and the boy he saw in Great Russell Street in 1792, were one and the same, but as the boy he saw in 1792, *had blue eyes and light-coloured hair*, and the boy he saw subsequently to the year 1794, having *brown eyes and brown hair*, we differ with him in recognising in this boy the same as he had seen in 1792, for it would be against the law of nature for a boy, who at the age of seven years possessed blue eyes, for such to change their colour after that age to brown, for they would retain the same colour from seven years of age throughout life, and their brightness would only dim through age, or under illness, therefore we say the boy Mr. George Meves saw in 1792 and 1802 was not the same, and that an exchange had been effected.

In referring to the special chapter of particulars respecting the colour of the eyes and hair of the Dauphin, it will be readily seen how this apparent change in the colour of the eyes had been effected, for it is evident that Augustus Meves, who possessed blue eyes, had taken the place of the Dauphin in the Temple in October 1793, and that the Dauphin, who possessed brown eyes, had taken the place of Augustus Meves in England. This will account for the change of the colour of the eyes of the reputed Augustus Meves.*

Respecting the colour of the hair changing, Mr. George Meves in this particular was correct, for as Augustus Meves possessed light-coloured hair at seven years of age, there would be nothing unnatural in such changing to a brown in the course of a few years. In referring to the Historical Records, page 156, it is seen when the prisoner of the Temple came under Laurent's charge, he possessed fair hair, nevertheless it is certain the true Dauphin possessed brown hair, through which fact we are made fully aware, "that this boy could not have been the Dauphin," and as the description again coincides with Augustus Meves, we naturally infer that such was in reality the case.

Although it is natural for fair hair to change to dark, it would be, quite contrary to the law of nature for a boy at seven years of age, possessing brown hair, for such to change its colour to fair hair. This would be decidedly unnatural ; nevertheless, the Dauphin assuredly possessed brown hair, and it is seen that the prisoner of the Temple, subsequent to October 1793, possessed fair hair, thus accounting why the reputed Augustus Meves possessed brown hair, for he was the Dauphin who was liberated from the Temple in October 1793, and at the same time accounts for the change of the colour of the prisoner of the Temple's hair, subsequent to October 1793, for in reality the captive of the Temple then was Augustus Meves.

Respecting the probability of eyes and hair changing colour, we refer our readers to Dr. Hancock's (Chief Ophthalmi Physician, appointed at Charing Cross) opinion thereon.*

In speaking of Mr. George Meves, how was it possible for him to know the actions of his brother, if they lived apart, and so seldom (in consequence of the position he held) saw each other ? If Mr. William Meves was so implicated with the Dauphin, is it feasible that he

* For subject "Colour of the Dauphin's eyes and hair," see Table of Contents for page.

would acquaint his brother with what he had been doing, if secrecy was desired? Depend upon it, Mr. William Meves was not the man to confide such a secret to his brother that he had effected the Dauphin's escape from the Temple, or of the incidents of his life connected with such, if his voice reached not the ears of his charge (the Dauphin). Certainly, had it been his own son there would have been nothing to reveal, but when the whole of the evidences of this work are justly weighed, namely, "the disclosure of Mrs. Meves—the personal identity, through the natural marks and accidental scars, from wounds that the Dauphin received—the apparent introduction of the deaf and dumb boy into the Temple—the startling particulars respecting the colour of the eyes and hair of the Dauphin, and the mystery surrounding the captive who was confined in the Temple, etc. ;"—these particulars manifest the greatest probability to conclude, that the boy who was under Mr. William Meves's care, subsequent to 1793, was in truth the son of Louis XVI.

At the time our father had arranged to proceed to Edinburgh in company with Le Comte Fontaine de Moreau, having communicated such to Mr. George Meves, who found he could not persuade him from undertaking this journey, what did he do, the assurance on his part of being his uncle giving him the power, but procured an order for his detention, as being incapable to see to himself?

In those days it was no difficult matter to obtain an order to deprive persons of their liberty, when such was essential for individual purposes, and the world at large has been made fully aware to what an extent, and what foul play was used in this most abominable practice, therefore it was no difficult matter for such a warrant to be issued under the representation of a person supposing himself to be a King, and on the point of travelling to Edinburgh to procure an interview with the Duchess of Angoulême on such apparent delusive claims, much to the annoyance of his friends. The assertion was quite sufficient to procure the necessary warrant for depriving the possessor of such seemingly incoherent ideas of his liberty. We believe Mr. George Meves's motive was good, for he thought he was doing what was proper in hindering him seeing the Duchess of Angoulême, nevertheless the limit of friendship was overstept, and his presumption unquestionably unpardonable for having recourse to such means, and we can only attribute such to his belief that he was befriending his brother's son. Thus, then, the interview, which in all probability he would have procured, through Le Comte Fontaine de Moreau, with the Duchess, was frustrated by this unforeseen and unwarrantable detention.

In this, there was no hesitation on his part in endeavouring to see the Duchess of Angoulême, for he knew within himself it was not his intention to deceive or impose upon the Duchess (his letters bear ample proof of such), but only to do that which was consistent and honourable, in placing before her the incidents of his life, his uprightness wearing no mask, and trusting to meet with openness and candour in return from the Duchess.

Acquaint a person who has been wronged of an inheritance with as much knowledge of his claim as our father possessed that he was the Dauphin, and would he not persevere by every means in his power to fathom the true counts of his cause? Such then could not be accomplished without much time and perseverance, for difficulties are not removed instantaneously. Supposing, after all his labours, he has been following the wrong course to obtain the desired clues; certainly such would be disheartening, still he would not give up his cause as lost, but would again contend with the difficulties, if he knew that in reality what he was seeking was a substance, and not a shadow, and although obstacles might again and again obstruct his efforts, hope would stimulate courage. Energy and renewed diligence would follow, with the conviction that success would be the ultimate reward. In the above manner our father has had to persevere, and now the proofs will be found that his was not a vain chimera, but a fact which history itself proves.

In referring to the Historical Records, from the period when the Princess-Royal last saw her brother in the Temple, namely the 8th October 1793, it must be apparent to the most sceptical, that soon after that date the Dauphin was no longer confined in the Temple, but that substitutes enacted his subsequent part in the Temple, which fact will still be more apparent when the reader recalls to mind, that the intervening period is "one year and eight months," of which the preceding Historical Records gives but a brief outline of the conduct pursued towards the unfortunate prisoner of the Temple,—how then, if the prisoner of the Temple's daily captivity is investigated, when such mystery is evident in the previous brief historical outline, how much more convincing and apparent will such be when investigated from day to day.

Since it is positive the Dauphin's liberation was effected from the Temple, and as we feel fully assured that in reality that Dauphin was the same as in life was known in England by the name of Augustus Meves, our course, as a matter of right, is to make public such conviction; and it is for public opinion to decide : whether or no we have not guaranteed warranty for such.

MONSIEUR LASSLEUR AND COLONEL BIGAULT DESFOUCHÈRES.

In reference to the proposal our father met with from Monsieur Lassleur and Colonel Bigault Desfouchères, and the means by which these gentlemen in the first instance became acquainted with him, is seen through the great resemblance he bore to Louis XVI., and the marks that existed upon him being identical with those known to have existed on the Dauphin.

It is seen he questions them to know what plans they would adopt were he to accept their offer and proceed to France. Their answer was : "that he would be well provided for, and all they requested of him was to remain silent, as the proofs of his identity must remain with them, as they knew perfectly well who he was, as such proofs existed on him, which fully convinced them that he was no other than the true Louis XVII. ; likewise, that whilst he was in Paris in 1816, his great resemblance to Louis xvi. had in certain circles caused much con-versation, as he had been observed whilst witnessing the performances at the different theatres, and likewise circumstances that had occurred to him whilst on his visit, of which they were cognisant. The reason of their desiring him to be silent, was on account of the time he stated he arrived in England, which they knew was incorrect.

In respect to their plan of making his claims known to the public, it was, as is seen in the Memoirs, to have gone to the theatre on some particular evening, when it would have been well filled with adhe-rents to the cause of Louis xvii., where he would have been seated in a conspicuous box, and recognised by their partisans as Louis xvii., on account of his great resemblance to Louis xvi. A French nobleman, who would have been present, would then have been appealed to, and had he answered, " that from his appearance he believed him to be the son of Louis xvi.," they would have raised the cry of " *Vive Louis XVII. /*" Several officers in the army and National Guard, who would have been present, and who were in his favour, would likewise have joined in the cry of " *Vive Louis XVII. /*" and they would then have carried their point, as the whole of Paris desired a change of Government, since the days of the Carlist's party were nearly at an end.

It is seen our father would not entertain such a scheme as proposed by Monsieur Lassleur and party, as it would have placed him on the footing of an adventurer, by having recourse to such means. He repudiated acting in a manner that would have been derogatory to his cause, or in any way that would have compromised him. He not con-senting to their wishes, and the political horizon in France increasing in ferment, which was to drive Charles x. from the throne, these gentle-men suddenly disappeared from the hotel in the Strand, and doubtless proceeded to France, to take part in the then coming struggle.

Our father had letters written to the Marquis Lafayette and Prince Perigord de Talleyrand, in which he acquainted them with what had come to his knowledge respecting his birth. Charles x. had to fly the kingdom of France. Then follows the insurrection, and the son of the regicide Egalité was placed on the throne, with the title of " King of the French."

Charles x.'s party arrived in Great Britain. Our father then forwarded two letters to the Duchess of Angoulême—one in 1830, and the other in 1831, in which he stated the particulars of the disclosures of Mrs. Meves, and of certain subjects that had come to his knowledge, and then follows his being introduced by Le Comte Fontaine de Moreau to the adherents of Charles x.'s party.

LE COMTE FONTAINE DE MOREAU.

What must have been the impression on Le Comte Fontaine de Moreau after he called on our father? Apparently he had directions from the Duchess of Angoulême, or from such sources, for the object of his visit,—as it was after our father had written to the Duchess he introduced himself, seemingly as having been commissioned to see him on account of the letters. After a brief interchange of courtesies, he requested to be permitted to see his (our father's) left wrist, in order to satisfy himself as to whether a scar existed there or no, which, after examining and satisfying himself that thereon existed a scar, he desired to know how such was occasioned. Our father's answer was: " He did not know by what means it came, but he supposed it was from the effect of some tumour that he had in his childhood."* *This is the scar, or one identical with that which the Dauphin received on the morning of his father's execution, when endeavouring to escape from the courtyard of the Temple, to plead for his father's life.*

Louis xvi. had promised the Royal Family, on the evening preceding his execution, that he would take his earthly adieu of them on the following morning. When the morning arrived the Royal Family were anxiously awaiting the expected interview, and as the King did not come as promised, they became impatient, and the Dauphin in his

* See Medical Certificates, Appendix, Note A.

anxiety made his way to the courtyard of the Temple, to supplicate for his father's life, when his farther passage was interrupted by the National Guard at the point of the bayonet; and it is here, though not stated in the Historical Records (page 119), that the Dauphin in his despair accidentally struck his left wrist on the point of one of the bayonets, from which he received a wound, and this wound, as a matter of course, was known to have existed on the wrist of the Dauphin by the Royal Family. This was the reason of the Count desiring to examine his left wrist, especially so as no allusion had been made to it in the letters that had been sent to the Duchess of Angoulême; therefore, the existence of this scar was strong evidence to those from whom he derived his mission, so likewise to himself, who in reality he was. Subsequently it is seen that the Marquis of Bonneval attached much importance to this scar.

The Count then requested to be permitted to examine his bosom, to which he was reluctant in complying with, remarking, "that he had some blood-spots and a dark-coloured mole on his right breast." The Count then observed: "He must pardon him, but he was like St. Thomas—he must see before he believed." He then complied with his request, and he then examined those singular appearances *on his breast coinciding with such which were known to have existed on the person of the Dauphin.**

The Count having fulfilled his mission, must he not have been highly impressed as to who in reality our father was, for the result of this visit was, he introduced him to the adherents of Charles x.'s party. He surely would not have done this unless there had been something very convincing in the marks he saw existing on our father. Depend upon it, his visit was not to be so easily convinced; but when identifying the marks upon his person, and such being identical with those which were known to have existed on the Dauphin, and such marks not having been described in his letters to the Duchess, he must then have been satisfied in a great measure who in truth our father was, and at once

* See Medical Certificates, Appendix, Note A.

perceived his personal ignorance as to the importance of these marks; and doubtless, had he not been brought up in the confused manner he was, it would have required but little explanation on his part to have established his unquestionable right to the title of Louis XVII.

LE COMTE DE JOUFFROY.

As to the Count de Jouffroy's opinion respecting our father's claims, he explains why the European Powers never sincerely wished to investigate this subject, namely, on account of the almost unlimited power Louis XVII. possessed in right of birth; for, by their tacitly acquiescing that Louis XVII. terminated his existence in the Temple, they frustrated the preponderance of power which would in right of birth have inevitably been vested in him. This was what insured Louis XVIII., and after him Charles X., the throne, their power, compared with that of the son of Louis XVI., being limited; whereas, had Louis XVII. been acknowledged, his power would have been unlimited.

Admit as a fact that Louis XVII. was liberated from the Temple, and was brought to England and reared as Augustus Meves, and that individuals who had known him by the name of Meves, whereupon his announcing himself as being in reality the true Louis XVII., those who have been thus acquainted with him, and the public generally, would be more inclined to discredit than credit such an assertion, whilst those who have but a superficial knowledge of the history in question, "we should say of that portion which concerns the Dauphin directly" exclaim, "This cannot be possible, for it is recorded that Louis XVII. died in the Temple." These conclusions not emanating from real conviction, but endorsing such simply because stated such by the Revolutionary Government of France, and tacitly acquiesced in "through political interests" by the European Powers. Is such a decision sensible or reasonable? How is it possible to form an equitable opinion before having read to see whether there are grounds sufficient to justify them in arriving at such a conclusion? If the world alike reasoned on all topics and repudiated investigation, unquestionably we should not be living in a very progressive age, and should but seldom arrive at definite conclusions on the most ordinary subjects. It is the fate of all ideas that revolutionize accepted ones to meet obstacles; nevertheless, nothing is impossible that is practicable. As to the liberation of the Dauphin from the Temple, there was no great difficulty surrounding the accomplishment of such, as everything facilitated it, and after these pages are unbiassedly perused, we presume few will question but that it was accomplished.

CAPTAIN CURTEN AND MONSIEUR ROGIERS.

In reference to Captain Curten and Monsieur Rogiers, and the communication received from Captain Curten as having come from the Cardinal de Latil, "the confessor of Charles x.," it has been antecedently explained, in commenting on Mr. George Meves's information, how our father made such a mis-statement, as that of saying an exchange of children took place at the Palace of Versailles, in October 1789, therefore, it would be useless to here recapitulate it, but acknowledging the error will be sufficient; but let it be remembered that this error did not originate as a recollection on his part, but only through misrepresentation of dates.

On the following, however, it is necessary to comment. The Duchess of Angoulême stated "she never lost sight of her brother from the time when the Royal Family quitted the Palace of Versailles till their unfortunate separation in the Tower of the Temple, and begged to assure the gentleman who wrote to her, that nothing on earth could afford a greater consolation to her heart than to know that her brother was still in existence, but Her Royal Highness fully believed that her brother died, and that his death was accelerated by poison. She admitted she did not see her brother in death, but the proofs were so positive as not to leave the slightest doubt on her mind." Such was Captain Curten's communication.

As there is great mystery surrounding the Dauphin after the last time the Duchess, " then Princess-Royal," saw her brother " in October 1793," this mystery we will explain.

What conclusions can be arrived at concerning the fact that the Princess-Royal and the Dauphin, who were both confined in the same prison, their tender ages rendering them harmless and unable to devise plots, being so cruelly separated from one another, and that after the 8th October 1793 they see each other no more during their confinement in the Temple, surely they would have been allowed to meet occasionally had there not been some stringent necessity why they should be entirely separated. In the historical portion of this work it is seen, p. 158, that the commissary Delboy expressed his indignation at this rule being strictly enforced, for he remarked, " Why prevent them from seeing each other under the reign of fraternity?" and then addressing himself to the captive he said, " Would you not like, my boy, would you not be very glad to go and play with your sister? I don't see why the Nation should recollect your origin if you forget it yourself." Had it been the Dauphin in reality who was confined in the Temple, there would have been no occasion to have enforced this rule, but as it was not the Dauphin who was confined there after October 1793, then there was on the part of the authorities a stringent necessity why the rule should be so strictly enforced,—for had the Princess and the captive been allowed to see each other, the secret of the Dauphin's escape from the Temple would have been manifest to the Princess-Royal, so this continued separation saved the authorities from being for a time detected ; and as the Princess had not seen her brother for so long a time, there was no apparent reason for her then to question the statement that her brother had succumbed under the rigours of the prison, more than to question the fate of her mother, " Marie Antoinette," or her aunt, " Madame Elizabeth," having fallen victims to the excesses of the time. These calamitous tidings were told to the Princess shortly before her liberation from the Temple. Sad indeed was such deplorable news to fall on the ears of a young and tender girl, and pitiless were the times that had occasioned such extreme barbarity.

There can be no question but that her Royal Highness, during her confinement in the Temple, believed it was her brother who died there, but in after life it is our firm belief, so likewise it was that of our late father, that the Duchess's eyes were opened as to the truth of her brother having been liberated from the Temple, and that she was fully cognisant that her brother was living under the assumed name of Augustus Meves, but on her marriage with the Duke of Angoulême, her policy thenceforth was in the interest of Charles x.'s party, the imperative orders of Louis xviii. and Charles x. being to discountenance any claim that might be advanced by the veritable Dauphin, for such would hinder the legitimate succession falling to the lot of the son of the Duke de Berri, "the Duke of Bordeaux," now known as "Le Comte de Chambord," however convinced the Duchess and they might be as to the reality of the existence of Louis xvii., for had the Duchess acknowledged our father it would have disinherited the son of Le Duc de Berri; therefore, in the first instance, the Duchess learned of her brother's death from a channel whose policy was to deceive, that is to say, its emanating source; and secondly, by a policy which commanded her secrecy.

As regards the communication respecting the enamel box, that apparently reminded the Duchess of some incident in her life, as she admitted such an occurrence. Upon Captain Curten questioning our father on this, he stated how Mrs. Meves accounted for this box, and gave his own opinion respecting such.

In this reminiscence, was there not something that awakened in the Duchess's mind some coincidence of her early captivity in the Tower of the Temple, as evidently the circumstance of the enamel box touched a chord of the Duchess's heart, by recalling an incident in her life too palpable to be mistaken?

These gentlemen asserted that the name of Marianne de Courville

Schroëder was known, and there were persons then living at Holyrood who remembered such a lady as being in the service of Marie Antoinette, as a confidential friend in whom the Queen placed great confidence—thus giving reasonable probability to conclude, together with the information of Messrs. Latour and Franks, and Mrs. Spence, Mrs. Fisher, and Miss Powell, that this said Madame de Courville Schroëder was in reality Mrs. Meves.

What could be more passively declaratory of the Duchess's belief in the existence of the Dauphin, than the announcement from Captain Curten of the sum of money that was placed in such hands as would be sure to reach our father, by order of the Duchess of Angoulême? Such a proceeding seems to confirm her acknowledgment that our father was her brother.

In the Memoirs, page 44, it is seen, after the decease of Mrs. Meves, a sum of money was placed to our father's account at his bankers', but he, being ignorant of its source, acquainted them with such ; and although they assured him they would be proud to honour any bills on the amount, he never availed himself of such an offer. Shortly after he was informed that the money had been placed to his account in mistake, which explanation at the time quite satisfied him, but after Captain Curten asserted that the Duchess of Angoulême had forwarded a sum of money for his use into such hands that would be sure to have reached him, he was under the impression that the sum of money which had been placed to his account at his former bankers'; and the sum forwarded for his use by the Duchess of Angoulême, were one and the same. Ten years having elapsed since the money was placed to his account, and the interview with Captain Curten and Monsieur Rogiers, and in the interim the banking-house of Messrs. Stephenson and Co. failed, and Mr. Rowland Stephenson fled the country on account of his defalcations, which conduct impressed our father that Mr. Stephenson, finding that he was in perfect ignorance from what source the above sum was placed to his credit, and his refusing to draw any cheques on this amount, that he had appropriated to his own use the sum which had been placed at the banking firm in the name of Augustus Meves.*

As regards the sum of money, does it not point out the Duchess's admission that our father was her brother, for it is as it were tantamount to a recognition of the fact, and doubtless Mrs. Meves had placed proofs in her hands to convince her of such?

What can be deduced from Charles x.'s party, but they being the adherents of his cause, it was not their policy to interfere in the cause of Louis xvii. The policy of the house of Charles x. did not admit of the public countenancing of the claims of Louis xvii., for had the supporters of Charles x. pressed the cause of Louis xvii., their own would have sunk into secondary consideration, therefore they were obliged to reflect before they acted, as they could not serve the cause of Louis xvii. and Charles x. at the same time, the two lines of policy being diametrically opposite; for the right of succession lay in the branch of Charles x.'s party so long as the cause of Louis xvii. was immured in obscurity, and therein accounts why the lips of the Duchess of Angoulême were sealed to all open acknowledgment of her brother's existence.

MONSIEUR LATOUR.

It is seen Latour stated that in his youth he was attached to the service of the chapel of Versailles, and attended the priests in their duties at the Palace, and that in 1786 he entered the office of Monsieur

---

* "That Rowland Stephenson carried on, under the cloak of religion, respectability, and morality, the most nefarious transactions, and made away with moneys intrusted to his care, cannot be denied. A more plausible or agreeable an acquaintance I never had, and although I could not help feeling gratified that an exposure had been made, which would warn others from placing any confidence in such men, I was grieved when I heard that he had been compelled to flee the country. Had I been possessed of wealth, so implicit was my faith in him, that I should probably have lost my whole fortune. He once asked me to remove my account from Cox and Greenwood to his house, but as I believed the balance was on the wrong side, I gratefully declined his offer."—Vide *Fifty Years' Biographical Reminiscences by Lord William Pitt Lennox,* vol. ii. p. 52, published in 1863.

Calonne, "Minister of Finance," and in 1787 became his private secretary.

Concluding such to have been the case, he in the routine of his occupations would have known a great deal in reference to the interior arrangements of the Court of France, and would therefore account for his acquaintance or knowledge of many persons in some way connected with the Court.   Therefore his knowledge of Marianne Crowley's position at the Court is easily understood ; and as he was subsequently well acquainted with Mrs. Meves whilst residing in England, he could not have been liable to error in recognising her as the lady who was attached to the service of Marie Antoinette, if this same Mrs. Meves was indeed the identical Marianne de Courville.

As regards the following, that the Queen was the mother of three male children, that is incorrect, for the Queen was the mother but of two sons and two daughters, and in no account is there any mention of the Queen having given birth to a son in 1783, named " Louis Auguste," and who, according to Latour, was created by the King "Duke of Bourgoyne." This is entirely a fabrication on his part, for did he attend the baptismal of a son of Louis XVI. when he was attached to the chapel of Versailles, it must have been either at the first Dauphin's, Louis Joseph Xavier François, or the Prince-Royal's, Louis Charles, Duke of Normandy ; and as there was no such son belonging to the family of Louis XVI. as the "Duke of Bourgoyne," it is apparent he had an object for such misrepresentation—probably for the reason attributed by Monsieur Chermant.*   However, there was a son of the Queen's who really became "*bossu*," but that was the eldest son, Louis Joseph Xavier François, who succumbed under his infirmity in October 1789.

As regards the diamonds that Latour stated were given to Madame de Courville, this we also believe to be entirely a fabrication, and only related in order to confuse ; therefore we conclude he had an object in making such a statement, attributable very possibly to what Monsieur Chermant stated ; nevertheless, had he been candid, doubtless he could

* See opposite page, Monsieur Chermant's information reviewed.

have given our father important information, for he said, he knew when he saw him in 1794 in Wilson Street, that he was not the Augustus Meves he had previously given lessons to on the pianoforte, in Great Russell Street.

Respecting Latour's entry into the National Guards in 1793, certainly what he has stated he could have accomplished with confederacy, for when the time is considered, and the interest that was felt in the Queen's favour, as is testified in the preceding Historical Records, there is no improbability in his assertion, namely, that the escape of the Queen might have been effected from the Conciergerie, for it is seen how many attempts were made, showing thereby her cell was accessible, and that devoted agency was acting in her favour in every direction, but at that time little did it require to baffle and disconcert well-laid plans when all but achieved.

MONSIEUR CHERMANT.

It is seen when our father spoke to Monsieur Chermant respecting what Latour had said, he cautioned him to be careful in placing reliance on what he stated, on account of his having entertained great regard for the late Duke of Berri, and, consequently, would be highly interested in the cause of his son Henri, "Duke of Bordeaux." It is not at all improbable that this was the real object Latour had in not giving our father accurate information.

THE MARQUIS OF BONNEVAL.

In commenting on the Marquis of Bonneval's information, we must, in the first instance, allude to the many projects that had been formed by loyalists to release the Royal Family from their captivity from the commencement of the Revolution, whilst the Royal Family were at the Palace of Versailles, till the period of the liberation of the Princess-Royal from the Tower of the Temple.

In reading the historical account of the Royal Family's flight from the Tuileries, does it not appear almost incredible that under the strict watch and peremptory orders that were issued for the safe custody of the Royal Family, and the extra vigilance that was aroused, both within and without the Palace, on the night of the 20th of June 1791, and that Lafayette himself (the commandant of the National Guard) having been informed the very night the escape was effected, and before its actual realization, by members of the Convention, that the reports and conversations at the clubs were, that this was the appointed night for the attempt to be made. How did this custodian of Royalty treat these rumours? He laughed at such, and advised these disturbed spirits to go home, as he considered such a thing impossible under the strict watch the Royal Family were subjected to. However, his assurance did not quell their suspicions, for these Revolutionary spirits obtained the password from him, and made all haste to the Tuileries. They inspected the different courts, etc., to see whether they could detect any indication or convenience that could facilitate the accomplishment of their fears. Yet their vigilance was evaded, and had it not been for the malignity of one person, the Royal party would have reached the frontier in safety.

On the night of the 20th of June the usual ceremonies took place at the Palace, and after the servants were dismissed, the Royal Family, when alone, habilitated themselves in all haste, in dresses that had been made to correspond to their assumed stations which they were to travel under, and they then left the Palace at intervals—the Queen leaving first, leaning on the arm of one of the body-guards, and leading the Princess-Royal by the hand. Whilst her Majesty was crossing the Carrousel, she passed Lafayette, with one or two officers, on their way to the Palace to insure the safety of incarcerated Royalty, and to see that his orders were strictly complied with. The Queen felt happy in eluding the vigilance of that apostate, that aristocratic jailer who held so often the destiny of France in his power, that dreamer of the impossible, amidst the raging elements of discord, sedition, corruption, dissemblance, and ambition, enrolled indiscriminately under the banner "Patriotism." Next followed Madame Elizabeth in company with one of the guards; then came the King with the Dauphin, while the devoted and faithful Count de Fersen, disguised as a coachman, preceded the King to show him the way. The Queen in her confusion crossed the Pont Royal and entered the Rue de Bac, then, perceiving the mistake, they had to retrace their steps, whilst the King and the Dauphin traversed the darkest and least frequented streets.

On the arrival of the King they got into the coach that was in readiness, and the Count de Fersen drove the Royal Family to Bondy, the first stage between Paris and Châlons, where in readiness were a berlin and a small travelling carriage to effect their anticipated freedom. The Queen's women and one of the disguised body-guard occupied the smaller carriage, whilst the King, the Queen, the Dauphin, Madame Royale, Madame Elizabeth, and the Marquise de Tourzel occupied the berlin, one of the body-guard sat on the box, and another behind. The Count de Fersen kissed the hands of the King and Queen, and bade the Royal party adieu. They proceeded on their route, and he returned to Paris, from whence the same night he took his route for Brussels.

On proceeded the carriages, reaching in safety the village of Sainte Menehould, and the King not having found the relays, which were to have been at certain stages, at their appointed posts, caused him great anxiety, and while at this village he put his head out of the carriage window, expecting to see some friend posted there to explain the reason of the absence of the several detachments that he ought to have met on the road. This one action caused the apprehension of the Royal Family, as the son of the postmaster "Drouet" recognised the King, from his likeness to the stamp on the coins. After the carriages had started on their way to the next town, this suspicion he circulated, when the national guard opposed the departure of the soldiers, who were there in readiness, to follow in the track of the King. During the confusion that ensued, Drouet "the malevolent" saddled his best horse and galloped as fast as possible to "Varennes," in order to acquaint the authorities with his suspicions, and arouse the inhabitants to arrest the occupants of the carriages ; and at which stage the Royal Family were arrested, and ultimately taken back to Paris.

Had the King found the relays at the appointed places, or had any one been stationed on the road between the different posts to explain any alteration that had taken place, or, failing such, had some trusty person been at the entrance of Varennes, or near such, to have given the information where the relay at this station was actually posted (which unquestionably should have been done), all would have ended well. The King, the Queen, and the three body-guard went themselves from door to door inquiring where the horses were stationed for more than half an hour, without gaining the slightest clue to where they were, whilst the relay was actually posted at the further end of the town, and those in charge of it anxiously awaiting the fugitives' arrival. Had the King been apprised of this, the bridge would have been crossed, and possibly their intended destination would have been reached in safety and without interruption. It appears Drouet, who had made all diligence from Sainte Menehould, passed the Royal party near the entrance of Varennes, called out to the postilions in passing who the party were, entered the town with all haste, aroused a few, and immediately blockaded the bridge. After the Royal party had searched in vain for the horses, they returned in despair to the carriages. The postilions now threatened to unharness the horses, but by bribes and promises, they relaxed, and again the carriages were in motion, but on arriving at the bridge the passage was blocked, and armed men seized the horses' heads, whilst others ran up to the carriage-doors and imperatively ordered the travellers to show their passports at the Municipality. Had the King been resolute and resented this audacity (which undoubtedly he should have done), their arrest would not have taken place, and their progress would not have been long delayed, for the body-guard, MM. de Valorg, de Moustier, and de Maldan, only awaited the order of the King to resist these desperadoes, and faithful men were rapidly approaching, and others near at hand, that the report of fire-arms would have hastened to the spot to have rescued the party if necessary, but the King forbade violence. Fatal indeed was his moderation to himself, his. family, and the Nation. Drouet and his party eventually succeeded in detaining and apprehending the Royal fugitives, and arousing the town and its vicinity, whilst Louis XVI. and the Royal party were kept prisoners at the house of the puritanical Sausse.

Count Charles de Damas arrived at Varennes with a few faithful dragoons, the others having revolted at the preceding stage (Clermont), and MM. de Choiseul and de Guoguelas, with a detachment of hussars, desired the King at once to force the passage, whilst the allegiance of the soldiers could be relied on, and before their mixing with the seditious. Likewise, M. Derlons, who commanded a squadron of hussars between Varennes and Stenay, learning the King's arrest, ordered his hussars to mount, and made all possible haste to Varennes to rescue the King by force. On his arrival the approaches were blockaded and guarded by National Guards, who refused to allow the hussars to enter the town, but M. Derlons was permitted to dismount and have an audience with the King. He placed his men at the King's disposal to attempt a rescue, as now the town was roused, and no time was to be lost. The King would not attempt such on account of the presence of women and children, fearing that some perfidious hand would in the rescue shoot the Queen, the children, or his sister. He trusted that the Marquis de Bouillé would have arrived in time, and with the superior force he commanded overcome all obstacles without endangering his family's lives, or without violence to any one, and that their deliverance would be promptly effected. The soldiers, by mixing and drinking with the seditious, turned treacherous. Sedition prevailed ; the King still would not have recourse to force ; his delay ultimately made it impossible had he consented. However, he did not consent. Lastly, officers arrived from Paris with an order for the King's arrest. Preparations were immediately hastened for their departure, and soon they were on the road to Paris, escorted by a formidable force.

The inquietude at Sainte Menehould and on the previous route, occasioned by the presence of soldiers, should have been allayed by their quitting such at a time when the multitude became uneasy by their presence, and concentrated at a given point where effectual assistance should if necessary have been given, and information through trusty persons stationed at by-places on the known route the King had to pass, acquainted him of the alterations that had unavoidably arisen. Had the King been accompanied, as the Marquis de Bouillé had originally planned, by the Marquis d'Agoult (a major in the French Guards), a man of energy and firmness, doubtless all would have ended successfully, especially if no further hindrance had happened, had he been present, than actually did arise. However, the Marquis de Bouillé's well-considered plan of that officer accompanying the Royal fugitives was laid aside, on account of the Marchioness de Tourzel (governess to the Royal children) asserting her privilege, in virtue of that capacity, of accompanying the Royal party. Therefore, instead of the presence of an intrepid, cool, and resolute man, to advise and act in case of emergency, a timid woman took his place, and the absence of that officer, considering what really transpired, was the cause of the failure. It was the unfortunate presence of women and children that made the King turn a deaf ear to all entreaties for a rescue. Had d'Agoult been present, his wariness as a man of the world would not have risked the slightest indiscretion which might have exposed any of the party to recognition. The King would not have looked out of the carriage-window at Varennes, surrounded by a concourse of people in agitation, and suspicious of something unusual stirring by the presence of troops. Had such a thing been necessary, d'Agoult would have been the person. His presence would have given all that was rendered necessary for the success of the undertaking. He would have allayed fears, and checked such from arising by his presence. The officers who commanded the troops on the road were intrepid and noble, but by unforeseen delays arising, their loyal efforts were of no avail. Their disposition to act, their courage, their fidelity, their unsullied honour as officers, deserve the highest commendation posterity can award a faithful soldier.

Had Napoleon I. been so situated, or were the present Emperor, "Napoleon III." so, the unlimited lives of Frenchmen would have been and would now be sacrificed to preserve their personal safety. France knows it, Europe knows it, the civilized world knows it; so likewise knows that the love, generosity, humanity, and clemency Louis XVI. had for his subjects' welfare effected his ruin. No tyrant was Louis XVI., but a veritable patriot-King, whose study was the happiness, prosperity, and amelioration of the nation; but hypocrisy and fanaticism by the seditious, thwarted his good intentions, and slaughtered without hesitation or mercy, so many thousand innocent persons.

REAL CAUSES OF THE FAILURE OF THE JOURNEY TO VARENNES.

"Various accidents doubtless contributed to disconcert this well-combined enterprise; but they might all have been surmounted save for the treachery or disgraceful irresolution of the Royal troops at Varennes, who revolted against their faithful officers, and the officious zeal with which the National Guard assembled to prevent the escape of their sovereign. History can supply no ground for pardon for such conduct. Patriotism cannot excuse the citizens, who sought to consign a virtuous monarch and his innocent family to the scaffold. Honour blushes for the soldiers, who forgot their loyalty amidst the cries of the populace, and permitted their sovereign, the heir of twenty kings, to be dragged captive from amidst their armed squadrons. The warmest friend of freedom, if he have a spark of humanity in his bosom, the most ardent republican, if not steeled against every sentiment of honour, must revolt against such baseness. Britain may well exult at the different conduct which her people exhibited to their fugitive monarchs under the same circumstances, and contrast with the arrest of Louis at Varennes, the fidelity of the western counties to Charles II. after the battle of Worcester, and the devotion of the Scotch Highlanders to the Pretender after the defeat of Culloden."*—Alison's *History of Europe*, vol. ii. p. 82.

It seems almost incredible that such a flight could have terminated successful in leaving Paris, after all the suspicions that had been

---

* The secret of Charles Edward's place of concealment was intrusted to above 200 persons, most of them in the very poorest circumstances. £30,000 was offered for his apprehension, confiscation and death pronounced against his adherents, yet not one Highlander was faithless to his Prince.

aroused of a meditated escape, and the strict guard which was kept at the Palace, and of the Queen having passed Lafayette himself, and more so, when the flight was so near a successful termination that the King was recognised by so singular a circumstance, and that his detector on suspicion alone used such exertions, malignity, and determination to arrest the fugitives. He possessed not the generosity of the magnanimous postmaster of Châlons, who, whilst the horses were being changed, recognised the King; but this worthy man felt that his sovereign's life was in his hands, and without manifesting the least surprise he helped to put to the horses, and ordered the postilions to drive on, silently wishing the Royal party God-speed on their journey.

As such an escape as that of the Royal Family from the Palace was rendered practicable, where could have existed any particular obstacle in effecting the Dauphin's liberation from the Temple? The greatest obstacle to overcome was his custodian Simon, therefore we appeal to public sense to inquire on what proofs they ratify the announcement that the Dauphin's demise took place in the Tower of the Temple; for we aver, that up to the present day, no public proof exists which can positively substantiate such; therefore, the public itself should not acknowledge such a political forgery, but assure itself as to the real history of the Dauphin.

In the antecedent Historical Records it is seen the many plans that were entered into to endeavour to liberate the Royal Family from the Temple, and all these undertaken at the risk of life, for detection would have been death; and possibly many other plans were formed that have not been publicly chronicled, which were entered into with zeal and rectitude for Royalty in captivity, amongst which, that of Mrs. Atkyns, as recounted by the Marquis of Bonneval, though entered into with all integrity on her part, was a failure, on account of the impracticability of the Queen's ultimatum. The period of the attempt, that while the Queen was confined in the Conciergerie, the Marquis being implicated in this, and though unsuccessful in liberating the Queen, he, and the party to which he belonged, were resolved, if possible, to effect the Dauphin's liberation from the Tower of the Temple.

It is seen the many efforts that were made to effect the Royal Family's escape at all hazards, and under such auspices that the world would be' more inclined to discredit than credit, had not the records of the time chronicled that such had really taken place, for the endeavours to release the captives from the Temple were adventurous indeed, and seem through their daring to belong rather to fiction than reality, did not history guarantee such. In what the Marquis of Bonneval stated there is no seeming inconsistency. His statement simply is, "that the Dauphin's escape was accomplished from the Temple by the means of bribes accepted by Simon, the guardian of the Dauphin, and the detestable Hébert."

Can Simon's republican principles be looked upon as incorruptible, when it is seen the firebrands of the Revolution itself bartered all for gold? In fact, the Revolution was carried by barterers for position from beginning to end ; therefore, was not Simon open to corruption, when gold, as stated by the Marquis of Bonneval, was the inducement which influenced him "and Hébert"? Entire confidence was placed in this man, thereby rendering the accomplishment of an exchange of boys easy, if he felt so inclined; and as Mr. Meves—we do not know whether by the name of Meves, "most probably an assumed name" —had placed his son, by influence from some quarter, in hands whereby the Dauphin's escape could be easily accomplished by waiting an available opportunity. Such an opportunity occurred during the Queen's trial, on account of public curiosity being concentrated in the direction of the Conciergerie, and absorbed in the fate of the Queen. It was then that the son of Mr. Meves (as is explained in page 175) took the Dauphin's place at the Temple, and the Dauphin was liberated therefrom.

In the Historical Records, page 142, it is seen—

"Hébert, with his party, went down into Simon's room, but the object of his visit was more the little prisoner than the captive ladies. He had a long conversation with Simon, looked at the child without speaking to him, took leave of the master with the words, '*Very soon,*' and withdrew.

"No official order or direction was given on that floor. '*Very soon*' is the sole portion of the visit we have heard of. A farewell word, simple and common enough, but which, under the circumstances, seems *frightfully significant*."—Beauchesne's *Louis XVII.*

So likewise on reflection they seem significant to us, for the Marquis of Bonneval stated that Hébert and Simon were bribed in order to allow the Dauphin's escape from the Temple, and as the Dauphin's deliverance was effected within three weeks after this visit, could these singular words, "*Very soon,*" have referred to the Dauphin's deliverance? "These frightfully significant words," as they are termed by Beauchesne, seem to imply, if there is any meaning in them, the carrying out of the stipulation of the Dauphin's release from the Temple.

The Marquis of Bonneval, on his own part, was sure that the Dauphin's escape had been effected from the Temple, for he averred, "that he guarded the carriage, which contained the heir and a person of approved courage, through a certain pass in Normandy, leading to the coast, and upon arriving at the coast in safety he left the carriage, as he was fearful of being recognised, as he was known as being a Royalist."

The carriage should have proceeded to the camp of General Charette, the Commander of the Vendean army, but it appears it did not, for when it arrived at a certain part of the coast, the Dauphin was placed in a boat, as may be seen in the Memoirs, page 6, and was brought to England by Mr. William Meves, and he then assumed the name of Augustus Meves. The Marquis not having received any communication that the Dauphin had reached the camp of General Charette, his doubts unquestionably were, whether he had again fallen into the hands of his tormentors; therefore he knew his escape had been effected from the Temple, but his location uncertain.

It appears singular, after the risk the Marquis had run, he did not in reality know the true destination of the Dauphin, but apparently he did not; and likewise, that he did not satisfy himself as to the presence of the Dauphin in the carriage, by certifying such with his own eyes, but he said he was perfectly satisfied that the carriage did contain the Dauphin, with a protector. The most probable inference why he did not have ocular demonstration of this, was the necessary caution that was required, for his province was not to arouse curiosity, but to have hindered all token that would have given rise to such. Had he then kept close to the carriage, suspicion on the route might have been aroused, and possibly the escape frustrated; but by following in the track of the carriage, if it had so happened that it had been stopt, he as a private gentleman may have rescued the occupants. Certainly, a signal from the parties who had compacted for the release of the Dauphin from the Temple would have been sufficient to have sufficed him that all had been accomplished, and the entry of the fugitives into the carriage would have assured him that all was correct. Let it then be assumed that the Marquis adopted the above plan, or one which would practically coincide with such.

As the Marquis then was cognisant that the Dauphin in reality had gained his deliverance from the Temple, it accounts for his caution how he proceeded in endeavouring to identify him.

It is seen when our father related the same statement to him as he had done to Charles x.'s party, and the Duchess of Angoulême, namely, his arrival in England in 1789, that the Marquis repudiated such an assertion, as he was personally aware that the Dauphin's escape had been effected during the trial of the innocent Marie Antoinette in 1793, and not in 1789.

When the Marquis questioned our father respecting his arrival in England, it is seen he replied that he was led to believe he first came under Mr. William Meves's care in 1792, from a boarding-school at Horsham. He did not say that he recollected this himself, but only that he was led to believe so. This led-to-believe-so statement emanated directly from persons whose object was to make him believe that such was in reality the case. However, his positive recollections were, that he was placed at Tempest's boarding-school at Wandsworth, and that during the vacation he was taken from this school to Vere Street, and it was from the windows of there, that he saw the illuminations given in honour of Lord Howe's victory. It was through witnessing these illuminations, and understanding that such took place in 1792, that he was positive he was in England at that time; but in this he was led astray as regards the date, for when in conversation with Mrs. Meves, and having alluded to these illuminations, she stated they took place in 1792. It was upon this information the error of date and place arose, for he recollected having been taken from a school just previously to having witnessed these illuminations; therefore, this fully accounts why in his letters to the Duchess of Angoulême, and to those who surrounded him, that he could trace his being in England in 1792.

How often is it the case that, when information is required, persons go every way but the right to gain that which is authentic? We must admit that our father, in the first instance, adopted this course, and as he was not aware what illuminations these were, he was led astray two years,—that is, the illuminations had really taken place in 1794, and he was under the impression they had taken place in 1792, and as Augustus Meves had left the school at Horsham (the Messrs. Thornton's) in 1792, and as the Dauphin had left Tempest's school in 1794, why, here is seen the similarity of coincidences by which he was open to be led astray !

As regards the correct date of these illuminations, our father ascertained such from the information he had received from Mrs. Fisher, who informed him that while Mrs. Meves was residing in Vere Street, Oxford Street, in the month of January 1794, she went to Holland with a deaf and dumb boy, the son of a Maria Dodd, and with this boy she proceeded from there to Paris, and that she did not return to England until the middle of May 1794. This information brings the correct solution of our father's recollections, for this was the month Mrs. Meves brought him from Tempest's boarding-school and took him to Vere Street, and from where he witnessed the illuminations, which on reference to history assured him were those given in honour of Lord Howe's victory, which took place in June 1794, for three successive days.* As these were his own recollections, he was aware of his former erroneous dates, and he then wrote, as is seen in the Authentic Memoirs, his life ; and as time passed, every additional particular that came to his knowledge made the fact more apparent of his being the son of Louis xvi., for time and experience were indispensable to unravel the mystery that surrounded him.

The Marquis, then, was positive our father had been misled as respected dates, and seeing there was no desire on his part to impose, he became additionally attached to him from the fact of the striking personal resemblance he bore to Louis xvi., and his manner and expression reminding him so much of the King. As respected his identification with the Dauphin, he was more and more convinced who in reality he was, for on his recognising the scar on his left wrist, this was demonstrative proof, as the Dauphin, on the morning of the execution of his father, having made his way into the court-yard of the Temple, he, whilst endeavouring to pass the guards, accidentally struck his left wrist upon the points of one of the guard's bayonets who obstructed his passage, and thereby inflicted a wound ; therefore, the existence of *this scar* guaranteed to the Marquis much more than words could have done in satisfying him who our father was.† This scar was the first thing le Comte Fontaine de Moreau, on his visit to our father at Bath Place, satisfied himself on, for it is evident without this scar he could not have been the Dauphin. In referring to the Marquis's evidence it is seen, he says, "Sir, it is extraordinary that you should have on your left wrist a scar corresponding with such as the Dauphin received in attempting to pass the guards on the morning of the King's execution," and then adding, "This scar, and your general appearance, particularly your features, which so exactly correspond with those of the

* On the 1st June 1794 a naval engagement took place between Lord Howe, commander of the English fleet, and the Revolutionary navy of France, which ended in a signal victory by Lord Howe. The arrival of this news excited the greatest sensation throughout Great Britain ; illuminations took place for three successive days—the 13th, 14th, and 15th June—all over the United Kingdom of Great Britain, in commemoration of this victory.

† See Medical Certificates, App. Note A ; likewise p. 119 Historical Records.

Dauphin, are to me the most convincing proofs, rather than your conversation, as you are certainly most ignorant of circumstances which regard yourself"

Furthermore, to verify his identity as Louis XVII., is the extraordinary appearance of the two teats on his right breast, which elicits evidence the most characteristic in identifying him as the Dauphin. Upon the Marquis questioning our father respecting this singular mark, he informed him, " that he certainly had many singular marks on his chest, but not two teats on his right breast," nevertheless, *over the nipple of his right breast was a kind of mole, which in his youth may have greatly resembled two teats.**

For the description of this double teat we refer our readers to the medical certificates of Doctors Newton, Andrews, Ringer, and Mr. Wakley, and of the special opinion of Dr. Andrews thereon. As all the natural marks and scars that were known to have existed on the Dauphin were found existing identically on our father, what is the natural inference that follows such ?

The many kindnesses the Marquis proffered our father shows he was highly interested in his cause, and at whose sudden demise he lost a stanch, warm, and trusty supporter of his cause.

DOCTOR RIOFREY BUREAUD.

In 1835 it is seen our father visited Dr. Riofrey Bureaud (who resided in Newman Street, Oxford Street), where he formed the acquaintance of several gentlemen, who were made acquainted with his pretensions. It was the Doctor who presented him with the work written by the Duchess of Angoulême, entitled *The Events of the Temple*, to which was appended Harmand's report of his official visit to the Temple in 1794,† wherein it is seen he could by no means or kind entreaty gain one word in reply from the captive.

---

* See Medical Certificates, Appendix, Note A.
† See Harmand's Report, *ante*, pp. 161-5.

On mature consideration of this report, our father saw, and not till then, the importance of the information Mrs. Fisher had previously given him, for it seemed to him that this boy, whom Harmand and the keepers of the Temple captive had reported they could not gain one word from, was no other than the deaf and dumb boy Mrs. Meves had taken to Paris in the month of January 1794. Harmand's report fully proves, that had the captive been capable of answering or hearing he would not have turned a deaf ear to the kind attentions of this stranger; therefore, there can be little doubt but that this was a deaf and dumb boy, and we infer that the boy Harmand saw, was in reality the son of Maria Dodd.

As regards our father having met Louis Napoleon at Dr. Riofrey Bureaud's, he is alive, and can answer this, and surrounded by those emblems of royalty which he and his uncle took arms against, but whom neither disdained to accept when the opportunity occurred of exalting them to the diadem; but as this has nothing to do with the question respecting the Dauphin, there is no necessity for argument, as it would lead to nothing, however discussed, except, that Napoleon is aware, and has been aware for many years, that the person called "Augustus Meves" was the veritable Louis XVII.

MR. FRANKS.

Admitting Mr. Franks held the functions at the Court of France as stated, and of his acquaintance with Cornelius Crowley, Esq., whom he saw in Paris with his daughter, with the object of placing her in a Convent, evidently Miss Crowley was in Paris for such a purpose, as the note of the Abbess of the Abbaye aux Bois * bears proof that it was so. As Mr. Franks was acquainted with Miss Crowley, of course he knew whether it was she who was subsequently in the service of Marie Antoinette. He attributed Miss Crowley's appointment at the Court to the influence of Signor Sacchini, who it will be recollected had been a

* See the Abbess's Note, Authentic Memoirs, p. 41.

pupil of his in London. Certainly his influence was sufficient to gain her an appointment at Court.*

In the letter written to Miss Crowley by her father, is stated, "that, should he survive his illness, he would return with his daughter to Paris," † thereby showing that Miss Crowley was in Paris in 1781.

It appears that when Miss Crowley returned to Paris in 1784, she re-entered the service of Marie Antoinette, and was known under the name of Madame de Courville Schroëder.

In reference to the severe wound the Dauphin received at his inoculation, on his right arm, as alluded to by Mr. Franks, and that such a corresponding scar existed on our father's right arm, identical in every particular to the one which must have existed on the veritable Dauphin's, this was demonstrative and irrefutable proof to him in concluding, through identity, who in reality he was, for had not such a large scar existed on him he could not have been the son of Louis xvi. and Marie Antoinette. The certainty that such a scar did exist on the Dauphin is indisputable, for the doctor who occasioned such an unnecessary incision was severely reproved.‡

What advantage could have accrued to Mr. Franks to state what was not true ? The only advantage, if such can be considered an advantage, was the knowledge of having deceived. Certainly investigation will test what is true, and what is untrue. Our desire in this cause is equity, and unworthy indeed should we be, did we not acquit ourselves of the responsible charge transmitted to us by the descent of blood.

* For biographical notice of Signor Sacchini, see footnote, p. 173.
† See Mr. Crowley's letter, Memoirs, p. 42.
‡ See Medical Certificates, Appendix, Note A.

END OF EVIDENCES OF THE MEMOIRS OF LOUIS CHARLES,
DAUPHIN OF FRANCE, REVIEWED.

V.

THE DAUPHIN'S RECOLLECTIONS OF THE PALACES OF VERSAILLES AND THE TUILERIES.

VERSAILLES AND THE TUILERIES.

IT is seen throughout our father's life that his thoughts were constantly dwelling on the incidents of his youth, as certain occurrences seemed so indelibly stamped on his mind that he could not satisfactorily account for, and it was then that he had recourse to Mr. and Mrs. Meves to have his natural curiosity satisfied, from what source in his youth such or such an event could have originated, and from the fact of the true Augustus Meves having in his youth attended a school at Horsham, which school had previously been a county prison, this school therefore in many respects coincided with the Tower of the Temple, and thereby enabled Mr. and Mrs. Meves to answer any questions he put to them in a most reasonable and satisfactory manner, inasmuch that he concluded that such incidents really must have occurred as they had represented; therefore, this accounts for the mystification that surrounded him, as all true recollections were as much as possible tampered with, in order to unsettle him, thus rendering him uncertain as to what in reality were his true recollections; for were he the Dauphin, which the facts connected with his life can leave but little doubt, evidently it was the policy of his supposed parents never to let such transpire—the conditions imposed most probably being such as commanded their silence; for how would it have been possible for his reputed father and mother to have reared him if certain knowledge had remained in him respecting the circumstances which had occurred to him in his youth had been palpable that they had happened in the Tower of the Temple, and never did he doubt their veracity till the disclosure made to him by Mrs. Meves: "that he was the lawful son of Marie Antoinette."

We will now describe our father's opinions respecting himself, after mature consideration on his part, and which were entertained by him up to the period of his demise.

On his visiting the Palace of Versailles in 1816, he has narrated how much he was struck with what there surrounded him, when looking over the balustrade of le Grand l'Escalier des Ambassades, listening to what the guide was reciting, as it seemed to him the very staircase from which he in his youth had witnessed some military band play in the hall, and of a kettle-drum having been strapped to the shoulders of a soldier. Upon his questioning Mr. and Mrs. Meves relative to this recollection, long prior to his visit to Versailles, they have stated "that during the time he attended Messrs. Thornton's boarding-school at Horsham, that at certain periods of the year there were village festivals given, and it must have been at one of these festivals that he had witnessed the incident as above related." This explanation was satisfactory, for such a circumstance in reality could have taken place there, nevertheless there can be little doubt, from what has transpired since this explanation, that it was in reality from the balustrade of le Grand l'Escalier des Ambassades he had witnessed the incident of the band playing, and the drum strapped on the shoulders of a soldier.

On his visiting the Salle du Théâtre at Versailles, it seemed as if he had some slight recollection of it, as it reminded him of a place where in his youth he had seen some fireworks displayed by some soldiers. The following very probably will elucidate this reminiscence :—

"The Flanders regiment having taken up their quarters at Versailles, a banquet was given by the King's Garde du Corps in the great theatre of Versailles (and not in the saloon of Hercules, as some chroniclers say), to the officers of the regiment of Flanders, on the 1st October 1789. Boxes were appropriated to various persons who wished to be present at the entertainment. On the night of entertainment tables were set out upon the stage. Around them were placed one of the body-guard and an officer of the Flanders regiment alternately. There was a numerous orchestra in the room, and the boxes were filled with spectators. The air, ' O Richard! O mon Roi!' was played, and shouts of ' *Vive le Roi*' shook the roof for several minutes. During the entertainment, the King, the Queen, and the Dauphin entered the chamber, when a general enthusiasm prevailed. The moment their Majesties arrived, the orchestra renewed the air just mentioned, and afterwards played a song in The Deserter, 'Can we grieve those whom we love?' which made a powerful impression upon those present. On all sides were heard praises of their Majesties, exclamations of affection, expressions of regret for what they had suffered, clapping of hands, and shouts of '*Vive le Roi! Vive la Reine! Vive le Dauphin!*' "—Madame Campan's *Memoirs of the Court of Marie Antoinette*, vol. ii. p. 70.

It is not therefore unlikely, surrounded as the Dauphin must have been at this entertainment, that it would have impressed him with some slight reminiscence of the theatre, and from our father's recollection of this place, it elicits the great probability that the above event was the means of making that impression on his mind.

Upon his visiting the Tuileries, the only object he imagined having seen previously, "was a large painting in the room of the Garde du Corps."

Respecting his remembrance of having seen in his youth a wonderful display on the water,* which, after what he had revealed to him of his being the son of Marie Antoinette, he imagined was the procession which bore the ashes of Voltaire to the Pantheon, for after his reading in *Prudhomme's Journal* the account therein given of this procession, it seemed in many instances to correspond with his recollections of the display he had seen when a youth. His reputed father accounted for the above as having taken place at Vauxhall Gardens, but if correct what Mrs. Meves revealed, it could not have taken place at Vauxhall, but the

* See Memoirs, pp. 16, 17.

incident which caused this reminiscence must have occurred in France. In comparing his recollection with Prudhomme's account, it will be seen it is not critically correct, for the procession was by land, and his recollection was a procession by water, but in reading Monsieur Lamartine's description of this procession,* which is fully detailed, and as far as regards the incidents therein given, his recollections, although defective, seems to correspond strikingly with such. Upon this procession arriving at the Quai Voltaire it stopped, and was visible to the occupants of the Palace of the Tuileries, and probably at this time the Dauphin may have been in the garden of the Palace, or adjacent thereto, and have witnessed this procession, as when the Royal Family were at the Tuileries they could take no open-air exercise, except on the terrace next to the river, therefore, this procession having passed over the water, and having come in such proximity to the gardens, shows the likelihood of its being the same which our father had seen in his youth. Though the procession was by land, nevertheless, it passing so near the water accounts why this procession had left such an impression on a child's mind, that it was a procession by water. Considering the preceding and subsequent tumultuous processions that took place in Paris, and the unsettled state wherein the Dauphin was placed, it easily accounts for mistakes that may arise in his narrations, as so many complicated and incomprehensible incidents must have happened, which were impossible for the understanding of a boy of his age to have retained with accuracy, and makes apparent the consistency "under such circumstances" of the reminiscences herein narrated.

* See Appendix, Note D.

END OF THE DAUPHIN'S RECOLLECTIONS OF THE PALACES OF
VERSAILLES AND TUILERIES.

VI.

THE DAUPHIN'S RECOLLECTIONS OF THE TOWER OF THE TEMPLE.

IN speaking of our father's recollection of the Tower of the Temple, there seems nothing unnatural in his reminiscences, as they are such as in reality would have made an impression on the mind of a youth,—such as the appearance of the place, the desolate garden, and the school at which he attended in the Rotunda of the Temple, and the boys attending him therefrom to the Temple, where he was received by Madame Simon, whose husband used to exercise him in a strangely built room, on the top of this Tower. Once when this person was stimulating him with a handkerchief, by accident it swang round his face, and tore the skin from his left cheek, and occasioned a wound which was some time in healing. The scar from this accident remained on our father up to the time of his decease.

In the Historical Records it is stated that the Dauphin received a blow from Simon with a towel, whilst waiting upon him.* How singular it is that the subject of the present Memoirs had a scar on his cheek occasioned from the result of such a blow as recorded, and of his recollection of such having been occasioned by Simon. Though this scar is not entered in the medical certificates, nevertheless it existed, and as no particular allusion had been made to it by those who attached importance to the several marks and scars accounts for the omission

* See Memoirs, page 2; likewise Historical Records, page 141.

in our not having directed medical attention to this scar, for it seemed
to us that enough was guaranteed to carry identity, without calling
attention to this; nevertheless, it existed as palpably as the other scars
on his person, but we admit it would have been more satisfactory for
medical testimony to have guaranteed its authenticity. The reason of
now alluding to this scar is on account of having lately read in
Lamartine's *History of the Girondists*, and Beauchesne's *Louis XVII.*,
that the Dauphin received a blow from Simon with a towel, and as there
existed a scar on the subject of these Memoirs, who accounted for such
having originated from a blow received from Simon with a towel, we
have therefore alluded to it, as its existence adds another link in proving him to be assuredly the son of Louis xvi.

Respecting the incident of the swing in the upper room of the
Temple, of the boy who whilst swinging striking the hooks which supported the tube that conveyed the smoke from an old iron stove in the
room, whereupon down came a portion of the worm-eaten old tube,
and with it the soot, the accumulation of years: to show the feasibility
of such having in reality occurred at the Temple, is, "that the upper
room of the Temple in which our father supposed the above event to
have occurred, had, upon the Royal Family's incarceration there, contained an old iron stove, which was afterwards removed, and a French
one took its place." There being some cause for such being done,
shows every probability that the above incident occasioned the necessity
of having a new stove, as, by our father's recollection of this tube, it
would require entirely replacing.

Whilst confined in this building he recollected having seen a kind of
play, and of being taken out by Simon to the house of a friend of his,
where, while in a room by himself, he got on a chair in order to reach
some comfiture from the cupboard, and not being able to reach the
desired article, he got on a high muff-box, which he overturned and fell
on the floor, which brought the company into the room. After which he
mounted Simon's shoulders and returned to the Temple, amidst a number
of persons who were attracted to them on account of their singing.

On the fourth day after the Dauphin's separation from his mother, a report was circulated in Paris that the son of Louis XVI. had been carried off from the Temple, and had been seen on the Boulevards, and that he had been carried in triumph to St. Cloud. Upon this startling report gaining ground all was commotion, and crowds hastened to the Temple to ascertain the particulars, when the Temple guard assured the inquirers, "that they had not seen Louis XVII. since he had been given up to Simon, and that they believed he was no longer in the Temple." This report caused a deputation from the Committee of Public Safety to repair to the Temple, in order to make an official report as to the safe custody of the Dauphin.

On their arrival at the Temple the Dauphin was taken into the garden in order to be seen by the guards, and for them to verify his safe custody in the Temple. After which Simon was taken into the council-room, where he fully ascertained the routine the authorities desired him to pursue towards the Dauphin (which was to get rid of him), and then followed the demoralizing treatment that was pursued towards the young captive. On the deputation's return to the Convention to report the particulars of their visit, they stated "that the Royal Family were quite safe, under the custodians of the Temple."*

The fact then of the Dauphin having been seen on the Boulevards is fully accounted for, as our father recollected such an incident that would satisfactorily account for such, for he has written, that in his youth he was taken out of the Temple by Simon to an acquaintance of his, and upon leaving the house he mounted Simon's shoulders and returned to the Temple amidst a number of persons attracted to them on account of their singing.†

The Historical Records prove that Simon had then the power of doing as he pleased with his charge, as full confidence was placed in him, or unquestionably he would not have been selected for such an office. The guards, as is seen, asserted that they had not seen the Dauphin since he had been under the custody of Simon; therefore, he

---

* See Historical Records, pp. 136 and 137.   † See Memoirs, pp. 2 and 3.

was the responsible person for the safe keeping of the captive prince. Evidently the incident which our father has narrated, was that which occasioned the report that the Dauphin had escaped from the Temple and had been seen on the Boulevards.

According to our father's recollections many persons used to visit Simon at the Temple, but Hébert and Danton were constant visitors, and especially so Danton, for whenever in the course of his life he was examining portraits of the French Revolutionists, the portrait of Danton always struck him as having been familiar to him in his youth, as he imagined he recognised in the features of that audacious republican the person who, when he was a prisoner in the Temple, used to explain to him, on a starlight night, the mysteries of the planetary system.*

Our father has stated, that the only time he recollected having met with ill-usage whilst under the care of Simon, was from one Jacques Réné Hébert, the immoral and depraved monster who endeavoured to sully the character of the noble and heroic Marie Antoinette by endeavouring, if possible, to ensnare the Dauphin and the Princess-Royal in a deposition of which they could not understand, only, that it was some stratagem to harm their mother. Upon this remorseless villain finding himself foiled in eliciting what he desired from the Dauphin, he seized him by the hair of his head and thrusted him against the door leading to the upper chambers, from which treatment he received a wound over his *left eye*,† and it was this brutality, in our father's opinion, that aroused the natural woman's nature in Madame Simon to use her influence in procuring his release from the Temple. He has described the manner how his escape was effected from the Temple, namely, " by the means of Madame Simon, his introduction to Mr. Meves, his arrival on the coast of Normandy, and subsequent arrival in London " (see Memoirs, pp. 6 and 7).‡

---

* Now, although he imagined he recognised his instructor in the portrait of Danton, in this he was mistaken, for it was the King who in reality was his instructor in the Temple.

† See Medical Certificates, Appendix, Note A.

‡ Deposition of a Medical Gentleman on the Trial of the Baron de Richemont:—
M. Rémusat.—One day on going my rounds at the hospital at Parma, a woman

Having portrayed the Dauphin's recollections of the Temple, we here remark, had it been his desire to impose he would have written quite different, for had he referred to books, and the writings of accredited chroniclers, for a guide, he could have, had his object been to deceive, coincided with many of the incidents narrated; but such was not his object; his object alone was to chronicle what he recollected had happened to him; he repudiated stating he recollected incidents of which he had no recollection, thereby manifesting that candour was his principle, and however much such would have served him, he repudiated stating anything but what he himself individually recollected. He trusted in public opinion, to judge whether there was not every reasonable assurance for him identifying himself as the Dauphin.

called Semas, who was in the hospital, in complaining of the regulations of the hospital, said to me, "If my children were acquainted with my position they would take me from here soon." I asked her if she had any children. "My children," she replied, "are the children of Louis XVI. and Marie Antoinette, whose governess I was." I said to her, "The Dauphin is dead." She replied, "No; he lives. He was released from the Tower of the Temple in a bundle of linen." Such was the disclosure of this person to me, and, to the best of my belief, such was her statement of the means employed in the Dauphin's deliverance. I inquired who this woman was, and was informed she was formerly the wife of the notorious Simon, the keeper of the children of Louis XVI. at the Tower of the Temple. When I learnt her actual capacity at the Tower of the Temple I then fully understood the woman's words, "I was the governess of the children of Louis XVI. and Marie Antoinette at the Tower of the Temple." (*Movement in the auditory.*)

M. le Président.—At what date did this circumstance occur?

M. Rémusat.—In 1811. I was a resident student at the hospital.

M. le Président.—Simon and his wife quitted the Temple in 1794, whilst the Prince died in 1795.

Baron de Richemont.—He was exchanged whilst Simon was keeper of the Temple, and was subsequently confided to the care of the Duke of Bourbon.

M. le Président.—That assertion is unfortunate, for in 1814 the Duke of Bourbon was the first to greet the royalty of Louis XVIII. (*Then addressing the witness*) At the time, did you speak of this revelation to any one?

M. Rémusat.—I have spoken of it to several persons, but I do not recollect their names. (*Much agitation in the auditory followed this evidence.*)

Le Constitutionnel, 2nd and 3rd November 1834.

For Richemont's Trial, see French papers of October and November 1834.

END OF "THE DAUPHIN'S RECOLLECTIONS OF THE TOWER OF THE TEMPLE."

VII.

HOW THE DAUPHIN WAS BROUGHT UP AFTER HIS ARRIVAL IN ENGLAND, TILL THE YEAR 1823.

AVING completed that portion of the Dauphin's recollections which constitutes his life till his escape from the Tower of the Temple and his subsequent arrival in England, we shall detail his subsequent career after his arrival in Great Russell Street. The incidents of his life from his arrival in England having been previously discussed,* renders it unnecessary to here recapitulate them, but to follow in order such as have not been commented on, namely :—

On finishing his schooling at Tempest's he returned to the care of Mr. Meves, when he studied music, and as he progressed in his pianoforte playing, his reputed father, seeing him frequently absorbed in thought whilst so engaged, adopted the habit of reading entertaining works to him, for Mr. Meves's desire was not to foster in any way his early recollections, but to hinder such coming in any way to his mind, therefore, he amused him in delightful narrations of the most pleasing to a boy's imagination, and thus his attention was drawn from ruminating on his early life by the extreme kindness of his reputed father.   His musical education was paid particular attention to.

Mr. Meves being an artist he took a portrait of his adopted son, at the latter end of 1797, which portrait our father had every reason to

* See page 198.

believe was the original from which the print, one of which he possessed, entitled, " L'Espoir des Français," " The hope of the French"—
had been engraved.

Our father, having made unusual progress as a pianoforte player,
was taken to Edinburgh, and appeared at Urbani's Concerts at the
Assembly Rooms in George Street, under the name of Master Augustus.
His performance at these Concerts met with a marked encomium
in a critique, likening him to the great Mozart.* One evening
after he had played Steibelt's Concerto of " The Storm," as he
passed down the room he was highly complimented by the Countess
de Lally, and by a stout French gentleman, who he was informed
was the Count of Provence, brother of Louis xvi., afterwards Louis
xviii.

On his return to London, one would suppose after such a success in
Edinburgh, that Mr. Meves would have endeavoured in every way to
have completed his musical education, by giving him first-rate masters ;
but no, his music instructor, who up to the time he went to Edinburgh,
had been giving him lessons on counterpoint and composition, was then
dispensed with, and Mr. Meves then desired to have him brought up
as a merchant, and with this object he placed him in the firm of Beland
and Co., where he was employed for some time.

It seems strange, after he had become a proficient instrumentalist,
and the general approbation he met with, and the high compliments
paid him at the Edinburgh Concerts, that after his return from Scotland,
he was placed by Mr. Meves at a counting-house, with the intention of
bringing him up as a merchant, which is seen did not at all agree with
his inclination, as it was a branch so opposite to that of the gratifying
study of music. The only reason we can attribute for Mr. Meves having
done such, is, that as a public character he would have been thrown
much into society, where he might have been recognised, whereas in an
office, this would have been obviated. The dull monotony of the counting-house, together with the uncourteous Beland, made him take a great

---

* See Appendix, Note C, for Biographical Notice of Meves' " Augustus."

dislike to his new vocation, which he represented to Mrs. Meves, who introduced him to Mr. John Broadwood, the celebrated pianoforte manufacturer.   He then quitted the counting-house and practised music assiduously, and by the recommendation of his kind patron he met with success in teaching in the highest circles ; likewise, Mrs. Meves having the teaching of many of the nobility, enabled her likewise to introduce him, and in a very short time he moved in society through invitation with the *élite.*

Mr. Meves had a great dislike to his visiting such society, remarking, that he would never gain money by it ; and he, desiring that he should have a settled income, purchased a musical walk, which occupied him thenceforth incessantly, for six days in the week.

In 1813 he took a dislike to the musical profession, on account of the wearisome humdrumming he had been subjected to in the teaching of schools, and became a speculator at the Rotunda of the Bank of England.

Respecting his visit to the Argyle Rooms in 1815, and of the lady whom he observed scrutinizing him after Mrs. Meves had left her seat, which lady he afterwards saw several ladies and gentlemen curtsey and bow to, and who, upon inquiry, he was informed was the Duchess of Angoulême,—in after years, when his eyes were opened as to his real origin, his opinion was, that he was taken intentionally to the Argyle Rooms by Mrs. Meves, so that her Royal Highness might see him, and be personally assured of his, "her brother's," existence.

Having fully alluded, in the Dauphin's recollections of the Palaces of Versailles and Tuileries, of his visit to Paris in 1816, these therefore we pass over, as it would be but a recapitulation, and follow his subsequent career.*   He again entered the musical profession, and published several compositions which became very popular, and at times visited the Bank of England, where he made some trifling speculations.

One afternoon when he was in the City some liberty had been taken

* See page 236.

with Mr. William Meves, whereupon his seeing him angry he inquired the cause? Having ascertained such, he left Mr. Meves to expostulate on such, in order to avert its recurrence, when he received no apology, and which ultimately ended in the insulter having the unpleasant satisfaction of being knocked down. For resenting this insult Mr. Meves promised to pay several expenses he was at, and placed about £3000 in their joint names in the Bank of England, and share property. Subsequent to his resenting this insult Mr. Meves became doubly attached to him, for since he had grown to manhood Mr. Meves had not over-indulged him, but this voluntary act of taking his part had acted in such a manner on him, that his kindness was immediately called into action for his welfare, and from that date, kindness towards him was his predominant characteristic.

Subsequent to the demise of Mr. Meves in 1818, on the reading of his will, it is seen he named our father therein as his natural reputed son, which caused Mrs. Meves to disclose his true origin, the consequence of which, together with the anxiety he experienced, determined him, however unnecessary, in fully and satisfactorily assuring himself of the true cause of his reputed father's demise, and from the depth of his thoughts consequent thereof he became indisposed, and placed himself under medical advice. The medicine prescribed unfortunately flew to the brain, and from the effects of which, it was some length of time before he recovered.

Since the demise of Mr. Meves he had never been able to gain from Mrs. Meves any more than what she had disclosed was true, and he having a delicacy in not forcing the subject upon her, awaited patiently to see what she would further disclose. One day whilst they were together she again assured him he was *the true Dauphin of France*, and son of Marie Antoinette ; and then follows the precautions she gave him, and how to make himself known to the Duchess of Angoulême.* She knew what historians had stated in reference to the Dauphin was incorrect, therefore she said, "Do not be led by what history has recorded,

* See Memoirs, page 37.

neither to enter into any particulars, for if he did he would be lost, for as a matter of course, the manner he had been brought up, and the misrepresentation to which he had been subjected, would in all cases have been contradictory to published Memoirs."

Upon the decease of Mrs. Meves it is seen she bequeathed her effects to Caroline Read. Evidently Mrs. Meves was interested from some cause or other to Caroline Read, and this cause was : that she was the daughter of Maria Dodd, and consequently the sister to the deaf and dumb boy Mrs. Meves had taken to Paris to extricate her son Augustus from the Temple; this is the reason of her making such a bequest, she having by doing so fulfilled the promise she had made to Maria Dodd respecting her daughter Caroline.*

Antecedent to the disclosure of Mrs. Meves, all the actions of the subject of the present Memoirs were compatible with the position in life wherein he was placed, and in no way prior to this period had he identified himself as being any other than the son of Mr. and Mrs. Meves. Who could possibly have known better than Mrs. Meves whether he was her own son, or that of another person? She could answer decidedly as regarded herself, and we see no reason whatever to discredit her revelation ; for that which has come to light, though it has taken time to see its applicability, will prove incontestably the sterling guaranty of such, for history in no way invalidates it, as the more assiduously the Records of the period the Royal Family were confined in the Temple are examined, the more apparent the fact of the Dauphin's liberation will be manifest. Let then the given history of the Dauphin at the Temple be closely investigated, with the determination of ascertaining precisely on what ground chroniclers have concluded that the Dauphin terminated his existence in the Temple, and it will be found that its foundation will not admit scrutiny, its supports are but superficial, and the fabric must fall to the ground, if assailed with the idea of testing its impregnableness. Assertions are not facts, and the history that has been made public up to the present date respecting the demise

* See Memoirs, page 51.

of the Dauphin in the Tower of the Temple, cannot be looked upon in any other light than that of assertion. Validity should not fear scrutiny, and if the demise of the Dauphin in the Temple comes under this denomination, investigation has nothing to fear, but reason proclaims validity backs it not, but alone assertion, and therefore investigation is not desirable, if such can be possibly postponed, for silence is preferable.

Taking the preceding Historical Records into consideration, and the present work, we cannot as matters stand acquiesce with such chroniclers who report the Dauphin as having ended his days in the Temple, for it is too palpably apparent, that they were in error when they concluded that it was the Dauphin who was confined in the Temple after October 1793.

END OF "CAREER OF THE DAUPHIN FROM HIS ARRIVAL IN ENGLAND TILL THE YEAR 1823."

VIII.

THE DAUPHIN'S CONVERSATIONS WITH THE PRETENDER NAÜNDORFF.

IN referring to the conversations our father had with Naün-dorff, it is seen he became acquainted with him through a Monsieur Auguste Desjardin, who was a warm supporter of Naündorff's pretensions.   After their being introduced the conversation very naturally turned on the Tower of the Temple, when our father informed Naündorff, on account of his having been led by his reputed parents to believe that he was brought up at a school at Horsham, which had formerly been a county prison, his positive recollections of the Tower of the Temple had been in a great measure destroyed, for the fact was apparent, that incidents which in reality had happened to him in the Tower of the Temple, had been represented as having hap-pened to him at this school at Horsham, and consequently gave rise to the mystification that surrounded him.   Having stated so much, he related the recollections he had of the Temple.*   After which it is seen the readiness he evinced in placing in Naündorff's hands works that he possessed, as a guide for him in writing his Life, which he stated he intended doing, thereby showing our father would have been happy could Naündorff have proved himself to have been the Dauphin, for if he indisputably could have done so, it would have relieved him of much anxiety, for with our father there was no desire to deceive, for his im-pression was candidly that he was the Dauphin ; nevertheless, he was

* See Memoirs, page 82.

personally aware from his own feelings the difficulties he had to contend with, for he seemed surrounded by a labyrinth of mystery, which would have occupied his whole time for its solution ; likewise, he felt convinced in many instances public opinion would have doubted his honour, as experience had made apparent to him the incredulousness ot the age. The Memoirs have been written at our special solicitation, as we knew his integrity, and it is upon our reading different works, and reflecting upon his Memoirs, that we see the consistency in his identifying himself as the true Dauphin.

Naündorff recounted what he himself recollected of the Temple, and it is from this, together with other particulars,* that our father imagined he recognised in Naündorff the true Augustus Meves.

We shall now give a sketch of Naündorff's published life, and then comment thereon, when it will be seen whether such is admissible.

* See Memoirs, page 85.

END OF " CONVERSATIONS WITH THE PRETENDER NAÜNDORFF."

IX.

AN OUTLINE OF THE PUBLISHED LIFE OF THE PRETENDER NAÜNDORFF.

IN Naündorff's published life he states he recollected events that occurred to the Royal Family of France, with wonderful accuracy, from a very early age till his consignment to the care of Simon and his wife. He then recollected being confined alone in the room that had formerly been occupied by Cléry (the King's valet-de-chambre) at the Temple—this room having been quite transformed into a prison, the door of which was fastened, and a wicket was made, through which his jailers placed him his food and uttered their invectives, even in the night, against his helpless and oppressed self, until he resolved rather to die than to answer them further. He became seriously ill through the condition he was reduced to and the privations he endured, he not having been provided with linen or clothes during his incarceration in this vile dungeon, the consequence of which was, that he soon became covered with vermin, and poisoned with the stench of this loathsome prison.

He then recollected some persons attending him, who he thought were doctors. They questioned and entreated him to speak, and tell them what he wanted. To these (he states) he made no answer, as he had many reasons for maintaining silence. Indeed his tongue seemed paralysed at the sight of those who were set over him as his guard. At last an attendant was sent, who was accompanied by several municipal officers, who asked him several questions, to which *he gave no answer.*

He was then cleaned, the room put in order, and a shutter which had obstructed the light from entering the room was taken down.

About this time he states some friends had formed the project of rescuing him from his persecutors, but they found too vigilant guard at the Temple to carry into operation their design, as there was only one access to him, for the turret which contained the staircase had but one door, at which a strict watch was kept day and night, inside as well as out, and every one previously to entering the Tower was searched, and likewise before leaving it, on account of the design of liberating him having been discovered. It being next to impossible to get him out of the Temple, his friends resolved to conceal him in it, in order to make his persecutors believe he had escaped therefrom. They conceived the project of taking him from the second floor, which he occupied, and concealing him in the fourth storey of the Temple.

Accordingly, one day his protectors gave him a dose of opium, which he took for medicine, and he was soon half-asleep. In this state he saw a child which they substituted for him in his bed, and he was laid in a basket in which this child had been concealed under the bed. He perceived as if in a dream that the child was only a wooden figure, the face of which was made to resemble his. This substitution was effected at the moment when the guard was changed. The one who succeeded was content with just looking at the bed to certify his presence, as it was enough for him seeing a sleeping figure. His habitual silence contributed further to strengthen the error of his new Argus. In the meantime he had lost all consciousness, and when his senses returned he found himself shut up in a large room, which was quite strange to him. It was the fourth storey of the Temple. This room was crowded with all kinds of old furniture, amongst which a space had been prepared for him, which communicated with a closet in the turret, where his food had been placed. All other approach was barricaded. Before concealing him there, one of his friends informed him how to act in order to be saved, viz., that he should bear all imaginable suffering without complaining, as a single imprudent step would bring destruction on him and on his benefactors, and insisted that when he was concealed he should ask for nothing, and act the part of a *deaf and dumb boy.*

When he awoke he recollected the injunctions of his friends, and he firmly resolved to die rather than betray them. He ate, slept, and waited with patience. He saw his protector from time to time at night, when he brought him what was necessary. The figure was discovered the same night the exchange took place, but the Government thought fit to conceal his escape. His friends, the better to deceive the sanguinary tyrants, *had sent off a boy under his name in the direction, he believed, of Strasburg.* The Government, in order to conceal the escape, put in the place of the wooden figure a *deaf and dumb boy,* and doubled the ordinary guard, endeavouring thus to make it appear that he was still in their safe custody. This increase of caution prevented his friends from completing the execution of their plan in the manner they had intended. He remained therefore in this vile hole, as if buried alive.

At this time he was about nine years and a half old, and already accustomed to hardship by his long sufferings. He cared little for the cold he endured, for it was in the winter that he was imprisoned in the fourth storey. No one could suspect his being there, this room being never opened; and if any one had entered it, they could not have seen him, as the friend who visited him could only reach him by going on all-fours, and when he did not come he waited patiently in his concealment. Frequently he had to wait for several days the arrival of the beneficent beings who provided him with food. "No doubt his readers will wish him to make known the names of these noble individuals, these magnanimous protectors." He states he cannot do so in his Narrative, caution being imposed upon him, through the intrigues of his political enemies, who intended to oppose an individual to him on his trial.

Orders were given not to admit into the Temple any of those who knew him, such persons only were sent there as were in the secret of his escape, or such as were unacquainted with him. He knew not how it happened, but in spite of all these precautions it was whispered about that the real Dauphin was no longer in the Tower of the Temple. The Government became alarmed, and it was decided that the deaf and dumb boy should die, and to effect this, deleterious ingredients were mixed with his food, which made him ill. In order to avert the suspicion of poison, M. Desault was called in, not to cure him, but to counterfeit humanity. Desault visited the captive and soon perceived that some kind of poison had been given to him; he ordered an antidote to be prepared by his friend the Apothecary "Choppart," telling him at the same time that the captive of the Temple *was not the son of Louis* XVI., whom he had formerly known. Desault's disclosure was repeated, and the assassins of his family, seeing that the life of the *deaf and dumb boy* was prolonged in spite of their attempts to poison him, substituted for him *a rickety boy from one of the hospitals* in Paris. This measure also quieted the apprehension they had entertained, that by some accident *the deaf and dumb boy might be discovered to be really such, and in order to secure themselves against any further betrayal of the secret, they poisoned Desault and Choppart, and the substituted rickety boy was attended by physicians, who, never having seen either the real Dauphin or the deaf and dumb prisoner, naturally believed that it was the Dauphin they were attending.*

He then states, a man, whom he recollected had rendered the King services during his confinement in the Temple, was employed to attempt his deliverance, for which purpose some individuals, high in the Revolutionary Government, had received large sums from a powerful personage. J. P. presented himself, and received not him, but the deaf and dumb boy in his stead. In accordance with the orders that had been given to him, he took the liberated deaf and dumb boy to Josephine Beauharnais (subsequently the wife of Napoleon Bonaparte), who, on seeing this boy, exclaimed, " Unhappy man, what have you done? By this mistake you have given up the son of Louis XVI. to his father's assassins." Josephine had been well acquainted with the real Dauphin, and also with the deaf and dumb boy, for it was she who had procured him for Barras when he was substituted in the place of the wooden figure. She was ignorant at that

time that the deaf and dumb boy had been exchanged for a rickety one.
Urgent motives constrained the Revolutionary Government to accelerate
the death of this unfortunate victim, who died, he was told, on the 8th
June 1795.   After the *post-mortem* examination, the body was placed in
a coffin.   Preparatory to interment, such was placed in the room formerly inhabited by the King.   While this was going on, a strong dose
of opium was given to him, the rickety boy was then withdrawn from
the coffin, and he took his place therein, all this being effected just at
the moment when the coffin was sent for, to be conveyed to the grave.
As soon as the dead child was concealed in the fourth storey, the coffin
was placed in a carriage.   This carriage had been prepared for the purpose.   On the way to the burial-ground he was withdrawn from the
coffin and placed in a box at the bottom of the carriage, and the coffin
was filled with rubbish to give it sufficient weight, and as soon as it was
deposited in the grave his friends re-entered Paris with him, there he was
intrusted to the hands of other friends, but he had not the slightest
recollection of any of the circumstances of the moment.   When he
awoke he found himself in a bed in a very neat apartment, along with
his nurse, who was a Madame * * *, the young sentinel of the
Temple Garden.   Fortunately this business was executed with despatch,
for scarcely was he in a place of safety when the whole secret was discovered.   All the endeavours of his persecutors to regain possession of
him were fruitless.   Soon it began to be publicly rumoured that it was not
the Dauphin who had been buried.   These reports alarmed the Government, who gave orders to its agents to disinter the coffin and to bury it
elsewhere.   His friends, fearing that he might be discovered, disguised
and sent him in a carriage out of Paris ; at the same time, to put his
enemies upon a wrong scent, they sent off a boy, a native of Versailles,
with his parents, intending him to pass for him.   Devoted friends
received him on the route with the tenderest care and greatest discretion.   It was intended to convey him to the Vendean army, but his
health gave way, and he remained with Madame * * *, who
never left him.   As soon as he became convalescent, she commenced

instructing him in the German language, that he might the more easily pass for her son. Whilst under this lady's care three persons in uniform visited him, with whom he was unacquainted, but who Madame * * * informed him were General Charette and two of his friends. He endures a long illness, and is recaptured one night by some gendarmes, and taken back to prison.

Whilst he was under Madame * * *'s care, a Mr. B., a Swiss, was in communication with her. He also had another friend, formerly Dame du Palais to Marie Antoinette; it was they who furnished Madame * * * and him with their requirements. Mr. B., being disguised as an old peasant, was in communication with Madame Beauharnais, who procured his escape from prison. When liberated he was placed into the hands of Mr. B., with whom was a young girl named Marie, and a huntsman named Jean, whose real name was Montmorin; thenceforth these protectors managed his affairs. They journeyed to Italy, where he was protected by the Pope, "Pius the Sixth." In Italy he was rejoined by Madame * * * and her second husband. The Revolutionary army penetrated Italy, and treachery obliged him and his friends to board a vessel sailing for England. Mr. B. and the young Marie were assassinated; he was captured at sea and brought back to France and placed in prison. He was still followed by Montmorin, the only one who escaped the treachery in Italy. He was then removed from this prison to another, where he remained till 1803, from where he was liberated by Josephine, and the minister Fouché, the faithful Montmorin breaking the chains of his captivity.

In 1804 he was again arrested in the environs of Strasburg, from where he was transferred to a prison and placed in a dungeon, where he endured the most agonizing sufferings till the spring of the year 1809. He was liberated from this dungeon by his friend, the faithful Montmorin, through the aid of Josephine. They travelled then for Frankfort-on-the-Maine. Montmorin then, he asserts, "sewed some papers in the collar of his greatcoat, which would form undeniable proofs of his identity to all the Sovereigns of Europe."

R

They then travelled to the domain of the Duke of Brunswick, from whom they obtained letters of recommendation for Prussia. They reached Prussia, and rested at an inn in some village. In the night they were arrested as spies, and taken before a Major de Schill, an officer in the service of the Duke of Brunswick, when Montmorin presented the Duke's letters, through which they were received kindly.

The Duke of Brunswick and the Westphalians being hostile, and Major de Schill, being hard pressed, he sent Naündorff and Montmorin away under an escort, when they fell into the hands of the enemy. A skirmish ensued, in which the trusty Montmorin was killed, and he was wounded and taken prisoner and placed in a hospital. He was then taken to the fortress of Wessel, on the frontier of France, and con-demned, amongst other prisoners, to the galleys at Toulon, by order of Napoleon. He was then transferred from one prison to another in the interior of France. At last he fell ill and was left behind at some village, and was conveyed to some tower where he met a soldier of Schill's hussar regiment, who soon recognised him, and persuaded him to endeavour to escape with him from the hands of their perse-cutors. Accordingly, one stormy night they effected their escape, and took refuge in a neighbouring wood. They reached the frontiers of Westphalia in safety, when his comrade Friedrichs went, as he usually did, in quest of provisions, whilst he took refuge in the hollow of an oak-tree. His retreat was found out by a shepherd's dog. The shepherd took compassion on him, imagining him to be a Westphalian deserter, and offered him refuge. He then acquainted the shepherd that he was not alone, and informed him of Friedrichs. The shepherd then relates he saw a person answering Friedrichs' description in the custody of the Cheva-liers de la Corde, on their way to the next town. Thus it was he lost his comrade Friedrichs. He accepted the proffered hospitality of the good old shepherd, and repaired to his habitation. On the third day he proceeded again on his journey to Berlin. On the road he met a carriage *en route* for Wittenberg, and its occupant, a young man, who offered him a seat, which he gladly accepted. Having arrived at Wittenberg the young man procured him conveyances, and he arrived safe in Berlin.

In 1810 he states he set up as a watchmaker, Schützenstrasse No. 52. He soon got on in business. The authorities then interfered, as they required the necessary credentials for his carrying on such a business. He was required to deposit in the magistrates' office his passport, the register of his birth, and a certificate of good conduct from his last residence. In this dilemma he received the advice of a confidant, who was in his secret, to write to the President of the General Police of the kingdom of Prussia, which advice he adopted.

This functionary visited him, and he then unsewed the collar of his greatcoat, in which Montmorin had sewed the proofs by which he might be recognised, with which the functionary was satisfied and took his departure. The next day the official called in order to procure the papers that they might be submitted to the King. He gave him the papers, from which he selected what he thought sufficient, and left, promising that he should experience no further annoyance. Notwithstanding he was annoyed, and obliged to adopt the name of his arrested companion, which was "Naündorff." In 1812 he quitted Berlin for Spandau, where he was attacked with illness, during which time the Prussians were bombarding the town. After his recovery he wrote to the European Powers respecting his claims.

In 1816 he sent a M. Marsin, or Marassin, an ex-officer in Napoleon's army, to the Duchess of Angoulême, furnishing him with proofs of his identity, and empowering him to assume his character. He never again saw this person after his departure, but he supposed, from what had transpired, that he had been arrested, and that the Government had procured the papers from him, and substituted for him one Mathurin Bruneau, whom the Government of Louis XVIII. brought to trial, in order to make his claims appear contemptible.

He married in 1818 Madlle. Jeanne Einers, and remained at Spandau till 1821, during which he was not able to regain the possession of the papers he had intrusted to the Prussian official. He espoused the quarrel of the burgomaster of Spandau against the Government, who wished to have him removed from his office by the authority of the Town-Council. All of a sudden the quarrel ceased, and the burgomaster was appointed to a situation in Brandenburg. Naündorff quitted Spandau for Brandenburg. Here he underwent much annoyance, and was accused of coining. During his examination he was questioned as to his birth. He replied he was a prince, and referred them for further information to the King of Prussia. He then went through a series of misfortunes, and was imprisoned till 1828.

After his liberation, and many difficulties, he arrived at Crossen, where his pretensions got circulated. From here the magistrate and himself addressed letters to the several crowned heads. His agent, M. Pezold, cited the judge of Brandenburg who had condemned him. Shortly after, M. Pezold (on the 16th March 1832) was poisoned.

He then wrote to the Royal Family of France, and shortly after was informed by an unknown friend that the King of Prussia, by the advice of his ministers, had issued an order for his arrest in order to place him in a fortress. He took friendly warning, and managed to evade being apprehended. He then set out and met with the ups and downs of a traveller's life. He fell in with a party of Poles. The priest of this fugitive band one evening accused him of being a spy, through which he was imprisoned by the police. The following day he received his liberty. In the meantime the malevolent priest and his party had departed. He arrived at Paris in May 1833, and was surrounded by a party of gentlemen. In 1834 M. Morel de St. Didier visited the Duchess of Angoulême, at Prague, in order to induce her to grant Naündorff an interview. During St. Didier's interview he handed the Duchess a portrait of Naündorff, which she examined attentively, when she remarked that she saw in it no resemblance to her family. After listening to St. Didier's petition, she replied, " It may be easily imagined how happy I should be to find my brother again, but I believe, unhappily, he is dead, unless another was substituted in his place, of which I am ignorant." St. Didier then resumed, " that a substitute had really been placed in the Temple, and that few persons in France doubted the escape of the Dauphin, as it appeared certain he had not died in the Temple." He then handed Madame the despatches which he had brought from Naündorff, which she promised to read, remarking, " This is too serious a matter to be lightly examined, and of such importance that it will be necessary to devote several days to the consideration of it." She gave him notice that she must mention the whole business to the King and to the Dauphin, for she never did anything without their knowledge and consent. Here ended the interview.

A few days after Her Royal Highness sent for St. Didier, when she informed him that she had read all that he had brought her, but in which she found nothing to grant the interview, observing,—" If anything could for a moment arrest her attention it would have been Madame de Rambaud's letter, because she remembered that she was her brother's attendant," but all that was nothing. He renewed his solicitation in his client's behalf, when the Duchess said, " She would reconsider the whole matter, but it was indispensably necessary that she should have sent her by a confidential messenger in writing, all that was refused to be told her except by word of mouth, then she would come to a decision about the desired interview," remarking, " That if she granted such it would take place in the presence of witnesses ; and above all, it was absolutely necessary to forward the details relative to his asserted escape from the Temple."

St. Didier observed to the Duchess, that if she made inquiries of the King of Prussia relative to Naündorff's antecedents, he thought that monarch would not speak satisfactorily of him, on account of the atrocious conduct of the Prussian Government towards him. He referred the Duchess to inquire his character amongst the citizens in the different towns in which he had resided. She promised she would make further inquiries, upon which he took his adieu.

St. Didier returned to Paris to consult Naündorff. In the meantime a remarkable and mysterious interview took place between the Duchess of Angoulême and the King of Prussia. Dresden was the spot fixed for the meeting ; the King travelled incognito, but not finding the Duchess there, continued his journey to Pilnitz, and then to Töplitz, where he met the Duchess ; and they had a long conference, concerning which nothing distinct can be ascertained, except, that the Duchess asked a variety of questions respecting Naündorff, which the King answered.

St. Didier went to Prague again in September, carrying with him a letter relative to the asserted escape of Naündorff. He was accompanied by Madame de Rambaud. This time he found the manner of the Duchess cold and reserved, and instead of the interest she had previously manifested, she now showed perfect indifference and contempt for Naündorff, observing, " that all he had stated had appeared in print, or must have been read by him." St. Didier spoke of a recent attempt to assassinate him. She smiled incredulously, yet on being assured it was a fact, she replied, " No one would think of assassinating an impostor," and then struggling between affected composure and irritation, exclaimed, " M. de St. Didier, this man is nothing but an impostor and an intriguer, but very clever." St. Didier replied, " He believed him no impostor, and if such an imputation were applicable to him, his friends and himself would be liable to it also." The Duchess then observed, " She was convinced of his (St. Didier's) integrity, nevertheless, he was under a delusion of which she did not partake."

During St. Didier's interview he presented the Pretender Richemont's portrait to the Duchess, which, according to St. Didier, after examining a few moments, she threw disdainfully on the table, saying, " No, no, Sir, this is not the thing."

Madame Rambaud, after travelling to Prague with St. Didier, was refused an interview with the Duchess, as she attached no importance to the pretensions of Naündorff.

The Pretender Richemont had a hearing to see on what grounds his claims were founded to the title of Louis xvii., he having been brought forward by the Government in order to disconcert and throw ridicule upon Naündorff's pretensions. He was opposed on his trial by St. Didier, who placed in Court, Naündorff's claims. Richemont was sentenced to twelve years' imprisonment, and subsequently Naündorff was suddenly arrested, and his papers seized, and he was forced to leave France on the plea of his not being a Frenchman. He came to England, where he published his life, and in the year 1844 he shook off the troubles of mortality, at Delft, in Holland.

END OF "AN OUTLINE OF THE PUBLISHED LIFE OF THE PRETENDER NAÜNDORFF."

X.

COMMENTARY AND INFERENCES ON THE PUBLISHED LIFE OF THE PRETENDER NAÜNDORFF.

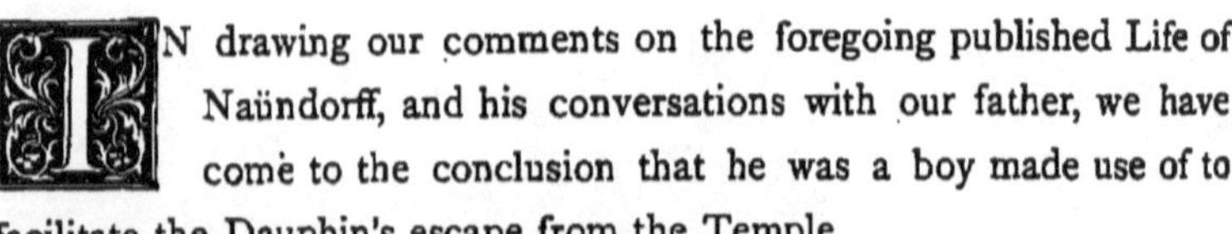

IN drawing our comments on the foregoing published Life of Naündorff, and his conversations with our father, we have come to the conclusion that he was a boy made use of to facilitate the Dauphin's escape from the Temple.

Having previously stated how the Dauphin was extricated from the Temple in the month of October 1793, during the trial of the noble Marie Antoinette, if the Records of the time are read it will be seen subsequent to the Queen's execution, that the captive of the Temple was solely under the guardianship of Simon and clique, and that the boy but seldom deigned to answer them ; he no longer roved about the garden of the Temple, but was kept to his room, ill-treatment became his doom, and the forfeiture of his life the desire of his keeper. What necessity was there for such seclusion ? The necessity was this :—The Dauphin had been liberated from the Temple, and a substitute having taken his place, such seclusion was necessary, in order to prevent the possibility arising where Simon and clique could have been detected in allowing the Dauphin to escape their custody. As respects the captive answering no questions, we have no doubt such was true to a certain extent, for after the exchange doubtless Simon imposed silence on the captive, in many instances as a matter of personal safety, when persons happened to be present whom he doubted; and the young prisoner was obliged to comply with the wishes of the rigid jailer, in order to avert the brutalities that his non-compliance would have subjected him to. This order of things was carried on till January 1794, when Simon quitted the Temple. Hébert and Chaumette then had the supreme authority at the Temple when the captive was placed in solitary confinement till July, and those whose duty it was to place the captive's food in the wicket, and who peered through to see that a boy was in the room, were unacquainted with the true Dauphin, or if otherwise, in the spirit of the times, merely looked through the wicket to see that a child was there, this being the only humanity the virtue of their office permitted.. It is evident this solitary confinement was to cover some mystery, and that mystery was " to save Simon Hébert and clique." During the time the captive was in this vile incarceration, Hébert and Danton were sent to the scaffold for favouring the cause of the royalists, and for attempting to restore the captives from the Temple. It was not till the execrable Robespierre was executed that the prison door of the captive was thrown open, when his vital powers were found all but exhausted, and then it was found, " *that the captive had blue eyes, which no longer reflected the azure light of heaven, but seemed to have taken a greyish, greenish tint in their dull immobility, and that his beautiful fair hair was stuck fast by an inveterate scurf like pitch.*" *

Should it lie in our power to prove the Dauphin, "the Duke of Normandy," possessed *brown or hazel-coloured eyes, and brown or chesnut-coloured hair*, then it will be evident that the boy confined in the Temple at this period was not the Dauphin, but a substitute.

It is seen in the information of Mrs. Spence, Miss Powell, and Mr. George Meves, that Augustus Meves possessed *blue eyes and light-coloured hair as a boy*, and that our father, say at twenty, possessed *brown eyes and brown hair*. When our father held the conversations with Naündorff, it is seen he was under the impression, through what transpired, that Naündorff was in reality the true Augustus Meves, for his eyes and

* See Historical Records, page 156.

hair corresponded with Augustus Meves's when a boy, and with those of the captive of the Temple in July 1794; his modulating on the pianoforte further strengthening the supposition,—for Augustus Meves had received lessons in his youth, and as so few people at that period learnt the pianoforte, it made the qualifications and identity of Naündorff agree so identically with Augustus Meves, likewise; his stated escape from the Temple, and his coming under the care of a family in Germany, where he was taught the trade of watchmaking, and in his eighteenth year entering the Prussian army, made our father imagine that the family Naündorff was really brought up with in Germany was that of Mr. Bouer, Mrs. Bouer being a sister of Mr. William Meves's.   Upon his questioning Naündorff to know whether indeed the persons under whose care he was placed in Germany were a family of the name of Bouer, he evaded a direct answer by saying, " He could not answer such, as it was necessary for him to be cautious in answering questions that were put to him," and interrogated our father in reply to know whether he did not receive a letter from Germany in 1818? To which he replied, " He did not, but he had been given to understand, subsequent to that date, that one answering such was at the Dead-Letter Office, in Lombard Street, City, but on account of his indisposition at the time he did not make the slightest inquiry about it."   Whatever this letter contained we know not, but evidently Naündorff knew our father by name whilst he was in Germany, and upon reflection our father thought it not unlikely that Naündorff was the true Augustus Meves; and if that was the case, it would account for his knowledge of incidents that occurred at the Temple from October 1793, till the substitution of the deaf and dumb boy. As respects his conversations with our father, it is seen his opinions respecting himself were greatly modified in his published Life, for therein he states, after he was released from the six months' solitary confinement, he came under the charge of Laurent. Now whether Laurent was or was not acquainted with the true Dauphin, he must have been aware of the substitution of the deaf and dumb boy, who was substituted for Augustus Meves, subsequent to the opening of the den in July 1794, for he was the responsible keeper of the Temple captive, and if correct what Naündorff writes of his having been hid in an upper storey of the Temple for eight months, he must likewise have known this. What Naündorff stated in his conversations respecting his escape from the Temple, and his published account, are diverse to a striking degree, for in his conversations he said, "That the evening after the substitution of the mannikin he was taken from the Temple in the disguise of one of the workmen's boys," but in his published Life he states, "That the mannikin, the same evening of the substitution, being discovered to be but a log of wood, the Government substituted a deaf and dumb boy, and he himself remained empanelled in an upper storey of the Temple for eight months."

Evidently when Harmand and colleagues visited the Temple in February 1795, it was a deaf and dumb boy who was personating the character of the Dauphin there, for not a single word could be gained from him, and the strange interrogatory Laurent made to Gomin on his entering on his duties at the Temple, namely, "*Whether he was acquainted with the Dauphin?*" to which he answered, "*He was not, and had never seen him.*" And the singular rejoinder, "*Then it will be some time before he will say a word to you,*" which notification seemed, from what subsequently transpired, was quite true, for the captive was speechless to all.

It is evident that the deaf and dumb boy was substituted in the place of Augustus Meves previous to Gomin entering on his duties at the Temple, and of this exchange Laurent must have been cognisant; but if such was effected, as Naündorff has stated, through the influence of Josephine Beauharnais and Barras, why, his silence was commanded.*

What Naündorff stated in the first instance of having escaped the first evening after the substitution, in the dress of one of the workmen's boys, seems more feasible altogether than to suppose he remained in

* Laurent died at Cayenne.

the upper storey of the Temple for *eight months*, for this seems incredible, and we do not hesitate a moment in pronouncing this a fabrication, and a most absurd one, for during the time he says he was confined, there can be no question, during so long a period, that some of his stated friends must have been detected in going to and fro to give him the necessaries of life, but in the first statement there is no such improbability, for if he were Augustus Meves, such in reality might have occurred as stated.

When Laurent gave up his position at the Temple, Lasne, much against his inclination, was appointed in his stead. He also relates that the captive replied to no questions put to him—" For," says he, "notwithstanding all my attentions, *I had not been able to extract a single word from him during three weeks that I had been at the Temple.*"* It is strange they all agree the captive did not speak ; and we conclude that if he was so reticent at first, he was so as long as the same boy impersonated the Dauphin in the Temple, and had the captive possessed the faculties of speech and hearing, it would have been impossible for him to have acted in the manner as described.

After reiterated solicitations for a surgeon to attend the captive, at last M. Desault was appointed. The same thing occurs again, "*No speech could be gained from the young invalid.*" Then followed the mysterious end of Desault, attributable, according to report, " through his not recognising in the captive of the Temple the son of Louis xvi.," and then followed the sudden end of the apothecary Choppart, which seems to confirm this opinion, for it is a remarkable coincidence.

Ultimately other doctors were appointed to attend the invalid, but apparently between the death of Desault and the appointment of Pelletan a further substitution was effected. It seems singular that up to the period of Desault's death, the captive never seems to have spoken to those who approached him (although every inducement was essayed to obtain such), should have so suddenly been full of conversation to those who approached him after the appointment of Pelletan,

* See Historical Records, page 166.

thereby showing the feasibility of what Naündorff states, "that a rickety boy was substituted in the place of the deaf and dumb boy," for such seems really to have been the case, if any reliance is to be put in the statements of the Temple captive's last keepers.

Although the captive's condition was ameliorated when Laurent was appointed his keeper, nevertheless he was left in loneliness, except at stated hours.* This routine was the order of the day up to the prisoner's decease, for the last two doctors, MM. Pelletan and Dumangin, who attended the captive, expressed their astonishment at the solitary state in which he was left during the night and part of the day,—thus showing there was an urgent necessity for keeping the captive in loneliness, and that urgent necessity was, "to prevent the detection of the Dauphin's liberation from the Temple transpiring."

Lasne, in whose arms the last captive of the Temple died, states, "*that his eyes shone as pure as the blue heaven, and his beautiful fair hair, which had not been cut for two months, fell like a frame around his face.*" †

Should it be admitted the son of Louis XVI. possessed brown eyes, or brown hair, it will be apparent the prisoner of the Temple in June 1795 was not the Dauphin.‡

As regards the proces-verbal of the doctors, it is seen they say, "On attaining the second floor, *they found a boy, apparently about ten years of age, whom the commissaries on duty declared to them to be the remains of the son of Louis XVI., and which two of their number (Pelletan and Dumangin) recognised as the child they had been attending.*" Thus then they did not affirm that the boy was the son of Louis XVI., but only, "*that they were given to understand it was the son of Louis XVI.*" It was on this authority alone that they testified the Dauphin's decease ; but this is no guaranty that it was the son of Louis XVI. Apparently none of them knew the Dauphin, therefore they could not testify that

---

* See Historical Records, pp. 157 and 168.   † See Historical Records, page 169.
‡ See subject " The Colour of the Eyes and Hair of the Dauphin," page 277.

the boy whom they saw was identified by them as the Dauphin, *but only as a boy whom they were given to understand was the Dauphin*, therefore they affirmed his death, but not his identity.

Then followed the mysterious interment of the child, which is a mystery, and for ever will remain such; but as for supposing Naündorff ever gained his deliverance from the Temple in the manner he describes in his published Life, this is too much to entertain. It is a Baron Munchausen story, to which we attach not the slightest credence, neither to his stated series of misfortunes, nor to the fatality that he states befell his asserted friends.

If our conjecture is right in supposing Naündorff to have been Augustus Meves, it would in a great measure account for his enacting the part he did, for through such might have originated the inducement for him to study the part of the Dauphin, and to learn from all sources recondite incidents which have been chronicled happened to the Dauphin, which would be impossible for the memory of any individual at the age he states to have retained with any degree of accuracy; for he states he remembered incidents prior to the journey from Versailles to Paris in 1789, and from that time the most minute personal knowledge of places, persons, names, the dresses he was in the habit of wearing, the situation of the furniture in the rooms the Royal Family occupied, and events which have been chronicled happened both private and public to the Dauphin, which we do not hesitate to say, though chronicled by writers of repute, are nevertheless mostly ideal. Then he had a perfect recollection of everything that took place at the Temple, with such an exactitude that shows these recollections could not have emanated from himself, but from the result of assiduous study only; therefore on such statements we place no reliance, for our opinion is, that he was one of the boys made use of to facilitate the Dauphin's escape from the Temple subsequently to October 1793, if, indeed, he was ever confined there.

The following paragraph appeared in the *Times* of September 7th, 1858 :—

"The History of a Chair.

"A Berlin journal has the following strange tale, of which it guarantees the truth :—'An old woman who lately died in the hospital, left, among other things, a very old arm-chair of Gothic style, and richly decorated. On the sale of her effects by auction a foreigner paid as much as 500 francs for the chair, and surprise having been expressed at his giving so large a sum, he made this explanation—The chair, with other things, was offered by the States of Molhren to the Empress Maria Theresa, and for many years figured in her boudoir. After her death, it, by her express desire, was sent to Queen Marie Antoinette in France, and afterwards was one of the principal pieces of furniture allowed to Louis XVI. in the Temple. The King's valet-de-chambre (Fleury) afterwards became possessed of the chair, and took it to England, where it became the property of the Prince Regent, and afterwards of the Duke of Cumberland. The latter took it to Berlin, and there it was given to an upholsterer to repair. The workman charged with the job found secreted in it a diamond pin, a portrait in pencil of a boy, and a number of small sheets of paper, filled with very small writing. The things he appropriated, the pin he sold, and the portrait and papers he gave to a watchmaker, a friend of his. Although the writing was in a foreign language, the watchmaker succeeded in making out that it consisted of a series of secret and very important instructions, drawn up by Louis XVI. for the Dauphin his son, the portrait being that of the latter. The watchmaker, whose name was Naündorff, some years after gave himself out as Louis XVII., and produced the papers and portrait in question to prove his allegation. After making some noise in France and Belgium, in which latter country he passed by the name of Morel de Saint Didier, this man died in 1849. His son, who called himself Duke of Normandy, went to Java in 1853. The Berlin workman who discovered the documents naturally did not state how Naündorff became possessed of them, but just before his death, which took place lately, he made a full disclosure to his family. They found out that the famous arm-chair had remained in Berlin, and had come into possession of the old woman ; and they caused it to be bought in order to sell it again in Austria.' "

The above is too problematic to attach much faith to ; however, did such take place, it would give a clue to the subsequent part Naündorff enacted.

Although St. Didier gained interviews with the Duchess of Angoulême in Naündorff's behalf, it is seen what opinion she had of his asserted claims; and doubtless she saw St. Didier to learn how far imposture dare proceed, and by what means he had enlisted such men as St. Didier in his behalf.

Previously to the Duchess of Angoulême having received the solicitations of Naündorff's supporters, our father had written to her in the years 1830 and 1831, and forwarded her a lithographic portrait of himself,* likewise, long previous to that period, we have every reason to conclude that the Duchess was perfectly well aware that he was her brother, through Mrs. Meves; therefore, if such was the case, she knew well that Naündorff, and all others who laid claim to the title of Louis XVII., were only adventurers and intriguants. If what we infer is correct, many may remark that, " Had the Duchess been positive that our father was her brother, nothing would have hindered her acknowledging him as such." The following is our opinion respecting such :—" Upon the Duchess of Angoulême's (then Princess-Royal) release from the Temple, she came under the care of Austria. At this period she was totally ignorant of her brother's liberation from the Temple; but such was not the case either with le Comte de Provence or le Comte d'Artois (the two younger brothers of Louis XVI.;) the policy they adopted was, 'that the only surviving daughter of Louis XVI. and Marie Antoinette should be espoused to the Duke of Angoulême, the eldest son of le Comte d'Artois, and then whatsoever thenceforth came to her knowledge respecting her brother's existence, her interests would be so identical with those of Charles X.'s family, that it would be impossible, or almost so, for her to countenance such.' " Thus the policy of non-recognition of her brother was forced upon her.

Far be it from us to desire to cast any unworthy imputations on the Duchess's memory, for we candidly believe her heart was in the right place, and we attribute solely her non-recognition of her brother to the position in which she was placed.

* See Authentic Memoirs, page 56.

The daughter of Louis XVI. married the Duke of Angoulême (the eldest son of le Comte d'Artois), the 10th June 1799, at Mittau in Courland, from which there was no issue. The Duke de Berri (second son of le Comte d'Artois), married the Princess Caroline, of the house of Naples, in 1816, the issue of which was Henri of Bordeaux, who was born the 29th September 1820.

In 1814, le Comte de Provence ascended the throne of France as Louis XVIII., and retained such till his decease in 1824. He leaving no issue, the crown descended to his brother le Comte d'Artois, who reigned as Charles X. He married in 1773 Maria Theresa of Savoy, the issue of which was two sons (the Duke of Angoulême, and the Duke de Berri).

The Ministry of Polignac, which issued in 1830 ordinances dissolving the Chambers, changing the mode of election, and suspending the liberty of the Press, caused in three days, the 27th to the 29th of July 1830, the overthrow of Charles X., who abdicated in favour of his grandson, the Duke of Bordeaux. Charles then retired, first to Scotland, then to Hradschin, near Prague, and lastly to Goritz, in Illyria, where he died in 1836, in his eightieth year. The son of l'Egalité (Louis Philippe) then took the post as Lieutenant-General of the kingdom, and subsequently that of King of the French. In 1848 he was obliged to fly the kingdom. He amassed great wealth whilst King of the French, and died in England in 1850, at Claremont. Thus, since the martyrdom of Louis XVI. the crown has not descended by legitimate succession, for the son of Louis XVI. certainly escaped from the Temple, so all since have been nothing but adventurers, who have occupied the throne of France under the title of Emperor or King; and from the revolution of 1789 has sprung the many parties that exist in France, namely, Legitimists, Orleanists, Napoleonists, and Republicanists, and the slightest fermentation places the power of the throne in uncertainty, for the populace always seem ready for insurrection, there being no true sincerity, as each is for the faction he represents; and though Henry of Bordeaux, the son of the Duke de Berri, now Comte de Chambord, is the acknowledged rightful possessor of the domains of France, nevertheless he has not as yet been able to secure a substantial footing during the many troubles and vicissitudes that have befallen France, since he, in hereditary right, if the Dauphin really died in the Temple, is the King of France.

How strange it is to find that in 1852 (fifty-seven years after the report that stated the Dauphin died in the Temple) a work was published, the author, M. Beauchesne, purporting to prove that the Dauphin died in the Temple, as the prevalent belief in well-informed circles up to that date was, that the Dauphin's escape had been effected from the Temple. As the public mind was not satisfied at that period, fifty-seven years after, it must be apparent, that the Dauphin's escape was based on more solid proofs than supposition, for had public curiosity been satisfied as to the certainty of the Dauphin's death, or had documents been handed down to posterity, which could have been relied upon as authentic, his death in the Temple would never have been questioned, and M. Beauchesne would have been spared a vast amount of anxiety and literary labour, amounting, as he states in his preface, to twenty years, in his attempt to appease the public mind on this point; his onerous efforts, however, have not in the slightest manner altered the popular belief of the Dauphin's deliverance from the Tower of the Temple. Although the purport of his work is to confirm the Dauphin's demise in the Temple, he has been signally unsuccessful in doing so,—for how is it possible to establish that which will not bear scrutiny? Intelligence will not confirm what the understanding repudiates. His work confirms most emphatically the Dauphin's evasion from the Tower of the Temple. It depicts the Royal Family in all their difficulties, and therein may be learnt the decrees of the authorities, and the sufferings of the captives of the Temple, and likewise clearly points out at what period the first exchange took place, and the further substitutions that took place in the Temple.

Of all the pretenders that have presumed to the title of the Dauphin, no substantial proof have they been able to advance which can lead to the supposition of their identity with the Dauphin; they have endeavoured to personate his character, and a sorry personification it has been. If their parts were conceived solely on their own assumption, it was a dangerous and desperate hazard,—for surely as impostors they would be unmasked, as positively they were, and which makes it appear not at all unlikely that Hervagault, in the reign of Napoleon I., that of Mathurin Bruneau, under Louis XVIII., and that of the Baron de Richemont, under Louis Philippe, were prompted to their parts, for the known antecedents of these men were easily ascertained, and the effect of giving them a public trial could only tend to render thenceforth the question notorious, ridiculous, and contemptible, and would make society cautious in giving a too ready or credulous ear to any future aspirant to such claim.

It is evident there existed great uncertainty, and that public opinion did not indorse the republican announcement of the demise of the son of Louis XVI. in the Tower of the Temple. The pretenders who endeavoured to personate the character of Louis XVII. strikingly prove what public opinion was on this subject. There must have been an incentive for such, and that incentive was, public opinion believed in the liberation of the Dauphin from the Temple. Let the unprejudiced but ascertain on what proofs Louis XVII.'s demise is founded, and they will be found utterly inconclusive.

When Naündorff called for a hearing, the Government was aware he was an adventurer, nevertheless it was not their policy to unmask him, as it may have led to unpleasant disclosures, for they were aware he held some clue as to the true Dauphin's destiny, which made him a dangerous Government antagonist, therefore he was not allowed a hearing, and was forced to leave France. Had Naündorff been so inclined, we believe he could have given accurate information respecting the Dauphin, but he was not fighting the battle of honesty, but that of desired gain,—his object was to sell his secret to the Government. Accordingly, he played his part, trusting to circumstances, for his motto was, " While there is life there is hope ; let others unmask me if they dare, I have nothing to lose, but much to gain, for I possess that which must eventually serve me, for I know the secret who and where may be found the true Dauphin, and therein lies my power, from which I have nought to fear."

Be the present question in reality irrefutable as regards its authenticity, yet doubtless the well-informed on this subject, not on account of their disbelief as to the escape of the Dauphin from the Temple, but through the above pretenders, whose pretensions have been based on grounds so characteristic of chicanery and imposture, that the probability is, that the present announcement is liable to be received with a smile of incredulousness on their parts, for they have, and not without reason, warrantable ground to be sceptical as to the identification of the veritable Dauphin until they have sterling guarantee to be otherwise, which sterling guarantee we presume will be found in the present pages.　We positively aver that imposture is not the incentive or object of the present work, but alone the desire to establish the truth respecting the real history of the son of Louis XVI.　Let reason then be the guide to judgment, and let sense, and that alone, overrule prejudice.

END OF " COMMENTARY AND INFERENCES ON THE PUBLISHED LIFE
OF THE PRETENDER NAÜNDORFF."

XI.

THE COLOUR OF THE EYES AND HAIR OF LOUIS CHARLES, DAUPHIN OF FRANCE.

WE state that Louis Charles, Duke of Normandy, had brown or hazel-coloured eyes, and brown or dark chesnut-coloured hair. Let such pictures then as the artist has had sittings of the Royal Family, or on which unquestionable reliance can be placed, be examined; this will elicit what colour the Dauphin's eyes and hair actually were up to October 1793. Reliance cannot be placed in the imaginative, but only in the literal. Those who describe the Dauphin as having possessed blue eyes and light-coloured hair derive their information from fallacious sources. After eight years of age the eyes do not materially change their colour, and at no period of life could they change from brown to blue, for by the law of nature they would change, if they changed at all, to a darker hue, and not to a lighter. As regards the colour of hair changing, we cannot suppose a child having at eight years of age brown hair, for that hair to change colour in the course of two years to fair hair, for instead of hair, if it changes at this age, getting lighter, it is the law of nature for it to get darker ; therefore brown hair could by no means (without artificial) change to fair hair. The boy who died in the Temple, the 8th June 1795, possessed blue eyes and fair hair : should it lie in our power to prove the Dauphin possessed brown eyes or brown hair, it will prove beyond doubt that the boy who died in the Temple was not the Dauphin, but a substitute, for it will then be conclusive the Dauphin's escape from the Temple was effected.

The following is the authority respecting the likelihood of eyes and hair changing their colour. In August 1861 we visited Dr. Hancock of Harley Street, London, the chief ophthalmic physician of the Charing Cross Institution, to know his professional opinion as to whether it would be possible for a lad at the age of eight years, whose eyes were brown, supposing such lad was confined and ill-treated for six months, whether there would be a possibility of his eyes changing their colour to light blue. To which he replied, "such a thing was not possible." We then handed him the following letter :—

"SIR,—As chief surgeon to the Royal Westminster Ophthalmic Hospital, I have to request your opinion to know whether it would be possible for a lad, at the age of eight years, whose eyes are brown, presuming such a boy was confined and neglected for six months, would there be a possibility in that period for brown eyes to change their colour to light blue, or would it be possible at his arriving at ten years of age,—if so, would it be according to the law of nature? Likewise, whether chesnut-brown hair could change its colour to fair hair, between the age of eight and ten under similar circumstances,—if so, is such change customary?—I have the honour to remain, Sir, yours respectfully,   AUGUSTUS MEVES.

"*August 24th*, 1861, 35 University St., Fitzroy Sq.
" HENRY HANCOCK, F.R.C.S."

To which he replied that such a thing would be impossible, as in the course of his experience he never heard of such a thing ; but brown eyes, from disease, might turn through inflammation to a reddish hue, or a greyish film might overspread them, which might assume a greyish-brown colour, but under no circumstances would they change their colour to a light blue. As respected brown hair,—"that in the course of time might possibly change its colour to a sandy or red or a grey, but it would be very improbable for it to change to a very light hue."

We then told him we were writing a work wherein this question arose, and asked him whether he had any objection to give his opinion on this subject in a certificate, to which he replied, " Such a thing was quite unnecessary, as no one could believe such a change possible."

Here then is seen that medical opinion states, that, under no circumstances, could brown eyes change to light blue, or brown hair to a light colour; therefore, if the Dauphin had either brown eyes or brown hair, the boy who died in the Temple could under no circumstances have been the Dauphin.

The reason Louis Charles the Dauphin has been chronicled by many as having possessed blue eyes, is, that they have confounded him with the first Dauphin (his brother), Louis Joseph Xavier François, who had blue eyes and light-coloured hair, or with the boy who was confined in the Temple after October 1793.

The following is one of the many paragraphs that our father directs our attention to, namely: Louis Joseph Xavier François, the first Dauphin, who died in June 1789, had blue eyes and flaxen hair, "there being several genuine portraits of this Dauphin." Louis Charles, the Prince-Royal, born the 27th March 1785, had brown eyes and brown hair, adding, "genuine portraits of this Dauphin are rather rare."

The following will elicit, in all probability, what colour the Dauphin's (the Duke of Normandy's) eyes and hair were :—

In 1859 we accidentally saw a copy of a work entitled *The Lost Prince*, written by John H. Hanson, Esq., which advocates the pretensions of a certain Rev. Eleazar Williams, who died in America, in reading which we found the following, in reference to the colour of the eyes of Louis Charles the Dauphin :—

" One feature I must not overlook. There is a marked discrepancy between the colour of his eyes, as described by many historians, and as represented in the pictures which have come down to us. The first say that they were of a brilliant blue, whereas the latter, the most trustworthy witnesses, especially where the artist is of the literal and unimaginative school, show them to have been a clear hazel, tinted perhaps slightly at the edges with a bluish colouring, but having nothing of the deep, clear azure which enhanced the aërial beauty of Marie Antoinette, by recalling the hues of a southern sky."—*The Lost Prince*, p. 42.

He further states, "that there is a portrait of the Dauphin in the Bryan Gallery, in which the eyes are painted hazel. I went, says Mr. Hanson, to the gallery, when Mr. Bryan said, he could pledge himself for the authenticity of the portrait, having purchased it at the sale of the collection of M. Prousteau de Mont Louis in Paris in 1851. This gentleman was a Royalist, and enjoyed a high reputation as a connoisseur and collector, and his name is a sufficient guarantee that whatever came from his collection is genuine."—*The Lost Prince*, p. 390.

He also states " that a M. B. A. Muller, residing in Howard Street, New York, who was a pupil of the revolutionist David, and also of Gros, was employed to take after death the picture of Louis xviii., of whom he still possessed an admirable crayon sketch. Upon inquiry, he stated that the Dauphin had hazel eyes. Upon him asking him how he knew, he replied, ' By seeing portraits of the Dauphin in France.' "—*The Lost Prince*, p. 393.

In 1859 there was on view, at Messrs. J. and R. Jenning's gallery in Cheapside, a painting entitled, " The Royal Family of France : Louis xvi. and Marie Antoinette in the Prison of the Temple in 1792." We viewed this celebrated painting, from the hand of E. M. Ward, R.A. This picture was exhibited at the Great Exhibition of Industry and Arts at Paris in 1855. The following is a description of the picture :— The time selected is that when Louis xvi. is taking his afternoon sleep on a sofa. His face is exceedingly calm. He is habited in his morning-gown. In the recess of the window, over his head, is placed a crucifix, and at the head of his couch lies open on a table *The History of England*, open at the page of Charles i.'s reign ; also a watch, and a Bible or Prayer-book is on the table. Such is the portrayal of the good and benevolent Louis. Near the sleeping monarch is the heroic Marie Antoinette, her face saddened by deep reflection, as she gazes on her devoted husband. Her whole faculties seem to be concentrated solely on his calmness. During his slumber she has been mending his coat, which now lies in her lap. She is in the act of biting the thread, to point it for the needle, but deep reflection has arrested her attention, reminding her of their then bitter position. She is habited in a light dress, and a small black dog is crouched at her feet, seemingly asleep. By her side is a table, on which rests her housewife, a winding-measure, and a work-box. The Princess-Royal is engaged watering a vase of lilies of the valley which stands on the table, her left hand resting upon the table, and her fair hair falls in ringlets over her bosom and shoulders. Around her head is a stripe of white satin. She is habited in a light-blue dress, wearing around her fair neck black lace; so likewise the sleeves of her dress are fringed with black lace, and there is discernible the features of her mother, the beauteous Marie Antoinette. Occupying the front part of the picture is the pious and good sister of Louis, " Madame Elizabeth," who is habited in a dark dress, wearing a white lace collar and apron. She is about occupying herself in knitting, for she holds the needles in her left hand, and her work-box is by her feet. Her sole attention seems centred in contemplating the Dauphin, who is seated on the floor by her feet, resting his arms on a stool, arranging the feathers of his shuttlecock. The Dauphin-Prince is habited in a dark-blue suit, and attached to his side is the republican colours. His hair flows in large ringlets about his shoulders, and is painted " *dark-brown or chesnut colour. His eyebrows and eyelashes are of the same hue*, but his eyes are downcast; nevertheless, from the tint, they reflect those of a dark colour." Behind Marie Antoinette and the Princess-Royal, placarded on the wall, is the declaration of the Rights of Man, and a bookcase is by the side, on the top of which is a globe, which the King used in instructing his son. Such then is the artist's portrayal of the Royal Family. The antechamber depicts another scene, in which the malign servants of the Revolution are portrayed. The ferocious Rocher, one of the turnkeys permanently appointed to guard the Royal captives, is gazing on the Royal Family, and blowing a long whiff of tobacco-smoke from his pipe into the apartment of the Royal party, in order to annoy the heroic Queen, who had a great objection to the smell of tobacco. This despicable barbarian E. M. Ward has portrayed with a visage which any physiognomist would not hesitate in pronouncing as capable of the direst actions if required, whilst behind this monster, at a table, are two muni-cipals engaged playing at cards.   One is a Jacobin, his piercing eyes being riveted on the Royal prisoners, whilst a pistol lies on the table, and a bottle and glass with liquor.   His ideas are on the captives, and his cards are but a secondary consideration ; whilst the other, a *sans-culotte*, is intent on his cards.   He is girdled with a sword and pistol, and behind is another municipal engaged in smoking, apparently ruminating on the scene before him.   On the wall is inscribed, " À bas Autrichienne, la Vêto."

In perusing the London papers in 1860, we observed in their columns remarks on an historical picture exhibited at the Royal Academy of Arts, a production of A. Elmore, R.A., of the Attack on the Tuileries on the 20th June 1792.   Our curiosity being aroused to see this picture, accordingly we visited the Royal Academy for that express purpose.   The subject is one most heartrending, which repre-sents the Queen and the Royal Family confronted with an infuriated mob, who have forced their way into the Palace and into the Queen's apartment, uttering their invectives against the Royal Family, during which a young girl came forward, and bitterly reviled, in the coarsest terms, the Queen.   Marie Antoinette, struck by the contrast between the rage of this young girl and the gentleness of her face, said to her in a kind tone, "Why do you hate me ?   Have I ever unknowingly done you any injury or offence ?"   "No, not to me," replied the incensed girl ; "but it is you who cause the misery of the nation."   "Poor child," replied the Queen, "some one has told you so, and deceived you. What interest can I have in making the people miserable ?   The wife of the King, mother of the Dauphin,—I am a Frenchwoman by all the feelings of my heart, as a wife and a mother.   I shall never again see my own country.   I can only be happy or unhappy in France.   I was happy when you loved me."

This gentle reproach affected the heart of the young girl, and her anger was effaced in a flood of tears.   She asked the Queen's pardon, saying, " I did not know you, but I see that you are good."

The artist has delineated the expressions of the motley mob at the time the young girl stands repentant for her act of virulence.*

A table and chair alone separate the Royal Family from the vengeance of their assailants. The Queen is standing erect, facing the mob, not fearing death, and behaving towards these malign persons with that magnanimity of soul becoming a Queen in so perilous a position. The Princess (her daughter) Marie Thérèse, is by her side, her countenance beaming with mistrust as to what might happen ; and the Princess Elizabeth (the King's sister) is in the recess of the window, beholding the mob with anxiety, while the Dauphin is seated on the table that separates the Royal Family from the fury of their assailants, clinging to his mother's arms with that natural fear which a boy of his tender years would exhibit under such circumstances. He wears the republican cap. *His eyes and hair are painted brown.*†

Our visit to the Royal Academy was especially to note what colour Mr. Elmore had painted the Dauphin's eyes, which we found he had

* Thus writes M. de Bourrienne respecting Bonaparte, on witnessing the attack on the Tuileries :—

"While Bonaparte and I were spending our time in a somewhat vagabond way, the 20th of June arrived. We met by appointment at a restaurateur's in the Rue St. Honoré, near the Palais Royal, to take one of our daily rambles. On going out we saw approaching, in the direction of the market, a mob, which Bonaparte calculated at five or six thousand men. They were all in rags, armed with weapons of every description, and were proceeding towards the Tuileries, vociferating all kinds of gross abuse. It was a collection of all that was most vile and abject in the purlieus of Paris. 'Let us follow this mob,' said Bonaparte. We got the start of them, and took up our station on the terrace of the banks of the river. It was there that he witnessed the scandalous scenes which took place ; and it would be difficult to describe the surprise and indignation which they excited in him. When the King showed himself at the windows overlooking the garden, with the red cap, which one of the mob had put on his head, he could no longer repress his indignation. 'Che Coglione !' he loudly exclaimed ; 'why have they let in all that rabble ? Why don't they sweep off four or five hundred of them with the cannon, the rest would then set off fast enough !'* When we sat down to dinner, which I paid for, as I generally did, for I was the richer of the two, he spoke of nothing but the scene we had witnessed. He discussed, with great good sense, the causes and consequences of this unrepressed insurrection. He foresaw and developed with sagacity all that would ensue. He was not mistaken."—*Memoirs of Napoleon Bonaparte*, by M. de Bourrienne, his private secretary and college companion.

† This picture was exhibited at the International Exhibition of 1862.

* Bonaparte lived to put his principles in practice near that very spot.

painted *brown*, thus corresponding with the description our father has so often especially directed our notice to. We have no doubt that this picture is painted from the most authentic sources as regards the features of the Royal Family and the colour of the eyes and hair, if not, it would be valueless as an historical portrait picture, and likewise would deteriorate much the artist's fame.

Many painters and historians have chronicled the Dauphin as having blue eyes. These gentlemen are mistaken, for they confound the eldest son of Louis XVI. and Marie Antoinette, "Louis Joseph Xavier François," who possessed blue eyes and flaxen hair, with the second son of the King, Louis Charles, who in reality possessed brown eyes and brown hair.

Here then is an historical painter who paints the colour of the eyes contrary to the above painters and historians. He would not take the responsibility of this unless he had sufficient grounds for so doing. We therefore direct especial attention to Mr. Elmore's historical picture, who can doubtless state *in propriâ personâ* the source from whence he derived his authenticity. He has positively rejected the authority of those that represent the Dauphin as possessing blue eyes, for he has represented him as possessing brown eyes and brown hair, thereby coinciding identically with our father's statement.

If Mr. Elmore's representation is admitted to be correct, it follows that the boy who terminated his existence in the Temple was not the Dauphin, for the boy who died there possessed *blue eyes and fair hair*.

We will now compare the different statements respecting the colour of the eyes and hair of the second son of Louis XVI. :—

BEAUCHESNE represents the Dauphin, when at the age of rather more than four years old, as possessing blue eyes fringed with long chesnut lashes, and dark chesnut hair which curled naturally, and fell in thick ringlets on his shoulders.—*Life of Louis* XVII., vol. ii. page 20.

LAMARTINE represents the Dauphin as possessing blue eyes and chesnut hair, divided on the top of his head, and descending in thick curls on his shoulders.—*History of the Girondists*, vol. ii. page 273.

E. M. WARD, R.A., represents the Dauphin as possessing dark-brown hair, flowing in large ringlets about his shoulders. On account of the position of the Dauphin he had no occasion to paint the eyes, but he represents him as possessing chesnut eyelashes.—*Historical Picture of the Royal Family of France in the Prison of the Temple*, see page 281.

A. ELMORE, R.A., represents the Dauphin as possessing brown eyes and brown hair.—*Historical Picture of the Attack on the Tuileries.* See page 283.

The extracts from *The Lost Prince* represent the Dauphin as possessing hazel eyes.—See pp. 279 and 280.

We will now give an account of the colour of the eyes and hair of the prisoner of the Temple subsequently to coming under Simon's charge, as recorded by Beauchesne in his Life of Louis XVII., published in 1852. Why alluding so pointedly to Beauchesne's work as a reference is, that after his studying well the substance of the most available documentary proofs that exists, for a period extending, as he states, to twenty years, his work in no way confirms the Dauphin's decease took place in the Temple, although it is written with the sole idea of substantiating such.

Whilst the Dauphin was under the charge of Simon, Madame Simon cut off his long ringlets (Historical Records, page 137).

After the resignation of Simon as guardian of the prisoner of the Temple, the captive was at once placed in solitary confinement, where he remained for six months.

On his deliverance from his solitary cell, and coming under the charge of Laurent, the captive is recorded as possessing blue eyes and fair hair (Historical Records, page 156).

Harmand's report likewise describes the captive of the Temple as possessing light-chesnut hair (Historical Records, page 163).

The prisoner of the Temple, who terminated his existence the 8th June 1795, is recorded as possessing blue eyes, which shone as pure as the blue heaven, and beautiful fair hair, which fell like a frame around his face (Historical Records, page 169).

What is to be inferred from the above ? Are those who represent the Dauphin as possessing blue eyes and fair hair, or, who represent him as possessing blue eyes and brown hair, or, who represent him as possessing brown eyes and brown hair, in error ? All cannot be correct. Which description then from the above is to be considered authentic ?

Speaking specially of the colour of the Dauphin's hair, Beauchesne, " describing the Dauphin at four years of age," Lamartine, Ward, R.A., Elmore, R.A., are unanimous in recording the Dauphin as possessing *brown hair;* but when attention is directed to the colour of the hair of the prisoner of the Temple, subsequent to coming under Simon's charge, it is seen he possessed fair hair, thus proving he could not have been the true Dauphin.

Allowance may be made as to error arising in the description given of the colour of the Dauphin's eyes, for that might easily occur ; but not so for the hair, as that was too palpably visible to admit of mistake, for no person, who was at all intimate with the Dauphin's appearance, could have had such defective eyesight as to mistake long dark hair, descending in long ringlets, on a gay boy's shoulders, for fair hair, or *vice versâ.*

It was physically impossible for either the boy who came under Laurent's charge, or the one who ended his days in the Temple, to have been the Dauphin, if it is admitted the Dauphin possessed brown hair.

We here suggest the solution of the mystery that surrounds the history of the captive of the Temple :—The colour of the Dauphin's hair was brown. After October 1793 the captive of the Temple was Augustus Meves ; he possessed fair hair and blue eyes, and was the lad, upon Simon giving up his position at the Temple, who was at once placed in solitary confinement, where he remained till the fall of Robespierre, and was the captive that came under Laurent's charge.* The captive Messrs. Harmand, Mathieu, and Reverchon saw, on their official visit, possessed light chesnut hair, this was the deaf and dumb boy (the son of Maria Dodd) whom Mrs. Meves had taken to Paris in 1794, thus showing it was not the same boy as came under Laurent's charge, for the boy who came under his care possessed fair hair. The captive who terminated his life in the Temple possessed fair hair, thereby showing a further exchange had been effected subsequent to Harmand's visit, and thus making evident by such singular means, the periods of the different substitutions that were effected at the Temple.

* See Historical Records, pp. 150 and 156.

END OF SUBJECT "COLOUR OF THE EYES AND HAIR OF LOUIS CHARLES, DAUPHIN OF FRANCE."

XII.

A WORD TO HISTORIANS: WHAT PROOFS AUTHENTICATE THE DAUPHIN'S DEMISE IN THE TOWER OF THE TEMPLE?

THE only reason the world has to credit that the Dauphin died in the Temple is, that the Republican Government specified such, which some historian of reputation has without examination related as a fact, when it has been repeated on his credit by his successors, and thus it has been handed down to posterity with all the authority of truth. When facts can be placed before the world which can substantiate that the Dauphin died in the Temple, then such should be believed, and not till then ; it is a mere political assertion as yet, and not a fact.

In speaking of historians, and persons of literary renown, are they never subjected to error ? is it not possible for them to be deceived as well as the rest of mankind ? They can only gain facts from authentic sources, and the authentic sources, if the Government of France at that period can be called authentic, was from a source whose desire was really to chronicle the Dauphin as having died in the Temple ; therefore, if they depended solely on acquiring their information from official report, they were quite as liable to be deceived as others. Was it not a subject of vital importance to the revolutionary party in France to endeavour to deceive the world on this subject, and likewise has it not been the policy of all succeeding Governments of France to acquiesce in this stroke of policy? What are the proofs that authenticate the Dauphin's decease in 1795? Are they incontestable? If so, let such be produced ; if they are unassailable they should have a stable foundation, and rely on stronger support than assertion. Let then the decided proofs be produced on which history settles this question, for what history up to the present period has made public, amounts only to assertion. From what source does the assertion emanate? From a revolutionary. Is this the sole corroborative proof? The only. Is there not a special guaranty of its authenticity? History furnishes it not ; refer to such, and it will be found to be futile ; it is a myth which stands not investigation ; it is an assertion, not a fact.

In the announcement we have made of our father having been the Dauphin of France, doubtless many will observe that as history has corroborated the Dauphin died in the Temple, such must be the case.

Those who reason thus, we refer to read the different works that have been written on this question, and at the same time, reminding them, if the Dauphin's death had been satisfactorily authenticated, there would never have been reason to question its accuracy ; therefore, in order to arrive at a just and satisfactory conclusion on this historical question, let such ascertain what solid proofs they have for acquiescing in the demise of the Dauphin in the Tower of the Temple, and if they peruse the Records from the Royal Family's incarceration in the Temple till the asserted death of the Dauphin, and make themselves familiar with the treatment the captive received in the Temple, they then will find that the liberation of the Dauphin from the Tower of the Temple is no charlatanical invention, and that the republican announcement of 1795 was but a political *ruse.*

What we desire to establish is nothing but truth, and to confirm a fact which should not be kept silent, and moreover must not be kept silent, therefore we desire historians and literary men to read with sincerity the pages here written, and to receive information which will open their eyes as to the delusion they have been labouring under. It is their province to be just, and to throw aside prejudice. Never had history more need of authentic proof than the demise of the Dauphin in the Temple. It was a republican fabrication, patent to all upon investigating fully the prisoner of the Temple's career.

END OF SUBJECT " A WORD TO HISTORIANS : WHAT PROOFS AUTHENTICATE THE DAUPHIN'S DEMISE IN THE TOWER OF THE TEMPLE ? "

XIII.

UNDER WHAT AUSPICES LOUIS XVIII. ASCENDED THE THRONE OF FRANCE.

ONSIEUR LABRELI DE FONTAINE, Librarian to the Duchess of Orleans, in his pamphlet entitled " Disclosures respecting the Existence of Louis XVII.," relates the following :—

The first article of the Secret Treaty of Paris 1814, explains the manner in which the Powers of Europe had permitted the Count of Provence to occupy the Throne of France. The following is the substance of the article :—

"That although the high contracting powers, the Allied Sovereigns, have no evidence of the death of the son of Louis XVI., ·the state of Europe and its political interests require that they should place at the head of the Government of France, Louis Xavier, Comte de Provence, ostensibly with the title of King, but being in fact considered in their secret transactions, only as Regent of the Kingdom for the two years next ensuing, reserving to themselves during that period, to obtain every possible certainty concerning a fact which must ultimately determine who shall be the Sovereign of France, etc. etc." *

Such then is Labreli de Fontaine's assertion, likewise he adds :—

"Being at Venice in 1812, Signor Erizzo, formerly a senator of Venice, showed me a proclamation of the Count de Provence, dated from Verona, the 14th October 1797, in which he only assumed the title of Regent of the Kingdom."

* See Court Journal, March 24th, 1832, respecting the Secret Treaty and the Proclamation, dated 14th October 1797.

From the above it may be fairly asked, why, if the nephew of Louis XVIII. died in the Temple, as had been given out, the uncle neither proclaimed himself, nor was proclaimed by the Allied Sovereigns (those who placed him on the throne), King of France. It is quite evident there existed the greatest possible doubt of the demise of Louis XVII., or certainly Louis XVIII. would never have issued such a proclamation, neither would the Allied Powers have come to such a resolution if there had not been the greatest possible reason to believe in the then existence of Louis XVII. Does not this one act on the part of the Allied Sovereigns show what opinion was prevalent respecting the son of Louis XVI.? There would never have been occasion for such a treaty if the facts in connexion with the Dauphin's demise had been conclusive. One-and-twenty years was a long period for the Allied Powers to be in doubt on such a subject. Doubtless the Governments had most substantial proofs for such a doubt, or they would never have questioned its authenticity; and there is no question but the Governments would have fully investigated its correctness, had it not been for the preponderating power Louis XVII. inherited, in right of birth.

END OF SUBJECT "UNDER WHAT AUSPICES LOUIS XVIII. ASCENDED THE
THRONE OF FRANCE."

XIV.

RECOGNITION OF THE SON OF LOUIS XVI. AND MARIE ANTOINETTE BY PERSONAL IDENTITY.

ACCORDING to the Chronological History of France, Charles Louis, second son of Louis XVI., King of France, and Marie Antoinette Josephe Jeanne of Lorraine, Archduchess of Austria, and Queen of France, was born at the Château of Versailles, on the 27th March 1785, at five minutes before seven in the evening, ' and, contrary to the ancient usage, he was baptized on the very day of his birth, at half-past eight, by the Cardinal de Rohan, Bishop of Strasburg, Grand Almoner, and the Abbe Brocquevièlle, Vicar of Versailles. He had for his godfather, Louis Stanislas Xavier, Count de Provence, and for his godmother, Marie Charlotte Louise of Lorraine, Archduchess of Austria, Queen of the Two Sicilies, represented by Madame Elizabeth.

The infant Prince was afterwards created Duc de Normandie, which no son of France had borne since the fourth son of Charles VII. He was usually called le Prince Royal. At the death of his elder brother in June 1789, he succeeded to the title of Dauphin, and was from thence called : Louis Charles, Dauphin of France.

Louis Charles had, at his birth, on his *right breast, an appearance,* "*comme deux mamelles*" *of two teats,* otherwise a mole over the nipple. Also, at the time of his inoculation he received from the lancet of the surgeon a deep wound, which left a large scar on *his right arm.* Likewise, during his confinement in the Tower of the Temple, upon attempt-ing to pass the guards to plead for his father's life, he accidentally struck *his left wrist on the point of one of the bayonets which obstructed his passage, thereby wounding himself.*   Also, whilst he was confined in the Temple in October 1793, Jacques Réné Hébert desired him to sign a paper relative to the dishonour of the Queen, and upon his refusal to comply, this barbarian ill-treated him, from the effects of which he received a *wound on the temple, over the left eye.*

The above marks are positively known to have existed on the body of the Dauphin, and it is on these that we establish the question of identity.

All the above marks were fully identified upon the body of our late father, for proof of which we submit the following medical certifi-cate, which was procured, during his lifetime, in order to place in his then finished Memoirs :—

" I hereby certify, that I have examined Mr. Augustus Meves, aged about seventy-three years, and that he has a slight scar on his left wrist, one over the left eye, another on the left instep, a large mark on his right arm, from the operation of inoculation, also a mole over the right nipple, another on the middle of the stomach, and several moles or blood-spots over the front of his chest.

" EDWARD NEWTON, F.R.C.S.

" 30 FITZROY SQUARE, *December* 13*th,* 1858."

The sudden demise of our father was a sad calamity to the whole of his family, by whom he was much and dearly beloved ; but as life could not be recalled, and being aware that if we allowed the period to pass without drawing medical attention to the marks and scars that existed on him, that it would hereafter have been impossible to have satisfied public credence, that such existed on him, when, by the existence of such, they would form material evidence in proving him to be the Dauphin of France ; therefore, on seeing Dr. Andrew, to whom the *post-mortem* was intrusted, we requested him to be particular in examin-ing certain marks and scars existing on our late father, as such were of particular consequence in proving his identity to property he should inherit in France. We then placed a copy of Dr. Newton's certificate into his hands as a reference, and requested him to note in his examination whether he identified such marks as therein specified? He replied he would direct his special attention to the marks therein referred to.

On the day of inquest, previously to the Coroner proceeding to ascertain the cause of death, we desired to speak with him privately, which request was complied with. On our seeing Mr. Wakley (the Coroner), we requested him to give us a certificate of the marks and scars that were found to exist on our late father. He inquired for what purpose we required such, or had we any suspicion that violence had been used? We replied, we had no reason to imagine violence had been used, but that the marks were from birth, and the scars had occurred from various accidents which had happened to him during his early youth. On his further inquiring our object for desiring such, and finding we were obliged to satisfy him as to the reality of our object, in order to obtain the certificate, which had not been our intention to have promulgated on this occasion; however, such was rendered necessary under the circumstances. We then informed him that we had every reason to believe, from the facts of our late father's life, that he was no other than "Louis Charles, the Dauphin of France, son of Louis XVI., King of France." Mr. Wakley then said, "He would call Dr. Andrew's attention to our request during the inquiry."

In the course of the inquiry Dr. Newton's certificate was placed in Mr. Wakley's hands. When Dr. Andrew was questioned separately on the different marks and scars, for which he stated he could vouch for the truth of the whole of Dr. Newton's certificate, with the exception of that of the "middle of the stomach." However, he found a mark corresponding midway between the navel and pubes, the same as specified by Dr. Newton, but apparently the term used to indicate its exact position was non-technical.

Mr. Wakley then desired to know whether we had any statement to place in Court, and said we could retire and consult upon it, which we did.   After what had transpired with Mr. Wakley we thought it necessary to write out a short statement and place it in Court, which we at once did, and then re-entered, when Mr. William Meves, as the eldest son, after having been duly sworn, stated—"The deceased gentleman was my father, who always led us to believe, from the marks on his person, and other circumstances, that he was Louis Charles de Bourbon, son of Louis XVI., King of France, and he had lately written his life, which is at the present time in the hands of Mr. Bentley the publisher, of New Burlington Street.

On calling on Dr. Andrew, he observed, had we informed him that we required the certificate for such a purpose, he would have instituted a committee of medical men to have been present during the *post-mortem*, and have taken notes on the different particulars.   After knowing for what purpose the certificate was desired, he again examined the different marks, etc., in company with Dr. Ringer, so as to enable him to give a defined and accurate description as to their appearance.   The following is Dr. Andrew's and Dr. Ringer's certificate :—

"Having been appointed by Mr. Wakley (Coroner) to make a *post-mortem* examination on the body of Mr. Augustus Meves, this gentleman having died suddenly while riding in a cab, my attention has been particularly called to the following external marks :—

"Four scars, quite apparent, but evidently of considerable age, the colour being nearly that of the surrounding skin.   One of these, irregular in outline, is on the left instep.

"Another, linear in form, one inch in length, and transverse in direction, is on the front of the left wrist, at the base of the thumb.

"The third, irregularly triangular, one inch and a quarter in length, is above and to the left of the left eye, extending inwards from the temple, and slightly encroaching on the eyebrow.

"The fourth, irregularly rounded, about three quarters of an inch in diameter, is on the outer side of the right arm, and at its upper third, seemingly from inoculation, but a larger scar than usual.

"A mole, well defined, about the size of half a small pea, very dark in colour, situated above the nipple, and about half-an-inch from it ; in addition, several blood-spots are scattered over the front of the chest, and one much larger than the rest is placed midway between the navel and pubes.

" Similar statements to these were made by me on oath before Mr. Wakley on the day of inquest.

" EDWYN ANDREW, M.D. LOND.,
" Resident Medical Officer at University College Hospital.

" *Saturday, May 14th, 1859.* "

" Having examined the body with Dr. Andrew, I certify that the above statements are quite correct.

" SYDNEY RINGER, M.R.C.S.,
" Physician-Assistant at University College Hospital.

" *May 14th, 1859.* "

Shortly after, we called on Dr. Andrew, on account of there being an omission in his certificate, as to which side the natural appearance on the breast of the two teats were, and at the same time we requested that he would explain the circumstance as to the manner we brought the subject respecting the marks under his notice, and if he would state his opinion as to the probability how these marks were occasioned—that is, by what agency, whether by blunt or sharp instruments. After putting the questions to him separately, and having received his answer, we then read from the Memoirs how these marks were occasioned, therefore his answers were in no way influenced, and in each instance they corresponded as to whether occasioned by blunt or sharp agency. We then placed the following letter in his hands, as a guide for what we in reality desired to call his attention to :—

" SIR,—At the time I desired you to give me the certificate for the marks on my late father's person, I drew your attention to them through Dr. Newton's certificate, it not being my intention then to have made public his claims, but only to have attested the certificate officially, knowing had I let the occasion pass I should never have been able to stamp the truth of his identity ; and as you found the marks, etc., as stated by Dr. Newton on his person, you not then knowing our motive for such a certificate until after the statement you made before Mr. Wakley ; therefore you would favour me by stating such, as it will show you could not have been influenced by any motive, or biassed from any remark I might have made to you, as I merely stated that I desired the certificate so as to claim property by identity in France. Likewise, whether you could remember what class of mole you nominate that which appeared on his breast, whether pustulous or otherwise, and which side of the breast the mole was on, as the side the mole was situated is omitted in your original certificate and Dr. Ringer's, as it is necessary to be critical on every minutia, and to refer to the photograph you and Dr. Ringer placed your signatures to, as being the portrait of Mr. Augustus Meves, for then it carries with it truth, as the generality are very apt to discredit things without they are placed beyond question ; and likewise to his stature, in reference to *embonpoint*, etc. ; and whether you think the scar on the right arm was one likely to be caused by inoculation, and the scar on the left instep might be such a wound received from the prong of a buckle? Also, whether the cut over the left eye was one likely to be occasioned by his being thrust against a door? also the mark on the left wrist was such from appearance that could be occasioned by a bayonet or some such similar instrument wounding him? Likewise whether such a mark could be caused as the appearance on his right breast, and whether age could in any way diminish its contour, and if at birth such could appear as another nipple or teat?

"About twenty years ago my father caught the scarlet fever, after which he thought the marks and scars were not near so visible.—Yours truly,   "AUGUSTUS MEVES.

"EDWYN ANDREW, M.D.,
   26th November 1859."

The following is Dr. Andrew's reply :—

"Being requested by the sons of the late Mr. Augustus Meves to explain more fully the circumstances connected with the official examination of their father's body, I may state, that on May the 9th I was summoned by the porter of University College Hospital to see a gentleman, supposed to be in a dying state, who had just been driven to the door in a cab. I at once proceeded to the spot, and found him seated in a corner of the vehicle, with his body in an upright position, but life was quite extinct, although the body was still warm.

" Finding that he had passed beyond all earthly means of restoration, I had him at once removed, and sent a message in due form to the Coroner. During the period which elapsed, before I received the necessary warrant from the Coroner, the son, Mr. William Meves, called on me to desire that I would be especially careful in noting any marks presenting themselves on his father's body, as these observations might be very important in supporting certain claims to property to which he considered his father had an undoubted right. At the same time he showed me the copy of a certificate given by a medical gentleman, a Mr. Newton, of Fitzroy Square. My attention being thus especially directed, I examined very closely the surface of the body, the results of which examination I have previously given in a medical certificate, and they were also stated by me on oath before the Coroner. On reading, however, my certificate a second time, I noticed one deficiency, which my memory readily supplied—viz., that with regard to the position of the large 'mole,' which should have been mentioned to have been situated over the 'right nipple.' This mole was very distinct and prominent at the *post-mortem*, and I can well conceive it might have been readily mistaken for a second nipple during childhood by a casual observer, especially, if it presented such a character at that period of life ; whether, however, it has remained stationary from birth, or became enlarged proportionally with the whole body, I should not feel justified, with my present experience, in offering an opinion.

"As to the scars, the most probable inference is, 'that the linear one,' situated on the left wrist, was produced by a sharp cutting instrument, while those on the instep and on the temple were caused by blunt agents. As to the form or nature of these instruments it would be impossible to make any trustworthy statement.

"Again as to the height and stature : Mr. Meves was above the middle height, rather corpulent, with features and hair, etc., indicating the age which he was considered to be ; but all the minute facts with reference to these points may be better ascertained by examining a photograph, to which I have placed my signature, after noting and observing the exact likeness to the face of the deceased.

"In conclusion, I may add, that these various statements and explanations have been made by me with the only motive of eliciting the truth of this apparent mystery, being perfectly unacquainted with any member of the Meves family, and being influenced by no remuneration, which I have not received or desired.

"EDWYN ANDREW, M.D. LOND.,
" Fellow of the Royal College of Surgeons.

"To Mr. W. MEVES,
 December 6th, 1859."

We also wrote to Mr. Wakley the following :—

"SIR,—If not troubling you too much, you would much oblige by giving me an account under what circumstances I brought the importance of the marks and scars on my late father's person before your notice, previous to the examination before the jury, as it was then absolutely necessary for me to have certificates officially corroborated, for had I not done so in that instance I should never have been able to gain credence respecting such marks, thereby being obliged to make the statement in order to make the subject clear to you why we needed such especial notification, and after the cross-examination of Mr. Andrew respecting these marks, etc., which were confirmed by him, and during the proceedings, when you desired to know if we had any statement to make, that we might retire to consider it, and what subsequent statement I placed in Court, and whether you could charge your memory of the appearance of the mole over the nipple on the right breast, and the general appearance of my late father.

"Would you do this, you would much oblige, as it is desirable for me to place every fact concerning my father beyond question.—Yours most respectfully,   "WILLIAM MEVES.

"T. WAKLEY, Esq.,
   10*th December* 1859."

The following is the reply :—

"On the 12th day of May last I held an inquest at 'The Wellington,' University Street, in the parish of St. Pancras, on the body of Mr. Augustus Antoine Cornelius Meves, late of 35 University Street.   Previously to my proceeding to view the body, a gentleman, who stated he was a son of the deceased, requested me to examine particularly certain marks on his father's body, which I did, in accordance with his desire. They strictly corresponded with the description given of them by Dr. Andrew in his evidence at the inquest.

"THOMAS WAKLEY,
Coroner for Middlesex.

"OFFICE, 1 BEDFORD STREET, STRAND, LONDON,
   December 27*th*, 1859."

In remarking on the question of Identity, is it not more than singular, we may say extraordinary, that each individual mark and scar that is attributed to the Dauphin, was found to have existed on our late father?   How are these marks to be accounted for, if he was not the Dauphin?   There is no supposition as regards these marks, for they are verified on the most unquestionable authority.   Perhaps not one in a generation would be born with such an extraordinary appearance on the right breast, as that which is stated to have existed on the Dauphin. This natural mark is of such characteristic meaning, that it alone, through its singularity, is sufficient to carry identity, and to stamp the truth of our late father's assertions, and especially so, when all the accidental scars, which are known to have existed on the Dauphin, were fully identified on him.

Established every fact in a case, with the exception of that of known identity, and what must the conclusion be, but defective in the most essential particular ?

Regarding the two teats on the right breast, it is the opinion of medical men, that while the natural teat, as common to man, has enlarged, that the appearance which we designate the second teat has remained stationary from birth, and that its appearance at that time would then have been as large as at any period of his life, therefore they would actually have presented the appearance of two teats on one breast in childhood, as in point of size possibly there was no difference, and there would be no difference, for many years. In reading Dr. Andrew's certificate and letter, we believe by his description of the mole over the nipple, and the contour of the scars, that there can be but one opinion with medical gentlemen as regards the agency how these marks were occasioned, that is, from blunt or sharp agency, for as Dr. Andrew remarks, " That as to the scars the most probable inference is, that the linear one situated on the left wrist, was produced by a sharp cutting instrument, while those on the instep and on the temple were caused by blunt agents." Thus all the marks that were known to exist on the Dauphin were identified on our father, which speaks much more than words can, who in reality he was.

The circumstance of our father's claims having gone the round of the London press, and we having despatched to the British Government, and the foreign Ambassadors at the Court of Saint James's, some of the leading facts respecting such claims, and finding a letter in these instances did not embrace sufficient in so complicated a question, we resolved to publish a brief account of his life, so that the world might see to a certain extent on what grounds his claims were founded. This resolution we carried into effect, and in 1860, published at Messrs.

Saunders, Otley, and Co., of Conduit Street, Hanover Square, an introductory account, under the title of "*The Prisoner of the Temple.*"

The following Opinions of the Press upon "*The Prisoner of the Temple,*" we submit to the reader :—

"The legitimate heir to the French Throne was, as every one knows, the son of Louis XVI. The son was a prisoner in the Temple with his mother, Marie Antoinette; but that he escaped thence is a well-known historical fact, and was admitted to be so in the treaty of the Four Powers in 1814, when his uncle was allowed to ascend the Throne as Regent, only until the place of L'Héritier's (as he was called) concealment was discovered. The unfortunate Prince had certain marks upon his person, and was intrusted to the care of a person high in the confidence of his mother. We think that any one reading this Pamphlet relative to Augustus Meves, a gentleman who expired suddenly in London a short time back, will admit that the chain of evidence it presents of his claim to the title of Louis Charles de Bourbon, the legitimate heir to the Throne of France, is complete. The personal marks are authenticated upon the oaths of some of our highest medical men, and the Coroner, Mr. Wakley; the history of his concealment and escape explained ; and lastly, his recognition during life as their Prince by the French Noblesse satisfactorily established. His sons have now discharged a just duty to their parent, whose feelings and conduct would have reflected credit upon the most exalted position. They have written this preliminary statement clearly, and without undue partiality ; and while they well convinced the world their father was a Prince, they have established his claim to what princes seldom possess, sense, truthfulness, and honesty."—*Court Circular*, April 21st, 1860.

"The object of this Pamphlet is the elucidation of the historical mystery in connexion with the demise of Louis XVII. of France. The work is dedicated to the Royalists of France, and all well-wishers to the cause of Louis XVII., by his two eldest sons, William Augustus Meves, and Augustus Meves. According to the accounts in this Pamphlet, Louis XVII. did not, as has been supposed by many, die when a child ; he, in fact, escaped from the Tower of the Temple, and the child who died there was an invalid substitute. He was placed under the care of a person named Meves, whom he was taught to look upon as his mother, and sent to England. The arguments which are brought forward in support of this statement are really very powerful. Great stress is laid upon the fact that even in 1814 the Allied Powers entertained great doubt regarding the death of the son of Louis XVI. To establish the personal identity of Augustus Meves with the son of Louis XVI., certificates signed by respectable medical men are given to prove that Augustus Meves, as a man, possessed those peculiar marks on his body, which were known to have been on the person of Louis XVI.'s son as a child. Of course much more is advanced to prove that Augustus Meves was really the son of Louis XVI. and the legitimate heir to the Throne of France, although we have not space to go into the matter more freely here. The compilers of this Pamphlet, who are the sons of Mr. Augustus Meves, intimate that they have communicated officially with the English and French Governments on this subject, and they are desirous that a judicial inquiry should be instituted to inquire into the truth of the statement that their late father was the true Louis XVII. We can hardly suppose it possible that these persons would make a mistake as to whether they were or were not King's sons."—*Literary Review*, April 14th, 1860.

" Lovers of the marvellous will find something to gratify them in these pages, which we think everybody will allow to be strange, if true.   We shall not ourselves attempt to pass judgment on their veracity at present.   Let all well-wishers to the cause of Louis XVII., read, mark, learn, and digest for themselves the hundred pages in which the Messrs. Meves have stated their claims to rank among the French Bourbons."— *The Critic*, March 31st, 1860.

" It may be in the recollection of our readers that a gentleman, known as Augustus Meves, died suddenly in London a twelvemonth ago, of whom it was reported at the time that he was no other than Louis Charles de Bourbon, the legitimate son of Louis XVI. and the unfortunate Marie Antoinette.   This gentleman's sons have collected in a portable form the arguments on which the claim may be considered to rest, and after a careful perusal of these pages it is scarcely possible to doubt the rank to which the authors of the work lay claim.   Admitting the indefeasible right of nations to select their rulers, should our versatile neighbours across the Channel ever think proper to return under Bourbon sway, one of these gentlemen may yet wield a sceptre."—*The Banbury Advertiser*, June 6th, 1860.

END OF SUBJECT " RECOGNITION OF THE SON OF LOUIS XVI. AND MARIE ANTOINETTE BY PERSONAL IDENTITY."

XV.

REASONS WHY THE DAUPHIN DID NOT PROCLAIM HIMSELF.

IT is evident throughout our father's life that he has had great mystification to dispel, and much of the information he has had to unravel has not been done *instanta*, but has been the work of time, even in knowing its applicability; therefore, in the first instance, it has been mystification that he has had to deal with, caused solely through following the information received, which has surrounded the question with complicities when really no complicity existed; and, secondly, through the property he inherited in the name of Augustus Meves he was obliged to be cautious how he proceeded, for if he had raised doubts of his not being the true Augustus Meves, he might have seriously involved himself,—therefore, he was obliged to act most circumspectly, for had he declared himself the son of Louis XVI., and not Augustus Meves, he might have invalidated his legal claims to any property left him in the name of Augustus Meves, therefore such a course needed mature consideration, as then it would have been a folly to have asserted, unless he himself could have fully proved his assertion, and he having great expectations before him he did not wish to raise any question as to the legality of his name, for had he done so, in all probability he would have involved himself, at the decease of Mrs. Higginson,* in law-suits as to the validity of his name, "Augustus

* See Memoirs, p. 52.

Meves," and likewise in other expectations ; therefore, as he was igno-rant of many circumstances at that time, he was forced to be cautious, and he thought it more to his advantage to remain contented as Augustus Meves. What would have been the probable consequence had he raised any doubt as to the legality of his name? Possibly he would have been involved in litigation, and would not have been able to have disposed of his inherited estate, etc. ; indeed, he might have been a ruined man, and as he was at that time worth about £12,000, and having a young family, he thought it much more to his advantage to remain as Augustus Meves than run the risk of declaring himself as being Louis XVII.

The following is a letter written by our father to le Comte de Jouffroy :—

"8 BATH PLACE, NEW ROAD, *December 28th*, 1831.

"DEAR SIR,—When I had the pleasure to meet you on Monday evening at Monsieur Camus's, I expected to have been introduced to Monsieur de La Revierre, who, I am informed, is a gentleman high in the Courts of Law in France, having held the position of judge. He would therefore understand and explain the necessity of a person who holds a freehold estate having by law a legal claim to his name. If any one doubts my name in a court of justice, I produce the baptismal register, and prove my title to such name. I must take great care by any written document, or conversation with persons, never to invalidate my right to my name, or I shall not legally be able to dispose of my freehold estate, or create a mortgage on it, in case of necessity. Had I been fortunate enough to have had an interview with Her Royal High-ness the Duchess of Angoulême, I could have at once stated my affair to her satisfaction and my own, the matter being completely confi-dential between us ; but as I am now placed I must be on my guard as to my own property, or I may be altogether ruined. I have always supported the character of, and supposed myself to be Augustus Meves, until my mother informed me to the contrary, but now I cannot believe that I am the person baptized at Saint James's Church. How is it possible after what has transpired?

"That my mother was with the Queen of France, and had the infant Duke of Normandy intrusted to her care, is true, and that she was in France in the autumn of 1789 for about three weeks, can be proved.—I remain, dear Sir, yours sincerely,

"AUGUSTUS MEVES.

"LE COMTE DE JOUFFROY."

Here then is seen that caution was necessary on his part how he acted, for it is one thing to assert, but another to prove, nevertheless our father's recollections are compatible with such as may reasonably be attributed to the Dauphin, and time and experience has proved to him and to us, that he was no other than the true Dauphin, whom the Revolutionary Government, for political ends, asserted died in the Temple. This being the case, it is our bounden duty to rectify this error in the history of France, and to advocate the cause of a father's right, as then we shall have fulfilled that homage that is expected from us, and had we, or did we neglect, our consciences would upbraid us with having neglected a just and honourable duty, due to the memory of a parent.

END OF SUBJECT " REASONS WHY THE DAUPHIN DID NOT PROCLAIM HIMSELF."

XVI.

CONCLUSION: WHAT IS THE DECISION?

HAVING thus far explained the mystery that surrounds the son of Louis xvi., little now remains to be said; it rests with public opinion, from what has transpired, to decide whether or no the escape of Louis Charles, the Dauphin of France, was effected from the Temple, and if so, whether in Augustus Meves he is recognised?

It is not presuming too much to say, the evidence brought forward is weighty enough to awaken the especial attention of those who feel an interest in the true destiny of the son of Louis xvi. and Marie Antoinette, and in his descendants, likewise of those whose principles are not ruled by party influence, but by that which is honourable and noble. The preceding pages, considered with equity, can leave little apprehension in concluding who, and what was the real career of the son of Louis xvi. and Marie Antoinette.

The history of the captive of the Temple, when fully inquired into, will emphatically prove that his liberation from the Temple was effected during the Queen's trial, whilst her assassin accusers and corrupt judges were busy in their fiendish malignity to divert sedition and immorality (which usurped all the executive power in France) in the immolation of that noble and high-born woman, the daughter of the ever memorable Maria Theresa, that captive Queen whom France herself had chosen from a foreign soil as the bride of the patriot King Louis xvi.* to ascend the scaffold and give up her life, which they, to the last man, for the

* See Appendix Note P, for reflections on the death of Louis XVI., p. 340.

national honour should have protected. Where breathes the French-man whose sympathy and heart does not glory in having possessed such a Queen as Marie Antoinette, and who does not execrate her ignoble assassins? From the palace to the dungeon her love for France was unabated. She suffered solely for being a Queen, and possessing a lofty and invincible spirit. She bequeathed to France, in her magnani-mity, love—not reproach, no, not even to her bitterest enemies. Had she lived in the halcyon days of the monarchy, how different her fate would have been! At the mention of her name sensibility is aroused; it is a talisman to courage and heroism.

The treatment that was pursued, and the solitary confinement the captive of the Temple was subjected to up to June 1795, makes apparent that there was a political reason for such, and likewise, makes manifest there existed some stringent necessity why the Princess-Royal, although incarcerated in the same tower as the captive, was so systematically refused on all occasions the gratification of an interview, or to attend him, although she was continually asking this favour from October 1793 till near her liberation from the Temple in December 1795. Had the true Dauphin during this period been confined in the Temple, this order would never have been so peremptory; for what detrimental effect could their meeting have occasioned to the authorities? None whatsoever, had it in reality been the Dauphin; but if a substitute, the contrary, for the exchange would have been at once detected.

What does history state in reference to the Dauphin's treatment after the month of October 1793, or from the month of October? He no longer roamed about in the open air, or in the garden of the Temple, where persons might approach him; all faithful friends, and those who were personally acquainted with the son of Louis XVI., including the loyal Hué, who petitioned the Committee of General Safety to be allowed to attend the captive, were strictly debarred from seeing him. From October 1793 the young prisoner was not accustomed to open doors and fresh air, but to the grat-ing of keys and loneliness. The originators of this routine, in the first instance, were those who had directly bartered the exchange, who resorted to such as a security for their personal safety, thinking that nature would succumb under such rigour; but in this they were mistaken, for he outlived them, whilst they, and many of his vile, depraved, powerful, tyrannical, and heartless oppressors, passed into eternity, leaving behind them a detestable monument of iniquities unparalleled. Secondly, the subsequent authorities enforced this routine, as a means to prevent the liberation transpiring.*

Respecting the demise of the captive on the 8th June 1795, it is seen in pages 158 and 159, that the Chevalier de Charette, the General-issimo of the Vendean Army, had stipulated with the Republican Government that the two imprisoned children of Louis xvi. should be given into his hands on the 13th June 1795; the captive died on the 8th June, and thus the policy of the Government was, that he had ceased to exist before the term expired.

In recurring to the Authentic Memoirs, it must be admitted that candour, from beginning to end, is its characteristic, and after what has transpired in the several subjects constituting the Commentary, it is for public opinion to decide whether sufficient proof has been brought forward to conclude, that the veritable Dauphin of France was in reality the person generally known as Augustus Meves, or whether he, and ourselves, have been under a delusion in this particular.

With the highest sentiments of respect, we subscribe ourselves, to all well-wishers of this cause, theirs faithfully,

WILLIAM MEVES.

AUGUSTUS MEVES.

Universiy Street, London,
   17th October 1862.

---

* For description of the lonely condition to which the captive of the Temple was subjected, see pp. 150, 156, 157, 168, and 169.

APPENDIX.

APPENDIX.

NOTE A.*

MEDICAL CERTIFICATES.

" I HEREBY certify, that I have examined Mr. Augustus Meves, aged about seventy-three years, and that he has a slight scar on his left wrist, one over the left eye, another on the left instep, a large mark on his right arm, from the operation of inoculation, also a mole over the right nipple, another on the middle of the stomach, and several moles or blood-spots over the front of his chest.

" EDWARD NEWTON, F.R.C.S.

" 30 FITZROY SQUARE, *December* 13*th*, 1858."

"Having been appointed by Mr. Wakley (Coroner) to make a *post-mortem* examination on the body of Mr. Augustus Meves, this gentleman having died suddenly while riding in a cab, my attention has been particularly called to the following external marks :—

"Four scars, quite apparent, but evidently of considerable age, the colour being nearly that of the surrounding skin.   One of these, irregular in outline, is on the left instep.

"Another, linear in form, one inch in length, and transverse in direction, is on the front of the left wrist, at the base of the thumb.

"The third, irregularly triangular, one inch and a quarter in length, is above and to the left of the left eye, extending inwards from the temple, and slightly encroaching on the eyebrow.

"The fourth, irregularly rounded, about three quarters of an inch in diameter, is on the outer side of the right arm, and at its upper third, seemingly from inoculation, but a larger scar than usual.

"A mole, well defined, about the size of half a small pea, very dark in colour, situated above the nipple, and about half-an-inch from it; in addition, several blood-spots are scattered over the front of the chest, and one much larger than the rest is placed midway between the navel and pubes.

* Referred to at pp. 4, 37, 60, 62, 76, 91, 175, 179, 210, 211, 231, 232, 234, and 242.

"Similar statements to these were made by me on oath before Mr. Wakley on the day of inquest.

"EDWYN ANDREW, M.D. LOND.,

"Resident Medical Officer at University College Hospital.

"*Saturday, May 14th, 1859.*"

"Having examined the body with Dr. Andrew, I certify that the above statements are quite correct.

"SYDNEY RINGER, M.R.C.S.,

"Physician-Assistant at University College Hospital.

"*May 14th, 1859.*"

"Being requested by the sons of the late Mr. Augustus Meves to explain more fully the circumstances connected with the official examination of their father's body, I may state, that on May the 9th I was summoned by the porter of University College Hospital to see a gentleman, supposed to be in a dying state, who had just been driven to the door in a cab. I at once proceeded to the spot, and found him seated in a corner of the vehicle, with his body in an upright position, but life was quite extinct, although the body was still warm.

"Finding that he had passed beyond all earthly means of restoration, I had him at once removed, and sent a message in due form to the Coroner. During the period which elapsed, before I received the necessary warrant from the Coroner, the son, Mr. William Meves, called on me to desire that I would be especially careful in noting any marks presenting themselves on his father's body, as these observations might be very important in supporting certain claims to property to which he considered his father had an undoubted right. At the same time he showed me the copy of a certificate given by a medical gentleman, a Mr. Newton, of Fitzroy Square. My attention being thus especially directed, I examined very closely the surface of the body, the results of which examination I have previously given in a medical certificate, and they were also stated by me on oath before the Coroner. On reading, however, my certificate a second time, I noticed one deficiency, which my memory readily supplied—viz., that with regard to the position of the large 'mole,' which should have been mentioned to have been situated over the 'right nipple.' This mole was very distinct and prominent at the *post-mortem*, and I can well conceive it might have been readily mistaken for a second nipple during childhood by a casual observer, especially if it presented such a character at that period of life ; whether, however, it has remained stationary from birth, or became enlarged proportionally with the whole body, I should not feel justified, with my present experience, in offering an opinion.

"As to the scars, the most probable inference is, 'that the linear one,' situated on the left wrist, was produced by a sharp cutting instrument, while those on the instep and on the temple were caused by blunt agents. As to the form or nature of these instruments it would be impossible to make any trustworthy statement.

"Again as to the height and stature : Mr. Meves was above the middle height, rather corpulent, with features and hair, etc., indicating the age which he was considered to be ; but all the minute facts with reference to these points may be better ascertained by examining a photograph, to which I have placed my signature, after noting and observing the exact likeness to the face of the deceased. '

"In conclusion, I may add, that these various statements and explanations have been made by me with the only motive of eliciting the truth of this apparent mystery, being perfectly unacquainted with any member of the Meves family, and being influenced by no remuneration, which I have not received or desired.

" EDWYN ANDREW, M.D. LOND.,

"To Mr. W. MEVES,   " Fellow of the Royal College of Surgeons.
  December 6th, 1859."

"On the 12th day of May last I held an inquest at 'The Wellington,' University Street, in the parish of St. Pancras, on the body of Mr. Augustus Antoine Cornelius Meves, late of 35 University Street. Previously to my proceeding to view the body, a gentleman, who stated he was a son of the deceased, requested me to examine particularly certain marks on his father's body, which I did, in accordance with his desire. They strictly corresponded with the description given of them by Dr. Andrew in his evidence at the inquest.

" THOMAS WAKLEY,
Coroner for Middlesex.

" OFFICE, 1 BEDFORD STREET, STRAND, LONDON,
  December 27th, 1859."

NOTE B.*

THE ABBÉ MORLET'S LETTER.

" MADAME,—I am not forgetful of the interest you took in my fate during my stay in London, and you have not limited it to that time : you have wished me to send news concerning myself. I have retained this desire with so much the more joy, as I should have greatly regretted to see my acquaintance with you brought to a termination. I shall always

* Referred to at pages 5 and 39.

remember having met in you all the intentions and considerations of friendship, accompanied by that delicacy which gives rise to something so delightful in the beneficence of your kindness. It will be sweet to me to cultivate this remembrance, and to pay homage to those virtues which have consoled me, and procured me some moments of happiness. I left London, Madame, my soul being divided. The hope of being able to procure refuge in my misfortunes strengthened from day to day; I felt that three or four persons who testified good-will could form another native land, and render the sky of your city more favourable to me; nevertheless I took my flight towards Valenciennes, and arrived there on the 3rd of September. I shall not stop to describe to you that complication of feeling which I experienced on approaching that city. It was gaiety, it was horror, my bosom dilated to breathe afar from France, and at the same time my thoughts became gloomy, as if I had approached the land of the Anthropophagi. I found my brother and a part of his family in the convalescence of the bombardment,—that is a dreadful malady, and there resulted a mortality at Valenciennes which continued during my stay there. One feels in the midst of the dead and dying, and ruins of all kinds heaped together, not much disposition for cheerfulness; the recital of the misfortunes that each had experienced formed the entire conversation, and if they allowed themselves any pauses, terror did not cease unless the risk of some sallies occurred to trouble it, and I have been many times witness of this good fortune; besides, the events of the day made us very attentive—sometimes it was the sight of a burning city, 'Le Quesnoi,' sometimes the passing by of Frenchmen, prisoners, at another time it was the wounded, preceded by carts which contained their arms; thus I saw pass by the tatters of my country, without being able to obtain news of our family remaining in France. We had some news of the Convention, which was very sorrowful, my brother having been denounced to it. It had one of his children, aged nineteen, arrested. At length I left Valenciennes the 18th of October; and behold I am at the house of another of my brother's emigrants, in a little town of the generality of the States of Holland, called Buren. I am there in the greatest solitude. My brother alone speaks French in his house; his wife, his children, his people, to the number of four, speak nothing but Dutch;—thus, as far as I am concerned, my whole society is reduced to one person only, and as that is to be shared by others there remains little for me. Had I been informed of this inconvenience I should have remained at Valenciennes, for this diversity of tongues is a great misfortune when one is obliged to bear it, as it makes a desert of a place even well peopled, and where an opportunity would be found of experiencing all kinds of delightful affection; notwithstanding I have

plenty of peace and tranquillity, which is an advantage not to be sufficiently appreciated at this time of confusions. I read a great deal. I
should like to keep up the little knowledge I have of English, but I have
no dictionary. I hope to have another soon. I am deprived of your
novel of Georgina, having left it at Valenciennes. Fortunately for me I
had read it during my journey to Gard.

"My respects to Madlle. Maricoure. Tell her I have done my
utmost to obtain news of her brother. Lady Annaly ought to go with
her into Brabant; I feel assured their health would be much better for it.
What opinion is formed in London of the state of our affairs? Is it
thought the step taken to check the French rage will be efficacious? A
poor secluded one like myself, tormented by his ignorance, is much
agitated by thinking, and has a strong desire to share the hopes of those
who have any; they must be questioned afar off—this is what vexes me.
I must solicit their kindness when there is an opportunity, or when there
is an occasion for it. It is that which determines me to request to say
a word on our political situation. At this moment there is a new insult
to the morality of the universe, the death of our Queen. In truth, one
cannot naturalize one's-self in such a world, and it is well to wish that the
generous English nation may overturn all these monsters during this
time of atrocities; one breathes a little, and the soul that is depressed
by it recovers a little energy; in cultivating friendship, and renewing precious relations founded on esteem, is the good I experience when I have
the advantage of writing to you. I ardently expect you to let me have
intelligence of your health and prosperity, and the condition of your
children. It is their education that is urgent, especially that of the
eldest. If I had remained in London, and you had thought my attention
would have been useful to them, I certainly would have proffered such
in homage to their mother.

"I should much like to know what becomes of the poor French
clergy in London. I put this question to you from sympathy with my
brethren. Should your servant be going to Brewer Street, Golden
Square, she might call at 38, the dwelling of Monsieur Bertrand, formerly steward of Bretagne, and likewise Minister of Marine; she might
present my compliments, and ask some information for me.

"I am, Madame, with respect, your very humble and obedient servant,

"MORLET, Canon of the Metropolitan of Rouen,
at Monsieur Morlet's, Knight of the Order of
Saint Louis, Bueren, near Utrecht, Guildre,
Hollondaise.

"*9th November* 1793.

' To Mrs. MEVES, 16 Vere Street, facing La Chappelle, Cavendish Square, London."

Note C.*

AUGUSTUS MEVES.

Vide " Biographical and Historical Dictionary of Musicians, selected from the works of Gerber, Choron, and Fayolle, Count Orloff, Dr. Burney, Sir John Hawkins, etc." published in 1827.

"MEVES (AUGUSTUS), a native of London, born in the year 1785. He is the son of the late Mr. William Meves, an artist of distinguished merit as a miniature-painter. His mother was a lady of acknowledged superior musical talent, and early observed a great partiality for music in her son, who seems indeed to have inherited this bias from both parents, his father having been also much attached to this enchanting science. On the occasion of his father giving a party to young John Hummel and his father of Vienna, together with Mr. Graeff and other musical gentlemen, young Hummel observed the facility with which Master Meves touched the piano, and thought that if he would study that instrument there was every prospect of his becoming a superior performer. From this recommendation Mrs. Meves taught him his notes, and his father induced him to practise by reading entertaining works while he was thus engaged, desisting the moment the boy ceased to play. In this manner he acquired a superior and easy touch upon the instrument. A similar practice was adopted to accustom his eye to the reading of music, his mother causing him to play whole ballets without allowing him to correct a single fault. Young Meves was notwithstanding intended by his father for the mercantile profession, until one of those slight incidents occurred which not unfrequently determine our future calling in life. He was accidentally playing at Broadwood's, when Mrs. C. Cramer, then present, inquired whether he had ever given lessons, which he had not then done. That lady became his pupil, and on leaving town for the season, made him a very handsome present. This agreeable surprise, for it was unexpected, induced him to prefer the cultivation of music as a pursuit to the dull monotony of a counting-house.

"Accordingly, we find him shortly after, in 1802, making his *début* at Edinburgh, under his Christian name only, and the newspapers of the day paying him the following most flattering compliments for so young a beginner:—'Mr. Augustus's fine touch and exquisite execution is only

* Referred to at pages 13, 93, and 245.

to be equalled by the great Mozart,' and on another occasion they remarked the force of his left hand.

"Meves, on the death of his father, quitted the profession of music as a teacher on account of its fatigues, but still continues to exercise his talent in the publication of various compositions, of which the following have met with great success :—'A Sonata,' dedicated to Mr. Cramer; 'L'Aline,' a rondo; 'German Air with Variations;' 'Within a Mile of Edinburgh,' harp; 'Auld Lang Syne;' 'Begone dull Care,' harp; 'Gente e qui l'Uccellatore;' and the Grand March from Mozart's opera of 'Il Flauto Magico;' a dramatic divertimento, 'My Lodging is on the Cold Ground,' air with variations."—Vide *Dictionary of Musicians*.

NOTE D.*

VOLTAIRE'S REMAINS REMOVED TO THE PANTHEON.

"An immense concourse of people followed the car that bore Voltaire to the Pantheon. This car was drawn by twelve white horses, harnessed four abreast, their manes plaited with flowers and golden tassels, and the reins held by men dressed in antique costumes, like those depicted on the medals of ancient triumphs. On the car was a funeral couch, extended on which was a statue of the philosopher crowned with a wreath. The National Assembly, the departmental and municipal bodies, the constituted authorities, the magistrates, and the army, surrounded, preceded, and followed the sarcophagus. The boulevards, the streets, the public places, the windows, the roofs of houses, even the trees, were crowded with spectators, and the suppressed murmurs of vanquished intolerance could not restrain this feeling of enthusiasm. Every eye was riveted on the car,—for the new school of ideas felt that it was the proof of their victory that was passing before them, and that philosophy remained mistress of the field of battle.

"The details of this ceremony were magnificent, and in spite of its profane and theatrical trappings, the features of every man that followed the car wore the expression of joy, arising from an intellectual triumph. A large body of cavalry, who seemed to have now offered their arms at the shrine of intelligence, opened the march. Then followed the

* Referred to at pages 17 and 238.

muffled drums, to whose notes were added the roar of the artillery that formed a part of the cortège. The scholars of the colleges of Paris, the patriotic societies, the battalions of the National Guard, the workmen of the different public journals, the persons employed to demolish the foundations of the Bastille, some bearing a portable press, which struck off different inscriptions in honour of Voltaire, as the procession moved on ; others carrying the chains, the collars, and bolts, and bullets found in the dungeons and arsenals of the state prisons ; and lastly, busts of Voltaire, Rousseau, and Mirabeau, marched between the troops and populace. On a litter was displayed the *procès-verbal* of the electors of '89, that Hegyra of the insurrection. On another stand, the citizens of the Faubourg Saint Antoine exhibited a plan in relief of the Bastille, a flag of the donjon, and a young girl in the costume of an Amazon, who had fought at the siege of this fortress. Here and there pikes surmounted with the Phrygian cap of liberty arose above the crowd, and on one of them was a scroll bearing the inscription, ' From this steel sprung liberty.'

"All the actors and actresses of the theatres of Paris followed the statue of him who for sixty years had inspired them. The titles of his principal works were inscribed on the sides of a pyramid that represented his immortality. His statue, formed of gold, and crowned with laurel, was borne on the shoulders of citizens wearing the costumes of the nations, and the times whose manners and customs he had depicted ; and the seventy volumes of his works were contained in a casket, also of gold. The members of the learned bodies and of the principal academies of the kingdom surrounded this ark of philosophy. Numerous bands of music, some marching with the troops, others stationed along the road of the procession, saluted the car as it passed with loud bursts of harmony, and filled the air with the enthusiastic strains of liberty. The procession stopped before the principal theatres, a hymn was sung in honour of his genius, and the car then resumed its march. On their arrival at the quai that bears his name, the car stopped before the house of M. de Villette, where Voltaire had breathed his last, and where his heart was preserved. Evergreen shrubs, garlands of leaves, and wreaths of roses decorated the front of the house, which bore the inscription, ' His fame is everywhere, and his heart is here.' Young girls, dressed in white, and wreaths of flowers on their heads, covered the steps of an amphitheatre erected before the house. Madame de Villette, to whom Voltaire had been a second father, in all the splendour of her beauty and the pathos of her tears, advanced and placed the noblest of all the wreaths, the wreath of filial affection, on the head of the great philosopher.

"At this moment the crowd burst into one of the hymns of the poet

Chenier, who, up to his death, most of all men cherished the memory of Voltaire. Madame de Villette and the young girls of the amphitheatre descended into the street, now strewed with flowers, and walked before the car. The Théâtre Français, then situated in the Faubourg Saint Germain, had erected a triumphal arch on its peristyle. On each pillar a medallion was fixed, bearing in letters of gilt bronze the titles of the principal dramas of the poet; on the pedestal of the statue erected before the door of the theatre was written, ' He wrote Irène at eighty-three years, at seventeen he wrote Œdipus.'

" The immense procession did not arrive at the Pantheon until ten o'clock at night, for the day had not been sufficiently long for this triumph. The coffin of Voltaire was deposited between those of Descartes and Mirabeau—the spot predestined for this intermediary genius, between philosophy and policy, between the design and the execution."—Lamartine's *History of the Girondists*, vol. i. page 149.

Note E.*

The Will of Francis Turner Blithe, late of Broseley Hall, in the County of Salop, deceased, dated 29th August 1770, has the following :—

(*Extracted from the Registry of the Prerogative Court of Canterbury.*)

"The rest, residue, and remainder of my estates, wheresoever and whatsoever, I give and bequeath unto my dear wife, Jane Elizabeth Blithe, and her heirs for ever, subject nevertheless to the payment of my debts and funeral expenses, and revoking all former wills by me made. I do nominate and appoint John Ashby, Esquire, George Goodwin of Colebrook Dale, in the said county of Salop, gent., and my dear wife, Jane Elizabeth Blithe, joint executors and executrix of this my last Will and Testament."

" Proved at London 8th March 1771 before the Judge, by the oaths of John Ashby, Esquire, George Goodwin, and Jane Elizabeth Blithe, widow of the relict, and executors to whom administration was granted, having been first sworn ' by commission ' duly to administer.

" Nath. Gostling.
Geo. Jenner, Deputy.
Chas. Dymley, Register."

(Ex^d. 930 Trevor.)

* Referred to at page 40.

x

Note F.[*]

LETTER FROM MR. DAVENPORT TO MR. AUGUSTUS MEVES.

" To Augustus Meves.

May 1824.

" Dear Sir,—Though it is a painful task to go over the ground of my late wife's unkind treatment of me on the disposal of her property personally, which I have forgiven, and wish to bury in oblivion, but at your desire I will once more explain the whole, that you may be informed of every circumstance relating to yourself. She had her virtues, and only failed in her want of gratitude towards me, as she acknowledged that I had always made her a kind and an indulgent husband, and never refused her a request till the last, that was fraught with so much injustice towards herself and cruelty towards me. It would have been the height of folly and madness to have consented. The coal and ironstone mines being out of lease, in which our principal income depended, she wished me to consent to let them for our lives to the present Mr. Harries, when I reasoned with her that he was her adopted heir to the property ; it would not be his interest to work the coal out of them in our time to pay a royalty, when in a few years probably they might become his own without payment of anything, or at least not to work them to that extent an indifferent person would be under a necessity of doing ; and if he failed in payment of rent, what advantage could she take of her adopted heir ? All she 'could do would be to put him in prison, which he knew she would not do ; and if I survived her, I should be so much in his power, that I may as well give him up the property at once, for I should have no control over him. However, all this reasoning would not avail, and she told me if I did not comply with her unreasonable wish it should be the worse for me ; and she was as good as her word, for she altered her will, and left everything she could to Harries, excepting her plate. Her jewels and plate she had secured to her in the marriage settlements. The plate she could not well separate, as there was a great deal of my own, and some of hers, charged with my arms upon it, therefore, there would have been some difficulty of ascertaining which had been hers or mine, so it was bequeathed to me.

" Mrs. Davenport, upon our marriage, was left by her late husband, in fee, her property at Broseley, and an estate near Shrewsbury, with a debt upon it of seven thousand pounds, which estate upon our marriage

[*] Referred to at page 41.

was vested in trustees' hands, to be sold to pay off the above debt, which instead of £7000, it sold for £10,000. The surplus £3000 she desired might be put on mortgage on my estate, and to oblige her I paid money off to make room for it, the interest of which you understand was her private property, and which she regularly received for her own use, with £200 a year. I regularly paid her for pin-money quarterly £200, of which she left to your mother, Mrs. Higginson, and yourself. £1000 she called in, and placed it in the East India Bonds, as she said at the time for her present expenditure, but at her decease it proved she had not spent a sixpence, but on the contrary several years' interest was due upon it. This £1000 she had left to me, but upon the alteration of her will she left it to Harries, with the rest of her accumulated property. Now, we supposed the accumulated property, which I had no idea of, nor her attorney, must have been a purse she had made in Mr. Blythe, her former husband's time, and if so, consequently *personally*, and belonging to me, as we had reason, and in fact by her receipts were satisfied, that she spent the interest of the £3000, and her pin-money, upon herself, and which as residuary legatee Harries could only claim by her will. However, our presumptive evidence was not admitted, and in consequence I lost the cause, by which unkind treatment she deprived me of my right to her personality, and involved me in a Chancery suit, the expenses of which, and the payment of the principal and interest, and lawyers' bills of £2000 for eight years, whilst the suit was pending, and which I have but lately discharged, and which so much disgusted me, that I gave up the executorship, and left the management of her affairs to Messrs. Harries. —I am, etc.,   " Davenport.

"To Augustus Meves, Esq.,
    " 13 Air Street, Piccadilly."

Note G.*

LETTER FROM MRS. CROWLEY TO HER DAUGHTER.

"To Miss Crowley, at Mrs. Faulkner's,
    50 Wells Street, Oxford Street, London.

        " Bath, *2nd January* 1777.
" Receive my thanks, my dearest Marianne, for the early notice you gave me of your safe arrival in London. I should have written to you

* Referred to at pages 41 and 172.

by last night's post, but I was obliged to answer a letter I received from Miss Ellison, with an enclosed bill, which she sent me. If I had not wrote the same post she would have thought the letter had miscarried. I am charmed with the account you give me of the kind reception good Mistress Faulkner gave you; it was truly like herself, all friendly, and truly polite. How kind it was in her to insist on your writing to me the same night that you got to London! I did not expect it, though I assure you that the early notice of your getting safe to the end of your journey gave me infinite pleasure, as also it did to your good father. I had forgot to give you the bracelet with his picture, but he had the goodness to put me in mind of it. He insists on my sending it by Miss Fitzpatrick, who leaves Bath to-morrow, I think. I need not doubt of your taking the greatest care of it. Excuse, my dear Marianne, the shortness of my letter, as it is almost 10 o'clock. Write soon, according to your promise. Our best compliments attend good Mrs. Faulkner; your father's blessing and mine attend you.—Your ever affectionate Mother, MARY CROWLEY.

"*N.B.*—Your trunk was sent per fly-waggon, and must arrive at the White Bear in Piccadilly to-morrow morning. Your music books shall be sent when you signify your place of settlement. Bocherini is added to your collection.

NOTE H.*

ROWLAND STEPHENSON.

"THAT Rowland Stephenson carried on, under the cloak of religion, respectability, and morality, the most nefarious transactions, and made away with moneys intrusted to his care, cannot be denied. A more plausible or agreeable an acquaintance I never had, and although I could not help feeling gratified that an exposure had been made, which would warn others from placing any confidence in such men, I was grieved when I heard that he had been compelled to flee the country. Had I been possessed of wealth, so implicit was my faith in him, that I should probably have lost my whole fortune. He once asked me to remove my account from Cox and Greenwood to his house, but as I believed the balance was on the wrong side, I gratefully declined his offer."—Vide *Fifty Years' Biographical Reminiscences by Lord William Pitt Lennox*, vol. ii. p. 52, published in 1863.

* Referred to at page 45.

Note I.*

NARRATIVE.

THIS Narrative, such as it is, full of faults, was written at the request of the Marquis of Bonneval and the Abbé Prince Charles de Broglie :—

"Cornelius Crowley, Esq., was the father of Jane Elizabeth and Marianne Crowley, by his wife Mary Ellison, daughter of Francis Ellison, Esq., of Newcastle-upon-Tyne.

"Jane Elizabeth Crowley was born in 1742, and subsequently married Francis Turner Blithe, Esq. of Broseley Hall, Shropshire. At his demise in 1771, she inherited by his will the whole of his valuable estates in Shropshire, called the Broseley estates, and an estate called the Whiteley estate, at Colebrook Dale.

"In 1772 the widow Jane Elizabeth Blithe married a second time William Yelverton Davenport, Esq. of Davenport House, near Bridgeworth, Shropshire.

"Mrs. Davenport died in the year 1811. 'Her will is proved at Doctors' Commons.'

"Mary Ann Crowley, the second daughter of Cornelius and Mary Crowley, was born at Bath, and baptized at the church of St. Peter and Paul, the 11th of April 1754.

"Mary Ann Crowley was educated at a Convent, 'St. Omer's,' in France, in the Holy Catholic faith. On her return to her father's house at Bath she studied music under Mr. Linley.

"Cornelius Crowley was nicknamed at Bath 'Musical Crowley,' on account of his extreme fondness for music, and his having dealings in Cremona violins. He was originally a dealer in Italian gems and jewellery, and having amassed a sufficient competency, he retired, and took up his abode at Bath. The latter years of his life he became a wine merchant.

"Mary Ann Crowley usually signed her name after the French manner, 'Marianne Crowley.' In January 1777 she came to London, as appears by the following letter, dated 2nd of January 1777, Bath :—

"'Receive my thanks, my dearest Marianne, for the early notice you gave me of your safe arrival in London. I am charmed with the account you gave me of the kind reception good Mrs. Faulkner gave you, as also it did to your good father. I had forgot to give you the bracelet with his picture, but he had the goodness to put me in mind of it. He insists on my sending it by Miss Fitzpatrick, who leaves Bath to-morrow, I think. I need not doubt your taking the greatest care of it. Mr. Piggot has this moment left me. He will be in London next

---

* Referred to at page 77.

Thursday fortnight,' etc. etc.—'I remain, my dearest Marianne, your affectionate mother,   MARY CROWLEY.

"'*N.B.* (in Mr. Crowley's handwriting).—Your trunks were sent per fly-waggon, and will arrive at the White Bear in Piccadilly to-morrow. Bocherini is added to your musical collection.'

"During Miss Crowley's residence in London she became the favourite pupil of Signor Sacchini, the celebrated Italian composer.

"Miss Crowley, from her great musical talent, and having a very fine deep-toned voice, was induced to make her appearance in an Opera, arranged expressly for her by Mr. Linley, under the assumed name of 'Miss Courtenay.' The afflicting news arriving of her mother's decease suddenly terminated her career as an operatic singer.

"Mr. Crowley came to London, and took his disconsolate daughter to Paris, for the purpose of placing her at a Convent. They resided when in Paris at Madame Gregson's, in La Rue Dauphine, as appears from the following note to Miss Crowley, chez Madame Gregson, Rue Dauphine, Paris :—

(*Translation.*)

"'Madame l'Abbesse de l'Abbaye aux Bois is very· sorry at not being able to receive Miss Crowley into the interior of the Convent. She suggests to her to take an apartment outside at 400 fr., on condition that she shall have a housekeeper, or lady's-maid, of mature age, and that she shall only receive the visits of those approved of by her father, of whom the Abbess shall have the list.'

"In June 1781, Mr. Crowley being ill, he wrote from Bath to his daughter Marianne in Paris, acquainting her with such. Upon her arrival at Bath in June 1781, she found her father had succumbed under his illness, and was buried. In the postscript of the letter Mr. Crowley wrote to his daughter, he says :—

"'If it is the will of God that I should survive this plunge, I will return along with you to France, and spend the remainder of my days in the bosom of the Holy Church. I have fully decided the point in my own mind.'

"Mr. Crowley spent, during his residence in Bath, the greater portion of his property. That which remained did not amount to £1000.

"Mrs. Jane Elizabeth Davenport allowed her sister 'Marianne' £200 a year.

"In January 1781 Miss Crowley was in London, and resided at No. 3 Little Maddox Street, Bond Street.

"Miss Crowley visited at the house of the Rev. Charles Wesley, where she became acquainted with the Dowager Duchess Caroline, Countess of Harrington, who much admired her manners and accomplishments. The following are letters from Lady Harrington :—

"'Lady Harrington's kind compliments to Miss Crowley. She will be glad of her company any time to-day she pleases. Lord Barrington is come to town, and Lady H. begs Miss Crowley will send his opera ticket.'

"'DEAR MISS CROWLEY,—I write to know how you are to-day, and to hope you did not increase your cold. I have had but a bad night, and am not out of bed. We were very comfortable yesterday, and if you think so, I shall hope to be so soon again.

"'I cannot let your pianoforte go away of a Sunday. What would the Wesleys say?—Your sincere friend, C. HARRINGTON.'

"The following letter is from Lady Anna Maria Lincoln to Miss Crowley :—

"'Give me leave to thank you, dear madam, for the music you sent me, and the songs you had the trouble of writing out for me. You have added much to my amusement by it; and could I hear you play them, I think I should like the music better afterwards. I rejoice extremely Lady Harrington has added so agreeable a person to her society, as all accounts agree in making you; and I hope some day or another to be presented to you, and, in the meantime, beg you will believe me your very humble servant, A. M. LINCOLN.'

"During the time Miss Crowley resided with Lady Harrington as companion to her ladyship, she became acquainted with Mr. Meves von Schroëder, a miniature painter, who came from Italy with Roger Palmer, Esq. of Rush House, near Dublin. Mr. Palmer was supposed to be the richest and most influential commoner of Ireland, and was said to have been concerned with a party who gave information to the French Government during the American War.

"In the year 1782 Mr. Meves von Schroëder had joined Mr. Palmer at Spaw, in Germany, from thence they went into Italy, where Mr. Palmer passed the winter months of the year 1782, at Portici, near Naples.

"In the spring of the year 1783, Mr. Palmer, accompanied by Mr. Meves von Schroëder, came to England. Shortly after his arrival Mr. Palmer went to Ireland to arrange the agency of his estates in the counties of Connaught and Mayo. Mr. Meves von Schroëder presented to Mr. Palmer a copy of Gawin Hamilton's picture of the Anger of Achilles for the Loss of Briseis, which he had painted during their stay in Italy.

"Mr. Meves established himself as a miniature painter in Half-Moon Street, Piccadilly, and found in Miss Crowley a great friend and patroness. She introduced him to a Mrs. Delaney, whose portrait he painted. Mrs. Delaney presented him to Madame Schwellensburg, when he copied a portrait of that lady, which gave great satisfaction, and occasioned an introduction to Mr. Romney, the celebrated portrait painter, and he copied several pictures painted by that artist.

"In 1784 Mr. Meves made an offer of marriage to Miss Crowley, and soon after it was reported that they were married 'privately,' according to the ritual of the Roman Catholic faith. Miss Crowley had thought to keep such a secret from her elder sister 'Mrs. Davenport.'

"After the decease of Lady Harrington in June 1784 it appears that Miss Crowley resided at No. 75 Portland Street, for the following note from Lady Sefton, one of the daughters of the Dowager Caroline, Countess of Harrington, bears that address :—

"'Lady Sefton presents her best compliments, and many thanks to Miss Crowley for her very obliging inquiries. She is pretty well, and hopes Miss Crowley is the same.

'HILL STREET, *Monday morning.*'

"When Miss Crowley went to France she travelled under Mr. Meves's family name of Schroëder, as 'Madame Schroëder.' On her arrival at Paris she made known to her friend Signor Sacchini (he was the Court musician to Marie Antoinette, Queen of France) the state of her circumstances, and he presented her to the Queen as a proper lady to attend upon Her Majesty. The Queen, on finding Madame Schroëder to be a lady of superior manners and education, was pleased to accept her services.

"On the 16th February 1785, Madame Crowley Schroëder was delivered of a son by a surgeon-accoucheur of the name of 'Vincent d'Etionville.' Permission was granted her to go to England for the purpose of having her son baptized and registered, in order to give him the rights of an Englishman in enabling him to inherit landed property, etc.

"On her arrival in London, Mr. Meves von Schroëder was out of town, he being at that time employed in Derbyshire, at Lord Scarsdale's, taking copies of some portraits for Lady Irving and Lady Pepper Arden.

"Mrs. Meves Schroëder, in her emergency, sent for Mr. George Meves (a brother of Mr. Meves von Schroëder), who, with a Mr. Kranke, stood as godfathers to the child. He was baptized the 25th March 1785, after early morning prayers, and named, 'Augustus Antoine Cornelius Meves,' at St James's Church, Piccadilly. After the ceremony, as there was no cause to detain Mrs. Meves Schroëder in London, she returned to France to fulfil her duties in the service of the Queen of France.

" The Queen, according to the Chronological History of France, was delivered of a son at Versailles the 27th March 1785, at seven o'clock in the evening. The child was baptized the same evening by the Cardinal Prince de Rohan, Grand Aumonier of France, and named ' Louis Charles de Bourbon Capet.' Subsequently he was created Duke of Normandy. He was usually called Prince-Royal, and succeeded to the title of Dauphin at the decease of his brother (Louis Joseph Xavier François, Dauphin of France), who died at Meudon the 4th June 1789, of a malady of the spine.

" Madame Schroeder was appointed one of the first women of the Chambers at the Petit Trianon, and remained attached to the service of the Queen till the month of July 1787, at which time she came to England in the suite of the Princesse de Lamballe. She was called at the Court of France ' Madame de Courville Schroëder.'

" Madame Meves Schroëder took apartments at Pimlico, near a tavern called Spring Gardens, where she resided for some time. Subsequently she went to France, and resided at Boulogne-sur-mer. About this time it was that some one informed Mrs. Davenport that her sister ' Marianne' had married a foreigner.

" Madame Meves Schroëder came to England in 1788, and resided for some time in Suffolk Street, Haymarket, and on the 26th February 1789 she gave birth to a daughter named ' Cecilia Marianne.'

" When Mrs. Davenport learnt that her sister had married clandestinely, she reduced the annuity she had been allowing her from £200 to £40.

" This resolution made it impossible for Madame Meves Schroëder to remain in London without contracting debts. She therefore placed her infant daughter under the care of a trustworthy nurse, and in the month of September 1789 she went to France with her son, and proceeded on to Versailles, and was appointed as one of the supernumerary waiting-women on Her Majesty. Here she remained until the month of October, when, on the morning of the attack and entrance into the Palace of Versailles by an infuriated populace, the Queen in an utter state of distraction, with the Dauphin in her arms, ran into the room where Madame Meves Schroëder, with her son, had taken refuge among a number of female attendants on the Queen, when Her Majesty tore from Mrs. Meves her son Augustus, and fled with him to the King's apartments, leaving the Dauphin to the care of the female attendants.

" In October 1789 Mrs. Meves Schroëder returned to England, and took apartments in Dartmouth Street, Westminster.

" Mrs. Davenport's allowance not being sufficient to keep her sister as a gentlewoman, she determined to make use of her musical talent for her support, and was greatly assisted in her endeavours by Mr. John Preston, a music-seller, who had been an intimate friend of Mr. Crowley's. He was at that time Mrs. Davenport's London agent. Amongst his recommendations was that of musical instructress to Miss Warner's boarding-school at Wandsworth in 1792. Mrs. Meves had also a kind friend in Mr John Broadwood, the eminent pianoforte-maker.

"In 1792 Mrs. Meves Schroëder lived under the name of Mrs. Meves, as her husband had at that time entirely given up the profession of a miniature painter, and frequented the Bank of England, where he transacted business solely under his name of 'William Meves' of the Stock Exchange.

"Mrs. Meves took apartments at 15 Great Marylebone Street; in the same house lived Dowager Lady Anneley, with her companion Madlle. Maricoure, and an emigrant French gentleman, the Abbé Morlet.

"A Captain Curten, and Monsieur Rogiers, brought the following message from Her Royal Highness the Duchess of Angoulême; the communication, however, did not come direct from her lips, but from the Cardinal de Latil, the confessor of the Royal Family at Holyrood. The above gentleman I had entrusted with a message bringing to the Duchess's knowledge my existence, and residence in London :—'They stated that the Duchess of Angoulême was quite positive that it was her own brother the Dauphin, who came with her from Versailles to Paris, on the 6th October 1789, and that she had never lost sight of him, but was in the constant habit of seeing him until the fatal separation in the Tower of the Temple at Paris in July 1793. That could positive proof be brought forward that her brother was still in existence, "nothing on earth could afford a greater consolation to her heart;" but she fully believed that her brother had died in the Tower of the Temple, from the cruelties he had experienced during his solitary confinement, likewise, she had been informed that poison had been administered to accelerate his death in June 1795.'"

COMMENTARY ON PRECEDING NARRATIVE.

Respecting the Narrative written for the Marquis of Bonneval, and the Abbé Prince Charles de Broglie, we have added such to the Memoirs, thinking that it would be satisfactory for our readers to know what was actually written, and the basis of the statement to the Duchess of Angoulême, and to Charles x.'s party. Certainly it was a most erroneous statement to make, that is "the Dauphin being exchanged in 1789 ;" however it will clearly prove that no imposition was really meant on the part of our father, and likewise be positive proof that he did not study his part from historical accounts, but that he founded such entirely on the revelation of Mrs. Meves, and the information as received from his reputed parents, and Mr. George Meves.

It is evident there was no desire on his part to deceive, but only to chronicle that which had come to his knowledge ; he left it to experts or qualified persons to solve the mystery, as all that was necessary for him, under the circumstances, to do, was to recapitulate what had been revealed to him, the facts being that Mrs. Meves owed her position at the Court of France to the influence of Signor Sacchini, and a brief account of her pedigree and career. It is a plain statement, made in a plain and unpretentious way, but most erroneous as regards the exchange, and the date of such. The origin of this palpable error is fully explained in Mr. George Meves's information reviewed, from page 194.

What he wrote to the Marquis of Bonneval concerning the exchange in 1789, and being brought to England, was not his personal recollection that such was really the case, but as tallying with information received. He was too young to have trustworthy recollection of such himself.

On the night of the attack on the Palace of Versailles, the Queen had but just time to escape the fury of a misguided populace, worked to frenzy by the machinations of the sanguinary enemies of France. Names are unnecessary, history has already recorded them. The heroic Marie Antoinette baffled her would-be assassins, the traitor Equality, " Philip Duke of Orleans," amongst the foremost.

Monsieur Hué, one of the faithful officers of the King's Chamber, has recorded the following in his work entitled *The Last Years of the Reign and Life of Louis XVI.*, page 130 :—

"Trembling for his son's life the King ran to his chamber, and carried him away in his arms. (The King, to get to the Dauphin's apartments, and avoid being seen by the brigands, was obliged to go through a dark subterraneous passage.) In his way the light went out. 'Take hold of my night-gown,' said the King calmly to the woman who attended the Dauphin. Having groped his way back to his apartment he there found the Queen, Madame Royale, Monsieur, Madame, Madam Elizabeth, and the Marquise de Tourzel. Thus united, the Royal Family waited with less terror the fate which threatened them."

Here then is seen that an incident did in reality occur at the Palace of Versailles on the night of the attack, bearing an affinity to that related in the foregoing Narrative to the Marquis of Bonneval.

The Narrative to the Marquis of Bonneval was written whilst its author was under an erroneous impression, for Mrs. Meves revealed only that he was the son of Louis XVI. and Marie Antoinette, but not the time the exchange was effected ; and Mr. George Meves informed him, as is seen in the Authentic Memoirs, and accounted for in the information reviewed of Mr. George Meves in Commentary, that Mrs. Meves arrived in England on the breaking out of the French Revolution.   After her arrival she had the care of her daughter, and Mr. Meves of his son.   Mr. Meves being an artist, was in the autumn of the year 1789 professionally at Lord Stamford's in Cheshire, having previously to setting out placed his son under the care of an old nurse.   During Mr. Meves's absence in Cheshire Mrs. Meves got possession of her son, and took him with her to France, and on her return to England she placed him at a boarding-school at Horsham.

Here then is seen how the mistake originated, of his stating he arrived in England in 1789, and of the incorrect dates that followed, the explanation of which is fully given in Mr. George Meves's information reviewed, from page 194.

NOTE K.*

THE ATKYNS FAMILY.

THE following epitaph is placed in Poets' Corner, Westminster Abbey :—

"TO THE MEMORY OF

"SIR EDWARD ATKYNS, one of the Barons of the Exchequer, in the reigns of King Charles the First and Second.   He was a person of such integrity that he resisted the many advantages and honours offered to him by the chiefs of the Grand Rebellion.   He departed this life in 1669, aged 82 years.

"SIR ROBERT ATKYNS, his eldest son, created Knight of the Bath at the Coronation of King Charles II., afterwards Lord Chief Baron of the Exchequer, under King William, and Speaker of the House of Lords in several Parliaments, which place he filled with distinguished abilities and dignity, as his learned writings abundantly prove.   He died in 1709, aged 88 years.

* Referred to at page 78.

"Sir Edward Atkyns, his youngest son, Lord Chief Baron of the Exchequer, which office he discharged with great honour and integrity; but retired upon the Revolution from public business to his seat in Norfolk, where he was revered for his piety to God and humanity to men. He employed himself in reconciling differences among his neighbours, in which he obtained so great a character, that few would refuse the most difficult cause to his decision, and the most litigious would not appeal from it. He died in 1698, aged 68 years.

AND OF

"Sir Robert Atkyns, eldest son of Sir Robert above mentioned. A gentleman versed in polite literature, and in the antiquities of this country, of which his History of Gloucestershire is a proof. He died in 1711, aged 65 years.

"In memory of his ancestors, who have so honourably presided in the Courts of Justice in Westminster Hall, Edward Atkyns, Esq., late of Kettringham, in Norfolk, second son of the last named Sir Edward, caused this monument to be erected. He died January the 20th, 1750, aged 79 years."

Note L.*

LAST WILL AND TESTAMENT OF LOUIS XVI.

"In the name of the most Holy Trinity, of the Father, the Son, and the Holy Ghost, the 25th day of December 1792, I, Louis the 16th of that name, King of France, having been for more than four months imprisoned with my family in the Tower of the Temple at Paris, by those who were my subjects, and being deprived of all communication whatever, since the 11th inst., with my family; being, moreover, implicated in proceedings the issue of which it is impossible to foresee, occasioned by the passions of men, and for which they can find no pretext or justification in any existing law, having God alone as witness of my thoughts, and to whom I can address myself, I here declare, in His presence, my last wishes and sentiments.

"I leave my soul to God my Creator. I pray Him to receive it into His mercy, not to judge it according to its merits, but by those of

---

* Referred to at page 120.

our Lord Jesus Christ, who offered himself a sacrifice to God his Father for us men, however unworthy we were of it, and I above all.

"I die in the union of our Holy Mother, the Apostolic and Roman Catholic Church, which holds its powers by an uninterrupted succession from Saint Peter, to whom Jesus Christ had confided them. I believe sincerely, and acknowledge all that is contained in the symbol and commandments of God, and of the Church, the Sacraments, and mysteries, such as the Church teaches and has always taught them. I have never pretended to make myself a judge in the different modes of explaining the dogmas which distract the Church of Jesus Christ, but I have agreed, and I will always agree, if God spares my life, with those decisions which the superior ecclesiastics, in union with the Holy Catholic Church, give and shall give, conformably with the discipline of the Church, followed since the time of Jesus Christ. I pity with all my heart those of our brethren who may be in error, but I do not pretend to judge them, and I do not love them the less in Jesus Christ, according to what Christian charity teaches us.

"I pray God to forgive me all my sins. I have sought to know them thoroughly, to detest them, and to humble myself in His presence. Not being able to avail myself of the services of a Catholic priest, I pray God to receive the confession which I have made of them, and especially of the profound repentance which I feel for having put my name, 'although it was against my will,' to acts contrary to the discipline and the belief of the Catholic Church, to which I have always remained sincerely attached in heart. I pray God to accept the firm resolution which I have adopted, if He spares my life, to avail myself as soon as I can of the services of a Catholic priest, in order to acknowledge all my sins, and to receive the sacrament of repentance.

"I pray all those whom I may have inadvertently offended (for I do not recollect having committed any intentional offence towards anybody), or those to whom I may have set any bad examples, or given any scandal, to pardon me for the evil which they may think I have done them.

"I beg all those who are charitable to join their prayers to mine, to obtain from God the forgiveness of my sins.

"I forgive, with all my heart, those who have become my enemies without my having given them any cause, and I pray God to forgive them, as well as those who from a false or ill-understood zeal have done me a great deal of harm.

"I recommend to God my wife, my children, my sister, my aunts, my brothers, and all those who are attached to me by ties of blood, or in any other manner whatsoever. I pray God particularly to cast eyes of mercy on my wife, my children, and my sister, should they happen to lose me, so long as they shall remain in this perishable world.

"I commend my children to my wife, whose maternal tenderness for them I have never doubted. I particularly enjoin her to instil into them honest and Christian principles, to make them look upon the grandeurs of this world, if they are condemned to bear them, as dangerous and perishable possessions, and to turn their thoughts towards the only solid and durable glory of eternity. I pray my sister to be good enough to continue her affection to my children, and to supply to them the place of a mother, should they have the misfortune to lose their natural parent.

"I pray my wife to pardon me for all the evils she suffers on my account, and the pain I may have given her during the period of our union, as she may rest assured that I entertain no ill-feeling towards her, should she have anything to reproach herself with.

"I earnestly entreat my children, next to the duty they owe to God, which must take precedence of all, to continue at all times united, submissive, and obedient to their mother, and grateful for all the cares and troubles she encounters for them, and in memory of me I pray them to look upon my sister as a second mother.

"Should my son have the misfortune to become King, I entreat him to reflect that he owes himself entirely to the happiness of his fellow-citizens; that he should forget all hatred and resentment, and especially everything that is connected with the misfortunes and the sufferings I undergo. That he can only accomplish the happiness of his people by reigning according to the laws, but at the same time to reflect that a King cannot make those laws respected, and accomplish the good that is in his heart, if not invested with the necessary authority; and that, on the contrary, being restricted in his operations, and unable to inspire respect, he must be more hurtful than otherwise.

"I entreat my son to protect all those persons who have been attached to me, as much as the circumstances in which he may be placed will enable him. To reflect that it is a sacred debt which I have contracted to the children or relations of those who have perished for me, and also to those who have suffered on my account. I know there are many persons amongst those who were attached to me who have not acted towards me as they ought to have done, and who have even shown ingratitude. But I pardon them (for frequently, in moments of trouble and agitation, we are not masters of ourselves), and I pray my son, should occasion offer itself, to think of nothing but their misfortunes.

" I should be happy could I now evince my gratitude to those who have displayed for me a real and disinterested attachment. On the one hand, if I was sensibly touched with the ingratitude and infidelity of people for whom I have never evinced anything but kindness to themselves, their relations, or friends, on the other, I have had the consolation to witness the attachment and gratuitous interest which many persons have shown me. I pray them all to accept my thanks for it. In the present state of affairs, I should be afraid of compromising them were I to speak more explicitly, but I especially enjoin my son to search for opportunities of knowing them.

" I should, however, consider it a calumny on the sentiments of the Nation, if I were not openly to recommend to my son MM. de Chamilly and Hué, whose real attachment for me induced them to shut themselves up with me in this gloomy abode, and who could only have looked forward to be its unhappy victims. I also recommend to him Cléry, whose attentions I have had every reason to praise since he has been with me. As he is the one who has remained with me to the last, I pray the officers of the Commune to deliver to him my clothes, my books, my watch, my purse, and the other trifling effects which have been lodged with the Council of the Commune.

" I also very willingly pardon those who have been placed to guard me for the ill-treatment and the restraint which they have felt it their duty to make me suffer. I have found some sensitive and compassionate souls—may they enjoy in their hearts that tranquillity which their mode of thinking must impart to them.

" I pray MM. de Malesherbes, Tronchet, and Desèze, to accept my thanks and gratitude for all the cares and trouble they have taken on my account.

" I conclude by declaring before God, and about to appear in His presence, that I cannot reproach myself with any of the crimes which are alleged against me.

Louis.

" Done in duplicate in the Tower of the Temple, December 25th, 1792."

Note M.*

LETTER FROM MRS. MEVES TO MR. MEVES.

"MADAME BOMBEAU having informed me that you are resolved to keep Auguste at your house, and to have a nurse at any rate, I answered that your will is mine, but, Sir, allow me to ask you, by what conduct towards my children have I lost the right to have them under my care in, as I think, the most critical period of their life, and how long it is that a mercenary nurse has been preferable to the cares of a fond mother? I think that my son is dearer to me than to you, notwithstanding all your protestations to the contrary. I have attended him during three sicknesses without you having deigned to be of any assistance to him. I ask you then, why he is now taken from my care? I consider you bold indeed to dare to take away a child from its mother, and trust him to a public nurse in preference, and to take upon yourself (you who know nothing of sickness, and who, I have heard you say, are without pity and compassion for the sick) the success of so delicate and dangerous a matter. I assure you I would not venture to do as much, and that resolute as I am in anything that concerns my children, I would not be so bold. You know that I never come to your house, and that the constitutions of my children are known to me—two things which with a man of reflection would have great weight. You have to answer for the life of your child, and you can confide it to a nurse in preference to its mother. Believe me, there exists not a being who prides himself in humanity and honour who would not condemn you. I have made you an offer to be his nurse, and ask you, what is your objection? I well know the service it would be to the child, and do not see why he should not come under my protection. If you will not come to any place in which I am, be it so. Believe that I neither request nor exact anything from you, which would be disagreeable to you with respect to me.

"If the child is with me, and all goes on well, it seems to me that you may confide in my care. If not, I have warned you, and I imagine it will be a sweeter reflection in time to come, that at least his mother cannot reproach you with his death, nor of having deprived her of the protection of her son at so critical a moment. I repeat, my will is yours, but after what I have said, reflect before deciding on it. The matter is a serious one, and is deserving your serious reflection. If your son dies at your house your regret will be eternal, and eternal will be my reproaches."

* Referred to at page 175.

Note N.*

LETTER FROM MR. MEVES TO MRS. HIGGINSON.

"Madam,—Part of a conversation which you have lately had with Mr. Vital having been communicated to me, I find that you and I have not clearly understood each other, for I do not reject a marriage with your cousin, and really, was it only out of consideration for the distressed and unprotected situation of her and children, I would not neglect every honourable reparation in my power that might alleviate them.

"I find, madam, you had a power to transact this affair, and conclude the marriage, beyond what I really ever understood till now; and you informed me in our last conversation that Mrs. Davenport had mentioned to you, in case the marriage should be brought about, the aid of a little money should not be wanting, which I should conclude to mean a small addition to her annuity. I also had your promise, when I presented to you her extreme want for clothes and other necessaries, that you would intercede to obtain such. I know your power of persuasion over Mrs. Davenport is unlimited, and as you have professed some friendship for me, I am confident that your friendship and your humanity for the children who never offended you, will overbalance your resentment.

"The request which your cousin at first made was granted, but Mrs. Davenport must, upon mature deliberation, be convinced that her present allowance never was sufficient without contracting debts. I might certainly expect that Mrs. Davenport's honour would (particularly in this case) look to the indemnification of her sister's maintenance at least; and in this request nobody can possibly suppose me to be unreasonable, therefore if Mrs. Higginson will but lay aside her anger, which cannot but be jointly felt by those who do not deserve it, and generously step forward with her exertions, the affair may be concluded.

"After this declaration, I think not only Mrs. Higginson, but everybody by whom I am taxed with unwillingness and indecision in this business, sufficiently assured of the integrity of my wishes.—I am, Madam."

* Referred to at page 176.

Note O.*

CHARACTER OF DANTON.

"DANTON, whom the Revolution had found an obscure barrister at the Châtelet, had increased with it in influence. He had already that celebrity which the multitude easily assigns to him whom it sees everywhere, and always listens to. He was one of those men who seem born of the stir of Revolutions, and which float on its surface, until it swallows them up. All in him was like the mass—athletic, rude, coarse. He pleased them, because he resembled them. His eloquence was like the loud clamour of the mob. His brief and decisive phrases had the martial curtness of command. His irresistible gestures gave impulse to his plebeian auditors. Ambition was his sole line of politics. Devoid of honour, principles, or morality, he only loved democracy because it was exciting. It was his element, and he plunged into it. He sought there not so much command, as that voluptuous sensuality which man finds in the rapid movement which bears him away with it. He was intoxicated with the Revolutionary vertigo, as a man becomes drunken with wine, yet he bore his intoxication well. He had that superiority of calmness in the confusion he created, which enabled him to control it, preserving *sang froid* in his excitement, and his temper; even in a moment of passion he jested with the clubs in their stormiest moods. A burst of laughter interrupted bitterest imprecations, and he amused the people even whilst he impelled them to the uttermost pitch of fury. Satisfied with his two-fold ascendency, he did not care to respect it himself, and neither spoke to it of principles nor of virtue, but solely of force. Himself, he adored force, and force only. His sole genius was contempt for honesty, and he esteemed himself above all the world, because he had trampled under foot all scruples. Everything was to him a means. He was a statesman of materialism, playing the popular game, with no end but the terrible game itself, with no stake but his life, and with no responsibility beyond nonentity. Such a man must be profoundly indifferent either to despotism or to liberty. His contempt of the people must incline him rather to the side of tyranny. When we can detect nothing divine in men, the better part to play is to make use of them. We can only serve well that which we respect. He was only with the people because he was of the

* Referred to at page 187.

people, and thus the people ought to triumph.   He would have betrayed
it, as he served it, unscrupulously.   The Court well knew the tariff of
his conscience.   He threatened it, in order to make it desirous of buying him; he only opened his mouth in order to have it stuffed with gold.
His most revolutionary movements were but the marked prices at which
he was purchaseable.   His hand was in every intrigue, and his honesty
was not checked by any offer of corruption.   He was bought daily, and
next morning was again for sale.   Mirabeau, La Fayette, Montmorin,
M. de Laporte, the intendant of the civil list, the Duc d'Orléans, the
King himself, all knew his price.   Money had flowed with him from all
sources, even the most impure, without remaining with him.   Any other
individual would have felt shame before men and parties who had the
secret of his dishonour, but he only was not ashamed, and looked them
in the face without a blush.   His was the quietude of vice.   He was
the focus of all those men who seek in events nothing but fortune and
impunity.   But others had only the baseness of crime.   Danton's vices
partook of the heroic—his intellect was all but genius.   He had upon
him the bright flash of circumstances, but it was as sinister as his face.
Immorality, which was the infirmity of his mind, was in his eyes the
essence of ambition; he cultivated it in himself as the element of future
greatness.   He pitied anybody who respected anything.   Such a man had,
of necessity, a vast ascendency over the bad passions of the multitude;
he kept them in continual agitation, and always boiling on the surface,
ready to flow into any event, even if it were of blood."—Lamartine's
History of the Girondists, vol. i. p. 139, Bohn's Edition.

NOTE P.[*]

REFLECTIONS ON THE DEATH OF LOUIS XVI.

"BUT truth is great and will prevail, the reign of injustice is not
eternal; no special interposition of Providence is required to arrest it;
no avenging angel need descend to terminate its wrathful course.   It
destroys itself by its own violence; the counteracting force arises from
its own iniquity; the avenging angel is found in the human heart.   In
vain the malice of his enemies subjected Louis to every indignity; in
vain the executioners bound his arms, and the Revolutionary drums
stifled his voice; in vain the edge of the guillotine destroyed his body,

* Referred to at page 307.

and his remains were consigned to unhallowed ground. His spirit has triumphed over the wickedness of his oppressors. From his death has begun a reaction in favour of order and religion throughout the globe. His sufferings have done more for the cause of monarchy than all the vices of his predecessors had undone. The corruptions had become such that they could be expiated, as has been finely said, only ' by the blood of the just ascending to heaven by the steps of the scaffold.'"

"*Its Unpardonable Atrocity.*

"It is by the last emotions that the great impression on mankind is made. In this view it was eminently favourable to the interests of society that the crisis of the French monarchy arrived in the reign of Louis. It fell not during the days of its splendour or its wickedness; under the haughtiness of Louis XIV. or the infamy of Du Barri. It perished in the person of a spotless monarch, who, most of all his subjects, loved the people; whose life had literally been spent in doing good; whose failings, equally with his virtues, should have protected him from popular violence. Had he possessed more daring, he would have been less unfortunate; had he strenuously supported the cause of royalty, he would not have suffered from the fury of the populace; had he been more prodigal of the blood of others, he would in all probability have saved his own. But such warlike or ambitious qualities could not with certainty have been relied upon to arrest the Revolution; they would have postponed it to another reign, but it might, under the rule of an equally irresolute prince, have then come under darker auspices, when the cessation of tyranny had not extinguished the real cause of popular complaint, and the virtues of the monarch had not made unpardonable the fury of the people. The catastrophe occurred when all the generous feelings of our nature were awakened on the suffering side, to a sovereign who had done more for the cause of freedom than all the ancestors of his race; whose forbearance had been rewarded by encroachment; his meekness by licentiousness; his aversion to violence by the thirst for human blood. A monarch of a more energetic character might have done more to postpone the Revolution; none could have done so much to prevent its recurrence."

"*Its Ultimate Beneficial Effects.*

"Nor has the martyrdom of Louis been lost to the immediate interests of the cause for which he suffered. His resignation in adversity, charity in suffering, heroism in death, will never be forgotten.

The terrors of the republican reign, the glories of the imperial throne, have passed away ; but the spotless termination of the monarchy has left an impression on mankind which will never be effaced.   In the darkest night of the moral world, a flame has appeared in the Tower of the Temple, at first feeble and struggling for existence, but which now burns with a steady ray, and has thrown a sainted light over the fall of the French Monarchy.   The days, indeed, of superstition are past ; multitudes of pilgrims will not throng to his tomb, and stone will not be worn by the knees of his worshippers ; but the days of admiration for departed excellence will never be past.   To his historic shrine will come the virtuous and the pious through every succeeding age ; his fate .will be commiserated, his memory revered, his murderers execrated, so long as justice and mercy shall prevail upon the earth."—Alison's *History of Europe*, vol. ii. p. 325.

EDINBURGH : T. CONSTABLE,
PRINTER TO THE QUEEN, AND TO THE UNIVERSITY.